REVENGE
in Paradise

REVENGE in *Paradise*

Terrye Robins

TATE PUBLISHING & *Enterprises*

Published by Tate Publishing & Enterprises, LLC
127 E. Trade Center Terrace | Mustang, Oklahoma 73064 USA
1.888.361.9473 | www.tatepublishing.com

Tate Publishing is committed to excellence in the publishing industry. The company reflects the philosophy established by the founders, based on Psalms 68:11,
"The Lord gave the word and great was the company of those who published it."

Published in the United States of America
ISBN: 978-1-60247-591-5
07.06.15

Other books by Terrye Robins
Trouble in Paradise

Revenge in Paradise is dedicated to my cousins, some of whom inspired certain scenes.

Rejoice, O ye nations, with His people: for He will avenge the blood of His servants, and will render vengeance to His adversaries, and will be merciful unto His land, and to His people. Deuteronomy 32:43

ACKNOWLEDGMENTS

I would like to thank my aunt, Freda Riggs, and my husband, Dan Robins, for their help in editing this book.

I would also like to thank Jackie Clarke and Julie Reynolds, who are members in the Lake Bloomers Gardening Club in Langley, Oklahoma, for their input regarding the Garden of Eden.

I also appreciate the guidance and help I received from all the kind folks at Tate Publishing, LLC. Thank you all for your hard work and encouragement!

CHAPTER 1

I'm not a fan of funerals. Though I don't know of anyone in our town of Paradise, Oklahoma, who looks forward to them, I only go when I have to. Don't get me wrong; I believe in paying final respects to the dead. I just don't like looking at them. I prefer to remember them laughing and full of life—not the empty shell that is left after death has robbed them of their spirit.

Perhaps I feel the way I do because I'm only twenty-five years old and excited about a new man in my life. I'm Allison Kane, but most folks call me Allie.

Despite my feelings, when my great-aunt Edith asked me to drive her to Paradise Cemetery for the graveside service of her good friend Pearl Bauer, I told her I would. Graveside services are safe; the casket stays closed.

I had always loved being around Miss Pearl. Even at eighty-seven years old, she could quiet a crowd in a heartbeat when she started singing. Every year at the town Fourth of July picnic, Miss Pearl was asked to sing "Somewhere Over the Rainbow." Her voice soared to the heavens and when the song was done, the cheers from the spectators were deafening. It was one of the highlights of the day.

As the rabbi from Temple Shalom said the final "Amen," everyone murmured in agreement. Only a few of Miss Pearl's relatives had attended. After I shook hands with them, I joined some of my own family members standing nearby.

"That was a nice service," Gramma Winters said. "I know Pearl would have been pleased that all the ladies from the church quilting circle made it."

"Yes, I'm glad there was such a large turnout," Mom said. "And I'm glad all the arrangements that came from the shop still look so nice. Since some of them are four days old, I was afraid the flowers would be wilting." My mother is the owner of Paradise Petals, the county's busiest flower shop.

"Well, ladies, if you'll excuse me, I'm going to see if Aunt Edith is ready to go," I said. "I still have some packing to get done."

Last March, I had the privilege of going to Hawaii to interview for a third-grade summer school position at the private school where my best friend, Traci Morris, teaches. The school paid all my expenses for the week and to top if off, I met the man of my dreams. I got the job and I fly to Oahu tomorrow.

"Thanks for helping us decorate the graves today, Allie," Nana Kane said. "The family plot has never looked more beautiful."

Since my great-great-grandparents founded the town of Paradise, many of my ancestors have been buried at Paradise Cemetery. When I graduated from college, I moved into a duplex that my Grandad Winters owns. I've been around for the last few years to help decorate the graves on Memorial Day weekend. I had to admit that the beautiful colors in the arrangements made the grounds look lovely.

"I'm glad I could join you," I said. After hugging both my grandmothers, I walked over to my mother and put my arms around her. "Thanks, Mom, for lunch today and for the money. I'll miss you and Dad while I'm gone."

"We'll miss you, too, honey. We wanted you to have the money to fly to another island besides Oahu while you were there. And even though I know you're going to be busy, call us now and then."

"I will. Now I'd better go check on Aunt Edith." After waving goodbye to all of them, I walked back to the canopy-covered area.

"Georgie, I appreciate you sticking around to help me," Aunt Edith said as I walked up beside her.

Help her? George Averd was my age and had been working for the county commissioner for the last several years as a backhoe operator opening and closing graves. If I had known what he was about to do, I would have grabbed Aunt Edith's hand and we would have made tracks out of there.

"Your request is a bit odd, Mrs. Patterson," George said. "But since you and Mrs. Bauer were such good friends, I reckon it's okay."

"Thanks, Georgie. I'm sure that Pearl will put in a good word for you with the Big Guy upstairs. Now, I'm ready anytime you are."

He walked over to the side of the casket and started fumbling with the lock.

A graveside service meant no open caskets! They were changing the rules! "Aunt Edith, what's he doing?"

"Allison, you know that Pearl and I became close friends. Her kids should have been tarred and feathered for sticking her in that nursing home and taking away her checkbook. She knew they'd never agree to her request, so she asked me to do it."

"What request?" If it involved opening the coffin, I was pretty sure I didn't want to know. I heard the click of the lock and started getting weak in the knees.

"She wanted to be buried with these things," Aunt Edith replied. She reached into her large purse and pulled out a necklace with a small, gold cross on it and a pair of worn pink house shoes.

I thought I knew why her children would have objected to the cross necklace. They were devout Orthodox Jews. Unlike Reform Jews, who often observe Christian holidays and traditions as well as their own Jewish holidays, the Orthodox branch didn't tend to be as accepting of

Christian traditions and symbols. I didn't have a clue about the slippers.

"Pearl was a Christian, but her kids and grandkids weren't keen on the idea. When we're finished here and on our way home, I'll tell you a secret that Pearl shared with me several years ago."

George had flipped the latch on the casket lid and was tipping it back. I looked around, half-expecting someone to walk up and ask what in the world we were doing.

"I took you to Miss Pearl's viewing," I said. "Why didn't you put the slippers and the necklace in the open casket while you were at the funeral home?"

"Well, I had them in my purse, but Billy was sticking to me like white on rice. Ever since that little misunderstanding with Juanita awhile back, he watches me like a hawk."

Billy Morton is one of the partners at Morton Brothers Funeral Home. The "little misunderstanding" Aunt Edith was referring to was the time he caught her rearranging Juanita Blair's hair at her viewing. Billy might not have been so upset about it, but a week earlier while Aunt Edith was at Clara Bacon's viewing, her hairdo also mysteriously changed.

All the ladies were regular customers at Gladys' Mane Event on Monday mornings. Aunt Edith said that Juanita would have had a fit with the style the young girl at the funeral home had given her.

"Well if you're set on doing this, please hurry and put the things in there before we get caught," I said.

She placed one of the slippers next to Miss Pearl's left arm, then the other one next to her right arm. I expected her to drape the necklace under the woman's chin, but instead, Aunt Edith started trying to lift up her head.

"Would you give me a hand here, Allie? I can't clasp the chain and hold up Pearl's head at the same time."

Oh, boy. "George, you've had more experience in this field. Would you mind helping her?" I asked. My hands were starting to sweat. "Please?" I would have offered to bear his children if it would have helped.

"Not in my job description, Allie," George said, grinning. "I bury them; I don't handle them."

Knowing there was no way out and wanting to rush this along, I walked over to the casket. "Okay, how do you want to do this?" I asked Aunt Edith.

"If you'll lift her head, I'll wrap the chain around her neck and hook the clasp."

Putting both my hands behind Miss Pearl's ears, I started lifting her head. While Aunt Edith fastened the chain, I avoided looking at the dead woman. *No dinner for me tonight,* I thought.

"Okay, you can let her down now," Aunt Edith said.

Laying her back on the pillow, I gasped when a large clump of hair came out in my hand.

"Don't worry about that," Aunt Edith said, taking it from me. "Pearl had Gladys add some hair plugs awhile back. Now that she's gone, I imagine they'll all start giving way."

Too much information.

"You can close her up, Georgie," Aunt Edith said. "Pearl will rest easier now."

"Sure thing, Mrs. Patterson. Glad I could help."

I didn't relax until we were in my Mustang heading out of the cemetery. As we drove toward Aunt Edith's house, she told me the story about her friend.

Miss Pearl had lived in an orphanage until a Jewish couple adopted her when she was seven years old. They were strict in their faith. When she was grown, her parents insisted that she marry a Jew, which she did. She and her husband raised two children. After he died, she started trying to find her biological family. She located her mother's youngest sister and was told that her mother had become pregnant when she was sixteen. Their family was poor and couldn't afford another mouth to feed, so they made her take the baby to an orphanage in a nearby town.

The aunt told her that her father was from Halo Heights, the ritzy neighborhood in Paradise.

"The necklace belonged to Pearl's mother, Velma," Aunt Edith said. "The aunt inherited it after Velma passed away, then was nice enough to give it to Pearl."

"Did Miss Pearl track down any relatives from her father's side of the family?"

"Yes, and it wasn't pretty. The guy had been a spoiled, rich kid apparently just out for fun on the other side of the tracks. The aunt said he sneaked over to see Velma for weeks and acted like he cared about her until she became pregnant. Then he quit coming. When Velma's father went to tell the boy's parents about the pregnancy, they said she was a liar."

"That's terrible," I said. "Despite all that, why didn't Miss Pearl give her own daughter the necklace before she died?"

"When Pearl told her kids about her heritage, they didn't want any part of it. Their daddy's family had money and I guess they didn't want to think that there were any poor people in their family tree."

I felt sorry for Miss Pearl. Though I knew she had attended services at Temple Shalom, she had been part of the quilting circle at our church for years. The ladies make quilts for babies infected with the AIDS virus. The finished quilts are sent to several different hospitals throughout Oklahoma.

Since Miss Pearl's health had deteriorated over the last few months, Aunt Edith had been taking her quilt blocks to the church for her. Though her fingers were gnarled with arthritis, the stitches were still tiny and even.

Once when we were at the nursing home visiting her, she told me, "Those poor babies don't deserve to have AIDS, Allison. God put people on this earth to show His love to others. The least I can do is offer those little children some comfort through my needlework while they're here."

"Aunt Edith, I understand about the necklace, but what was the deal with the pink slippers? Did they belong to her mother, too?"

"No, but they brought Pearl lots of comfort through the years. She said she didn't think the good Lord would mind if she wore them while she walked on the golden streets in heaven."

It sounded good to me. Though the saying goes "You can't take it with you," I thought God might make an exception for Miss Pearl's slippers.

I pulled into Aunt Edith's driveway. "Thanks for the ride," she said. "Would you like to come in? Linda took the boys fishing at your Grandpa A.J.'s place and I don't expect them back for a while."

Grandpa A.J. and Nana Kane own an eleven-hundred-acre ranch called the Circle K. Because there are several thousand head of cattle on it, there are numerous ponds and a couple are stocked with fish.

"I appreciate the invitation, but you might want to rest while you've got the house to yourself. Besides, I still have more packing to do."

"I love having Bennie and his family here, but those grandsons of mine wear me out!" she said. "Bennie was a quiet boy, but his sons are live wires. I guess they get their rambunctious behavior from Linda's side of the family."

Bennie was Aunt Edith's only child and hadn't married until he was in his late thirties. He and Linda had their first child, David, within a year after their wedding. Derrick came along two years later. Bennie had recently retired from his job with an oil company in Alaska and moved his family to Paradise to be closer to Aunt Edith. He planned to continue to do some part-time work at Kane Energy, the company that Grandpa A.J. started forty years ago.

"Is Bennie having any luck finding a house?" I asked. His family had been staying at Aunt Edith's for the past two weeks.

"Not yet. I've been putting the newspaper ads at his place at the table every morning, but so far they've only looked at three houses. I love them to death, but they're starting to cramp my style."

Aunt Edith has an active social life. Since the weather had turned warm, she had taken two day trips with the Screaming Eagles, her over-fifties motorcycle club. On one of them, they traveled down Route 66 to Arcadia to see the Round Barn and also stopped at several other attractions along the way. She brought back a neat mug for me from Frankoma Pottery in Sapulpa. She had also been dating a new man at church, but I knew that since Bennie and his family had arrived, she hadn't had a single date with him.

"The Eagles left yesterday for an overnight trip to Wichita," she said. "Bennie threw a fit when I mentioned going with them. 'You're not a spring chicken anymore, Mother,' he said. Well, he's not putting me out to pasture yet!"

"I'm sure he's just concerned about your welfare, like we all are."

"Maybe. But since his daddy has been gone, God rest his soul, and Bennie lived way up in Alaska all these years, I've enjoyed my independence and I don't plan to give it up. Thank goodness I get to come and be with you in Hawaii for a couple of weeks. Maybe by the time I get back, they'll have a place of their own."

I was going to be staying with my friend Traci while I taught summer school. She and her husband, Tommy, were coming back to Oklahoma to visit their parents the last part of June. With their approval, I had invited Aunt Edith to come and stay with me then.

"We'll have a great time," I said. "You won't need to bring a lot of clothes. There's a laundry room in their building."

"I went to Mary Jane's Boutique last week and found some great walking shorts and a new swimsuit," she said, smiling. "I looked at some of the new string bikinis that had just arrived, but I settled on a fuchsia one-piece instead."

Thank goodness, I thought. The other people on the beach might not be ready for a seventy-eight-year-old woman in a string bikini strutting her stuff.

"I'll meet your plane when you get there on the 16th," I said as she climbed out of my car.

"Okay. You have a nice trip tomorrow. And thanks for helping me with Pearl."

I smiled and nodded. *A typical day with Aunt Edith,* I thought. I watched her walk up her front steps and into the house, and then I left.

🐾 🐾 🐾

As I got out of the car inside my garage, I could hear the phone ringing and my two dachshunds, Rowdy and Precious, barking. I rushed into the house and waded through the welcoming committee as they jumped up on my legs.

"I'm glad to see you guys, too," I said. I reached for the phone on the end table.

"I was beginning to think you weren't home," the male voice on the line said. "And I was going to be very disappointed if I didn't get to talk to you before I left."

"Hello, handsome," I said, plopping down in my recliner. "It's good to hear from you."

Simon Kahala is the new love in my life. We spent a lot of time together the week I was in Hawaii for the summer school interview. When I returned home, he paid me a short visit after I had some trouble with a neighbor, and my family got to meet him. Since then, our only source of communication has been through phone calls and e-mails.

"I've been plowing through evidence files all morning and decided I needed a break," he said. "You're the prettiest distraction I could think of."

Simon is a detective for the Hawaii State Bureau of Investigation, or HSBI, on the island of Oahu. The agency assists local law enforcement agencies throughout the Islands with felony person crimes.

"Glad I can help. And speaking of that, is there anything I can do to help you with this case that's been giving you fits for the last three months?" He had been tight-lipped about the details that kept him flying back and forth to Maui.

"It will help having you here; I miss you. But when you arrive tomorrow, you'll have to hit the ground running to be ready for school on Wednesday. It's too bad you didn't get more time off."

I had just completed another school year at Elliott Kane Elementary, where I teach third grade. I knew when I accepted the summer job in Hawaii that there would only be a few days of down time, but I didn't care. Prince Kuhio Elementary was picking up most of my expenses and a month-long visit in paradise was a once-in-a-lifetime opportunity!

"I don't mind," I said. "Since I'll be using Traci's classroom, I know everything will be organized. She'll give me any help I need on Tuesday. I'm thrilled to get to be there, even if it's only for five weeks."

"I know Aunt Nalani is tickled to have you. She came to Mom and Dad's for dinner last Sunday after church and couldn't stop talking about you." Nalani Kahala was the principal at Prince Kuhio and also Simon's aunt.

"You said you were glad to reach me before you left. Are you off to Maui again?"

"In less than two hours. But I'll be back in time to meet your plane tomorrow afternoon. You're supposed to get in at 4:00, right?"

"That's right. By any chance will you be free the rest of the evening? I was hoping you could join Traci, Tommy and me for dinner."

"I made it a point to be off. I know you'll be tired from traveling, so Tommy and I made arrangements to take you girls somewhere special."

Since I introduced Simon to Tommy back in March, they've become best buddies. They both enjoy watching basketball on television and have been playing golf together at least once a week. Traci told me that a few weeks ago they went deep-sea fishing with Simon's brother, Richard. I figured that it wouldn't be long before Simon was teaching Tommy to surf, since he loved that sport as well.

I told him about helping Aunt Edith fulfill Pearl Bauer's requests after the funeral. He had met Aunt Edith when he was here and seemed to like her a lot.

"From what I know about your aunt, I'm not surprised that she did that for her friend," he said. "But you know, you two could have been in a lot of trouble if you'd been caught."

"The thought did cross my mind." *What an understatement!*

"This case in front of me now is dealing with an item that was buried with its owner," Simon said. "About three months ago, someone dug up a grave in one of the cemeteries on Maui and stole an expensive ring out of the casket. The HSBI detective there, Eddie Zantini, is coming here on Wednesday. I was hoping that you would join us for dinner that evening. I've been telling him about you and he can't believe that a blonde, blue-eyed angel really lives in Oklahoma."

"I'll try to live up to the expectations," I said, laughing.

"Oh, I'm sorry, but I've got another call on the other line. Would you please hold on a minute?"

"Sure, I'll wait for you. Go ahead and get it."

While I had been on the phone, Rowdy and Precious had been lounging in my lap letting me scratch their tummies. My cousin, Doug Blessing, lives in the unit on the other side of the duplex, and we share joint custody of the dogs. Since Doug is studying to be a pediatrician and has a demanding social life, I usually care for the pups. But while I'm gone to Hawaii, they would be his responsibility.

"Are you still there?" Simon asked when he came back on the line.

"Waiting patiently. Someone at work needing your help?"

"That was Marshall calling. He and Dave just finished interviewing a landscape artist who reported some vandalism to one of his projects. They were leaving from there and wanted to know if I'd like to meet them for an early lunch. I only had some pancakes, ham, grits and juice with my coffee this morning, so I'm glad for their invitation."

Marshall and Dave are detectives for the Honolulu Police Department. I met them during my earlier visit to Oahu. I looked at my cuckoo clock on the wall and saw that is was 4:00. With the five-hour time difference, it was 11:00 a.m. in Hawaii.

"Yeah, after eating *only* that amount of food, I don't know how you're able to hold up the phone," I said, smiling.

"Hey, you know I like to eat, and I have to keep up my strength to chase down the bad guys."

"Well, before you go, you said that Marshall and Dave had been interviewing a landscape artist. What is that? I've never heard that term."

"There's a guy named Maynard Desmond who was born and raised here. He creates artistic exhibits using flowers, shrubs, lava rock and a host of other things. He's been asked by the state to work his magic in some of the parks. I'm not sure if he considers landscape artist an official title, but he does impressive work and that's what a lot of people call him."

"I'd like to see some of the things he's done. Maybe you could show me some of his work when I arrive."

"Sure, I'll be glad to. I hate to go, but if I'm going to make that plane, I'd better get on the road."

"Be safe, and good luck catching the bad guys."

"Thanks. Have a good flight and stay away from good-looking strangers. I'll see you tomorrow at the airport."

After hanging up, I nudged the dogs out of my lap. "Come on you two. You need to go outside for a while. And no digging!"

Famous last words, I thought. Their digging had created a world of trouble for me awhile back. I had a gruesome experience with body parts when they brought home the toes of two different dead men. I was stalked by the neighbor whose yard the men were buried in, and it had been a harrowing experience for me. After the ordeal, Simon insisted on coming to visit me. He had been a soothing balm for my emotional wounds. The neighbor was now in prison, and a nice family with three young children was living in the house.

I opened the sliding glass door and watched the dogs dart toward the fence. My neighbor, Mrs. Googan, and her Pomeranian, Ginger, were in their backyard. I waved at her as the dogs greeted each other and started running the fence.

Confident that Ginger would keep the pups busy for a while, I walked back into the house to continue my packing. I was trying to adhere to my advice to Aunt Edith by taking only necessary outfits. Miss Kahala had told me that for summer school, casual attire was the norm. I had purchased several new outfits before going for the interview, thanks to some money that my dad had given to me. After adding some other clothes I had purchased last summer, the large bag was ready to close.

As I wheeled the suitcase to the front door, the phone started ringing.

"Hello."

"Aloha, Allie. Sung Masaki here."

"Mr. Masaki, what a nice surprise! It's great to hear from you!"

"I hope you don't mind that I called Nalani Kahala for your phone number," he said. "I was anxious to find out if you would be coming back to Hawaii this summer." Mr. Masaki was the owner of the *Hawaiian Star* newspaper on Oahu. I had met him on the plane in March.

"Yes, I landed the job and I'm flying over tomorrow morning. I planned to come and see you after I settled in at school. How have you been?"

"Doing great for an old man. News on the island has been flooding in. That's one reason I'm calling. Are you still interested in discussing that part-time job I mentioned to you when you were here? I could really use your help."

"I'm game, if you are. Are you still planning to use me to write human interest pieces?"

"Yes and no. I hired a talented young journalist from St. Louis about a month ago. I was hoping the two of you could work together covering general assignments like accidents, civic events, human-interest stories and an occasional crime piece. I have several beat reporters that cover the courts, education and business news. You'll still have the opportunity to do some individual pieces, though. But after I hired Kyle, and became familiar with his writing style, I felt like the two of you would make a dynamite team."

"I'll be glad to work with someone else. In fact, since my experience is limited, it would probably be a good idea. When would you like me to come in to discuss the details?"

"I hate to rush you, but would Tuesday afternoon be too soon? There was a grave robbery several months ago and my staff hasn't made much headway on the story. We haven't been able to get much from Honolulu P.D. I know you have some acquaintances in the department, and I was hoping you might be able to get an inside scoop."

I was silent for a moment. "I wouldn't feel comfortable trying to weasel information out of my friends, Mr. Masaki."

"Oh, no, don't misunderstand me. I would never ask you to do anything underhanded. I don't approve of that kind of behavior, and the *Hawaiian Star* doesn't operate that way. I was just hoping that since you know some of the officers, they might prefer giving you the story, rather than talking to someone else."

Now that I understood him, I felt better. "Tuesday it is, then," I said. "I'll be working at the school all morning, but I should be able to come and see you after lunch. How's that?"

"Mahalo, Allie, that's wonderful. I'm looking forward to it. Now, I won't keep you any longer. Have a safe flight, and I'll see you on Tuesday."

"Thank you, Mr. Masaki. Have a great weekend!"

After hanging up, I was more excited than ever about my trip. My past writing experience had been limited to school events and other minor articles for our hometown newspaper, the *Paradise Progress*. I figured that if a seasoned editor like Mr. Masaki saw some potential in me, I had a chance to develop my skills further.

I let the dogs inside and fed them, then I set to work giving the house a good cleaning. By 7:30, the place was spotless and I was pooped.

Though I thought for sure that I wouldn't want any dinner after the ordeal at the cemetery, I was famished. The refrigerator was bare because I didn't want to leave any food in it while I was gone. I looked in the freezer and saw two frozen dinners. Hungry enough to eat them both, I carried them to the microwave oven. As I removed the first one from the box, the phone rang.

When I answered it, my cousin Kristin said, "How about a pizza? It's my treat since this will be your last meal here for a while."

"Sounds yummy. I've been cleaning, so I'm a mess. Do you mind bringing it over here?"

"That's what I had in mind. Joey is spending the night at Mom and Dad's, so it will just be me." Joey is her five-year-old son. "Is a supreme okay?"

"Great! Now I won't have to eat the TV dinners from the freezer."

She started giggling. "Dinners, as in more than one?"

"Hey, I was hungry."

Just then there was a knock on my front door. I walked over and looked out the peephole and saw Doug standing there. I opened the door and waved at him to come in.

"Kristin, Doug just walked in. You'd better get two pizzas. I'll pay you for the second one."

"That's okay," she said. "I have a coupon for a free medium if I buy a large one. I'll call it in and be there in a few minutes."

"See you then."

"Pizza's coming? It looks like I picked the right time to drop in," Doug said. "I was coming over for the dogs because I figured you'd get to bed early tonight, but I could go for a little nourishment while I'm here."

"You're like me, Doug; always ready to eat," I said, grinning.

"While we're waiting for Kristin to get here, why don't we go ahead and move the dogs' stuff and your plant to my place," he said. "I'll let them finish the dog food you have here, then buy a fresh bag to replace it when you get back."

"Sounds fine to me. Let's go."

Doug promised to pick up my mail and keep my peace lily plant alive while I was gone. I lifted the heavy brass pot containing the plant into my arms. Balancing it on my hip, I headed out the door and across the yard to his front porch. While carrying the dog crate in one hand and the half-empty bag of dog food on his shoulder, Doug followed me over. Rowdy and Precious kept getting under our feet as usual.

By the time things were settled inside his place and we were walking back to mine, Kristin had arrived and was getting out of her car with the food. Doug and I walked over to meet her.

"Mmmm, this smells good," I said, taking the pizza boxes from her. "I've got a two-liter bottle of Pepsi we can have with it."

With Doug corralling the pups, we all managed to get inside. He poured the drinks while Kristin and I put paper towels and plates on the table. Once we were all seated, I said grace, then we dug in. Rowdy and Precious settled close by with expectant expressions on their faces.

Between bites of pizza, we talked and laughed about all kinds of things. Kristin was happy because her husband Kevin, who is a chaplain in the army and currently stationed in Iraq, was coming home for a two-week visit. I was happy because I was leaving for Hawaii tomorrow. Rowdy and Precious were happy because we kept slipping them scraps of pizza, and Doug was happy because he didn't have to cook his own dinner.

After we finished eating and the dishes were washed, I kissed the puppies before relinquishing them to their Uncle Doug. Before they left, each of my cousins gave me a hug and wishes for a good journey. We all knew that our routines would be different over the next few weeks. But for the most part, different would be a nice change. Or so we thought at the time.

CHAPTER 2

My dad picked me up at my house at 6:00 a.m. and took me to the Tulsa International Airport. The flight was set to leave at 8:15. After breezing through security, I bought a carton of milk and a blueberry donut at one of the coffee shops. I settled into a seat in the area near my gate and watched the ground crew load luggage onto the plane while I ate.

Though it was still early, the workers were wiping sweat from their faces. The weather in Oklahoma had been unseasonably warm for the past week. Forecasters were predicting a break in the heat wave if storms that were building out west made it here.

"Those guys look like they could use a cool drink," the man beside me said. I looked at him and saw that he was watching the workmen outside, too. He was dressed in an expensive-looking navy blue suit, pale blue shirt and maroon silk tie. His hair looked like he had recently seen a talented stylist and his face was clean-shaven.

"Yes, they would probably appreciate that," I said. "I don't envy them working out in this heat."

The man handed me one of his business cards. "Mel Shuman," he said. "I'm a sales representative for the Pandora Juice Company. A cup of icy lemonade or orange juice would probably hit the spot for those young fellas out there."

I glanced at the card and saw that he lived in Salt Lake City, Utah. "Traveling home, Mr. Shuman?"

"Yes, I've been gone for a week and though I've loved being in the Sooner state, I'm ready to head back to the coolness of the mountains. This heat is hard on a chubby guy."

Though a bit hefty, I wouldn't have called him chubby. "I've always liked lemonade myself," I said. "When I was nine years old, my cousin Kristin and I set up a stand in front of her house. We didn't get rich from the sales, but we did get our picture in the local paper."

"Impressive," Mr. Shuman replied. "So many kids today want everything handed to them and don't know the meaning of hard work. You became a young entrepreneur, and I'm sure you've been rewarded for it."

"I've never been afraid to work hard," I said. "I had odd jobs while I was growing up. I was babysitting by the time I was ten, and I was writing 'Kids in the News' articles for our hometown newspaper when I was thirteen. I'm going to get more journalism experience writing part-time for a newspaper while I'm teaching summer school in Hawaii."

The flight attendant started calling for boarding. "Well, I enjoyed visiting with you, young lady, and I wish you good luck in your endeavors." He stood up and picked up his carryon bag. "They just called my section. If I don't see you again, have a safe flight on to Hawaii and a nice time once you get there."

"Thanks, Mr. Shuman."

Since he was in first class and I was in coach, I doubted that our paths would cross again.

After a two-hour layover in Salt Lake City, I boarded a 767 and was glad to have a window seat. There were only a handful of empty seats on the large plane and one of them was next to mine. Enjoying the extra space after being cramped on the earlier flight from Tulsa, I settled in with a crossword puzzle book while waiting for lunch to be served.

There were several in-flight movies to choose from and I decided on a romantic drama. More than once I found myself in tears when the heroine thought her handsome lover had betrayed her. When the movie was over, an hour remained until the plane would arrive in Honolulu, so I decided to take a little nap.

I woke up refreshed. The plane had begun its descent, so I went to the lavatory to check my makeup. Pulling a brush through my shoulder-length hair, I smiled when I thought of my last plane ride to Oahu. While trying to help another passenger with his carryon bag, I had lost my balance and tumbled into Simon's lap. Little did either of us know at the time that a relationship would emerge from my clumsiness.

After I returned to my seat, the "fasten seatbelts" sign came on. I could hear the whine of the landing gear as I peered through a break in the clouds. When I spotted the tips of Oahu's mist-covered mountains, I felt excitement run through me. We were flying in on the windward side of the island. I smiled when I recognized the pristine beach that ran close to the Kaneohe Bay Military Base where Tommy worked.

The sparkling, aquamarine-colored water was gorgeous and the gentle waves were inviting. Several sailboats bobbed offshore, and I could see people lounging on the beach. At that moment, I realized how much I had missed the splendor of the island and was anxious to set my feet down again on its soil.

A few minutes before 4:00, the wheels of the plane touched down at Honolulu International Airport. I began to get nervous at the thought of seeing Simon, and I started trying to smooth the wrinkles out of my slacks. It had been two months since his visit to Oklahoma, and I couldn't wait to see him again.

When the plane stopped at the gate, I gathered my things and waited in line for my turn to disembark. I was expecting Simon to meet me in the baggage claim area, so I planned to head in that direction. I followed the slow-moving crowd down the tunnel, and as I exited it, I heard his voice.

"My prayers have been answered. A handsome stranger didn't steal you away from me."

I turned around and saw him standing a few yards away from me. "Well, you'd better come over here and take me away before one does," I said, laughing.

He walked over and took hold of my hand. "Come on. I'm not taking any chances."

He led me to the nearest corner of the room, then put his arms around me and kissed me. Though I had expected a warm welcome, he was holding me like he didn't plan to let me go. When our lips separated, I was breathless.

Still holding me close, he said, "I've been looking forward to doing that for weeks. I was beginning to think I wasn't going to make it with just phone calls until you arrived."

"I'm glad you missed me. I've missed you, too."

Turning me so that our hips were touching, he placed his arm around my waist. "Let's go get your stuff. It's way too crowded in this place."

We chatted all the way to the baggage area, then after picking up my bags, we walked to his Jeep. With my things in the back, we buckled up and headed toward Kamehameha Highway. Tommy and Traci live about six miles from the airport in a high-rise apartment building in Aiea.

As Simon turned onto the highway, I spotted something in the small park on our left. "That's new since I was here," I said. "How unique!"

He pulled onto the park road and stopped the car "Yes, this project was just finished a couple of weeks ago. Maynard Desmond created it. He's the artist who reported the vandalism yesterday."

Through the car window, I could see a large statue of a rooster. Its body was covered with pieces of black lava rock. The long tail feathers, in assorted shades of red, orange and gold, curved away from the body and almost reached the ground. The crimson comb on top of the figure's head was made of cut glass and colored stones.

"I'd like to get out and take a closer look," I said.

"Let's go."

We walked the short distance to the display. English ivy and plumeria were planted on two elevated hills in the background. Stepping-stones led through a break in the shrubbery that had been planted to form a big circle. The bird and a fifteen-foot-tall apple tree stood in the middle of it. The tree was covered in blooms, and the details on the rooster were extraordinary. I couldn't resist touching the feathery plume on the bird.

"These feel like real feathers," I said. Most of the strands were three to four feet long. "What kind of material could Mr. Desmond have used to make them seem so real?"

Simon walked up beside me and felt of one. "They are real. The only bird I know of with feathers this long would be an ostrich. Since the natural color would be brown or black, he must have bleached them, then dyed them to look like a rooster's plume."

A lone branch on the apple tree pointed toward the bird. I noticed a rope dangling from it. When I walked over to take a closer look, I was surprised to see that it formed a hangman's noose.

I pointed toward the noose. "That's an odd thing to add to the display, don't you think?"

He joined me beside the tree. "Maynard's exhibits represent legends from the different cultures that immigrated to Hawaii. If I recall, this one is from a Portuguese tale. There's a placard posted over there, if you want to read more about it."

We walked to the sign standing on the left side of the exhibit. It read:

In the town of Barcelo, a crime was committed and the authorities didn't have a suspect. A stranger from another country was traveling through and was accused of the crime. Despite his claims that he was innocent, he was sentenced to hang.

The man begged to see the judge before his sentence was carried out. The authorities took him to the judge's house, where he was hosting a dinner. In the middle of the table sat a platter of roasted rooster. The accused man shouted that if he was hanged, the bird from that platter would crow in protest.

Sure enough, when the rope jerked around the man's neck, the rooster crowed. The judge was horrified and rushed to the gallows. He was relieved to find that the knot had caught and prevented the man from strangling. The traveler was released and from that time forward, the Portuguese considered the rooster to be good luck.

"That's an interesting tale," I said when I finished reading it.

"The Portuguese are the ones who introduced the ukulele and slack-key guitar to the Islands," Simon said. "Each culture added something when they settled here. All the exhibits have become popular with the locals as well as tourists."

"I can understand why. The artist is very talented."

We walked back to the Jeep and I took one last look at the display as Simon pulled onto the highway.

"So how was your trip to Maui?" I asked. "Are you getting any closer to finding the missing ring you've been looking for?"

"One more piece fell into place. The detective I told you about yesterday went to see a pawnshop dealer in Los Angeles. We got a call from a detective with the L.A. Police Department that a young woman tried to sell an antique gold ring to the dealer. He became suspicious when he saw the ancient symbol on the inside of the band. The girl claimed the ring belonged to her grandmother."

"That's sad that she was trying to hock a family heirloom," I said. "But these days that's not so unusual."

"No, but the girl was Jamaican and the symbol engraved in the ring was a Hawaiian family crest. So the dealer doubted that the story about the grandmother was true. He asked her to wait while he checked on some prices in the back room. He found the description of the ring on a stolen property list that we had sent to the police department there."

"That's great!"

"Well, it would have been, but when the dealer came back out front, the girl and the ring were gone."

"Gee, that's too bad."

"This case involves more than stolen jewelry," Simon said. "We think that whoever dug up the grave has a personal vendetta against the owner. Not only was the ring stolen, but the finger it was on was taken, too."

My mouth dropped open. "You mean the robber stole the person's finger?"

"Twisted it off right at the knuckle. As sick as it sounds, we're fairly sure the crime is connected to another grave robbing that happened here two years ago. The two victims were related."

"Was that person's finger taken, also?"

"Three of them were. The burial records show that the woman was buried with three rings and a necklace. In today's market, the collection of pieces would easily bring a half-million dollars."

"That's some incentive for digging up a grave," I said.

"You can say that again. Now, that's enough shoptalk. Here we are."

Simon turned off the street and into the parking lot of my friends' complex. He drove past the row of garden apartments to the tower.

"A sight for sore eyes," I said.

"The building won't look so desolate now that you'll be back in it," Simon said. "Every time I drove by it, I thought of you."

"That's sweet," I said, squeezing his hand.

After he parked, I grabbed my purse and carryon bag and jumped out of the Jeep. Simon walked around to the back and started unloading my suitcases.

"Sorry those are so heavy. Though I'm sure it feels like it, I didn't pack the kitchen sink."

He pulled the handles out so he could roll the bags. "I guess you're worth the effort," he said, grinning. "A lot of things are needed when you're going to be away from home for over a month."

"A girl has to be prepared. I wouldn't want you to get tired of seeing me over and over in the same outfits."

"You could wear a flour sack and I'd still think you were beautiful."

We walked to the front door of the tower. I pushed the buzzer on the building, then turned toward him. "Thank you, kind sir, for the compliment and for the ride from the airport."

Traci's voice sounded on the intercom. "Allie, is that you?"

"Yes, ma'am. My escort and I are here. Would you please open the door for us?"

"I can't wait to see you!" Traci said. "Hurry up, you two."

The security door buzzed and we walked into the cool foyer. Once everything was inside the elevator, I pushed the button for the seventeenth floor. We started moving, and Simon pulled me into his arms. "Welcome back to Hawaii, Miss Kane."

It seemed that fireworks were exploding all around us as he kissed me. The circle of his arms was a refuge and I felt like I was home again. I knew right then that it was going to be hard to leave this security when my job was finished.

❧ ❧ ❧

"It's so good to see you!" Traci squealed as we hugged in the hallway. "I've been beside myself with excitement all weekend!"

"You can say that again," Tommy said, walking up behind her. "Last night I didn't think Traci was ever going to come to bed. She was cooking and cleaning until almost midnight."

"You don't have to tell everything you know," Traci said, elbowing him in the ribs. "You're excited, too. You left work early today so that you would be here when Allie arrived."

"Yeah, I did," he admitted. "Now, if Simon doesn't mind, how about a hug?"

"Well if you insist," Simon said. He started walking toward Tommy.

"Oh, you're hilarious," Tommy said. "I meant from Allie, Mr. Golf Pro."

"Mr. Golf Pro?" I said. "You mean Simon is giving you a run for your money on the golf course? Just for that, you get two hugs from me." I walked over and put my arms around his waist.

"It's great when we're partners against some of the other guys, because if my game is off, I know Simon will pull us through," Tommy said when we parted. "But he's murder when we're playing each other. I'm glad I'm a friend and not an enemy."

"Why are we standing here in the hall talking?" Traci said. "Allie, let's get you inside and settled."

"Since I'm due back here in less than two hours to pick up all of you, I'm going to go home to shower and change clothes," Simon said. "Traci, I'll leave Allie in your capable hands."

"We'll be ready when you return," Traci said.

"See you soon," he replied, then he gave me a kiss.

Not soon enough, I thought as I watched him walk back toward the elevator.

Traci and I walked into the apartment. "Thanks for letting me stay here for the next few weeks," I said. "Considering your condition, I'll try to clean up after myself and not cause any extra work for you." Traci was due to have their first baby in October.

"You're not going to cause any extra work for me," she said. "When you left here after spring break, the bedroom and bathroom you used were cleaner than they had been before you came. Besides, the school is paying me to keep you, remember?"

The principal at Prince Kuhio was able to hire me because the school was awarded a federal grant for the purpose of "helping mainland teachers become more culturally aware of the Polynesian student's study habits." Though the school would pay my salary and provide a car for me to use, the grant paid for all my travel and food expenses. Traci would receive a stipend for providing a room in her home for me.

"It's a sweet deal," I said. "I couldn't have asked for anything better to start my summer."

"Now, I hate to rush you, but Simon will be back before you know it and we all have to get ready," Traci said. "You know where everything is, so just make yourself at home."

While she and I had been talking, Tommy had carried my suitcases into the guest bedroom. "I think I'll take a shower to get the travel grime off," I said.

"What are you wearing tonight?" Traci asked. When we were growing up we often wore the same styles and colors of clothes.

"Though Simon didn't give me a lot of clues, he said to dress casually. Have you been able to get anything more out of Tommy?"

"Not a word. Usually he can't keep a secret to save his life, but he's been close-mouthed about the plans he and Simon made for tonight."

"Well, I guess I'll wear the new pink capri pants I brought and a coordinating top," I said. "What did you have in mind?"

"Since I'm wearing maternity clothes now, my selection is somewhat limited. But I also have a new pair of capris and that sounds like a good choice. See you in a bit."

After Traci left, I unpacked my suitcases and put away all my clothes. Then I gathered up my makeup bag and hair stuff and headed to the bathroom to take a shower.

I don't know if it was the thrill of getting to see Simon and my friends again, or if I was just hungry, but I was ready in record time. Traci was still dressing, so I used my phone card to call my parents to let them know I had arrived safely. As I hung up, I heard Tommy talking on the intercom.

"We'll be right down," he said. "Is everything all set?"

I didn't hear a reply because someone on the freeway below started honking their horn. H-1 is one of the island's three major expressways and runs alongside the apartment building.

"Come on, Traci," Tommy hollered. "Simon is waiting."

I watched Tommy put on a pair of sandals. He was dressed in cut-off jean shorts and a loose-fitting shirt. When Traci came into the room, it looked like we had gone shopping together for our matching outfits. Both of us had put our hair in a twist on the top of our heads and our pink sandals were identical.

"You girls look like twins," Tommy said. "If your hair and eyes were the same color and if Traci didn't have that cute little bulge in the front, it would be hard to tell you apart." In contrast to my blonde hair, Traci's hair was dark brown and curly and she had big brown eyes.

"Thank you, sweetheart," she said. She gave Tommy's arm a squeeze. "I've always wanted to look more like Allie. And I'm proud of this cute little bulge." She lovingly patted the front of her blouse.

"I'm glad to be your twin," I told her. "But I don't plan on having a bulge like yours for a while. I've got to get the wedding ring first."

The three of us walked out the door into the hallway. "Your wedding day may not be as far away as you think," Traci said. "The handsome guy waiting downstairs might surprise you while you're here."

The thought of being married to Simon had crossed my mind a few times, though I never dwelled on it. Neither of us had ever said the "L" word to each other.

When we stepped off the elevator, Simon was waiting outside the front door for us. He was dressed in khaki shorts, a blue-flowered aloha shirt, and he was wearing sneakers. After planting a kiss on my cheek, he took my hand and led the way to his Jeep.

"I hope you girls are ready for a fun evening," he said as he started the car. "Tom and I have been working on this plan for a while."

"I'm just thrilled to be here," I said. "Any restaurant is fine with me as long as there's lots of food. It's way past my dinner time." In Oklahoma it was already 11:00 p.m. and the lunch I had eaten on the plane was long gone.

"There will be lots of good food and fresh air," Tommy said. "But that's all I'm saying about the place until we get there."

As we pulled out of the complex onto Moanalua Road, Simon's cell phone started ringing. He glanced at the display of numbers, then answered it. "Yeah, Dave, what's up?"

While Simon listened, he started slowing down the Jeep. When he pulled into an alleyway next to a gas station and stopped, I had the feeling that our dinner was going to be delayed.

"Okay, I have guests with me, but if they don't mind, we'll swing by there. I'd like you and Marshall to start questioning the workers who might have seen people coming in and out today. I'll see you in a few minutes." He was about to hang up when he glanced at me. "Thanks, Dave."

Before Simon met me, he was pure business with the detectives he worked with. It's not that he was unappreciative of their efforts, or that he set out to be rude—he just didn't take the time to add "please" and "thank you" in his conversations with them. I had pointed out to him that a little sugar sprinkled along the way could pay big benefits in the long run.

He looked at me, then turned around to face Traci and Tommy in the back seat. "I'm sorry to have to hold up our party, but something has happened at the Shady Palms Cemetery. The evening security guard found a disturbed grave. If you all don't mind, I need to run by there for a few minutes."

"What do you mean by 'disturbed?'" I asked. "You're not normally involved in cases regarding destruction of property."

Simon glanced at Tommy in the rearview mirror before looking at me. "This involves a person," he said.

A person and a disturbed grave? This can't be good, I thought.

"Don't worry about delaying dinner," Tommy said. "You need to go to work, so if you don't mind having us tag along, let's go."

"We're with you," Traci said. "There will be plenty of time to eat when you're finished."

"People at Shady Palms are waiting for us," I said to Simon. "Let's go."

🐾   🐾   🐾

The sun was sinking low on the horizon and shades of peach and indigo were swirled across the sky. We traveled south on H-1, then exited onto Keeaumoku Street. After winding through a residential area, Simon headed directly north toward the mountains. The evening mist was settling on the peaks, forming an eerie site.

He pulled off the street and drove through an arch into the cemetery. The main road into the graveyard was paved, but after going only a few hundred yards, he made a right turn onto a gravel one-lane road. I noticed that many of the headstones running along each side of it were very old. A few of them had dates from the 1800s engraved on them and most were weatherworn from decades of rain and wind.

Simon drove down a small hill and I saw two state government vehicles parked along the side of the road. He pulled in behind one of them and turned off the engine.

"Dave said the grave is in an area behind that long hedge over there," he said, pointing toward the right side of the car. "I won't be long."

"I saw some restrooms back there, and I need to go to the little girl's room," Traci said.

"I'll walk with you," Tommy said to her, then he looked at Simon. "We'll kill a little time going over there, then we'll come back here and wait for you."

"What about you?" Simon asked, looking at me. "Do you mind waiting here alone for a while?"

"I'd rather come along with you. I won't get in the way and I'd like to say hello to Dave and Marshall."

"Okay, come on. The sooner I check this out, the sooner we can get out of here."

Simon held my hand as we walked between the rows of graves. Some of them were adorned with lush plants and fresh floral arrangements while others had plastic flowers on them. A child's grave had toys on it and another one was topped with a basket of apples. Regardless of the ornaments, or lack of them, each plot was neatly trimmed and looked well cared for. It was easy to see that the loved ones left behind still remembered those who had gone on.

As we rounded the end of the hedge, it was like we stepped into a different world. There were only a dozen graves in this section and it was gloomy and barren. Unlike the other part of the cemetery where huge monuments seemed to protect the occupants, the headstones here laid flat on the ground. Only the name and date of death was engraved on them. None of the graves had flowers or any other decorations on them. Though the grass had been mowed, the plots looked forsaken, as if no one cared to do anything more.

As we neared a mound of dirt at the far edge of the section, Marshall spotted us. He walked toward us, then stretched out his hand to me. "It's good to see you again, Allie. Sorry it's under these circumstances. I hear you're back on the island for a while."

I shook his hand. "Thanks, Marshall. It's good to be back and to see you again, too. Have you lost some weight since I saw you last?"

A look of pride came on his face. "As a matter of fact, I've lost twenty-five pounds. I've been working out four times a week at the P.D.'s fitness center. My hard work is starting to show."

I wondered if the race he had run and lost with Sammy Cho back in March had anything to do with his new fitness habits. Sammy ran into me, literally, after he was involved in a shooting on the beach. He had hidden the gun in one of the toilets, and I found it when I used the facilities. The day I went to visit Mr. Masaki at the *Hawaiian Star*, I saw Sammy drive by. Simon had advised me to stay clear of him, but I was too hardheaded to heed his warning.

Marshall and Dave had been on a stakeout watching for Sammy that day and weren't thrilled when I found him first. When Sammy took off running, the two detectives chased him, but he scaled a fence and escaped. Simon had been after Marshall to get in shape and I shouldn't have been there in the first place. We agreed not to bother Simon with the details of the encounter.

Simon pointed toward a mound of dirt near the area where Marshall had been standing. "Dave told me the name of the deceased on the phone, so I'm glad you called me. What else have you discovered?"

"I had the caretaker check the burial records. Other than the clothes the guy was buried in, nothing else was in the casket." Marshall looked at me and hesitated. He seemed to be weighing his next statement. "Some things were taken, though."

I couldn't imagine anyone stealing the clothes off a corpse! Sure, I had heard about soldiers taking boots or articles of clothing from the enemy in cold weather to survive. But this was Hawaii. What would make anyone desperate enough to risk digging up a person to steal his clothes?

I saw some kind of unspoken message pass between Marshall and Simon. "Allie, please stay here for a minute while I go talk to the caretaker," Simon said.

He and Marshall walked toward a cluster of men on the other side of the mound. Floodlights had been set up around the perimeter of the grave. Despite their glow, it felt like the cold fingers of death were all around me, and I was anxious to leave.

The grass beneath my pink sandals was damp. I didn't want them to get messed up, so I moved to a dry spot a short distance away. As I looked down at the ground, it reminded me of a checkerboard. A dry patch was followed by a square of wet grass. I followed the unusual path until I reached the tall hedge. In the shadows, I spotted something lying on the ground.

I knelt down and saw that it was a gardening glove. Unlike the cotton version that I had worn when I planted daffodil bulbs along my sidewalk in the spring, this one was made of canvas. The brand name "Heman" was stitched across the back of it. The creases in the cloth made by the wearer's fingers were caked with mud. The palm area and the cuff of it were damp.

Concentrating on my find, I jumped when Simon said, "What are you doing down there?"

I lost my balance and toppled headfirst into the hedge. I wasn't hurt, but I felt like an idiot. He took hold of my arm and pulled me out of the bush. Twigs and leaves were stuck in my hair. He apologized for scaring me while he helped me brush the leaves and gunk from my shirt.

"It's okay, I'm fine," I told him. "Nothing's hurt, but my pride. You might want to take a look at this, though."

Simon stooped down and looked under the bush. He picked up a nearby stick and stuck it inside the cuff of the glove. He lifted it out, then held it up to take a better look.

"I'll give it to Marshall to take to the lab for a soil analysis," he said. "If the dirt from the grave matches the crusted dirt here, it's possible that it could have been used by the person who dug up the grave. But since this section of the cemetery isn't visited much, it could have been lost by someone a long time ago and not noticed."

"What about testing for fingerprints, or skin cells left inside it?"

Simon grinned at me. "If this had been a latex or leather glove, the wearer's fingers might have conformed to it and left a print inside. However, with this type of cloth, the alleles left will be our best bet for identification."

"Alleles?"

"The DNA makeup of the cell," he said. "Because most people are a mixture of races, DNA evidence alone isn't enough to convict someone of a crime. However, it does help narrow down the suspects if you have other evidence available."

"Well, then let me show you something else that might help," I said.

I pointed out the wet and dry checkerboard pattern on the ground. We followed it to the gravel road where it stopped. We turned around and backtracked along the path, and it led us to the open gravesite.

"I don't know what to make of it," Simon said, shaking his head. "Except for this stretch of grass from the road to here, there aren't any damp places. This part of the island hasn't had any rain for over a week, but we noticed that the soil taken out of the grave is pretty moist."

Something occurred to me. "Are you sure someone dug up the grave by hand?"

Simon nodded. "There are no tire tracks or signs of machinery in here. Whoever did this put in some sweat and elbow grease to dig down far enough to open that casket."

"What if he wanted to make the job a little easier?"

"What do you mean?"

"Last winter, I made an egg custard pie for one of our family dinners," I said. "When I was ready to bake it, I carried it slowly to the oven because the mixture is so thin, it tends to slosh out of the crust. When I reached the oven, I had forgotten to open the door first. Instead of setting the pie down, I tried to open the door while holding it with one hand."

He started smiling. "I'm not an expert when it comes to baking, but I bet I can imagine what happened to your floor."

"Not the floor," I said, shaking my head. "I managed to get the oven door partially open, but in the process, I tilted the pie. Some gooey egg mixture sloshed out of the shell and slid down the hot surface of the door. Then just like waves in a bathtub, the mixture moved back the other way, sending more sticky filling down between the glass and the partition. It was a mess! I never did get it all cleaned out. I still have streaks of baked egg custard between the glass and the inside of the door."

"So you think someone was sloshing something liquid along this path?"

"It's a theory. If I was going to dig in hard, dry soil, I'd wet it down first so it would be easier."

Taking a step toward me, Simon said, "It's worth considering. I'm glad you joined me, or the clues you found might have been overlooked. I'm going to give this glove to Marshall, then we're leaving. He's in charge of this show, and we have some fun things to do."

CHAPTER 3

As we drove out of the cemetery, Simon said, "I'm sorry for the delay in starting our relaxing evening. It should get better from here, right Tom?"

"You bet," Tommy replied. "It's a surprise worth waiting for."

Aside from telling our friends that someone had disturbed a grave, Simon didn't say anything more about the case. We drove along the shoreline heading toward Waikiki Beach. I thought we might be returning to a fun restaurant that my friends had taken me to back in March, but we passed it by.

A couple of miles before we reached the heavy tourist area of Waikiki, Simon turned off the highway into a small park. He stopped in a secluded area a short distance from the shoreline.

"Here we are," Tommy said. He climbed out of the car. "I hope you girls are hungry."

Traci and I looked at each other with confused expressions on our faces.

"This is a gorgeous stretch of beach and the sunset is really romantic, but I'm starving," Traci said. "I don't see a restaurant, or even a food vendor anywhere near here. I've seen both you men eat and I know you're probably hungrier than I am. What's up?"

Simon had walked around and opened my door for me. He was helping me out when he said, "Don't worry, ladies. You're going to love this."

He led me to the back of the Jeep where Tommy was already opening the door. Inside the area behind the seat, I saw a quilt draped over something. When Tommy pulled it off, I was shocked at what was there. The back end was packed with a picnic basket, a large ice chest, several Chinese lanterns, a CD player and more.

"Traci, you've got to see this!" I said. "Look what these two have been hiding!"

She walked up beside me as the guys started lugging out all the goodies.

"That basket is from Mr. Omura's deli," Traci said, leaning over to lift the lid. The mouth-watering aroma of yeasty bread, fish and spices escaped from the small opening. "Come on, Allie. Don't just stand there. Let's help these wonderful men set out the grub!"

We each carried a load to an empty spot on the beach. Tommy spread out the quilt and a large blanket. The rest of us started setting things down on them. The fragrance of the food was working its magic, because it only took about five minutes to get things arranged. As Simon pulled trays and bowls of food from the ice chest and basket, I filled glasses with ice and lemonade. Traci put out the plates, napkins and silverware, then she unwrapped a warm loaf of buttered French bread. Tommy arranged the lanterns around our cozy area and lit them.

We filled our plates with teriyaki ono fish steaks, lobster, fresh pineapple and papaya, green bean casserole and lots of other goodies. Only the sound of gentle waves slapping the beach and contented sighs from the four of us could be heard for several minutes. After half of the food on his plate was consumed, Simon asked, "So was it worth the wait?"

"Food from Mr. Omura's is always worth the wait," Tommy said, brushing crumbs from his shirt. Traci nodded in agreement.

"I appreciate you ordering everything, Tom," Simon said. "You did a good job."

"You mean the job of ordering was left up to you?" Traci asked, looking at her husband. "Sweetheart, I'm very proud of you. You even bought some vegetables."

"I'm learning the value of good nutrition," he said. "With the baby coming, our days of fast food and chips needs some revamping. But I didn't order that good-looking cake in the ice chest. Where did that come from?"

Simon wiped his mouth with his napkin. "An offering from my mom. It's a 'Welcome Back' gift to Allie."

"Oh, that's so sweet of her," I said. "I'm anxious to see her again."

I had met Simon's mother and father at a birthday party back in March. Charlene was a short, slim woman and had the same chocolate-brown eyes that Simon possessed. His father, Dennis, was a tall, robust man with a kind smile.

As Simon lifted the velvety strawberry cake from the ice chest, I noticed two men walking across the beach toward us. One was carrying a guitar and the other one had a ukulele in his hand. When they stopped a few yards from us, Simon waved at them. They said "Aloha," then began to play a soft Hawaiian ballad.

"Just in time," Tommy said, standing up. "May I have this dance, my dear?" He stuck out his hand toward Traci.

She gave him a bewildered look, but soon recovered and reached up to him. Pulling her into his arms, they began swaying with the music.

"If it's alright with you, we'll have the cake later," Simon said to me. "Would you join me in this dance?"

I smiled at him, and he took my hand. He pulled me into his arms and I laid my head against his shoulder. I closed my eyes and breathed in the soft cologne that was on his shirt. The sweet music floated around us as my body molded against his. We flowed as one through the soft sand on the beach. A few rays of sunlight remained on the horizon. I had never felt so content.

"It sure feels good having you back in Hawaii," Simon whispered.

"Hmmm," was the only reply I could muster. Words couldn't describe how great I felt.

The music stopped and Simon pulled back slightly. Cupping my chin in his right hand, he kissed me. It was a good thing his other arm was holding me, because I would have melted into a puddle on the beach right then and there.

"I'm ready for cake," I heard Tommy say. "How about you guys?"

"What do you say, Allie?" Simon whispered into my hair. "Do you need an energy boost?"

Man, do I ever! Dragging myself out of the fog his kiss had put me into, I said, "I could use a little pick-me-up. Bring on the sugar."

Simon smiled and led me back to the blanket. As I plopped down next to Traci, he glanced at his watch. "The evening isn't over yet, girls. If you'll look over there toward the hotels lining the beach, we're about to have more entertainment."

The two musicians had slipped away. I couldn't imagine anything better than being serenaded by your own duet. But just as Tommy handed me a piece of cake, a huge spectacle of light lit up the night sky. A fireworks display was being shot off at one of the nearby Waikiki hotels. Brilliant red, gold and orange fireballs were shooting high above the water. Before they drifted away, bursts of silver and gold exploded overhead.

We enjoyed the display while eating Charlene's luscious dessert, then started packing up to go home.

"Thank you, guys, for a wonderful evening," Traci said when we reached the apartment building. "I enjoyed it immensely."

"Me, too," I said. "I'll never forget it."

"It was our pleasure, wasn't it Tom?" Simon said. "Nothing is too good for our girls."

Our girls? Yes, it's good to be back in Hawaii!

The next morning I woke up to the sound of traffic coming from H-1 and the aroma of bacon frying in the kitchen. It took me a minute to orient myself to my surroundings, but when I did, I smiled and jumped out of bed. I grabbed my robe from the bedpost, then stopped in the bathroom to splash water on my face. When I entered the kitchen, Traci was standing at the stove gathering slices of crisp bacon from the frying pan.

"Good morning, sunshine," she said as she turned off the burner. "Sleep well?"

"Like a dream. Can I help?"

"If you want to grab the toast on that saucer, I'll bring the bacon. The juice is already on the table."

Following Traci into the small dining area, I felt giddy with excitement. We would be leaving soon to go to school to get the room ready for my students. *My students.* I liked the sound of it. Though this was a short-term assignment, I was anxious to work with children from another culture. I hoped to learn things that I would be able to take back to my job in Paradise.

"Miss Kahala said she would be in the office by 8:00 this morning," Traci said. "I assured her we would probably be there by 9:00 at the latest. I know you want to get some lesson plans done, and I'll help you change the bulletin boards. Feel free to use everything in the room just like it's your own."

"I appreciate that. I have an interactive bulletin board set that I brought with me for that small board behind your desk, but I intend to let the kids display their own work on the two larger ones."

"That's a good idea. The kids love seeing their own handiwork around the room."

After we finished eating, we both showered and were dressed and ready to leave by 8:15. As we pulled onto Moanalua Road, we passed a group of people standing at the bus stop across from the building. I couldn't help but notice the baby-faced young man standing close to the curb. He was dressed in "high-water jeans" as the boys back home call them. The cuffs of the pants were several inches above the top of the work boots he was wearing, and his shirt buttons were barely holding the opening together. He looked directly at me as we drove past.

"Do you know that guy?" I asked Traci. I continued observing him in the side mirror.

She looked in the rearview mirror and shook her head. "No, but I've seen him at the bus stop a lot. He's there like clockwork. I usually leave the house by 7:15 to get to school and he's always there. He must be running late today."

I dismissed the man from my thoughts as we crawled along with the heavy flow of traffic. There was a lot to be accomplished in the classroom before the students came tomorrow, and I needed to focus on the tasks ahead.

When we reached the school, I grabbed the sack that I had placed in the back seat and my purse, then we walked inside the building. We met Miss Kahala coming out of her office. She was dressed in a green and white muumuu and she had a white orchid pinned in her hair.

"Welcome, Allie," she said as we walked up to her. "It's good to have you here."

"Thank you, Miss Kahala." I stretched out my hand to her. "It's good to be here. I can't wait to get started."

Shaking my hand, she said, "I've had my assistant put together all the final paperwork that you'll need to sign. She also has your class list ready. You'll have ten students in all."

"I was hoping to take a look at the students' files today. From the information your assistant e-mailed to me, I understand that working on reading skills is the primary focus for the group."

"Yes, fortunately I was allowed enough teachers to be able to group the children so that emphasis could be directed to their particular needs. Hawaii doesn't normally have summer school since the school system offers tutoring through the year. However, most of the students that will be here for this June session needed some extra help beyond that.

Your group of students has problems with reading, while the other third grade class will be focusing on difficulties with math."

"Well, I love teaching reading, so I'm happy it worked out that way."

"I'm glad to hear that. Now, regarding the car that you will be given to use, there was a problem with the air conditioner. The mechanic assured me that he would have it repaired and here around 10:00 a.m. tomorrow. If you can find another way to school in the morning, you'll have transportation by the time your class is dismissed at noon."

"I'll be happy to bring her," Traci said. "I hadn't told Allie, but I had planned to come and show her some things around the building that she might find helpful."

"Thanks, Traci. I appreciate that," I said.

"Yes, thank you, Traci," the principal said. "Now that the car matter is settled, Allie, let's get you signed in so you can start drawing a paycheck."

After taking care of the necessary paperwork, the secretary showed me where the students' files were stored, then Traci and I headed to the school library. She had told me that the librarian kept multiple copies of a variety of books for the teachers to use with reading groups. One of my favorites, *The Giving Tree* by Shel Silverstein, was among the selections.

After signing out ten copies, Traci and I headed for her classroom. The custodian had washed the blackboards and mopped the floor until it shone. I got to work reviewing the story and in no time I had lesson plans done for the short week. Traci kept busy cleaning out closets in between answering my questions. She showed me where she kept things in her desk and made me feel right at home.

I looked around the room. "I guess the only things left to do now are to put up the bulletin board I brought, take a look at the students' files and copy a few sets of papers."

"I'll be glad to go run the papers for you," Traci said. "It's already 11:30 and I heard your stomach growling awhile ago."

"Yes, I'm ready for lunch and that would speed things along. I'll put up the bulletin board while you're in the workroom, then we can go look at those files."

Traci nodded. She picked up the original worksheets that I had set aside for copying, then headed down the hall. I pulled the decorative materials that I had brought with me out of the bag, then started putting them up. Traci walked back into the room just as I finished.

"That bulletin board looks great!" she said. "The kids are going to love it."

"Thanks. I remembered how curious your students were about Indians when I visited in March, and I felt like this would be a great icebreaker. I'm proud of how it turned out."

The hundredth anniversary of the Five Civilized Tribes Act was coming up soon. I had brought a display showing the various groups that had traveled to Oklahoma during the march called the Trail of Tears. The students would be able to learn about the different cultures by manipulating pieces showing the types of clothing, housing, and tools used by the tribes.

With everything in place, we gathered up our things and walked down to the office. I pulled the files and we sat down at a small table to review them. Since the children were coming from several different schools, Traci wasn't familiar with some of them. But it was nice to have her sitting beside me in the reviewing process. When we finished, I refiled the information and we left.

"From the teacher's comments that I saw, it looks like you're going to have a varied group of kids," Traci said as we drove away from the school. "It will be a challenge, but I know you're up to it."

"It looks like the majority of them have faced some tough times. But I love turning kids on to reading. Hopefully, this group will respond to the fun activities I've planned for them."

"I have to hand it to our parent association for the amount of money that has been raised for books," Traci said. "The librarian has had a ball this year ordering literature sets for us to use. On the last day of school, she told the teachers to be sure and let the summer school staff know that they were welcome to use the books and the teaching materials.

"Well, I plan to take advantage of them," I said. "I've used several of the titles I saw in there and have some great ideas for activities to go along with them."

Traci pulled into a parking space in front of a small grocery store on Beretania Street and stopped. "This is where the food from last night's picnic came from," she said. "Mr. Omura is a sweet Japanese-American man who has a wonderful take-out menu and deli. His parents started the grocery store decades ago and he worked for them. When they retired in the mid-1980s, he took it over and added the deli. Lucky for us, there's a couple of empty tables in the park over there."

I looked across the busy street toward the small park about a block away. Tall buildings formed a barrier around the grassy area that was nestled in the middle. There were people sitting at most of the dozen or so tables scattered in it.

I followed Traci into the store. We had to step aside to let four men dressed in suits carrying Styrofoam boxes squeeze past us. "This is a busy place to be so small," I said, looking at the crowd around the counter.

"It's swamped at both lunch and dinner time," Traci said. "Mr. Omura has such good food, he usually sells out if you don't get here when it first goes into the display case. I eat here at least twice a week during the school year."

As we moved along in the line, I took in the aromas of the tempting cuisine I could see displayed in the glass cases. Despite the many people coming in and out of the store, the man and the plus-sized woman behind the counter were filling orders quickly. As he rang up the order for the couple standing in front of us, he was joking and laughing with them.

Traci and I stepped up to the counter. "Mr. Omura, this is my friend Allie. She's visiting from the mainland and got to taste your ono and lobster last night."

He looked at me and smiled, then turned his attention back to her. "Ah, Miss Traci," he said. "Yes, your husband came in and we had fun putting together your surprise picnic. Did you and your friend enjoy it?" He glanced my way.

I smiled and nodded at him.

"Very much," Traci said. "It was romantic. Did Tommy share the plans they had for us with you?"

"He told me that your friend was coming here to teach summer school and that he and his buddy wanted her first night here to be memorable. I hope the music, sunset and my good food did the trick," he said looking at me.

"Oh, yes, Mr. Omura," I said. "I'll never forget it. Thank you."

He smiled and nodded his head. "Now, what will you have today?"

Looking into the case, I ordered the teriyaki chicken and vegetable combination dish. As he scooped a large portion into a take-out carton, Traci asked him to add a couple of pieces of rumaki to mine. After ordering the same items for herself, she pulled out her billfold.

"No, let me get this," I said, unlatching my purse.

"Lunch is on the house," Mr. Omura said to us. "Call it a 'Welcome to Hawai'i' gift from me to you, Miss Allie."

"Thank you, Mr. Omura," I said, smiling. "That's very kind of you, but you don't need to do that."

"I don't, but I want to. Just come back often while you're here. Pick up a bottled drink in the cooler over there and have a nice lunch you two."

We thanked him again, then walked to the cooler to get our drinks.

"What a nice man!" I told Traci as we walked outside. "I'll have to bring Aunt Edith here when she comes to stay with me. She loves Japanese cooking."

"He has some of the best," Traci said. "Wait until you try the rumaki."

"What is rumaki? I recognize the bacon wrapping, but that's about it."

"It's a Hawaiian hor d'eoeuvre. They serve it at some of the luaus. I'll tell you what it contains after you've had a taste."

We grabbed the only vacant table left in the park and dug into our lunches. I tasted the rumaki and decided that I liked it, but couldn't figure out what it had in it. After eating both pieces, I said, "Okay, what was in those tasty little morsels?"

Traci looked at me and smiled. "Chicken liver and water chestnuts."

If I hadn't already swallowed the pieces, I would have spit them out. "Eeewww. You know I hate chicken livers. Gizzards, I love, but not livers."

"Yeah, but you liked that, didn't you? Your palate overcame the preconceived dislike you had. The livers aren't fixed like they are in Oklahoma. These are marinated in soy sauce and sugar. Then you add a water chestnut and wrap the whole thing in a slice of bacon. Put them on a skewer and grill or broil them for fifteen minutes and 'Wahlah!,' you have rumaki."

"Well, I have to admit they didn't taste like the fried ones I ate as a kid at Nana's house. I guess you're forgiven."

As we gathered up our trash, Traci said, "Now, if you're ready to go talk to your new boss at the *Hawaiian Star,* we'll be on our way."

"Let's go," I said. "We probably won't be there long."

🦋   🦋   🦋

When Traci turned left off McCully Street, I told her to take the next left into the alley that ran alongside the *Hawaiian Star* offices. Blacktop had replaced the gravel that had covered the drive last March. When we reached the small lot behind the offices, she pulled into an empty parking space between a late-model silver Chrysler and a rusted 1996 Honda.

As I climbed out of her car, I could smell fabric softener in the air. I glanced at the laundromat across the way. Last spring, I had hidden behind the open door and eavesdropped on a conversation between Sammy Cho and his uncle. When my shoelaces became entangled in the old rusty wire that was still lying next to it, I fell headfirst into the door. Sammy walked out and caught me.

Traci and I walked across the parking lot toward the office building. "I'm anxious for you to meet Mr. Masaki," I said. "I think I'll enjoy working for him."

When we reached the back door, I tried to pull it open, but it was locked.

"Should we go around to the front?" Traci asked.

"Mr. Masaki was expecting me, and he said that if the door was locked to knock on it and someone would let me in."

I rapped on the steel door. After several seconds, a tall, blonde man with the darkest blue eyes I had ever seen opened it. His muscular frame filled out the yellow polo shirt and khaki slacks that he wore. I glanced down at the tanned arm holding the door open and saw that the fabric of his shirtsleeve was stretched to the limit around his bulging muscles.

"You must be Allie," he said. "Come right in. We've been expecting you."

We've been expecting you? Looking at the attractive face, I got a nervous feeling in the pit of my stomach. I realized he was waiting for us to come inside, so I nodded at Traci to go in ahead of me. She was staring at him with her mouth hanging open, so I nudged her with my elbow. I didn't blame her for her reaction; he was a sight to behold!

As he held the door open for us, he pressed his body against the doorframe so that we could get through the space. Having regained her composure, Traci motioned toward the entrance. Assuming she wanted me to enter first, I stepped forward, but at the same time, so did she. Before I realized what was happening, I was standing sideways in the opening and Traci was wedged in behind me. The entire front of my body was pressed against the man. Traci was holding me against him with the length of her arm while my back was pinning her against the opposite doorframe.

I heard footsteps in the hallway, then Mr. Masaki's voice. "Well hello, Allison. I see you've met your new partner, Kyle Messenger."

It was embarrassing to be seen by my new boss in such a predicament. But I was also embarrassed because Kyle's body was molded to mine.

I turned my head to the left. "Hello, Mr. Masaki." He had an amused expression on his face. I turned back toward my new partner and smiled up at him. "Nice to meet you, Mr. Messenger."

He grinned at me. "The pleasure is all mine, Miss Kane, but please call me Kyle."

"Okay, I'm Allie."

"I think I can get us out of this, if you two girls work with me," he said.

"I'm for that. Traci's elbow is poking into my back and it doesn't look like that piece around the doorframe is too comfortable for yours. How are you doing back there, Traci?"

"I feel like a sardine squeezed into a very crowded can," she said. "Whatever he has in mind to get us out of here, I'm all for it."

Mr. Masaki covered his mouth with his hand. Though he was trying to hide it, I could tell from the twinkle in his eyes that he was probably grinning ear to ear.

"What do you want us to do?" I asked Kyle.

"If you and I suck in our stomachs at the same time, we'll be pressed closer together. By doing that, I think we can get enough space between this doorframe and your friend to move out together sideways."

Every part of me, from my neck down to my knees, was pressed tightly against him. Thank goodness Simon wasn't here to see this. "Tell me when," I said.

"Okay, we'll do it on the count of three," he said. "One...two... three!"

I sucked in my stomach at the same time that he did, and for a few seconds, my breasts were flattened even tighter against his chest. My face was on fire as we both took two steps sideways.

Breathing a sigh of relief when I was finally free, I turned and walked over to Traci, who was leaning against the wall. "Are you okay?" I asked her.

Taking a deep breath, she nodded. "I'm fine. I'm just glad it was my arms wedged in and not my stomach."

"Me, too."

Mr. Masaki stepped forward. "Now that that is over, welcome to your new job, Allison. Please introduce Kyle and me to your friend."

"Oh, I'm sorry. This is Traci Morris. We grew up together and she's being kind enough to let me stay with her in Aiea while I'm here."

Both men shook hands with her. "It's nice to meet you, Ms. Morris," Mr. Masaki said. "Would you like a tour of the *Star* facility before I send Allison out on her first assignment?"

"I didn't realize you'd want me to start today," I said to him. "I don't have the car from the school yet, so Traci brought me. I hate to impose on her to make another trip over here this evening to pick me up."

"Oh, that's no problem," Traci said. "But I am interested in seeing this newspaper operation before I go. I've been reading the *Hawaiian Star* ever since we moved here."

Looking at me, Mr. Masaki said, "As I told you on the phone Sunday afternoon, I'm anxious for you and Kyle to get started on this grave-robbing piece. I had intended to wait until tomorrow to put you to work. However, the caretaker for the cemetery at the Byodo-In Temple agreed to an interview about new security that he's implemented to keep such a thing from happening there. He's only available this afternoon. Kyle has been using the company car for assignments." He looked at my new partner. "You wouldn't mind giving Allison a lift back to her friend's place this evening, would you, Kyle?" We all looked at him.

"I'd be glad to," he said, smiling. "My apartment is in Waipahu, so Aiea is right on the way."

The journalist in me was itching to get started and everything seemed to be falling into place. "No time like the present," I said. "If you'll give me a notepad, I'm ready to start."

"I can do a little better than that," Mr. Masaki said, smiling. "Kyle, if you wouldn't mind giving Ms. Morris a tour, I'll visit with Allison and show her the office she'll be using."

"Sure thing," Kyle said. "Right this way, Ms. Morris." With a sweep of his hand, they started down the hall together.

"Traci, I'll walk you to your car when you're ready to leave," I said to her.

She turned and nodded at me, then focused her attention back on Kyle. "Call me Traci, please," I heard her tell him. "Only my students call me Ms. Morris."

"Now, Allison, if you'll come with me, I'll show you the office where you'll be working and we'll discuss your salary," Mr. Masaki said.

Walking beside him down the narrow hallway, the hum of the huge presses grew louder. I had taken a tour when I had been there in March and had been amazed at the efficiency of the operation. Like most newspapers today, the *Hawaiian Star* used offset printing where images are etched onto thin aluminum plates. Positive images are developed from a full-page photographic negative, then are mounted onto the offset printing press. A twenty-foot tall web press sat in the center of the spacious room. A monstrous roll of newsprint streamed through it. In addition to putting ink on the paper, the web press also assembled the pages in the correct sequence.

Twice a week, over forty thousand copies of the *Hawaiian Star* were produced and distributed throughout the Islands. There were more than twenty thousand subscribers who received their copies by mail or by carrier. The remainder of the papers were distributed through coin boxes and retail outlets. With my limited experience at the *Paradise Progress,* I realized that Mr. Masaki was taking a risk hiring me. I was determined that he wouldn't be sorry about his decision.

He led me up two flights of stairs and down a short hallway. "We've been using this building ever since it was built more than forty years ago," he said. "Until last year, the rooms on this floor had been used for storing records. My staff has offices on the second floor, but as the paper has continued to grow, it was necessary to make some changes. This floor was remodeled last fall and three new offices were created. I hope the one I've fixed up for you will suit your needs."

Since I was only going to be there for a month, I didn't expect any special treatment. A table to write on and access to a computer and phone was all that I really needed. I was overwhelmed when we stopped at the doorway of a large office that had a gorgeous view of the ocean and a park across the street. The walls were painted a soothing eggshell color and a wide border with various shades of burgundy and mauve in it ran along the edge close to the ceiling. Set in the center of the room was a polished oak desk with a comfy-looking leather chair pushed beneath it. A matching armoire was sitting against one wall with a couple of file trays on it. A variety of office supplies were stacked beside the trays. A computer and printer, that both looked brand new, were sitting on the desk.

Stepping into the room, I said, "Oh, Mr. Masaki, it's beautiful!"

He smiled, but didn't say anything. I ran my hand over the smooth finish of the desktop, then sat down in the comfortable chair and looked around the room. I noticed a framed copy of an old *Hawaiian Star* newspaper hanging on the wall in front of me. The paper had yellowed with time. A picture at the top showed a much younger version of my new boss. He was looking at the camera and smiling while shaking hands with another man. The headline above the picture read, "*Hea-hea to Ko Hawaii Pae'Aina.*" Since my Hawaiian dictionary was still at Traci's, I asked Mr. Masaki what the headline said.

"It means 'Welcome to the Hawaiian Islands,'" he replied. "That's a copy of the first edition ever printed. The man in the picture with me was the mayor at the time, who also happened to be one of my cousins. Back then, I had one assistant to help me get the paper out twice a week. I thought it would be an appropriate addition to the room, though you're welcome to add any other pictures, if you'd like to."

"It's perfect," I said. I stood up and walked to the window. Down below, in the middle of the park, I could see a massive garden filled with orchids, birds of paradise and a host of other tropical plants. Children and dogs were running and playing and the park benches were filled with people of all ages.

Mr. Masaki walked up behind me. "To do his or her best work, a writer needs inspiration. With some help from some of the ladies who work here, we fixed up the offices. Only God could have created this spectacular view."

"Amen," I said. The sun was shining down on the swaying palm trees and the scene was alive with color. In the distance, I could see the waves rushing toward the shore and a few surfers dotted the swells.

After discussing my salary and getting an overview of the afternoon assignment ahead, I grabbed a new pad and pen from the stack of supplies. Mr. Masaki and I walked back downstairs together. We met Traci and Kyle coming back up the hallway toward us.

"I enjoyed the tour very much," Traci said to Kyle. "Thanks for being a great guide."

"My pleasure." He turned and looked at me. "So, how did you like your new office? Pretty cool, huh?"

"I love it! I'm anxious to try out that new computer. After I walk Traci to her car, I'm ready to head out if you are."

"I'll be ready to go by the time you return," he said.

Traci thanked Mr. Masaki for the tour, then she and I walked out to the parking lot.

"You couldn't have asked for a nicer partner than Kyle," she said. "And he's drop-dead gorgeous to boot! If you didn't already have a love interest, I'd suggest you go after him, post haste!"

"Yes, he seems like a nice guy, but I'm very happy with Simon, thank you."

"Speaking of Simon, are the two of you going out tonight?"

"We had planned to go to dinner, but I didn't expect to start working here today. I told him I'd be hard to reach, so he asked me to call him when I got back to your apartment. I'll see how it goes at the graveyard, then give him a call."

"Okay, have fun. I'll see you later tonight," Traci said.

"See you."

CHAPTER 4

"Mr. Masaki likes us to use the Honda for company business," Kyle said. "It's a little beat up, but it gets thirty-five miles to a gallon of gas. With gasoline over three bucks a gallon here now, it really adds up. When we're done with the interview, we'll come back here and get my car and I'll take you home in it." He motioned toward the silver Chrysler sitting two spaces away.

The sleekness and glamour of the car seemed to fit him. As I watched him fold his long legs into the driver's side of the old Honda, he looked like a fish out of water.

We drove on the Likelike Highway toward the other side of the island. Kyle pointed out some sites along the way.

"When I first came here, I called this the 'like-like' highway, using a long vowel sound," he said. "Mr. Masaki is the one who told me it's pronounced 'leaky-leaky.' He said the highway was named after Princess Miriam Likelike, a younger sister of Hawaii's last two monarchs. I don't recall their names."

"King David Kalakaua and Queen Lydia Liliuokalani," I said.

He glanced at me and smiled. "So, you're not only pretty, but smart, too," he said. "Most of the teachers I had in school were old hags that rode my case every chance they got."

"I do my homework."

When we reached the Wilson Tunnel that would take us through the Koolau Mountain range, I told him some things I had learned when I had visited back in March. "This tunnel was completed in the early 1960s, right after the Pali Tunnels were done. Until then, people had to drive around the island on the Kamehameha Highway to get from one side to the other."

"That would take a lot of time," Kyle said.

We pulled into the Valley of the Temples Cemetery, and I couldn't help comparing it to the one in Paradise. Like the plots at home, most of the graves here were adorned with flowers, but some of the additional decorations were a bit unusual. As we drove along, I saw bottles of beer and saki propped against some headstones. Balloons and toys were on a few of the mounds and one of the graves near the road had a baseball mitt and bat lying on it. As we pulled into the parking lot in front of the Byodo-In Temple, I could hear music coming from a radio lying on a grave a short distance away.

"These people believe in going all out for Memorial Day, don't they?" I said.

"Not just on Memorial Day. Christmas, Easter, Mother's Day and birthdays are all big decoration days over here. Look at those four plots clustered together over there." He pointed to a group of graves about twenty feet away. "You don't normally see something like that in cemeteries on the mainland."

I looked where he was pointing and saw dinner plates sitting on each of the four graves. At this distance, I couldn't make out the specific items on them, but I could tell they were all covered with food.

"What's the theory behind it?" I asked. "Are people trying to feed their dead ancestors?"

"Some cultures believe the dead will feed the poor with it."

I couldn't fathom a belief like that, so I didn't comment. As we walked across the wooden bridge that spanned a stream in front of the majestic temple, I glanced down into the water. Hundreds of bright orange, yellow and spotted carp were swimming close to the planks holding up the bridge.

"Those fish are beautiful!" I said. "Both my grandfathers would have a ball here with a rod and reel. Though I can't imagine eating any of them. They look like overgrown versions of the pet goldfish I had in my aquarium when I was a kid."

Leaning against the railing, Kyle looked over and said, "They say there are close to two thousand koi fish in this stream. There's a place inside where visitors can purchase food for them if they want to. From the looks of these guys, I'd say they've been eating pretty well."

We walked toward the temple, and I was amazed at the detail in the Chinese architecture. The structure was crimson and had a slate-colored molded tile roof on each section. A person could enter it either through one of the hundred-foot-long covered walkways extending along each side, or by using the steps leading up from the sidewalk at the center of the building. Manicured shrubs and gardens were all over the place.

"Have you ever been here before?" Kyle asked.

"Traci and her husband and I passed it going to church the week I was here for spring break. But too much happened to get back over when it was open. How about you?"

"I visited here when I came over on vacation three years ago. The temple was built in the late 1960s and is an exact replica of the nine-hundred-year-old Byodo-In Temple in Uji, Japan. Though only Buddhists were buried in the cemetery in the beginning, many of their descendants converted to Christianity, so it's open to all faiths now. A Christian Church was built along one side of the cemetery a few years ago."

"I'd like to walk through it if we have time after the interview," I said.

"Sure thing. It shouldn't take long to get the information we need for the story."

We started climbing the stone steps leading to a small cottage behind the temple. When we neared the top, a tall, redheaded man with a bushy mustache was standing on the landing.

I was huffing and puffing by the time we reached him. Embarrassed because Kyle wasn't even breathing hard, I decided I'd better start taking advantage of the stairs in Traci's apartment building instead of using the elevator all the time. *Adding some long walks wouldn't hurt either,* I thought.

Kyle walked toward the man and extended his hand. "Mr. MacGregor? I'm Kyle Messenger and this is Allison Kane from the *Hawaiian Star.* I spoke with you on the phone on Friday."

"Nice to meet you, Mr. Messenger," the man replied, shaking his hand. "Ms. Kane, it's a pleasure."

"We appreciate you taking the time to visit with us about the increased security out here," Kyle said. "Please rest assured that nothing will be revealed that you don't want known. The purpose of our piece is to dissuade any would-be vandals from striking here."

"I appreciate you clarifying that for me," Mr. MacGregor said. "I was hesitant to reveal any system upgrades, but then I got to thinking that getting the news out might be a deterrent. First, I need to check out a problem that was reported by the Buddha statue. If you and Ms. Kane would like to join me on the walk over there, I can fill you in along the way."

"Sounds good," Kyle said. "I brought along a tape recorder to tape our conversation, if you don't mind."

"Sure, that's fine with me. Are you ready, Ms. Kane?"

"Yes, sir. I'm anxious to take a look around.

Mr. MacGregor led the way down the steps and through a winding garden path. Along the way, he told us that since the last grave-robbing incident on Maui, motion detectors and multiple floodlights had been installed all over the grounds. In the past, one security guard patrolling at night had been sufficient, but now a second one had been added to help with the rounds.

"Back when it first began, this cemetery was a quiet place," Mr. MacGregor said. "Now it's a popular tourist attraction. Not only does the beautiful temple draw visitors, but the interest in the former Philippine dictator, Ferdinand Marcos, also brings people here."

"I didn't realize he was entombed here," Kyle said.

"He's not, now. His remains were finally allowed back into the Philippines in 2001."

"I remember studying about Marcos in world history class in high school," I said. "He was forced out of the Philippines, so he and his wife came to Honolulu. He brought bags of gold and jewels with him, and his wife had even more bags filled with her hundreds of pairs of shoes."

"Yes, there was quite a controversy when they moved here," Mr. MacGregor said. "Though it died down for a while, when he passed away in 1989, things got stirred up again. His wife insisted that he be put in an air-conditioned mausoleum here and the people of Oahu had to pick up the electric bill. Eventually the payments stopped and the power company threatened to cut off the juice. Now he's in a refrigerated crypt in his home country. I've heard that his wife and others still come regularly to view him and pay their respects."

"That's so bizarre," I said. "When I go, I don't want anyone looking at me. If they didn't see me while I was alive, then they're out of luck."

"Same here," Kyle said.

The three of us walked into the main temple, then into the room where the statue of Buddha presided. Mr. MacGregor said that the statue was made of wood and weighed over two tons. A small marble-topped table holding two pewter vases filled with flowers and a large copper bowl sat in front of the statue. Several dollar bills and coins were lying in the bowl.

The caretaker walked behind the table and pulled a red floral scarf from beneath one of the vases. Holding it up, he said, "People give all types of offerings. The money given helps maintain the facility. One of the groundskeepers reported finding this. They've been instructed to remove any foreign objects and place them in a room in the meditation house. However, the caretaker who found this is a practicing Buddhist. He refuses to touch another person's offering, though he is quick to let me know about them. We don't want to offend anyone, regardless of what they leave. But because of the quantity of items left each day, we try to remove them right away."

Mr. MacGregor carefully folded the floral scarf, then led us through the breezeway. The gardens were magnificent and the paper-like trunks on the eucalyptus trees were amazing.

As we ended the tour, Kyle said, "I appreciate the information you've given to us for our story. You mentioned on the phone that you also oversee another smaller cemetery close by. Do you have time to show us that security system?"

"Yes, I'll be glad to take you there," Mr. MacGregor said. "My red Volkswagen is parked on the far end of the parking lot. You can follow me to the other place in your car, if you like."

The three of us walked to the parking lot. Kyle pulled in behind Mr. MacGregor's car and we drove a couple of miles down the road. When we reached the entrance of the small cemetery, I said, "*Kapuo'io'ina.*"

"What did you say?" Kyle asked, looking at me.

"The sign at the entrance said *Kapuo'io'ina.* In the Hawaiian language it means 'sacred resting place.'"

"Uh huh, if you say so," he said, grinning. "I have a hard enough time keeping up with English. I have no desire to try to learn a foreign language."

"I'm picking up a word or two now and then. I love it here and it's fun trying to learn the language."

As we drove into the parking area, I saw a few people tending to their loved ones' graves. An elderly couple holding hands was sitting on a bench under one of the shade trees. A small Japanese tour group was taking pictures near a large concrete fountain.

Mr. MacGregor led us through the cemetery and told us about the security system. Though the grounds were much less elaborate than at the Valley of the Temples, they were decorated nicely and well groomed. A mausoleum was the only building there. Several wooden benches were scattered along the pebble walkways near it. A statue of King Kalakaua stood beneath a Banyan tree off to one side, and he seemed to be keeping guard over the grounds. I walked the short distance to the statue to take a closer look.

The details carved into the stone were unique. The facial features reflected strength, and the man looked like a brave warrior ready for battle. The feathers on the stone cape that he wore had intricate designs and must have taken weeks to carve. I ran my hand along the base of the statue, then stopped. Where stone toes met the concrete stand, I saw two thumbs!

Oh, boy! Leave it to me to discover something gross!

"Mr. MacGregor?" I called. "Would you mind coming over here for a minute?"

He and Kyle stopped talking and looked my way. They started walking toward me. I was concentrating on my breathing and kept swallowing hard to keep the lunch that I had eaten earlier from coming up.

When the two men reached me, a sick look came across Kyle's face. I heard Mr. MacGregor whisper, "Dear Lord in heaven!"

Kyle took a step back and looked like he might pass out. Mr. MacGregor just stood staring at the appendages.

It was time for someone to take some action. "Kyle, may I borrow your cell phone?" I asked. "I'm going to call a detective friend of mine and report this. Mr. MacGregor, you might want to avert that group of sightseers from coming this way." I nodded toward the tourists heading toward us.

"By all means," he said. He ran his hand over his face and took a couple of deep breaths before walking away.

Some color had begun coming back into Kyle's face as he pulled his phone from his pocket. He handed it to me and said, "I'm sorry about that. It was just such a shock!"

Remembering how I felt the first time I saw a severed body part, I didn't blame him for his reaction. I dialed Simon's cell phone number and was glad when he answered after the fourth ring.

"Kahala," he said, hesitantly. Not many people had Simon's cell phone number. When he gave it to me, he told me that co-workers and family members had the number, but other calls were channeled through the main dispatcher at Honolulu P.D. I knew he always checked the display before answering his phone. Since Kyle's number wouldn't be familiar to him, I was thankful that he didn't let it roll over to voicemail to screen it.

"Hi, it's me," I said.

"I almost didn't answer, but now I'm glad I did," Simon said. "This isn't Traci's number. Where are you calling from?"

"Mr. Masaki wanted me to start today, so I borrowed my partner's cell phone."

"So, he's paired you up with a partner, huh? What's her name?"

I wasn't sure what to tell Simon about Kyle yet. I didn't think he was the jealous type, and I knew he'd find out soon enough. But the issue of the thumbs was more pressing at the moment, so I dodged the question.

"You'll get to meet my partner later," I said. "We're at the Sacred Resting Place Cemetery. I found something you need to come and check out."

There was silence on the line, and I figured that Simon's smile had changed to a frown. "Okay, I know I'm probably not going to like it, but tell me what you found."

The details of my discovery came pouring out, and I was wet with sweat by the time I finished.

"I'm sorry you had to find those things, but please try to relax," he said, soothingly. "I'll contact Marshall and Dave. We should be there in about fifteen minutes."

"We'll be waiting." I hung up, then gave Kyle's phone back to him. I looked at my watch; it was 3:45. "My friend and some others will be here soon. I'll wait here so that no one bothers the evidence."

"I'm going to run back to the car and get a notebook to jot down some notes," Kyle said. "You know, this is a lucky break for us. We'll be the only reporters on the scene for this story. Mr. Masaki will be thrilled that we got the scoop!"

"It may be a dream come true for a reporter," I said, "but I can't help thinking about the poor person who lost his thumbs. I don't like to get stories at someone else's expense."

"Yeah, it's a bummer for the guy, but a sweet break for us! This story is bound to make the front page! I'll see you back here in a few minutes."

As I watched him jog toward the parking lot, I was beginning to have my doubts about our partnership. I wasn't the kind of person to get a story at any cost, but I wasn't so sure about Kyle.

At 4:00, I heard a siren and saw the flashing lights on Simon's car as it pulled into the entrance of the cemetery. Another police vehicle with its lights flashing, and a van with "Honolulu County Medical Examiner" written on the side followed him in. When they reached the parking lot, I waved.

Simon stepped out of his car and waved back at me. He waited for the other men to join him, then the group started walking toward me. As they drew closer, I saw Simon say something to Marshall and Dave. When they reached me, they both nodded, then proceeded on past with the coroner. Simon pulled me into his arms and held me close.

I looked over his shoulder and saw Kyle walking toward us. Though I was reluctant to pull away from Simon, I knew he had a job to do and so did I. Stepping away, I said, "Come on. Before you get tied up with your work, I want to introduce you to my new partner."

Simon turned around, but didn't move as I started walking toward Kyle. When I looked back to see why he wasn't coming, I saw that his fists were clenched. An angry scowl covered his face. If looks could kill, Kyle would have been a dead man.

Kyle had stopped where he was and seemed to be torn about whether or not to come any closer. I knew Simon didn't get mad easily, so I figured something had happened between the two men that I wasn't aware of.

Uneasy with the standoff and not sure how to bridge the gap, I decided to try good manners. "Kyle, I'd like you to meet my friend, Simon Kahala. Simon, this is Kyle Messenger."

As the two men stood sizing each other up, Simon said, "We've met."

I was surprised by his abruptness, but even more so by his next statement to Kyle.

"I realize you have a story to get here, *Mr. Messenger,* but I hope you haven't forgotten what I told you last time."

Kyle's stance relaxed a little as he walked over to us. "No, sir, I haven't. But I hope that for Allie's sake, you'll believe me and let bygones be bygones."

Even though there was only a couple of years separating them, it didn't seem inappropriate to hear Kyle call Simon "sir." From the moment I had met Simon, he had commanded respect, and I hadn't seen anyone yet who didn't act like he deserved it.

Simon stood silent for a few moments, then glanced at me. Looking back at Kyle, he said, "I'll give you the benefit of the doubt. Don't make me sorry for that."

"No, Detective, I won't."

"Now, if you two will excuse me, I need to find out what's going on with the thumbs," Simon said.

"I'll come and find you before we leave," I said to him. "You may think of something you need to ask me. Kyle and I are going back to the *Star* to get his car, then he's giving me a lift to Traci's."

I could tell by Simon's expression that that bit of news wasn't something he was happy to hear. "*I'll* give you a ride to Traci's." He looked at Kyle. "Then I'll go home and change clothes while you get ready for *our date.*"

I was sure that the emphasis on "our date" wasn't a mistake and was meant to send Kyle a message. As chauvinistic as it sounded, I let it slide. If I was going to be possessed by anyone, I was glad to let it be Simon.

🦋 🦋 🦋

"I'm not crazy about your new partner," Simon said to me in the car on our way to the apartment.

"Yeah, I kind of got that impression. You're not the kind of person to jump to conclusions. What happened between you two?"

"For starters, he almost compromised a crime scene a couple of weeks ago. One of my men caught him picking up some evidence. When I questioned Kyle about it, he claimed he was just looking at it. I read him the riot act and threatened to take him to jail if he ever tried anything like that again."

"Did you notify Mr. Masaki about his conduct?"

"No, because though I suspected he was intending to take it with him, I didn't have absolute proof. But I'll tell you, I'm not keen about you working with him."

Ignoring his last remark, I said, "You said 'for starters.' What else has turned you against him?"

"He twisted the facts on another case when he wrote the story. He made a couple of talented detectives look like the Keystone Cops."

"If he reported it wrong, why didn't you demand a retraction?"

"Well, it wasn't *what* he said, but *how* he said it. It could have been a positive piece to show a job well done, but instead, his bias remarks made some people look incompetent. When he did that, he created an enemy in me."

I could understand Simon's frustration because he was a hardworking detective who strived to maintain high morale among his workers. Oftentimes it didn't take much criticism to deflate someone who was already feeling stressed in a thankless job.

Simon pulled into the parking lot of Traci's apartment building and stopped by the front door. He shut off the car engine, then turned to look at me.

"Hopefully, your talk with Kyle did the trick," I said. "Mr. Masaki thinks he's a good reporter, or he wouldn't have paired me up with him. If there is anything unethical about his methods, maybe my charm will rub off on him and help him change." I reached over and squeezed Simon's hand that was lying on the console between us.

"That's just one more thing for me to worry about," he said. "Your charm works magic on men. I should know."

So, his reaction today hadn't just been related to Kyle's work ethics. "You don't have a thing to worry about," I said. "I may be working with Kyle, but I prefer dating handsome Hawaiian detectives."

"In contrast to handsome blonde reporters?" He stroked my cheek with the back of his free hand. "It's a good thing. Just be sure you remember that when he tries to make a move on you."

My heart was beating a mile a minute. I was about to tell him that Kyle wouldn't do that, but I forgot what I was going to say as I stared into his dark brown eyes. His right arm rested on the seat behind my head. When I reached up to brush back the wisp of black hair that had fallen across his forehead, he took hold of my hand and guided it to his chest. The hard muscles under his shirt couldn't hide the quickened beat I felt beneath my fingertips.

Simon leaned over the console and pulled me toward him. The clean scent of his cologne surrounded us. Enjoying everything about him, I closed my eyes and all thoughts of Kyle were lost.

He kissed me gently at first, then hugging me tighter, the kiss grew deeper and I was a goner. No drug on earth could create such a sweet euphoria. At that moment, I didn't want the high to ever end.

CHAPTER 5

When I walked into the apartment, Traci was lying on the couch watching the evening news with Tommy.

"Here's Lois Lane, now," Tommy said. "How did your first assignment go?"

"You're not going to believe what I found on a statue," I said. "But before I tell you, what's the matter with my best friend? She doesn't look well."

Traci looked up and smiled, but I could tell by the look in her eyes that it was an effort for her. "Oh, I'm having some mild cramping and Tommy is making me stay on the sofa," she said.

"This isn't the first time it's happened and the doctor said you needed to rest more," he said. He walked over and knelt down beside her. "Whatever has to be done to keep you and the baby safe is worth it."

I could tell Traci was touched by her husband's concern. "I know and I will," she said. "I just overdid it today, I guess. I'm sure the cramps will stop in a few minutes."

"Well, if they don't, I'm calling the doctor again," Tommy said.

He stood back up and walked back to his recliner. "No arguments about it."

"Yes, dear."

"Is there anything I can do for you?" I asked. "I could make you some soup, or I'll cancel my date with Simon if you'd like me to stay in and sit with you."

"I'll take you up on the soup, but you aren't canceling your date on my account. I'll go to bed early, and I'm sure I'll be fine to take you to school in the morning."

"I'll go in right now and fix you guys something to eat before I get ready."

"I'll help you," Tommy said. "I brought home some vegetable rice soup from Mr. Omura's deli, so supper is already halfway done."

The two of us worked side by side preparing the meal. Tommy warmed up the soup while I sliced some cheese, leftover roast beef and French bread for sandwiches. He fixed their drinks and I cut up a salad. Soon dinner was served.

"So how did your first day with Kyle go?" Traci asked as she bit into her sandwich.

"We went to interview the caretaker at the Byodo-In Temple and that went well. After that, the caretaker took us to a smaller cemetery. Things got a bit strained when I found two thumbs at the base of King Kalakaua's statue."

Tommy started coughing and Traci looked up at me and stopped chewing. I guess my discovery wasn't the best choice for dinner conversation.

After swallowing her food, Traci took a big gulp of her drink. "I'll bet that was a real eye opener for your new partner. You're going to make him work for his salary."

Having composed himself after his coughing fit, Tommy said, "I hope you called Simon."

"Yes, he and his team came out to investigate. But he wasn't too talkative after I introduced him to Kyle."

"I'll bet," Traci said, grinning. "I imagine he wasn't too happy to see you with the blonde Mr. Wonderful, was he?"

"Not too much, no." I looked down at my hands lying on the table-top. "I assured him that Kyle was only a working partner and nothing else."

"Yeah, but does Kyle know that?" Traci asked.

"I'll make sure he understands, if it ever comes up. Now, I better get ready for my date."

"Thanks for dinner. It was great," Traci said, rising from the table. "I'm starting to feel better."

"I'm glad to hear it," I said.

Tommy was carrying all the dishes to the kitchen, so I turned around and walked to my bedroom. Gathering up some clean clothes, I took a quick shower and brushed my hair until it shone. I put on a little blue eye shadow, some blush and mascara, then hurried to get dressed. Simon was calling on the intercom from downstairs when I walked back into the living room.

"She just walked back in," I heard Tommy say into the speaker.

"Please tell Simon I'll be right down," I told him.

I checked on Traci to see how she was feeling and told her I wouldn't be late coming in. I wanted to be rested when I met my new students the next morning.

I rode the elevator down and when the doors opened in the lobby, Simon was standing there dressed in jeans and a short-sleeved navy blue shirt. His hair was still damp from his shower and his five o'clock shadow was gone. Even though I had just left him about an hour before, I was still glad to see him.

"Hi, beautiful," he said. He reached for my hand. "I know this is a school night for you, so I thought I'd take you to a place only the locals know about. It's called The Oasis Café and I've been going there for years. They have all kinds of food and you rarely have to wait for a table."

"Sounds like a good place," I said.

Once we were in the Jeep headed out of the apartment complex, I asked Simon how the Shady Palms case was coming. Since I had found the glove under the hedge near the disturbed grave, I felt like I had a vested interest.

"The deceased was Ray Franklin, the son of the guy in the Maui cemetery who lost his ring and left finger three months ago," he said. "Eddie and I have been pounding our heads against a wall with that case. Now, this one comes along to add fuel to the fire. Whoever is opening these graves has to be eaten up with hate for this family. The others were bad, but Ray's grave disturbance makes no sense at all."

"I agree with you," I said, looking at him. "Anyone who would dig up someone just to steal their clothes has got to have a screw loose. I'm sure there are agencies here like we have in Oklahoma where people who need clothes can get them free."

Simon looked at me oddly. "What makes you think the person took Ray's clothes?"

Shrugging, I said, "Because Marshall said that according to the burial records, the only thing buried with him were the clothes he was wearing. But he did say that something was taken. If there was nothing else buried with him, what else could it be?"

Simon smiled at me and reached for my hand. "Sweetheart, I understand how you could have drawn that conclusion, but Ray didn't lose any clothes. He's still dressed like he was when the state buried him."

I frowned at him. "Then what else could have been taken?"

Simon hesitated for a moment. "All of his fingers."

I gasped. *His fingers?* I looked down at my free hand. I started rolling my fingers in and out, then hid them in my lap. The desire to protect them was overwhelming.

"Simon, that's crazy!"

"There is no logical reason for a lot of human behavior and especially something like this," he said. "I didn't say anything when I brought you home today, but did you notice anything unusual about the two thumbs you found?"

Thinking back, I hadn't touched them, or even taken a second look after my discovery. "I remember there was some decomposition, and I don't recall any blood."

He squeezed my hand. "The pieces of flesh on the thumbs contained traces of formaldehyde."

I stared at him for a minute. "You mean they were embalmed?"

Simon nodded his head. "I won't be surprised if the thumbs turn out to be Ray Franklin's. Aside from his dad's case, we haven't had any other cases regarding severed limbs on the island in over two years."

"Well, I hope they do belong to Ray. That will be one less puzzle for you to solve."

"You're right about that," he said. "Now, we're almost to the restaurant, so let's talk about something more pleasant, shall we?"

The food at The Oasis Café was fabulous. There's a barbecue restaurant near Paradise and I didn't think any place could beat it. But after eating the barbecued brisket, I had to re-evaluate.

Remembering my breathlessness after climbing the steps at the Byodo-In Temple, as we left the restaurant I suggested we walk off some of the meal. The Ala Moana Center was only a couple of blocks away, so we drove there. We window-shopped for over an hour before Simon took me home.

He walked me to the door of the tower. "We're still on for dinner tomorrow night with Eddie Zantini, right?"

"You bet," I said.

"He likes the Red Reef, so I'll make reservations for 7:00."

Traci and Tommy had taken me to the Red Reef Café when I came for the summer school interview. It was located a short distance from Waikiki. The specialty was shrimp and oysters served with greens grown in nearby Waimanalo. A live band played every night.

After kissing me good night, Simon said, "Eddie and I will pick you up about 6:30 tomorrow evening. Have a wonderful first day at school and stay at least ten feet away from Kyle Messenger when you go to the *Hawaiian Star* tomorrow."

Laughing, I said, "That will be a little hard to do, but I'll try. Sleep well and I'll see you tomorrow."

He nodded, then headed back toward his car. I walked inside the lobby to the elevator and pushed the button. The stairs would have to wait until another day; I was too tired to face them tonight.

It was 10:30 when I slipped into the apartment. Traci had left the bathroom light on for me. I tiptoed to my bedroom and put on my pajamas, then went into the bathroom to wash my face and brush my teeth.

When I came out, I could hear both of my friends snoring. *That's a good sign,* I thought. I hoped that the cramping Traci had experienced earlier in the evening was gone for good. But just to be safe, I said a special prayer for her before I fell asleep.

🐾 🐾 🐾

"Allie. Alliieee." I was trying to wake up, but I couldn't make myself open my eyes. When I felt someone touch my shoulder, I sat straight up in bed.

"Sorry to have to wake you so early, but Tommy is insisting on taking me to the doctor," Traci said.

I looked out the window and could see the first signs of daylight. Alarmed when I realized she had said "doctor" I looked at her. "Are you still cramping, Traci? I'll get dressed and come with you."

I started trying to shove back the covers, but they wouldn't budge because she was sitting on the edge of them.

"I had a little light cramping before I went to bed. Just to be sure there's nothing amiss, I want the doctor to check me out. Tommy has a 9:00 a.m. meeting at the military base, but he wants to be with me during the examination. So in order to do that, the doctor is meeting us at the hospital at 7:00. I hate to ask you to do it, but would you mind taking the bus to school this morning? One stops on the road out front at 7:20."

"No, of course not." I reached over and took her hand. "But I still want to come to the doctor with you."

"I appreciate your concern, but you've got commitments. Tommy will bring me back home when we're finished."

"What if you get sick today while both Tommy and I are gone?" I was torn between my obligation to the school and my friend.

"I'm sure I won't. However, that's one reason I'm asking you to take the bus instead of using my car. I'd hate to be without transportation in case something did happen." She stood up beside the bed. "Now, it's only 6:00, so go back to sleep for a while. We'll be leaving for the hospital in a few minutes."

"I'll call you to see how your examination went before I go to the newspaper today," I said. "Better yet, I'll bring home some lunch for you."

"You're a sweetheart for offering, but Tommy already has it covered. He's coming home at noon to check on me and he said he'd bring home some burgers. Now, stop worrying about me. Get some rest and I'll talk to you later."

After she walked out and closed my door, I laid my head down on the pillow. Though I tried, I couldn't go back to sleep. I was restless due to concern for my friend and in anticipation of the day ahead. Jumping out of bed, I took a warm shower and was ready to go in no time. I spread up the bed, then walked to the kitchen.

Traci had set a pastry box on the kitchen counter and left a note on top of it telling me to help myself to the muffins inside. I poured a glass of milk, then took a couple of blueberry muffins from the box and put them on a plate. With time to spare before catching the bus, I carried my breakfast onto the lanai.

As I munched on the muffins, I watched the sunrise in the distance. The traffic on H-1 was picking up as people made their way to work. *At least I won't have to deal with the heavy traffic this morning*, I thought.

I carried my dishes back inside, put them into the dishwasher, then grabbed my purse. Instead of taking the elevator, I walked to the end of the hallway and took the stairs down the seventeen flights to the lobby. Even though my legs were a bit shaky from the workout, I was pleased with my effort.

It was a few minutes after seven when I reached the bus stop. Several people were already there waiting. The long bench under the canopy was full. An old woman that looked to be at least eighty years old was leaning on her cane next to it. A couple of men in suits were standing on the sidewalk looking at newspapers. The hefty young man that I had seen waiting there the day before was standing by himself near a street sign.

Not sure of my connecting bus number, I took a chance that the young guy might be able to help me. I walked up behind him and said, "Good morning."

He jumped. When he turned around and looked at me, he seemed surprised that I was talking to him.

"Sorry," I said, smiling. "I didn't mean to startle you."

Stuffing his pudgy hands into his pockets, he looked uncomfortable. "Oh that's alright. I was daydreaming again and didn't hear you walk up."

Wanting to put him at ease, I said, "I'm Allison Kane and I need to get to Prince Kuhio Elementary. I know that Ala Moana Center is the hub, but would you happen to know which bus goes from there to the school?"

All the trepidation he may have felt seemed to disappear. A look of pride replaced it. "That used to be my school," he said, smiling. "At Ala Moana, you need to get on the same bus that I do." He pulled his hands from his pockets and raised them up in front of me. "We'll get on number forty-three." On his left hand he had raised four fingers and on the right hand he had raised three. Both hands were free of jewelry except for a gold ring set with some red gemstones that he wore on his right pinkie finger.

He seemed to be waiting for a response from me. I nodded and said, "Bus Number 43."

He smiled and lowered his hands. "Watch where I get off, then go one more mile up the road. Pull the cord right in front of the school. The bus driver will let you off there."

He appeared to be a bit slow. The instructions seemed to have been drilled into him. Evidently, when he had attended the school, someone must have gone over the travel plan with him until he had it down pat.

"Thanks for your help," I said. "What's your name?"

He hesitated a moment and glanced down at the pavement. I thought perhaps he had been cautioned about talking to strangers. I guess I passed the test because he looked up and smiled again, then stuck out his hand to me. "I'm Nathan. Glad to meet you."

I shook his hand. "It's very nice to meet you, too, Nathan."

The bus rolled over the hill and stopped next to us. As we filed onto it, I could see that there were only a few empty seats available. I stepped aside so that the old woman with the cane could have one of them. I reached for the bar above my head, just as the bus lurched forward.

I was squeezed in between Nathan and one of the businessmen, who was still reading his newspaper. After several minutes of bumping into my new acquaintance, I decided to take a stab at small talk.

"Where do you work, Nathan?"

"I'm the day janitor at the Nahoa Nursing Home. I like it because the people there are really nice."

"Do you ride the bus to work every day?"

"Most of the time. My brother Ronald works different hours than I do. He and I live together."

"That's nice," I said. "I have two brothers myself."

"Yeah, Ronald is great." He held up his hand in front of me. "He gave me this neat ring yesterday for my birthday."

"It's beautiful."

"Thanks." He glanced out the side window. "Here is where we change buses."

The bus made a right-hand turn behind the shopping center and pulled in behind another group of buses stopped in the loading zone. The walkways were crowded with people waiting for passengers to disembark. I followed Nathan down the steps of our bus and stayed close behind him as he led me to Bus Number 43. When we stepped inside it, I was glad to see some empty seats. I slid into one, then Nathan sat down beside me.

As we traveled along, he talked about being a student at Prince Kuhio. I could tell that his time there had been very special and that Miss Kahala had been a positive force in his life. He went on and on about how nice she had been to him.

The bus started slowing down as we came to Wilder Avenue. "Here is where I get off," Nathan said. He stood up in the aisle.

"I've enjoyed chatting with you," I said. "I hope we see each other again."

"Me, too. Those kids are lucky to have you as their teacher. If you see her, please tell Miss Kahala I said hello."

"I will. Have a great day at work!"

Nathan turned and walked toward the door. He waved at me before stepping off the bus.

🐾   🐾   🐾

I walked into the office at school. The secretary looked up and smiled at me. "Good morning, Miss Kane," she said. "Ready for your first day?"

"Looking forward to it, and please call me Allie."

"I'm Diane," she said. She picked up some papers from the corner of her desk. "Here is your class attendance sheet and parent contact information form. I set up your e-mail account in the system this morning. You're welcome to use it for personal e-mails, as well as for communicating with the students' parents."

"Thanks," I said. "That will save some minutes on my long distance phone card."

I took the papers from her, signed in, and then headed to the class-room. The students would be arriving soon. When I got there, I put my purse away, then laid a copy of *The Giving Tree* on each desk.

As I set the last copy down, two dark-haired boys stuck their heads inside the door. I could hear voices in the hallway. I walked over to the boys and saw several children huddled together behind them. I smiled at the group. "Welcome, everyone. I'm Miss Kane. Please come in and choose a locker."

Grins replaced most of the apprehensive expressions. The ten chil-dren clambered into the classroom. They put up their backpacks, then each child chose a desk.

The group was a mixture of seven boys and three girls. Their appearance was as diverse as night and day. Hawaii is considered to be a melting pot, and this group was a prime example. Two of the boys had the distinct features of Samoan ancestry. Another boy had red hair and green eyes, and two others had blonde hair and blue eyes. The three girls were of Oriental descent with black hair and dark eyes. The two boys who had earlier led the group in had the same golden brown skin that Simon did, so I assumed they were part Hawaiian. One was named Seth and the other one was Steven.

Leaning against the teacher's desk with the attendance sheet in my hand, I said, "I'm going to tell you a little about myself. Then I would like you to introduce yourself to the group and tell us what you enjoy doing most."

I told the students where I was from and answered several of their questions. Each child told me his or her name, then they talked about their hobbies, playing video games and other fun things they liked to do. Considering the reason they were here, I wasn't surprised that no one mentioned reading books as a favorite thing to do.

"Many of you talked about games you like to play," I said. "What if I tell you that by the time you get out of this class, you'll enjoy reading books as much as you like playing some of those games?"

They looked at me like I had lost my mind. A couple of them rolled their eyes.

"I stink at reading," a boy named Mareko said. "I hate it!"

"Me, too," a girl named Annie said. "I'd rather clean the bathroom than have to try to read a book."

Seth spoke up. "I like hearing stories, but when I try to read them myself, it's too hard. The words get all jumbled up inside my head." Several other students nodded in agreement.

Having taught children with reading difficulties in the past, I understood the frustration they were feeling. Changing their negative feelings about books would be the first step. Making them successful with reading and feeling good about themselves was the ultimate goal.

"Well, let me ask you a question," I said. "Do any of you like to climb trees?"

"I do," several of them answered.

"I'm the best climber in my neighborhood," a dark-headed boy named David said. "We've got a coconut palm tree in our front yard, and I can climb it faster than anybody in my family."

"I climbed trees when I was your age," I said. "My grandparents have a huge pear tree in their back yard, and my cousins and I loved eating the juicy fruit off of it. We'd pick everything that we could reach from the ground, but then we'd have to climb up into it to reach the pears on the higher branches. One day I got stuck on a high limb and couldn't get down."

I'm sure it was hard for these children to imagine that I was ever their age and had climbed trees. I didn't say anything more as I walked around the desk and picked up my copy of *The Giving Tree*.

Seth raised his hand. "What happened, Miss Kane? How did you get down?"

"I'm going to read this book to you, Seth, then I'll tell you what happened. Everyone just sit back and relax."

The book was a tale of friendship between an apple tree and a boy about their age. When he was young, the boy climbed the tree, ate the apples, jumped in the autumn leaves and took naps in her shade. When he became a man, he no longer played in the tree, but the tree continued giving her apples to him to sell. She gave her branches to him so that he could build a house, and she gave her trunk to him so that he could build a boat. Finally, nothing was left but a stump.

The man left and was gone for many years. The tree was sad that she had lost her friend. Returning home again when he is old, one day the man sat down on the stump to rest. He remembered all that the tree had given to him. He is sad that he took so much. However, the tree is happy again because her friend has returned, and she can still give him a nice place to sit and rest.

While I was reading the book, Miss Kahala stepped into the classroom. I saw her look around. The students didn't seem to notice her and she indicated to me that she didn't want to interrupt. She slipped back out as I was finishing the story.

When I closed the book, Annie raised her hand. "I feel sorry for that tree, Miss Kane. It just kept giving and giving."

"Yes, Annie, that's true. That's what friends do. Now before we do some fun activities with this book, I'll tell you how I got out of the pear tree that summer."

I told the students that I had climbed too far out on a thin branch, and it had broken with my weight. I was able to catch a larger limb as I fell. It saved me from falling to the ground. However, the bark and the twigs had scraped my arms and legs. The closest branch was too far away for me to reach it, and it scared me to look down, so I just hung there.

My arms were getting tired, and I was sure I was going to fall. But then through the leaves of the tree, I saw the light from Gramma's back porch come on. I heard my cousin Michael call my name. Someone had missed me, and he had volunteered to come out to look for me. Along with my other cousins, I had always looked up to Michael, and I was embarrassed that he had to be the one to find me hanging in the tree. But in my predicament, the fear overcame the embarrassment.

I called to him and he hurried over and started climbing up the pear tree. He didn't make fun of me, or tell me how silly I was to be stuck up there. He just kept assuring me that he would get me down and that everything would be all right. When we reached the ground, he insisted on carrying me inside, though I told him I could walk. He helped put bandages on the scrapes on my arms and legs.

"He was a hero, wasn't he Miss Kane?" Danielle asked.

"He was to me," I said. "We're still close today. Now, can anyone tell me how you can be like the tree in the story, or like my cousin Michael to your classmates this summer?"

Several ideas were offered, but Mareko gave the answer I was hoping for. "We can help each other and not laugh if someone makes a mistake."

"That's right, and we're going to start right now," I said. "Everyone please pick up your copy of the book and follow along while I read it to you again."

Everyone followed my instructions. When I finished reading, I said, "Now, we're going to do some fun activities. How would you like to build a palm tree on the wall?" I saw skeptical expressions on some of their faces. "Well, that's what we're going to do. Then we're going to cover the branches with the hard words we found in the book."

After the tree was built, I paired up the students. They seemed anxious to try to read the book to each other. I walked among the pairs to assist with occasional words, but found I was rarely needed. They continued to refer back to the words we had written on the palm branches. When dismissal time came, they asked to take their books home to read again to their parents that night. Mareko said he'd be reading to his dog, Zippy. Though I had already planned to assign the rereading project, it worked out nicely that they thought it was their idea instead of mine.

CHAPTER 6

I was due at the paper by 1:00, so I asked Diane for help getting into my e-mail account. First, I wrote to Doug. I asked about Rowdy and Precious and told him to give them a hug for me. I told him a little about my "unusual" discovery at the Sacred Resting Place Cemetery and that I would give him more details about it later.

After sending the letter to Doug, I started a message to Kristin. I gave her a brief rundown about school and the fun things I had done since arriving. I inquired about her visit with Kevin and asked her to give him and Joey my love.

On the phone call to my parents the night before, Dad had said that thunderstorms were heading toward Paradise. I asked her to let me know if there had been any damage. Before sending the letter, I also asked her to please forward my e-mail address to other family members. After I logged off, I walked to the workroom to call Traci.

On the third ring she answered. "How did your examination go?" I asked.

"The doctor scolded me for not relaxing more, but he said the baby was fine. I haven't had any more cramps, so I'm hoping it was a one-time thing."

"I hope so, too, but you can't be too careful. As long as I'm here, I'll take care of the cleaning and marketing. If Tommy will help me with the cooking, you can stay off your feet and rest more."

"Oh, Allie, I appreciate your offer, but I don't want you to have to wait on me. You're holding down two jobs, and I want you to get out and have some fun, too. Now enough about me. How did your first day at school go? Any discipline problems?"

"No, everything went well. The kids loved the book we chose. Did you think there might be some problems?"

"Well, I didn't want to put you on your guard needlessly, but Mareko Folora and Seth Morgan can be a handful."

"They were both fine today. In fact, they offered to help take charge when we were building the word tree."

"I'm glad to hear it," Traci said. "Mareko is a smart kid, but his home life has been pretty rough. His parents fight a lot; I'm talking real knock down drag outs. He and his sister have been put into foster care more than once in the last couple of years. He has some self-esteem issues, but if anyone can help him, you can."

"Thanks for the heads up and for the vote of confidence."

"You're going out with Simon and his friend for dinner tonight, right?"

"That's right. I'm anxious to meet Eddie Zantini. From what Simon has told me about him, he's quite a character. I'll be home about 5:00 to get ready."

"See you then," Traci said.

I walked into the office and asked Diane for the keys to the Chevy Malibu that the school was loaning me. Heading out the door toward the dark brown coupe, I was anxious to get to the *Hawaiian Star* and help Kyle start writing the severed thumbs story.

When I climbed into the car, I noticed that the interior was a bit drab, but spotless. Someone had hung a six-inch hula girl figurine on the rearview mirror. Not one for having dangling items on my mirror, I lifted it off and slipped it onto the volume knob on the radio. The colorful flowers of the doll's lei and shimmering grass skirt added some brightness to the dreary interior.

I pulled onto Manoa Road and followed it until I came to the stoplight at the Wilder Avenue intersection. Taking a left, my attention was drawn to a sign shaped like a big potato. All types of yummy toppings covered the vegetable. The sign was sitting on top of a small restaurant. The name of the place was Duke's Tator Shack. Being a sucker for butter, cheese and sour cream on a spud, I decided to pull in and give it a whirl.

When I stepped into the shaded interior of the restaurant, it took a moment before my eyes adjusted to the dim light. I noticed several men sitting on stools along the counter and a few other customers sitting at tables scattered throughout the room. A sign that said, "Order Here," loomed ahead of me, so I started navigating through the maze of tables to that spot. When I was almost there, I heard someone call out my name.

Searching for the source, I saw Nathan waving at me from the end of the counter. I smiled and waved back.

"Come on over; I want you to meet my brother," he hollered. All eyes in the place turned my way.

As I walked toward him, I noticed a man dressed in short-sleeved beige overalls sitting beside him. He didn't seem too happy with Nathan's outburst.

Oblivious to the man's frown, Nathan said, "Allie, this is my brother Ronald. Ronald, this is my new friend, Allie. We met this morning while I was waiting for the bus."

The dark-haired man looked up at me and his mouth curved into a charming grin. "Pleased to meet you, Allie," he said. "Nathan hasn't stopped talking about you since I picked him up for lunch. When he told me he had a new teacher friend, I wasn't expecting someone as pretty as you."

"Thank you," I said. "Nathan was helpful this morning, and visiting with him made the trip on the bus more enjoyable."

Ronald wiped his hands on a napkin lying next to his plate, then stretched out his right one to me. It was tanned and his fingernails were well manicured. As I placed my hand in his, he laid his other one on top of mine. The simple handshake turned into something almost sensual. Pulling my hand from his, I saw something in his eyes that gave me the creeps.

"Please excuse my appearance," he said, dropping his hand onto the counter and glancing down at his feet. "I helped someone else do their job this morning and I haven't had a chance to change clothes yet." The legs of his overalls and his work boots were encrusted with mud.

"No problem. It was nice meeting you, but I need to order some lunch and be on my way." I stepped away from the counter. "It was nice seeing you again, Nathan. Enjoy your lunch." Nathan waved at me, then I hurried to the order window.

While I was waiting in line, I glanced toward the two men. Ronald was staring right at me. I turned my attention to the menu posted on the wall in front of the slow-moving line. When it was finally my turn, I chose a beef stroganoff baked potato with extra sour cream and a Diet Dr. Pepper. Glad when my lunch was ready, I hurried out the door.

When I reached the *Hawaiian Star,* I walked inside and said hello to Mr. Masaki as I passed by his office. I headed upstairs and paused in front of Kyle's doorway. He was talking on the phone, so I just waved at him.

Settling into my new desk chair, I spread out some napkins on the desk, then took out the enormous potato from the sack. As I peeled back the heavy foil wrapping, the scrumptious aroma from the mushroom sauce filled the room.

When my lunch was half gone, I heard Kyle holler from the other room. "Allie, I smell something mighty good in there. Was that sack from Duke's?"

I swallowed the bite I was chewing. "Yes. This is the best potato I've ever tasted! You're welcome to a bite."

Kyle stepped to the doorway of my office. "Duke's is great! If I hadn't stuffed myself with seafood pasta from The Roasted Duck at lunchtime, I might take you up on your offer. But right now, I'm full of shrimp and scallops."

Pushing back the rest of the potato, I said, "That was delicious, but I can't eat another bite. Though I'm full, that pasta dish sounds good. I've never heard of The Roasted Duck."

"We'll go there for lunch sometime," Kyle said. "It's a bit expensive, but the newspaper has an expense account, so it won't cost us anything."

I frowned at him. "Mr. Masaki didn't say anything about free lunches being included in my benefit package."

"Oh, it's all a tax write-off, so the old guy won't say anything," Kyle said.

"Well, I wouldn't want to take advantage of such a *great* guy." I didn't appreciate his reference to our boss as "the old guy." "Are you ready to start working on the thumbs story?"

"Sure. I've been typing up some information, so why don't we work in my office. Bring along whatever you have and we'll compare notes."

Nodding, I picked up my notebook and pen and followed Kyle to his office. After I pulled a chair around to his side of the desk, we set to work.

Despite our clashes when I insisted that we get all the facts right, the afternoon flew by. By 5:00, we had written several pages of good script. Kyle said he would be gone the next afternoon for a dental appointment, so we agreed that he'd work on the story in the morning, then I would pick up where he left off in the afternoon.

Anxious to get back to Traci's to dress for dinner, I set my notebook on my desk and left.

The traffic was bumper-to-bumper up McCully Street to H-1. It didn't move along much better once I was westbound on the expressway. Each of the six lanes was packed with vehicles. When I reached the apartment complex, I parked in a guest space in front of the tower. I buzzed Traci's apartment, and in a few seconds I heard Tommy's voice.

"Who goes there?" he asked.

"It's me. Would you please let me in?"

"Sure thing," he answered. "I got a couple of extra keys from the building super today, so you'll be able to come and go as you please."

"That's great." The door latch clicked, and I walked inside.

Tommy opened the apartment door for me. "Here you go," he said. He dropped two keys into my hand. "The silver one opens the front door, and the gold one is for our apartment door."

"Thanks, Tommy. I'll be sure and not lose them." I walked into the kitchen and saw Traci fixing supper. "Hey, you. Do you feel like doing that?" I gave her shoulder a squeeze. "I'll be glad to fix you guys something before I go out."

"Hey, yourself," she said. She was dressed in blue jeans and a mauve knit top. Her hair was pulled into a ponytail and she looked rested. "I appreciate your offer, but I'm feeling much better. I sat out in the sunshine on the lanai this afternoon, per Dr. Tommy's orders. Watching all the activity around Pearl Harbor perked me up."

Tommy walked in and put his arms around Traci's waist. "She's been a good girl today and she promised me she would lie down if she started hurting again," he said. "I'll clean up the kitchen after we eat, so she won't have to be on her feet too long."

Knowing Traci enjoyed a busy lifestyle, I sympathized with her that she needed to stay off her feet. I knew it wasn't easy for her.

She glanced at the clock on the stove, then turned to look at me. "You'd better go get ready for your date. You know Simon is always on time."

I looked at the clock and saw that it was already after 6:00. "Yikes, you're right! He'll be here any minute! I'm going to go change clothes and freshen up."

I hurried into the bathroom and plugged in my curling iron. While it heated, I washed my face, then put on new makeup.

I curled the ends of my hair into a soft flip, then scooped up each side and fastened them with some jeweled clips. After giving my bangs and some stray strands around the front a quick curling, I was done.

When I walked into my bedroom, I could hear Traci talking to Simon on the intercom. I pulled off my clothes and hurried to the closet to pick out a dress to wear. Wanting to make a good impression, I decided on a dark purple sheath with a fitted waist. After slipping it on, I began zipping it, but the zipper caught on a loose thread halfway up my back. As I stood tugging at it, I heard Simon's voice in the living room. He was introducing his friend to Traci and Tommy. Something else was said, then I heard everyone laughing. Finally managing to get the zipper to the top, I put on some black heels, took one last look in the mirror, then headed down the hallway.

"Eddie and I have been friends for years," I heard Simon say as I walked into the room. "He's a Yankee, but I don't hold that against him."

"Yeah, this kid was still wet behind the ears when I met him five years ago," the man standing beside him said. He patted Simon on the back. "He had just made detective when a buddy and I came to Oahu on vacation."

Simon was six foot two, but this man stood at least two inches taller and was several pounds heavier. He was wearing a green and white floral aloha shirt, and the muscles in his upper arms held the fabric on the short sleeves taut.

Simon spotted me and started walking toward me. "That was quite an experience, let me tell you," Simon said, shaking his head. "But since my girl is here now, I won't go into the gory details. I wouldn't want Allie to get a bad first impression of you." He took hold of my hand and led me to the man. "Allie, this is my good friend and colleague, Eddie Zantini. Z, this is the angel from Oklahoma that I told you about."

"I can see now why you've been hiding her from me," Eddie said, smiling. "I'm pleased to meet you, Allie." Before I knew what was happening, I was wrapped in a bear hug. When he stepped away from me, he looked at Simon. "You know I can't resist beautiful, blonde, blue-eyed ladies. You must have been afraid that I'd steal her away from you."

"You'd have a fight on your hands if you tried," Simon said, grinning. He put his arm possessively around my shoulders.

Though I knew their banter was all in fun, it gave me a nice feeling. "I'm pleased to meet you too, Eddie," I said.

"If we're going to make those 7:00 reservations, we'd better get going," Simon said.

Walking us to the door, Tommy said to Simon, "I know you're busy on this case right now, but I'm ready for another game of golf. Let me know when you can tear yourself away from work and we'll go play."

Simon snapped his fingers. "I'm glad you mentioned that. Eddie loves to play golf, too, and we had discussed hitting the course about 4:00 tomorrow. If you can get away, why don't we make it a three-some?"

"Yeah, you can watch me beat the old pro here," Eddie said. "I still owe him a round from the last time he came to Maui and beat me at Ka'anapali. I was among the top five players for that particular course until Simon came and played. He blew us all out of the water and took the number one spot on the board."

"He's a tough one to beat, that's for sure," Tommy said. "I've only won two times in the last four months."

"Well, maybe tomorrow will be the lucky day for one of you," Simon said, smiling. "Tom, meet us at the Aiea course about 3:30, and may the best man win."

After saying good night to Traci and Tommy, we headed toward Simon's Jeep. Eddie kept Simon and me laughing all the way to the restaurant. By the time our food came, my cheeks were hurting from smiling so much.

Turning toward Eddie, I said, "So how did you and Simon happen to meet?"

"I'm not sure you want to embarrass yourself with the story, do you Z?" Simon asked.

"Hey, we're all family here, right?" he said. "I don't mind if you fill her in."

Simon looked at me. "Allie, this big, bad New York City detective and his friend came to Oahu for a vacation. I had just been promoted to detective. One evening, I was called out to work a robbery case at a Waikiki hotel. While I was there, one of the managers alerted me that two men were turning cartwheels on a nearby beach."

Eddie chuckled. "And that's not easy for a man my size and in the sand, no less."

Simon rolled his eyes and grinned. "Yes, you guys were quite the acrobats. But to continue my story, I went to check it out. These two burly guys had been tipping back mai tai's all afternoon and were feeling no pain. I ended up hauling them to jail for drunken disorderly conduct."

"Well, that's not exactly all that we went to jail for," Eddie said.

I looked at Simon and he seemed reluctant to elaborate. Shaking his head he said, "Allie, from what I could piece together, the two of them had been swimming and had some trouble with the undertow. According to them, their bathing suits were sucked off. They were jumping around on the beach buck-naked." He looked at Eddie. "I still shudder when I think about your bare rear end shining in the moonlight."

I started laughing. "That must have been quite a show for the tourists," I said to Eddie. "How long did you have to stay in jail?"

"Oh, after Simon confirmed that we were detectives with NYPD and had just had a lapse in judgement, we were released. But I decided after that little incident, I should probably cut back on the booze. Other than an occasional beer now and then, I'm alcohol free."

"How did you end up moving to Hawaii?" I asked him.

"I fell in love with the Islands. I had worked the senseless muggings, rapes and murders in Brooklyn for ten years and I was sick of it. When I got back home from that vacation, I gave a month's notice at work, sublet my apartment to my younger brother, then moved my meager belongings to a one-room apartment in Honolulu. I received a good recommendation from my boss in New York, so the HSBI decided to take a chance on me. A few months later, the governor gave me the head job on Maui."

"And you've made a pretty good hand ever since," Simon said.

"I've done okay until this severed finger case came up," Eddie said. "I can't seem to buy a break on this one."

We talked about the cases over coffee and dessert. The victim from the two-year-old Oahu case was a woman named Alhoi Akau. She was a descendant of a rich family who had owned a lot of land on Kauai. Being the only heir, she had inherited all the family wealth and lived lavishly until she died in 1921.

The Maui case that Eddie was working on involved one of her grandchildren, Gerald Franklin. His mother and her siblings, the children of Alhoi Akau, squandered away most of the fortune they had inherited. The only thing of value that Gerald possessed when he died was a ring worth nearly thirty thousand dollars, and he had worn it to his grave. That ring was the one reported being seen by the Los Angeles pawnshop owner a few days earlier.

"If it is a vendetta, have you considered watching other graves connected to this family?" I asked. Before either man answered, I realized that wasn't practical. "But, since it was over a year between the two incidents, you couldn't have someone watching twenty-four hours a day, could you?"

"For about a month, men patrolled the gravesites of the family members who had been interred with valuables," Simon said. "But after a few weeks, we just couldn't spare them anymore."

The conversation shifted from their work to my first day of summer school. Simon also wanted to know how my afternoon at the *Star* had gone, so I gave them a short review.

"Well, kiddies, I've enjoyed this, but it's time the old man got some shuteye," Eddie said. He tried to stifle a yawn. "I need to be in my best form tomorrow afternoon if I'm going to win that golf game."

The three of us were talked out and lost in our own thoughts as we rode back to Traci's. The windows were down on each side of the Jeep, and the balmy breezes swept through my hair. I closed my eyes and listened to the soft jazz playing on the radio while enjoying the touch of Simon's fingers stroking mine.

It was the end of a wonderful evening, and I should have been content. But the grave-robbing cases were nagging at me. It was time to do some research on my own.

When I woke up the next morning, I could hear rain spattering against my bedroom window. Easing open one eye, I saw rivulets coursing down the pane. The digital clock on the nightstand next to the bed read 6:30, so I pushed back the blanket and put on my robe before padding to the bathroom. After a warm shower, I quickly got ready for school. As I walked toward the kitchen, I could smell coffee brewing.

"Good morning, sunshine," Traci said. She set some cereal boxes on the counter.

"Good morning. How do you feel today?"

"I'm much better, thanks. I had intended to get up and fix some bacon and eggs for you, but I was dead to the world this morning."

"That's okay," I said, grabbing a cereal bowl from the cabinet. "I love Cheerios. Is Tommy gone?"

"Yes, he left around 6:00." She followed me to the dining room table. "He wanted to be sure he finished all his work so that he could make it to the big golf game today."

"Those guys really take it seriously, don't they?" I said.

"Like a heart attack. But, if you think about it, you and I took our own hobbies pretty seriously, too. From the time I was ten years old until I got married, I wouldn't miss a rodeo or a chance to show one of my horses at a fair. If I remember correctly, you were always practicing for some music contest at school or church. The guys' interests lie elsewhere, that's all."

"You're right," I said. "To each his own. Speaking of that, what are your plans for the day?"

"Shopping for the nursery. We can't afford to buy all the furniture and accessories for the baby outright, so I have to find what I want and then put the items in layaway. That way I can pay for them over time. Since that won't take all day, I thought I'd come to the school for a while this morning and give you a hand, if you'd like me to."

"I'd appreciate that. The kids loved *The Giving Tree,* and we'll be doing some activities with it today. If you wouldn't mind browsing through the school library and bringing me some more titles to pick from, they'll have something new to start working on tomorrow."

"Sounds good," she said. We carried the dirty dishes to the sink. "I'll try to get there around 10:00."

After brushing my teeth, I said good-bye to Traci, then headed toward the parking garage. The rain had lightened up, but the air was still heavy with moisture. I buckled myself into the car, then headed out of the complex.

Before pulling onto Moanalua Road, I glanced toward the bus stop and saw many of the same people from the morning before waiting for the bus. Nathan was standing alone with his head bent against the persistent drizzle. His hair was plastered to his head, and I didn't have the heart to let him get any wetter.

I tooted the horn on the Chevy, and he looked up at me. I waved, but realized he couldn't see me through the fog on the windshield. I rolled down the window and stuck out my head. "Nathan, how about a lift to work?" I hollered.

At first he didn't respond, but after recognition set in, a big smile appeared on his face. Nodding, he yelled back, "I'd like that."

I motioned to him to come and get in, then watched as he loped across the street to my car. I leaned over and unlocked the passenger door, and he climbed inside.

"Kind of messy out today, isn't it?" I said. I turned left onto the street. "You need an umbrella."

Wiping droplets from his face with his shirtsleeve, he said, "Yeah, the pretty yellow one that my mom gave me disappeared one day from my locker at work."

"That's too bad."

"Yeah, since it was hers it was special to me. Her Uncle Hiram gave it to her when she was a teenager. She told me that he never had any kids, and since she was an only child, he was always giving her presents."

"Why don't you ask Ronald to buy you another one?" I asked.

"I have, but he's busy and keeps forgetting to pick up one for me."

But he doesn't seem to mind letting you get drenched in the rain, I thought. I berated myself for being judgmental and made a mental note to look for a new umbrella for Nathan myself.

He asked me if I had told Miss Kahala "hello" for him. I promised that I would if I saw her today. I inquired about the kind of job his brother Ronald had. He told me that he drove a machine that digs up dirt. Assuming he must work in construction, it explained the mud-covered overalls and boots I had seen him in the day before. Soon I was pulling in front of the Nahoa Nursing Home.

"Gee, thanks a lot for the ride, Allie," Nathan said as he opened the door. "It sure was a lot nicer than standing on that old bus all the way. I hardly ever get a seat."

"You're welcome. I enjoyed the company."

Nathan stepped out of the car onto the sidewalk, then turned around. "Have a good day at school. I hope to see you around again sometime."

As he was about to shut the door, I said, "Hey, Nathan? Since I come by here on my way to school every morning, would you like to ride with me the rest of the month?"

It only took him a moment to respond. "That would be awesome! Where do you want me to meet you?"

"How about where I picked you up this morning?"

"I'll be there. See you tomorrow!"

He slammed the door, and I watched him walk toward the building. Halfway there, he bent down and pulled some weeds from the pansies that were blooming along the edge of the sidewalk.

I pulled away from the curb back into traffic. Before I reached the school, I realized I had just offered to be alone in a car with a man that I only knew by his first name. To keep myself out of trouble with Simon, I thought I'd better try to find out a little more about my new friend.

CHAPTER 7

When I reached the school, I saw Miss Kahala's car in her reserved parking spot. Knowing I might miss her if I waited until noon, I signed in, then walked over and knocked on her open office door.

Glancing up from the newspaper she was reading, she smiled at me. "Allison, come in and have a seat. How did things go yesterday?"

"Very well." I sat down in the chair across from her. "I'm anxious to try some new things with the students today."

"No discipline problems?"

"Not a single one. I hope to keep them so wrapped up in reading and doing fun activities that no one will have time to get into trouble."

"I'm glad to hear it. Now, what can I do for you?"

"I wanted to ask you about a former student who came to school here several years ago. His name was Nathan. I met him at the bus stop yesterday and have run into him several times since then. He spoke highly of you and asked me to tell you hello, then I realized on the way here that I didn't know his last name."

"Is he a quiet, young man in his early twenties and a bit slow?" she asked.

"I wouldn't say he's quiet. I gave him a ride this morning to the nursing home where he works, and we both talked a blue streak all the way there."

Frowning, Miss Kahala said, "You gave him a ride? Hawaii is a friendly place, Allison, but unfortunately there are some bad seeds. If you haven't yet, I'm sure you'll hear about some of them from Simon."

"Normally I'm cautious and wouldn't offer rides to strangers, but from the moment I met Nathan, I found him to be one of the gentlest people I've ever met."

"You've got to be talking about Nathan Nowicki," the principal said. "And, yes, he is a jewel and wouldn't hurt anyone, though I can't say the same about his brother, Ronald."

"I met him, too, and I have to agree that he seems a little rough around the edges."

Miss Kahala told me that she had been the counselor at Prince Kuhio Elementary when Ronald came through the school. He often started fights and though he could be charming when he wanted to be, he had an underlying dark nature about him.

Though he was happy when his new stepfather adopted him, he had told Miss Kahala that he still felt cheated by his biological father. Apparently, the man had denied that Ronald was his child and had never offered support of any kind. But Ronald changed when his baby brother was born during his fifth-grade year.

"He was like a new kid," Miss Kahala said. "His mother, Lorraine, had come in for meetings many times regarding Ronald's problems, but after the baby came, I never had to call her in again. Ronald's grades improved, he quit fighting and he smiled a lot more."

"You mentioned that Nathan was a bit slow. Do you know anything about the circumstances of his condition?"

"When Lorraine was pregnant with him, she came down with measles. Nathan was born with severe learning disabilities and a below average I.Q. But despite his struggles in school, that boy never gave up! He accepted all the help we would give him and tried hard to do well in school. I'll never forget him, I can tell you that."

"From the nice things he has told me about you, he'll never forget all you did for him, either." I stood up. "Thanks for the information. I've got students coming soon, so I'd better get to the classroom."

"You're welcome. Let me know if I can do anything else for you."

As I walked down the hallway to the classroom, I thought about Ronald. It was understandable that he would feel hurt and angry that his father had rejected him. But Nathan seemed to have come to his rescue and had helped to turn Ronald's life around.

When I reached the classroom, I gathered up several sheets of different colored construction paper, glue and ten pairs of scissors from the cupboard. I located a few paintbrushes, some boxes of watercolors, a large bag of crayons, and some other supplies that we would need. By the time the students were in the room and seated, I had everything on the activity table ready to go.

I asked the children to get out their copies of *The Giving Tree* and join me in a circle on the floor. We discussed the story, then I separated them into three groups. After assigning them roles, they spent some time practicing their parts.

When it was time to perform for the whole group, Seth and Mareko became quite the entertainers. Seth played the part of the forgotten apple tree, and his passion for the role was amazing. Mareko came in a close second as he portrayed the selfish man. Everyone enjoyed performing for the group, and by the time they were finished, they knew the story inside and out.

"Excellent job, everyone," I said. "Now it's time to take a break before we start the craft project."

As I led the students down the hall, I saw Traci carrying an armload of books out of the library. "Here let me give you a hand," I said. I took some of them from her.

"I kind of got carried away in there," she said. "There are tons of great choices, but I picked out a few of my favorites. Do you want to take a look to see if any of them strike your fancy?"

Glancing through the selections, I saw several of my own favorites.

"You've made some great choices. I've used some of these in my class-room back home, so it will be easy to come up with activities to go along with them."

"I thought you'd like them," she said.

I held up the copy of *Where the Sidewalk Ends*. "I'd like to read aloud some of the poems about friendship from this book," I told her. "The material is great for journal writing."

"I agree. Some of the other titles in that stack are good for teaching sequencing, cause-and-effect and other reading skills."

"Would you please check out ten copies of each one of these while I get started with the lesson plans on them? If they are as big a hit as the first book was, we'll be checking them all in and moving on to the next set in no time."

"I'll have them to you in a few minutes." Traci turned and walked back into the library.

After leading the students back to the classroom, I gave them some brief instructions, then set them free to create their masterpieces. When Traci brought the sets of books to me, I began jotting down ideas.

By the time the noon bell rang, the students' pictures were mounted on the bulletin board for all to admire. I had passed out copies of *Love You Forever* by Robert Munsch for them to read that night. Though I had planned to collect the other books and return them to the library, everyone wanted to take them home and read them again. The more they read the better, so I agreed.

Traci had taken off to do some shopping for the nursery. After I straightened the room, I headed to the office to check my e-mail.

I had two messages: one from Doug and the other one from Kris-tin. Doug told me that he and the dogs missed me a lot. He also said that hail from Monday night's storm had damaged several roofs around town. He told me to be sure and tell him more about my Sacred Resting Place discovery when I wrote back to him.

Kristin had written that she was loving every minute of Kevin's visit and was dreading when he would have to go back to Iraq. She said they were leaving Saturday morning to go visit his parents. Kevin had grown up in southern Oklahoma in a town called Lawton, which was about two hundred miles from Paradise.

I decided to wait and respond to their letters on Monday. I logged off, then grabbed my purse and headed out the door.

As I drove to the *Hawaiian Star*, I realized I was famished. Since I had been a good girl and had eaten whole-grain cereal for breakfast, I opted for a cheeseburger, onion rings and a chocolate shake from a drive-in along the way.

Continuing to the newspaper, I munched on the rings. They didn't compare to the yummy ones that the drive-in back home served, but they filled the gap. By the time I pulled into the parking lot, only crumbs remained in the package they had come in.

I got out of the car and saw Sammy Cho coming out the back door of his uncle's laundromat. He spotted me and started walking my way.

We hadn't parted on the best terms in March, so I wasn't sure what kind of a reunion he was planning. For a moment, I debated about whether or not I should cut and run toward the door of the newspaper. But I realized that Sammy was in such good shape, if he chose to, he could probably catch me before I got there.

His sister's boyfriend had almost beat her to death with Sammy's gun. Sammy went after him, found him on Ewa beach and tried to take the gun away from him. During the scuffle, the boyfriend had been shot and killed.

The whole week I was here, I kept running into Sammy. I figured God wanted me to keep hounding him to turn himself in to the authorities. Simon strongly disagreed with my theory. But hey, in the end Sammy called Simon, and he didn't get any jail time out of the deal.

I started easing toward him and tried the friendly approach. "Hey, Sammy. How are you doing?" Holding my lunch bag in one hand and my purse in the other, I decided that if he started punching me, I was going to bonk him on the head with my purse.

"Aloha, Miss Kane. I thought I saw you drive through the alley yesterday." He stopped in front of me. "What are you doing back on Oahu? Here to offer your assistance to Hawaii's finest?"

"I help when I can. But the main reason I'm back is to teach summer school."

"Still working with the *kamali'i,* huh? That's honorable."

"Yes, I love children. I'm also working part-time here." I pointed toward the building. "What are you doing these days?"

He ran his fingers through his thick, black hair. "After my little brush with the law in March, I've been trying to walk the straight and narrow. I'm working part-time at a gas station over on Wilder Avenue, but I need more hours. I'm looking for a full time job, but I may have to settle for another part-time position to supplement the one I have."

"It sounds like you're on the right track." My hand was throbbing from holding my purse so tightly. Deciding that Sammy wasn't going to try anything, I relaxed my grip.

"So, Mr. Masaki hired you?" Sammy asked. "He's a good guy. I've been reading his paper since I was in the third grade. It gets to the grit of the news."

"Yes, the *Star* has won a lot of awards for good writing and professional style. It was an honor to be hired by him. He wants me to help cover some unusual stories."

"If you chase down your stories like you chased me last spring, he'll be getting his money's worth," Sammy said wryly. "And speaking of unusual, I haven't seen much about those cemetery disturbances in the *Star.* The competition has been riding law enforcement pretty hard for their lack of progress."

"That's one thing I'm working on right now with another reporter. We hope to have something new for the Saturday edition."

"Well, I won't hold you up any longer, Miss Kane. It was nice talking to you."

"It was nice seeing you again, Sammy, and please call me Allie."

He took a few steps toward the laundromat, then stopped and turned back around. "About the missing finger thing, you might want to see what you can find out about a similar event that happened on Kauai a few years back. My dad was raised there, and I overheard him and my uncle talking about it."

"Thanks for the information. I'll check into it."

He nodded and waved, then walked away.

As I walked inside the building, I could hear some of the small presses running. Since the *Hawaiian Star* was only published on Wednesdays and Saturdays, I had been told that some clubs on the island paid to have their newspapers run on other days. I said hello to some other staff members that I met along the way, then headed toward my office. Kyle wasn't back from lunch yet, so I nibbled my soggy cheeseburger while waiting for my computer to boot.

I was searching through the *Star* archives for stories related to the grave-robbing cases, when the phone rang. "Hello, this is Allie."

"How about a date?" a smooth, male voice said.

I grinned. "Well, I already have a date tonight. He's bringing a golf buddy over for dinner, but after they leave, I might be able to squeeze you in."

"Hey, that's not funny," Simon said. "I'm the only man you're seeing tonight, so don't plan any romantic rendezvous after Eddie and I leave."

"Oh, Simon, it's you." I started giggling.

The line went quiet. "You knew it was me all along, didn't you, Allie? You had me worried there for a minute."

"Of course I knew it was you, silly. I'm just trying to keep you on your toes. What's going on?"

"Eddie and I have been wading through old case files," he said. "But we're about to call it a day and go meet Tommy to play golf."

"I ran into an old friend of ours when I was coming into work today," I said. "He mentioned something about an incident on Kauai a few years ago that might be related to the grave-robbing cases you're working on."

"Oh? Who was that?"

"Sammy Cho. He didn't give me any specifics, but he said that he overheard his father and uncle talking about it. I've dug through two years' worth of newspaper stories, but so far I've come up empty."

"That's interesting," Simon said. "I'll contact the HSBI agent on Kauai and see if he knows anything about it. He's been there for four years, and I'm sure he would remember a case like that."

"I'll keep looking on this end." I glanced up at the clock. "Have a good game, but try not to beat your friends too badly."

"Okay. I'll take it easy on them. We should be finished by 6:00. We'll bring home some food so that you and Traci won't have to cook."

"Sounds like a winner," I said. "See you then."

During our conversation, I had heard Kyle rummaging around in his office. When I hung up, he stuck his head in my doorway.

"Hey, Allie. I had lunch downtown with a friend and the time got away from me. How's the missing fingers piece coming?"

"Very slowly. But today I found out an interesting tidbit that might be connected to it. I've been searching through the archives, but haven't hit pay dirt yet. Why don't you grab a chair and I'll fill you in."

I relayed what Sammy had told me, then we worked for a few minutes together. We weren't making much headway, so we decided to split up and research separate years. Kyle went back to his office to use his own computer. By 5:00, we had gone through four years' worth of material and still hadn't found a story linking the current cases to anything from the past.

I thumbed through the thin folder containing the information we had accumulated so far. With the small amount, I knew it was going to be difficult to write a decent story for the next edition of the paper. In less than forty-eight hours, the finished product would be rolling off the presses, and we had very little new information to report.

"Well, I'm taking off," Kyle said. "I'll see you tomorrow."

"Have a nice evening."

After straightening my desk, I shut down my computer, then grabbed my purse. On the way down the stairs, I decided to check and see if Mr. Masaki was still in his office. I was anxious to share with him what Sammy had told me and to see if he might be able to corroborate it.

"Knock, knock," I said as I poked my head inside his doorway.

He looked up from some copy he was proofing and smiled. "Come in, Allie. How is the grave-robbing story coming?"

"A lead came in this afternoon. Kyle and I have been trying to track down more information about it. I wanted to bounce some ideas off you to see what you think."

"Yes, Kyle stopped by and said that he found out about a possible related incident on Kauai," Mr. Masaki said. "He's quite the talented journalist, isn't he? I told you he was a go-getter."

Kyle got the new lead? Irritated that he had stolen my thunder, I debated whether or not to set the record straight. But since Mr. Masaki seemed so pleased and we were going to share the glory when the story was written, I decided to let it drop. I would handle Kyle myself.

"Yes, he's something," I replied, though talented journalist wasn't what I had in mind.

We visited awhile longer about that piece, then I told him what I had written about the thumbs on the statue. Since Kyle was rarely around, I had done it alone. I told Mr. Masaki I hoped that I would have something more from the police before the piece ran on Saturday.

"It sounds like you've got that story under control. On Monday, there's a human-interest story that I'd like you to pursue. A new exhibit is being built in a park near the Diamond Head State Monument. The artist isn't fond of the press, but since you have a special way with people, I'm hoping he'll let you interview him."

"Is the project being done by Maynard Desmond?"

"Yes, it is. Are you familiar with his work?"

"As a matter of fact, when I arrived last Monday, a friend showed me a beautiful creation that Mr. Desmond had recently completed. He does remarkable work."

"He's very talented," Mr. Masaki said. "According to the Parks Department, for this new exhibit he has been given triple the amount of space he usually gets. Our readers enjoy seeing stories about locals, and Maynard Desmond is very popular here."

"I'd love to do the interview. My mother owns a flower shop and nursery back home. Though I'm not as knowledgeable about plants as she is, perhaps I can spark his interest enough to talk to me."

"Wonderful! Here are the directions to the park."

After getting a few more details, he gave me a map for that part of the island, then I left.

Lost in thought about whether or not to confront Kyle the next day, I drove onto H-1 and crawled with the other cars toward Traci's. After taking the Aiea exit, I was about to turn into the complex, when I remembered Nathan's umbrella. Darn it! I had passed several ABC stores along the way, but now my only choice was to pull into the Pearlridge Center.

Traffic was bumper-to-bumper in the left lane, so I slowed down to wait until someone would let me in. The driver in a black Ford Taurus behind me tapped on his horn. In my rearview mirror, I could see that traffic was backing up behind me. I knew I'd have to wedge my way into the left lane so that I could turn into the shopping center.

Glancing into my side mirror, there was a slight break, so I cut into the left lane. I jumped when a horned blared. I turned around and saw a Nissan pickup sitting just inches from my back bumper. It had been in my blind spot and I never saw it. The driver was waving his hands and mouthing something at me. I could tell he wasn't calling me a good woman driver. I shrugged and mouthed "sorry," then drove another block and turned into the shopping center.

I parked on the lower level, then walked toward an entrance to the mall. I thought I'd try to find an umbrella at the store where I had found some souvenirs for family members last spring. Just inside the mall entrance, I saw Ronald Nowicki standing at the counter of a snack bar. Two girls, dressed in striped pinafores with matching hats, were laughing at whatever he was saying.

Since his back was toward me and I was rushed for time, I didn't want to attract his attention. Putting my hand along the side of my face, I hurried past the group. Glancing back at them as I turned the corner, I was sure he hadn't seen me.

Inside the shop, I walked past the T-shirt tables and flip-flop shoe racks searching for the umbrellas. After circling two counters full of photo supplies and various snack items, I found a tall, round basket with umbrellas and walking canes in it.

Sorting through the array of designs and colors, I settled on a yellow one with a picture of a smiling sun wearing sunglasses printed on it. I thought that Nathan would be happy with my choice, so I walked to the register to pay for it.

When the purchase was complete, I picked up the sack and headed back into the mall. As I rounded a corner, I ran smack into Ronald! I tripped over his foot and fell to the ground, landing on my knees. If he hadn't grabbed my arm, I would have fallen flat on my face.

The tip of the umbrella ripped the sack, then skidded across the tile floor. A teenage girl talking on her cell phone sidestepped it as it came to rest against the wall. Never missing a beat in her conversation, she left it lying where it was and continued on her way.

"Are you okay, Allie?" Ronald asked. He reached out his hand and pulled me back onto my feet. "You had quite a spill. Good thing I was here to catch you."

If you hadn't been here, I wouldn't have tripped in the first place, I thought. Holding up the tattered sack, I said, "I'll be okay. I'd better go get the umbrella before someone falls over it."

"Allow me." He walked over and retrieved it.

I looked at my bruised knees. The skin wasn't broken, but I was sure they would be tender for a couple of days.

When Ronald came back, he handed me the umbrella. "Thanks," I said, taking it from him. I looked it over. It had a dirty spot where it had skidded across the floor, but otherwise it seemed fine.

Before I knew what was happening, he crouched down and began examining my knees. His hand moved toward one of them, but I jumped back out of his reach.

"I'd better help you to your car," he said, standing back up. "I wouldn't want you to fall and skin those pretty knees any further."

"That's okay. I'll be fine." I started walking away from him.

"I insist," he said, falling into step beside me.

Though I wasn't thrilled with his company, a lot of people were milling around inside the mall, so I decided not to make a scene.

As we walked, he asked me some questions about school. My brusque "yes" and "no" answers didn't deter his attempt for further conversation. He said that Nathan had told him that I had given him a ride to work that morning. Even though his brother had shared that information with him, I didn't tell him that the yellow umbrella I was holding between us was for Nathan.

Tired of answering his questions, I decided to ask one of my own. "Nathan said he rides the bus because your working hours are different from his. What do you do?"

Hesitating, Ronald said, "I work for the State of Hawaii. I don't usually get off until 6:00 p.m., but things were a little slow today so I left early. Nathan works from 8:00 in the morning until 2:00 at the nursing home and enjoys the bus ride home. Of course, he'll feel like a king riding with you every morning this month."

We had reached the row where my car was parked. I wasn't keen on him knowing the kind I drove. I turned toward him. "I'm glad to do it. Now, I need to be going, so if you'll excuse me…"

This time he took the hint. "It was good to see you again, Allie. I'm sure we'll bump into each other again before you go back to the mainland."

Not if I have anything to do with it, I thought. I turned and walked slowly toward my car. He gave me the creeps. Regardless of his smooth words, there was something disturbing in his eyes.

When I reached my car, he hadn't moved from the spot where I had left him. Having no other choice, I climbed in, then locked the door. As I drove by him, he waved at me and I just nodded. At least he didn't know where I was staying.

❦ ❦ ❦

"That guy sounds like bad news," Traci said to me. My mouth started watering as I watched her pull a big loaf of eggnog macadamia nut bread from the oven. I had told her about Nathan and the encounter with his brother. "Do you think it was an accident that he was walking by that store at the same time you were leaving it?"

"It's hard to say. He could have seen me I suppose, though he looked awfully busy trying to charm a couple of girls when I arrived." Traci cut off a bite of the warm bread and handed it to me. I popped it into my mouth and savored the flavor of the spicy nutmeg and crunchy nuts. "I didn't realize how much I missed macadamia nuts until I tasted these. I need to take some back to Paradise with me."

"I just received two packages in the mail from Purdy's Farm on Molokai," Traci said. "Tommy loves to munch on the roasted ones while he's watching sports on TV, and I like to bake with the plain ones. Mr. Purdy has the freshest stock around." She started slicing the loaf with a sharp knife. "You know, since that guy knows where you teach, you need to make sure he's not lurking around somewhere in the parking lot before you leave school each day."

"Yes, Mother. I'll be careful."

She walked toward the cabinet where the plates were kept. As she passed me, she swatted my behind. "Don't be sassy."

I grinned at her. Though I didn't think she had any reason to worry about Ronald, I was touched by her concern.

I set plates, eating utensils and napkins on the dining room table.

When I returned to the kitchen and began putting ice into glasses, I told Traci about running into Sammy Cho. I also mentioned how Kyle had gone to Mr. Masaki with the tip Sammy had given to me.

"That sneak," Traci said. Before I could respond, the apartment door flew open and the guys walked in.

"Who's a sneak?" Tommy asked. He set a bucket of chicken on the counter.

"Allie's new partner at the newspaper," Traci said. "He's trying to take credit for her work."

Simon walked over and set a large bag down next to the bucket, then he put his hand on my shoulder. "I told you that guy was worth watching," he said. He planted a soft kiss on my lips.

A pleasant shiver passed through me. "That was a nice welcome," I said. "How was the game?"

"Maybe you should ask Tom," he said, grinning. "He's been bursting at the seams to brag about his victory to someone besides Eddie and me."

"I can hardly believe it, but I beat Mr. Golf Pro!" Tommy said, slapping Simon on the back. "Until the fourteenth hole, Eddie and I were competing against each other for second place because Simon was staying at least four strokes ahead of us. Then I switched to a seven iron and birdied on the fourteenth. After that, I eagled on the fifteenth. Man, I was on fire!"

"He sure was," Eddie said, leaning against the doorjamb leading into the kitchen. "He ran off and left me. I was lucky to make par all day. When he beat Simon by a stroke, you would have thought he had won the lottery!"

"So what happened to you?" I asked Simon.

"Well, I have to be nice and let my buddies win once in a while," he said, smiling. "No, actually I started feeling a little guilty about playing golf when I should have been working."

"That guilt trip turned into luck for me," Tommy said. "If you hadn't bogeyed on that hole, you would have beat us for sure."

Traci was unloading the food from the sack. "Well, this calls for a celebration," she said. "Here, sweetie. Take the baked beans and coleslaw into the dining room. Allie, will you please bring the biscuits? If Simon and Eddie will grab the chicken and the drinks, we're ready to party!"

Marching into the dining room with food in hand, we all found a place at the table and sat down. A small flower arrangement in a pewter bowl had been placed in the center, along with two pale green candles in crystal holders. Before we filled our plates, Tommy said grace. He thanked God for his big win on the golf course, for good friends, and for the tasty food we were about to receive. After a round of "Amens," we started passing the containers.

Though not the best dinner conversation, I asked Simon if he had any new information about the missing fingers' cases.

He wiped his mouth with his napkin. "On the record, Miss Reporter?"

"If you don't mind. Mr. Masaki is going to think he made a bad choice if I don't start pulling my weight."

"Well, we can't let him think that. The thumbs you found belonged to Ray Franklin."

"Yes!" I said, making a fist and pulling my bent arm down in triumph. "Now, if we can just figure out who left them on the statue, why they were cut off in the first place, and if the glove belongs to the guy who did it, the case will be solved!"

"That's a lot of ifs," Simon said. "And where is this *we* coming from? Whoever is doing this is nuts, and I don't want you within a hundred miles of him."

I looked at him and frowned. "Well, naturally I'm going to do everything I can to help you find this guy."

"Allie, I agree with Simon that you shouldn't get more involved than you already are in this," Traci said. She stood up and started picking up some dirty plates. "Tommy and I were discussing it last night. We concluded that someone with a sick sense of humor is playing games here."

"That makes three of us," Simon said.

"Make that four," Eddie said.

I decided not to pursue it any further right then. But I knew I wasn't finished with this. The conversation turned to more pleasant things while we ate dessert. Traci had outdone herself with the eggnog nut bread. The guys couldn't stop raving as they ate thick slices topped with whipped cream. Not a crumb of the loaf was left by the time we were finished.

I told Traci that I would clean up the kitchen and Simon offered to help me. Eddie offered, too, but didn't seem a bit disappointed when I told him we could handle it. While I loaded the dishwasher, Simon wiped down the counters. He bumped into me a number of times and apologized by wrapping his arms around me and nuzzling my neck. Though the job took three times as long, it was worth it.

As he bundled up the trash, he said, "Have you made any plans for this weekend?"

"Not really." I hung the dishtowel on the rack to dry. "Do you have something fun in mind?"

"I'd like to take you to Maui to meet my grandparents and show you some sites over there. Grandmother has been after me to come for a visit. I told her a couple of weeks ago that my girlfriend was coming back to the island, and she said she'd like to meet you. They have two spare bedrooms and she loves to cook for guests. Would you be interested?"

His girlfriend? And he wants to introduce me to more members of his family? That's got to be good! "I'd love to meet them," I said. "And this will give me a chance to see Maui. My dad gave me some money to spend on sightseeing, so I can pay for my own plane ticket."

"Don't worry about that," he said. "I'll take care of all the expenses. HSBI agents fly free on inter-island flights, so it won't cost that much.

Grandpa will pick us up at the airport, then let us use his pickup for sightseeing."

"You're going to let them know we're coming aren't you? What if they have other plans for the weekend?"

He looked like he had been caught with his hand in the cookie jar. "Well, I was hoping you would agree to the trip, so I called them last night. Was I presuming too much?"

I grinned at him. "Not at all. It sounds like fun."

Relieved, he said, "I'm glad to hear you say that. The plane leaves a little after six tomorrow evening. Since you're with me, you won't have to go through the security checkpoint. I'll pick you up about 5:00."

We walked to the end of the hallway and deposited the bag of trash into the chute, then rejoined our friends on the lanai to watch the sunset. There were only four chairs, so I sat on Simon's lap and leaned back against him. A cool breeze was blowing, but I wasn't a bit cold. In the shelter of his arms, I was comfortable and content.

On the horizon, the sky was the color of apricots. Blue-gray clouds above Pearl Harbor were floating out to sea. The sounds of someone playing Chopin on the piano a few floors above us drowned out the traffic noises on H-1. I recognized the piece being played. It was "Three Ecossaises," which translated into "Three Scotch Dances." When I was fourteen years old, it had given me fits!

Darkness enveloped the terrace. We walked inside and decided to play dominoes for a while. We all had a ball and Eddie ended up the big winner.

"I never win games," he said, laughing. "Now I understand the rush that Tom felt after the golf game today. It's something I could get used to."

It was after 10:00 when Simon announced that he and Eddie needed to leave. After thanking Traci and Tommy for their hospitality, Eddie walked down the hall to push the button for the elevator. Simon thanked them, too, then took my hand and led me out into the hallway. He took his time kissing me good night.

As I watched him walk toward the elevator, I thought about the great evening we had shared. Though I hated to see it end, the excitement of going to Maui the next day made it a whole lot better.

CHAPTER 8

It was sunny the next morning, and Nathan was all smiles when I picked him up. He glanced into the back seat as he got inside the car. "Your umbrella is the same color that mine was," he said. "I love yellow."

I reached over the edge of the seat and picked it up. "I bought this for you. It won't replace the special one that your mother gave you, but it will keep you from getting drenched when you have to wait in the rain for the bus."

His smile grew bigger as he took it from me. "Gee, thanks, Allie! That's really nice of you. Now Ronald won't have to get one for me."

"You're welcome, Nathan. I'm glad you like it."

Thinking of my encounter with his brother at the shopping mall, I knew that he could have picked up a new umbrella for Nathan yesterday. But from what I had witnessed at the food counter, his priority seemed to be himself. It made me wonder about Nathan's living arrangements.

"Nathan, you mentioned your mother yesterday. Do your parents live close to you?"

The smile disappeared from his face. "Our mom died of breast cancer five years ago. Our dad was killed in a car wreck two years before that."

Good job, Allie! Ruin his morning by bringing up unhappy memories! "I'm so sorry to hear that," I said, berating myself. "I'm sure you miss them very much."

"It's been tough, but I still have my brother. If he hadn't let me move in with him, I don't know what would have happened to me. I'm different than most people."

My heart ached for him. If I hadn't been driving, I would have given him a hug. He was gazing out the window looking like a little lost boy.

"You're very unique, Nathan, and you're one of the sweetest, kindest, gentlest people I've ever met. In fact, yesterday when I told Miss Kahala that you said hello, she said lots of nice things about you."

He perked up and his smile returned. "She did? I wasn't sure if she would remember me."

"She told me that she would never forget you! I could tell that you're special to her."

I let him ponder that for a while, then we started discussing our plans for the weekend. I pulled up in front of the nursing home and stopped.

He pressed the umbrella against his chest. "The first thing I'm going to do is ask my supervisor for a new lock for my locker door," he said. "I don't want to take any chances of losing this."

I smiled at him. "Have a good day, Nathan," I said as he climbed out of the car. "I'll pick you on Monday morning."

"Same time; same place," he said. "Have a great weekend!"

"Thanks. You, too."

At school, I paired up the students and they reread *Love You Forever.* When they were finished, we did group activities related to the story, and the morning flew by. Since they had been working hard all week, I decided to give them a weekend free of a reading assignment. But they wouldn't hear of it. They begged me to pass out the next book, so I gave each of them a copy of *Amelia Bedelia* by Peggy Parish.

When they were gone, I straightened the room and jotted down some plans for the following week. Since I was focusing on hands-on activities more than worksheets, there was much less paperwork for me to do. Pleased with the progress each child was making, I planned to check out sets of more difficult books the next week. I locked the classroom, then walked to the office to check my e-mail.

There was only one message in my inbox. It was from my cousin, Frankie Janson, who is a detective with the Paradise Police Department.

The subject line read "I miss you!"

My cousins and I are close, but I suspected that since I had been gone for less than a week, there was something more behind the statement. Frankie hated writing letters, and I couldn't remember ever receiving an e-mail from him. We talked on the phone a lot, but few written words had ever passed between us. A little concerned, I opened the message and read:

Dear Allie,

I hope you're enjoying yourself. We're busy cleaning up after the storms that came through here on Monday night. Huge tree limbs knocked down power lines and the electricity was out all over town for ten to twelve hours. There was golf-ball-sized hail in the outlying areas, including at the Circle K. Doug told me that lightning struck one of the Bradford pear trees in your yard and split it down the middle. The town crews have been working around the clock hauling off limbs, picking up debris and trimming the salvageable trees.

The big pecan tree in Aunt Edith's front yard had several broken branches. The wind ripped off one and it only missed her garage by a few feet. Yesterday, her neighbor across the street called the fire department to come to her house.

Sorry, but I've got to go now. Johnny Ramsey down at the Wash

'N Go just called the dispatcher and said that some coin boxes in a couple of the stalls have been vandalized.

Don't be a stranger.

Love, Frankie

"Well, thank you Frankie!" I said out loud. It sounded like the storms had ripped my hometown apart and he was leaving me hanging! And why would Aunt Edith's neighbor call the fire department to come to her house? I wished that I could call him right then to get more details, but Kyle and I had a story to write for tomorrow's paper and I needed to be home by 5:00.

I sent a short reply to Frankie that I would be in touch, then I logged off.

Driving to the *Star*, I thought about the new information that Simon had given to me the night before. When I pulled into the parking lot of the paper, I was surprised to see Kyle's car. I walked in the back door, smiled and waved at Mr. Masaki, then hurried upstairs. Nearing the closed door of Kyle's office, I raised my hand to knock, but stopped when I heard his loud, angry voice. At first I thought his words were directed toward me, but then realized he was talking to someone on the phone. Turning around, I walked to my own office and unlocked the door.

While setting my purse down on the credenza, I could hear Kyle's voice through the paper-thin wall. "But you promised me," he shouted. The frustration in his tone was clear.

Not wanting to eavesdrop, I started humming to myself while I waited for my computer to boot. As Kyle's voice grew louder, so did my humming. The buzzing vibration from the increased volume made my whole mouth start tingling, so I started singing instead. My cousin Michael had led "How Great Thou Art" at church the previous Sunday, so that was the first song I thought of. As I belted out, "Then sings my soul, my Savior, God to Thee," for the third time, there was a loud knock on my door.

Kyle stuck his head in and grinned. "Are you having church in here?"

Looking up at him with my mouth hanging open, I know I must have turned ten shades of red. I was embarrassed because our little competition had gotten out of hand.

"Not exactly," I said, sitting up straighter. "But singing is better than shouting at people, don't you think?"

I guess he realized that I had overheard him, because he started shifting his feet. "Sorry about that. An acquaintance isn't following through on something she promised to do, and I got a little carried away on the phone."

"So I heard." I changed the subject. "I've been adding some new information to the thumbs-on-the-statue piece. Want to take a look and see what you think?"

"Sure." He pulled around a chair and sat down next to me. "I have to leave by 3:00, so I was hoping we could get this thing cranked out."

I waited while Kyle read what I had written. He nodded a couple of times, then added a note in the margin before handing it back to me.

"You have quite a flair for the written word," he said. "Where did you get the additional details?"

Knowing the conflict between him and Simon, I just said, "I made some more inquiries with law enforcement. Their spokesperson was kind enough to help me."

"Well, it sounds good," Kyle said. "Let's go see if Mr. Masaki can visit with us about it. I know he's planning on running it on the front page tomorrow."

Though I have confidence in my own writing ability, it felt good to have a professional journalist's approval. The note he had added said to be sure to add the source's name.

When we reached Mr. Masaki's office, he was hanging up the phone.

He motioned for us to come in. "Here's my new energetic team," he said. "Is your piece finished?"

"Yes, and it's pretty good if I do say so myself," Kyle said. "We're ready for you to take a look at it. It's been a tough one, but we think you'll be pleased."

I gave him an odd look. *A tough one? How would he know?* I thought. Aside from being at the cemetery when I had found the thumbs and reading the piece once I had it written, he hadn't contributed anything.

Mr. Masaki leaned back in his chair and propped his feet on the edge of his desk. Recalling the pose from the day of my interview with him, I remembered why I was here. I loved to write and Mr. Masaki had shown that he believed in me by giving me this job. Though Kyle was trying to take credit for everything, I knew what I had done. It would look childish if I started saying who did what. I figured it was best just to forget it.

Our boss underlined a few phrases and jotted down some questions on the top of the first page. He suggested some better ways to express certain things, then we discussed the layout and overall theme of the presentation. He seemed pleased with the way that it flowed and that it didn't appear biased.

"A good front page story," he said. "Honolulu P.D. should be happy with this article. You're giving credit to whom credit is due. That's quite a turnaround for you, Kyle, considering what happened last time."

Kyle cleared his throat. "Yes, I thought it would be better to humor the cops, instead of crossing them. It took some digging to get this information from them, but they finally gave us what we needed."

I stared at him, but he didn't seem to notice.

"Allison, I detect a lot of you in this story," the editor said.

I looked at my boss. "I'm trying, Mr. Masaki, but it's far from over. I'm anxious to see the culprit who's doing this get caught."

"And knowing you're helping the authorities, I'm sure he will be." He turned his attention to Kyle. "Now Kyle, just whom did you get the information from? I noticed that you put a note in the margin here about the source."

Turning in my chair to face my partner, I was anxious to hear his response. I suspected that he wasn't used to being questioned about his work, because he seemed to be at a loss for words. He looked at me and appeared to want my help to get him out of the hole that he had dug for himself.

I let him squirm for a few moments, then decided to be a nice girl. "He didn't get his name, Mr. Masaki. Detective Kahala is overseeing the case and gave me that information."

A look of relief spread across Kyle's face.

Mr. Masaki looked at me, then back at Kyle. I wasn't sure if he realized that Kyle was playing him, but it wasn't my place to set the record straight. At least not yet.

"I see. Well, as soon as these minor corrections are made, this piece is ready for tomorrow's edition," Mr. Masaki said. "I won't keep you two any longer."

As we stood to leave, Kyle looked at the clock on the wall behind the editor's desk. "If you don't mind finishing that up, Allie, I'm going to head to my appointment now," he said. "Have a nice weekend, you two." Without waiting for a reply from either of us, Kyle headed out the door.

I stood up to leave. "Before you go, Allie, I want to tell you that I'm proud of the work you're doing here," Mr. Masaki said. "The *Hawaiian Star* is lucky to have you."

"Thanks. I'm enjoying working here," I said, smiling. "Now, I'm going to go get this piece finished. Have a nice weekend."

I walked back to my office and wondered if Kyle had learned his lesson earlier. I guess time would tell.

After the third ring, I heard, "Frank Janson."

"Aloha," I said, twirling the phone cord. "*Pehea 'oe?*

"Aloha I know," he said, "but you're going to have to interpret the next part."

"It means 'How are you?' Some of my students are fluent in both English and Hawaiian, so they've been teaching me a few phrases."

"I didn't know if you would still be associating with us commoners," he said.

"Yes, but not because you deserve it. I can't believe you left out so many important details in your e-mail message."

"I didn't intend to worry you, but you know I'm not great with correspondence. I was on a roll, when the Wash 'N Go call came in. I didn't have any choice but to send you what I had already written."

"Okay, I'll forgive you since you needed to go out and fight crime. But only if you give me all the scoop now." I was determined to keep the upper hand in this conversation, because with Frankie, I rarely got the chance.

"Conditional forgiveness," he said. "I guess I deserve it since I left you hanging like I did."

"So, how badly was the Circle K damaged? Was any of the livestock hurt?"

"I drove out Tuesday morning and Grandpa said that four calves took a beating from the hail and had to be put down. Some of the cows were skittish and a little skinned up, but seemed to be okay otherwise. The vet came out and patched up old Goliath while I was there. That old bull must have been trying to take refuge under the big catalpa tree in the east pasture when a limb broke off and hit him across the back."

Goliath was a nineteen hundred-pound Black Angus bull that had been born on the Circle K. He was Grandpa's favorite breeder because he was a descendant of a bull that his grandfather, Elliott Kane, had bought in the late 1800s. Great-great-grandpa Elliott's bull was one of the first four introduced into the United States by a man from Scotland who had settled in Kansas.

"I hate to think of those poor babies enduring that," I said, sadly. "What about Goliath? Is he going to be alright?"

"The vet thinks so. Two of the discs in his back were fractured, but he said they should heal over time. Goliath had some abrasions on his right side, so the limb must have hit him at an angle, then veered off. Grandpa said he was going to keep him in the paddock on the north side of the barn for a few days so he can tend to him."

"Well, I'm sure Grandpa is relieved to know that Goliath will be okay. Now what was the deal with Aunt Edith? You said her neighbor called the fire department."

"Yeah, that," Frankie said, sighing. "As I mentioned in the e-mail, the town cleanup crews have been working like mad hauling off limbs. A couple of guys have been using the cherry picker to trim mangled trees. But Aunt Edith got tired of waiting on them to get to her pecan tree."

Uh-oh. This didn't sound good.

"When the fire truck arrived, one of the guys called in and asked for help with crowd control. Rita was working the phones, and when they told her they were at Aunt Edith's house, she called me."

Rita was my favorite dispatcher at Paradise P.D. She had known most of my family all her life and though she knew that some of us were a little nuts, she never appeared judgmental.

"Crowd control? What was going on?"

"When I arrived, cars and people were everywhere! Everyone was looking at something in the sky and didn't notice me. Even after I tapped the horn and got on the loud speaker and told them to move, they just gave me enough room to get through. When I climbed out of the car in front of Aunt Edith's, the sun was shining in my eyes. I couldn't figure out what everyone was staring at—then I spotted her." He let out a sigh.

"I probably don't want to hear this, but tell me what she was doing."

"Thirty feet off the ground with her legs wrapped around a branch of that pecan tree, Aunt Edith was going to town!" he said. "Her chainsaw was open full blast and wood chips were flying everywhere! She was covered in sawdust. But I have to hand it to her; she did have on some safety goggles. The firemen on the ground were yelling at her to shut off the saw, but she wasn't paying them any mind. Her friend, Daisy Johnson, was so upset that I was afraid she was going to have a heart attack right there on the sidewalk."

Aunt Edith's guardian angels had been run ragged over the years. I imagine God must have assigned a whole band to watch over her, because I don't think just one could keep up.

"She didn't hurt herself, did she?" I asked.

"No. Remarkably, she seemed to know what she was doing. She had tied a heavy rope to the limb she was cutting, then looped it several times around the trunk of the tree. Two limbs were already down, and she had cut them into nice-sized pieces of firewood. One of the firemen was stacking them on the front porch for her. After she lowered the branch that she had cut to the ground, she let one of the guys in the ladder truck swing over and take it from there. He took the chainsaw from her, then she rode on the platform with him to the ground."

"Thank goodness she didn't fall out of the tree," I said.

"You can say that again," Frankie replied. "I asked her to please not work on the tree anymore on her own. I told her I'd bring over some help on Saturday and we'd finish the job for her. She wasn't thrilled with the prospect, but when I drove by this afternoon, things were still as we had left them. Jamie, Michael and I are going to meet over there in the morning." Jamie is my older brother and is the Sr. Computer Staff Engineer at Kane Energy.

"You're a good boy, Frankie Janson. By the way, where was Bennie during all of this?" I couldn't imagine that Aunt Edith's son would let her get up in the tree to begin with.

"I asked Aunt Edith where her guests were, and she said that Bennie and his family had gone house hunting in Tulsa. I'm sure she didn't share her tree-trimming plans with him before they left, or he would have nixed it."

"She's been wanting them to start looking for a house of their own," I said. "Maybe something will turn up before long. She's coming here in two weeks, but until then, you had better keep an eye on her. Savvy?"

"Yes, ma'am."

Aunt Edith could be a handful. She was her own woman; all one hundred pounds of her.

"Well, I'd like to visit with you longer, but I need to get back to work," I said. "In less than two hours Simon is picking me up, and we're going to Maui for the weekend."

"Oh, really." The line was silent for a moment. "And just what are his intentions in this romantic getaway?"

Frankie knew that I would never compromise myself, but I couldn't help smiling when he shifted into protective cousin mode.

"Simon's been working hard and needs a break, so he's taking the weekend off. We're flying over so that he can show me some of the sites. But you don't need to be concerned about my reputation, because we'll be staying with his grandparents."

"Well, it sounds proper, so I guess it will be alright."

"I'm glad you approve. Now, since that's settled, have a good weekend and I'll talk to you later."

"You too. Have fun."

After hanging up, I made corrections to the story, proofread it twice, then forwarded it to the copy editor. I straightened my desk, then headed out the door.

🐾 🐾 🐾

At 5:00, Simon was loading my overnight bag into the back seat of his Jeep. After he got inside, he buckled his seatbelt and we were on our way.

"Our flight leaves at 6:20," he said. "It takes forty minutes to get to the Kahului airport on Maui. Grandpa is supposed to pick us up there.

He and Grandmother usually eat supper early, but she said she would hold it until after we arrive."

"That's nice of her to do that. My Gramma and Grandad Winters usually eat supper around 5:00. If I ate that early, I'd need another meal before bedtime."

"As you know, I'm not your typical three-meal-a-day person," Simon said. "Someone is always going out for barbecue, or burgers, or calling in pizza at the police department. If the snacks in the kitchen get low, everybody chips in a few bucks. Then someone goes shopping to fill the cabinets and fridge again. And of course, there's never a lack for company if I want to go out to eat. I eat five or six meals a day on the average."

"I'd weigh a ton if I ate that much! I imagine your parents' grocery bill dropped like a rock after you left home," I said, smiling at him.

He grinned at me. "Yeah, they were able to start traveling more once Richard and I left. I guess the several hundred dollars a month they paid out to feed us started adding up once we were gone."

I told Simon about the storm that passed through Paradise and about Aunt Edith's adventure with the chainsaw. By the time I had finished, we were pulling into the security parking lot at the Honolulu International Airport.

Though I told Simon that I was capable of carrying my own bag, he insisted on carrying both of our bags to the Hawaiian Airlines ticket counter. After we picked up our boarding passes, we walked toward the security check-in area.

We bypassed all the people waiting in line to send their belongings through the X-ray machine. Though we got some dirty looks from a couple of them, their expressions changed when they spotted Simon's badge clipped to his belt.

Several Transportation Security Administration agents were assisting passengers with their belongings. Simon walked up behind the one standing in front of the X-ray machine conveyor belt. He was a thin, dark-haired man and he was wearing glasses. A large silver and black German shepherd was lying beneath the machine next to his feet.

He turned around. "Hey, Simon. I just saw you last Sunday, didn't I?" he asked. "Are you taking up residence on Maui now?"

"Hi, Kelly. No, but I have been spending a lot of time there. If you've got a second, I'd like you to meet my girlfriend, Allison Kane."

"Sure thing," he said. He stepped away from the machine and another agent took his place.

Simon turned toward me. "Allie, this is Kelly Hugo, an ace when it comes to airport security."

Kelly smiled as he stretched his hand out toward me. "I don't know if I'd say *ace*, Miss Kane. Simon keeps such a tight reign on the criminals here on Oahu, my job is a breeze."

"Allie, don't listen to him," Simon said, grinning. "He's just being modest. Last month he and his canine helper down there caught two different people trying to smuggle drugs onto the plane."

Kelly motioned toward the dog. "Abbie is the one who deserves the credit. It may not look like she's paying attention, but believe me, she knows everything that's happening within fifty feet of this line. Those two druggies picked the wrong day to travel if they thought they could get their dope past Abbie."

"She's a beautiful dog," I said. "My two dachshunds are pretty good detectives, too."

"Yes, they're real bloodhounds in the truest sense of the word," Simon said, smiling. He knew all about Rowdy and Precious digging up and dragging home the toes of the two men who had been found buried in my neighbor's yard a few months back.

"Dogs have a keen instinct when it comes to trouble," Kelly said. He reached down and stroked Abbie's head. "I wouldn't know what to do without her." The dog nuzzled his hand. It was clear to see that there was a strong bond between the two. The agent stood back up. "It was nice meeting you, Miss Kane. I know you'll have your work cut out for you, but try to keep this guy in line if you can." He patted Simon on the back.

"Be safe, Kelly," Simon said. "I'll see you again soon, I'm sure."

We walked on toward our gate. "He seems like a nice guy," I said.

"Nice doesn't begin to describe him. Kelly would give you the shirt off his back, then offer you his shoes and socks, too, if he thought you needed them."

When we reached the gate, we handed our boarding passes to the flight attendant. The other passengers were already on board the Boeing 717 aircraft. We found our seats and Simon stowed our carryon bags in the overhead compartment. Within five minutes, the plane was taxiing out to the runway.

I had the window seat, and I couldn't get enough of the spectacular view as we flew away from Oahu. The evening sun was casting its last rays across the foam-tipped waves, and lights from some of the hotels lining Waikiki beach were starting to come on.

Simon took my hand. We talked softly and just enjoyed each other's company. The flight attendant brought some refreshments. She had to scurry to serve everyone before the end of the short flight, but not a drop of guava juice was spilled and no trash remained by the time the captain came on the intercom. He told us we would be landing at the Kahului International Airport within ten minutes.

After leaving the plane, Simon and I headed through the terminal and outside the front door. His grandpa pulled up beside us in a tan, extended-cab Ford pickup.

"How about a ride, you two?" he called out the passenger side window.

"Hi, Grandpa. This is Allie. Thanks for picking us up."

"Hello, Mr. Kahala. It's nice to meet you," I said.

Simon opened the door and put our bags in the back seat. He gave me a hand into the front seat, then climbed in beside me.

"Please call me Trip," his grandfather said. Though still hefty, he was a slimmer version of Simon's dad and had hazel eyes. He had a bit more gray in his dark hair, but it was easy to tell that they were closely related. He pulled out of the airport onto a busy highway. "Allie, you're as pretty as a picture. Welcome to Maui."

"Thank you, sir. I'm very excited about getting to come here to meet you and your wife. I've heard good things about you from Simon. Now it will be nice to put faces with the names."

"We're mighty glad to have you," he said. "Ella is back at the house fussing over supper. I hope you're hungry because she fixed enough food to feed a small army."

"I'm starving," Simon said. "I hope Grandmother fixes caldereta and corn muffins this weekend. I've had a craving for them for days."

"Caldereta? What's that?" I asked.

"It's a stew made with meat and vegetables in a very spicy tomato base," he replied. "The recipe came from the Filipinos."

"Hmmm. In the winter, my family has beef stew and cornbread a lot," I said. "I guess our cultures aren't that different when it comes to comfort foods."

Simon leaned forward and looked around me at his grandfather. "Do you think I ought to tell her what kind of meat is used in caldereta, or just let her try to guess after she tastes it?"

Trip grinned. "You might ought to tell her. In the past, I've encountered some mainland folks that don't like our recipes."

"Though I would never eat it, some people in Oklahoma hunt down and eat rattlesnakes," I said. "As long as your stew doesn't have snake, horse or dog meat in it, I'm sure I won't have any objections."

Simon reached for my hand. "It's made with goat meat. Grandmother makes the base with tomatoes from her garden, then adds other fresh vegetables and herbs to it. She simmers the meat for several hours and it's so tender, you can cut it with a fork. Caldereta is delicious."

Goat meat? Well, why not? I thought. "I'm game," I said. "When in Rome, or in this case Hawaii, do as the locals do."

"That's my girl," Simon said. "Now, we'll have to put in our order and see if Grandmother will fix it while we're here."

We drove through the central part of the island toward the West Coast. Sugarcane fields stretched for miles on both sides of the highway. One of the fields was on fire. Smoke billowed toward the sky and twisted stalks of cane were lying all over the ground.

"Oh, it's too bad they lost that field," I said. "I imagine the owner is sorry to see his crop go up in flames."

"They set the fire on purpose," Trip said. "The cane stalks contain a lot of moisture, so they don't burn. The leaves and chaff burn off leaving only the useable portion of the plant. See that tractor sitting at the edge of the field?" I looked where he was pointing and saw a monstrous tractor with a crane attached to the front of it. Dangling on the end of the crane's long arm was a large, curved, iron object. "That contraption hanging off the end there is called a push rake. It grabs and picks up big bundles of stalks. They're loaded into trailers, then trucks hook onto the trailers and haul them to the mill."

The huge metal containers reminded me of the beds on the dump trucks I had seen coming from a rock quarry close to Paradise. Two of them were stacked high with cane stalks. "Those are big loads," I said.

"They get about sixty-four tons of cane into one trailer," Trip said.

"We passed the Alexander and Baldwin Sugar Mill and Museum back by the airport," Simon said to me. "I didn't think about it, or I would have pointed it out to you. Next to the museum, they have a push rake as well as some other equipment used in processing the sugarcane. If you want to, we'll stop by there tomorrow and look around."

"I'd love to," I said. "I know that sugarcane used to be the biggest contributor to Hawaii's economy before tourism took that spot. But is it still the largest agricultural crop?"

"Not anymore," Trip said. "Several plantations closed in the 1990s causing the crop value to fall below that of pineapples."

We passed several beach parks as we headed north along the shoreline. Though it was getting dark, a few board and wind surfers still dotted the water.

"If you don't mind me asking, what were you planning on showing Allie this weekend?" Trip asked Simon.

"We haven't discussed it yet, but I thought we'd go to the Maui Tropical Plantation, then drive to the top of the Haleakala Crater tomorrow. We'll pass right by the Sugar Museum, so we can add that to the list, too. When we get back, if we're not too tired, we might hit some hot spots along the water front tomorrow night."

"There's a new supper club down on Front Street that has a terrific band," Trip said. "Ella and I checked it out last weekend. That place was hoppin'!"

Trip reminded me a lot of my great-uncle Clarence, Gramma's and Aunt Edith's older brother. It was nice to see older people get out and have a good time.

We passed through the center of Lahaina, then Trip turned right into a residential neighborhood. After driving several blocks, he turned into the driveway of a brown frame house. He pulled into an empty spot beneath the carport, then turned off the engine.

"Home sweet home," he said.

We got out of the truck and Simon pulled our bags from the back seat. When we reached the front porch, a woman about my height opened the door.

"Aloha, Simon," she said, stepping onto the porch.

"Aloha, Grandmother." He leaned down and kissed her cheek. She put her arms around his neck and hugged him. When he stepped back, he said, "I'd like you to meet Allison Kane."

"Aloha and welcome, Allison," his grandmother said, stepping toward me. She put her arms around me and gave me a hug.

"Thank you for having me, Mrs. Kahala."

"Come in and I'll show you where you'll be sleeping. Simon, you'll be in your father's old room, if you want to go ahead and set your bag in there."

"Yes, ma'am."

We slipped off our shoes inside the front entryway, then followed her into a modest-sized living room. The hardwood floors gleamed from a fresh coat of wax. An Oriental rug covered the middle portion of the floor. Rattan couches with brightly-colored, comfy-looking cushions on them sat against two different walls. Airy curtains framed the sliding glass door that led to a spacious back yard.

Ella led us down a short hallway and stopped outside the door of a lime-green bedroom. Inside the room, there was a beautiful oak sleigh bed covered in a yellow and green floral bedspread. A chest of drawers and a nightstand that matched the bed sat against one wall. A six-drawer dresser completed the suit. The louvered doors on the closet were shut.

"I hope you'll be comfortable in here," she said. "This room used to belong to one of Simon's aunts before she left home to get married."

I stepped into the room. "It's very nice." A cool breeze was blowing through the window causing the pale yellow curtains to flutter. There wasn't a speck of dust on any of the furniture, and the carpet looked like it had just been vacuumed. On the opposite side of the room, a door with a full-length mirror attached to it was standing ajar.

Simon walked into the room toward the closet. "I'll set your bag here in case you need to hang up something," he said. He pointed toward the mirrored door. "You have your own bathroom right through there, if you need to freshen up before we eat."

"Yes, just make yourself at home," his grandmother said. "There are fresh towels, soap and washcloths on the vanity."

"Thank you very much."

Simon gave me a kiss on the cheek, then left the room and walked down the hallway. Mrs. Kahala paused at the doorway. "Both my son, Dennis, and my grandson speak highly of you, Allison. Though Simon has dated a lot over the years, he has never brought a girl to our house for an overnight visit."

I sensed that she had something more on her mind. "Simon is very special to me, Mrs. Kahala."

She nodded and smiled. "That's good to hear, and please call me

Ella. Now, dinner isn't going to get itself on the table. I'll leave so that you can freshen up. Come and join us when you're ready."

"Thanks. I'll be right there."

🌺 🌺 🌺

The caldereta was delicious! Ella had also fixed a large salad using a variety of greens, tomatoes, Maui onions and carrots grown in her garden. Long rice, which was actually noodles made from a type of bean flour, and a plate full of fresh papaya, pineapple and passion fruit slices rounded out the meal. Much to Simon's delight, she had also made corn muffins, and he put away six of them. He soaked up every drop of stew remaining in his bowl with the last muffin from the basket.

"Now for dessert," Ella said. She started picking up our empty plates from the table.

"I don't know where I'll put it," I said. "The meal was wonderful, but I'm stuffed!"

"Did you make haupia, Grandmother?" Simon asked.

"It's your favorite pudding, isn't it?" she said, smiling at him.

I noticed she didn't say favorite "dessert." Simon loves sweets and I was finding out that he had a lot of "favorite" flavors of ice cream, pie and cake.

I helped her clear the table, then we carried in individual dishes filled with a thick, white pudding. When I tasted mine, the creamy, coconut mixture melted in my mouth. Ella said she had picked one of the coconuts from their tree in the backyard to use for the dessert.

"This sure is tasty," Trip said, licking his spoon. "You can't beat fresh coconut for haupia."

"I hope you don't get fined someday for keeping that tree," Simon said. "So far the state isn't cracking down too hard in the residential areas, so maybe the officials will leave you alone."

"Cracking down for having coconut palms?" I said. "Driving here from the airport, I saw palm trees in almost every yard we passed."

"I didn't mean the actual tree," he said, "but the coconuts on it. A few years ago, a tourist was hit on the head with a coconut and sued the state. After the government had to pay out a bunch of money, they passed a law that all coconuts had to be cut from trees in public places."

"It seems that people will sue for just about anything these days," Simon's grandpa said, shaking his head. "It's a shame that the locals have to eliminate what nature has provided for their people for thousands of years. If you ask me, that knucklehead should have been watching where he was going."

Simon looked at me and grinned. I felt the same way that Trip did about it, and I suspected that Simon did, too.

After Ella and I cleaned up the kitchen, we all walked into the backyard to sit for a while. The sun had been down for over an hour. Trip lit two tiki lanterns that were mounted on poles a short distance from the back door. Together with the stars scattered across the clear sky and the full moon, a soft glow covered the yard. A gentle breeze blowing across the ocean less than a mile away was cool and refreshing. We all talked and laughed until 10:00. The news was coming on television, so Simon's grandparents excused themselves to go back inside to watch it.

Simon was holding my hand and playing with my fingers. He stood up and pulled me to my feet. "Let's go for a moonlight stroll."

He wrapped his left arm around my waist and pulled me against him so that our sides were touching. We started walking across the yard into the shadows.

Though there wasn't much light, when we reached the gate, I saw that it had a lock on it. "Are we going to climb over the fence, or do you have a key for this lock?" I asked him.

"Oops, no key." I could see a grin on his face. "I guess we'll just have to stand here for a while until we figure out how to open it."

Simon turned me so that I was facing him. He pulled me close and looped one of his arms around my back. With his other hand, he placed his fingers beneath my chin. His chest was pressed against mine, and I could feel the steady beat of his heart.

I looked into his eyes and whispered, "You didn't really have a moonlight stroll in mind, did you?"

He gently kissed one cheek, then the other one. "I didn't say we'd walk very far." He slowly moved his fingers down the side of my neck. I tilted my head and enjoyed the gentle caress.

Cupping the back of my head in his hand, he pulled me toward him. When his lips touched mine, I was lost. Only Simon filled my thoughts, and it was a wonderful feeling.

"As bad as I hate to let you go, I think we'd better get inside," he said, taking a step back. "We'll need to start out by 9:00 in the morning, if we're going to see very much. Besides, my will to overcome temptation is getting pretty thin right now."

I know what you mean, I thought.

We walked hand in hand into the house. Simon's grandparents had already turned in. He walked me to my bedroom door, gave me one last kiss, then headed to his own room.

While I got ready for bed, I couldn't help smiling. My heart hadn't yet settled into its normal rhythm when I drifted off to sleep.

CHAPTER 9

"Good morning, everyone," I said as I walked into the kitchen.

"Good morning," Simon and his grandparents said in unison.

Simon stood up from the table and walked around to pull out a chair for me. "Did you sleep well?" he asked.

"Like a rock," I said. He squeezed my shoulder, then walked over to the coffeemaker.

"Would anyone like more coffee?" he asked.

"I'm good," Trip said.

"My cup is still half full, but the biscuits in the oven should be ready," Ella said. She started pushing back her chair.

"Stay where you are, Grandmother. I'll get them."

Simon grabbed an oven mitt from a hook above the stove. He pulled out a big pan of homemade biscuits from the oven, then carried them to the table. A saucer with butter on it, and an assortment of jams were already sitting in the middle. A platter of bacon, link sausage and scrambled eggs was sitting beside Trip.

Simon said grace, then we all filled our plates. I realized that the fluffy biscuits tasted as good as Gramma Winters' biscuits, though I would never tell her that.

After everyone was finished, I stood up and started to clear the table.

"You leave that stuff where it is," Ella said to me. "You two have a busy day planned. I'll take care of the dishes."

"Well, if you're sure. Thank you for the good breakfast," I said. I looked at Simon. "After I brush my teeth, I'll be ready to go when you are."

He took a last drink of his coffee, then pushed back his chair. "I'll meet you at the front door in five minutes."

I had made my bed and straightened the room before going to breakfast. After I finished in the bathroom, I pulled a disposable camera from my overnight bag and dropped it into my purse. I looked in the dresser mirror one last time, adjusted my ponytail, and then headed toward the front door.

Simon was already there waiting for me. "We'll see you two sometime this evening," he told his grandparents as he opened the door. "If Allie wants to, we'll probably go down to Front Street tonight to eat, so don't cook anything for us."

"There's a new restaurant with a classy band down there that your grandpa and I went to last weekend," Ella said. "It's called Big Kahuna's Place. You might want to check it out."

"Thanks. We might do that. We'll see you this evening," Simon said.

I waved at them, then he and I walked outside to the pickup and left.

We drove through Lahaina past the L.K. & P.R. Sugarcane Train depot. The old-style steam engine was noisy as it pulled away from the station with its cars loaded with passengers. Simon said it was a popular tourist attraction that offered roundtrip rides from Ka'anapali to Lahaina several times a day. They also offered a dinner tour each evening.

As we traveled south along the coast, I couldn't get enough of the gorgeous scenery. When we reached McGregor Point, Simon pulled into the parking lot and we got out. The small island of Lanai stood off in the distance. Even though the wind was mild, it was causing the waves to pound the boulders in the cove below us. The turquoise water in the lagoon splashed against the jagged rocks, then receded in a swirl of white foam. As the ocean melted into the horizon, the aqua color changed to a deep royal blue.

"This is a good location to watch the humpback whales in the winter and spring months," Simon said. "They start coming down from Alaska in late December to give birth. They stay in these warm waters until May to give the babies time to put on some weight, which they do at a rate of almost a hundred pounds a day."

"That's a lot of weight gain!" I said. "The mother's milk must really be rich."

"Yes, it is, and a baby will drink about eighty gallons of it a day."

Though the whales were gone now, I noticed a lot of boats in the water. "I doubt if the mother whales like boats getting close to their babies. Are there any special regulations when the animals are in the area?"

"Yes. There have been as many as seven hundred whales living out there during that five-month period. Boats aren't allowed within one hundred yards of them. Of course, that rule doesn't stop the whales from swimming closer than that to the boats. The ferries that carry working folks from Lanai and Molokai to Maui every day have to be extra careful during that time. But overall, most sailors are cautious when the whales are out there."

We got back into the car and drove a few miles to the Maui Tropical Plantation. As we walked inside the door of the large country store, the smell of fruit, coffee and assorted goodies from the grill filled the air. We wandered up and down the aisles, and I couldn't resist buying a bag of chocolate-covered macadamia nuts. While munching on the crunchy snack, I browsed through the racks of books in the center of the store. Needing both hands to look through the selections, I handed the half-eaten bag of nuts to Simon. He took off toward the T-shirts while I sorted through the books about the Hawaiian monarchy.

Twenty minutes later we met at the register. Simon had picked out matching his-and-her T-shirts for us to wear sightseeing the next day. They each had colorful sailboats and palm tress on them, and Maui, Hawaii was written across the front of each one. I had settled on two books. Between the two of us, we spent almost fifty dollars.

The plantation offered a tram tour of the grounds. Simon paid for our two tickets, then we headed out the back door of the gift shop. As we walked toward the tram pickup point, I admired the manicured lawn and lush flowers lining the sidewalks. The handiwork of hardworking gardeners could be seen everywhere.

Along with about twenty other guests, we climbed aboard the tram. The driver slowly pulled away, then started telling us interesting facts about the different varieties of trees and plants growing throughout the plantation. Acres of banana, mango, star fruit, papaya, and macadamia nut trees stretched ahead of us.

The driver stopped the tram by a coconut grove, and we all got off. He demonstrated how to husk a coconut using a sharp long garden pick mounted on a platform. He said that even with today's technology, coconuts still have to be husked by hand. No machine has been invented to do the job. He explained that an average coconut contains about two cups of water and that the liquid is good for the kidneys. One tree can bear seventy to eighty coconuts a year, and it can live to be a hundred years old.

After the coconut husking demonstration, everyone climbed back aboard the tram. We slowly trekked through the rest of the orchard. As we neared the end of the ride, we passed some guava trees. Our guide said that guava fruit contains iron, calcium and five times more vitamin C than orange juice.

When the ride concluded, Simon and I wandered past the nursery and by the small lagoon. We stood and watched some kids tossing fish food into the pond.

"Now to the Alexander and Baldwin Sugar Museum," Simon said. He took my hand and we walked to the car.

We headed north on Highway 3o, then drove east on Highway 32 toward the airport in Kahului. Simon said that the mill and museum were just a few miles south of the airport.

When we pulled into the museum's parking lot, I saw a monstrous push rake sitting at the edge of the lot. I asked Simon to take a picture of me in front of it. I was always looking for unusual things to spice up units for my students. If I decided to integrate some facts about sugarcane into my plant unit, this would be a nice addition.

For a few minutes, we looked at some heavy equipment that was sitting in the yard beside the building, then we walked inside.

"Welcome to the Alexander and Baldwin Sugar Museum," a woman sitting at a table said. "Please sign our guest book, and I'll give you some information about the facility."

I signed the book for Simon and myself, then took the brochure the woman offered to me.

"This building was built in 1902 and was originally the plantation superintendent's home," she said. "There are six rooms full of artifacts, photos, and interactive displays that you are welcome to look at." She motioned toward a double-doorway on her right. "A ten-minute video is continuously playing in this room behind me. It will give you some history about sugarcane and the processing procedures. If you have any questions when you're finished with the tour, please feel free to ask."

Simon and I walked through the refurbished home, and I felt like I had stepped back in time. The rooms were full of murals, yellowed letters and documents, tools, old photographs and more from a bygone era. The Plantation Room contained religious artifacts and household items used by former workers. It also had a scale model of a worker's camp house.

According to various displays, Polynesian settlers introduced sugarcane to Hawaii more than a thousand years earlier. The state's largest sugar mill, operated by the Hawaiian Commercial & Sugar Company, was just across the road. Not only did it produce raw sugar, but it also produced large quantities of molasses. In addition to that, seven percent of Maui's electrical power was generated there.

After watching the informative video, Simon and I each picked up a sample packet of raw sugar that was in a basket near the exit. The grains were coarse and tan in color. When I tasted it, I could tell a difference between it and the white refined version I was used to eating.

"I enjoyed the tour," Simon said as we walked toward the pickup. "I learned some of that when I was in school, but seeing that video and the other things in there brought it to life."

"Yes, it was very interesting and I learned a lot, too," I said. "I know that all types of field workers have had to endure hot, backbreaking conditions to earn their wages. I've been told that picking cotton was a hard job, but I can't imagine that working in the sugarcane fields was much easier."

"I'm sure it wasn't," Simon said. "One time I was questioning Mom about her background. She told me that her grandfather was among the first to come here from the Philippines to work in the sugarcane fields. They were called sakadas, and they started migrating to Hawaii in the early 1900s."

"So he had firsthand experience," I said.

"Yes, and according to her, he had a hard life. The white plantation owners encouraged Filipinos to come here because they would work hard for very little wages. Another advantage was that unlike some of the other workers, Filipinos shied away from the unions that were prone to strike. Mom's grandfather married and settled here and only went back to the Philippines for an occasional visit."

"It's sad that many white landowners in the United States took advantage of other races in order to prosper," I said. "Heartache and despair was endured by a lot of people just because their skin was a different color."

"Yes, but some of those people rose above that and turned their hardships into greatness and prosperity. Many inventors, statesmen, scholars, doctors and lawyers of all races might not have had the opportunities to do what they did if they hadn't been living in the greatest nation on earth. They worked hard and reaped the benefits."

"They took lemons and turned them into lemonade," I said. "Whatsoever a man sows, that shall he also reap. Galatians 6:7."

"And let us not be weary in well doing; for in due season we shall reap, if we faint not," Simon replied, smiling. "Galatians 6:9. I bet you didn't think I knew that scripture."

I looked at him and smiled. "I'm impressed. I was in a Bible quiz group at church from the time I was nine years old until I graduated from high school. I could remember a lot of scriptures, but I had a hard time remembering the chapter and verse references."

"Well, my favorite ones stuck with me," Simon said. "But I'm sorry to say that I don't read the Bible nearly as often as I should." He turned right onto the Haleakala Highway. "Now we're going to the House of the Sun. With an elevation of over ten thousand feet, you can't get much closer to heaven than that."

"House of the Sun?"

"That's what Haleakala means. According to an old Hawaiian myth, one day the demigod, Maui, went to the top of the crater and lassoed the sun. He beat it with the rope because it wasn't giving the natives on the island enough daylight to plant their crops. Before letting it go, he broke the sun's legs. With broken legs, it could only crawl across the sky, causing daylight to last longer."

"That sounds like another story I've heard before," I said.

"When God made the sun stand still so that Joshua and the Israelites could finish off the Amorites?"

"You got it."

The curvy road circled through Maui's oldest and largest family-owned cattle ranch. Simon said that it consisted of approximately 30,000 acres. Several times he had to slow down to go over the cattle guard grates in the road. The pastureland reminded me of the Circle K, and I felt a twinge of homesickness. I made a mental note to call my parents and both sets of grandparents when I got back to Traci's the next evening.

We met a group of about forty bike riders cycling down the mountain road toward us. Simon said that several tour companies on the island offered sunrise bike tours. Their vans would pick up tourists at their hotels around 3:00 a.m., then take them to the top of Haleakala. Everyone had breakfast on the summit, then most companies paid for a second breakfast after the thirty-eight mile trip down the mountain was completed.

"If I got up that early and rode a bicycle thirty-eight miles, I would need a super-sized second breakfast," I said. "What does a trip like that cost?"

"It varies, but depending on the package, it runs between fifty to one hundred dollars. The tour company provides all the gear, like helmets, gloves, jackets and good quality bikes." After the group passed us, Simon pulled off the road onto a narrow stretch of pavement. "Let's get out and stretch our legs. I want you to see the view from here."

I pulled my camera from my purse, then slid across the seat and out his door.

"Wow! That's magnificent!" I said as I gazed across the valley below.

We were standing more than a mile above sea level. From our vantage point, we could see cattle grazing, thick patches of colorful wild flowers mixed with the long grass, and flowering trees. Small villages dotted the coastline. The ocean, crowned with low-hanging, puffy clouds, added the final touch to the picture-perfect view.

"It's magnificent, all right," Simon said. He draped his arm around my shoulders. To my surprise, he started singing. "On a clear day, you can see forever." I smiled as I listened to him sing the verse of the old song. I harmonized with him on the chorus.

"You have a lovely voice," I told him. "And you even know Broadway show tunes to boot."

He grinned at me. "Mom has been a lover of music all her life. She plays the violin, and she studied music in college. In fact, she was in the Royal Hawaiian Band for three years. Since music was playing in our house a lot when I was growing up, it rubbed off on me, I guess."

"Music is another thing we have in common, then," I said, smiling at him. I mentally added that item to the plus side of our compatibility list.

"Besides good food, acquaintances and enjoying detective work? Yes, I love music."

"So your mother played in the Royal Hawaiian Band? That's where I saw Sammy Cho last spring when I gave him your phone number. If I hadn't been there helping to chaperone Traci's class, it might have taken you longer to get Sammy to turn himself in."

Simon grinned. "That's true. I give you credit for helping to solve that case. However, as I told you then, I get very uncomfortable when you put yourself in dangerous situations. So I want you to watch your back while you're gathering facts about these grave-robbing cases for the *Star*."

"Oh, don't worry. I'm always careful."

I took several pictures of the scenery, then we drove on up the road to the top of the mountain.

The fifty-space parking lot was almost full when we pulled into it. Simon stepped out of the pickup, then reached behind his seat and pulled out two jackets. "Here," he said, handing the smallest one to me. "You're going to need this. It's thirty degrees cooler up here than it was down below where we started."

We climbed the half-mile rocky trail that led to the summit. Though we walked slowly, I was huffing and puffing. The oxygen-thin air made breathing more difficult. But once we arrived on top, it was well worth the climb. It felt like I was on top of the world! I could see the islands of Lanai, Molokai, the Big Island and the western part of Maui. The view was breathtaking!

The wind had swept small lava rocks to the base of the mountain. Drifts of red, yellow, black and gray stones were piled in the center of the valley. Swirls of loosened particles rested in gullies that had cascaded down the mountain to the trough below. Mineral-rich, red soil on one side of the crater reminded me of the clay found in the panhandle of Oklahoma. The region there is aptly named "Red Carpet Country."

I pointed toward the valley. "It's hard to imagine that we're standing on a mountain that spewed out all that rock thousands of years ago."

"Actually, it was only about two hundred years ago when this volcano erupted the last time," Simon said. "It happened near Makena, which is located along the coastline due west of here. This is a shield volcano, and the magma beneath it is like hot, thick syrup. Rock and soil is pushed upward to form a cone, but the gases escape through vents, so explosions are rare."

"Rare, huh?" Driving up here, it hadn't dawned on me that we would be standing on top of an active inferno.

I guess I must have had a worried expression on my face, because Simon squeezed my hand. "Don't fret. Though Haleakala is bound to erupt again, I don't think it's going to be today."

"That's good to know," I said, grinning. I pointed toward a building about a half-mile away from us. "What's that?"

"It's the Pu'u Ula'ula Observatory, or Science City as it's sometimes called. There are thirteen telescopes in there operated by NASA, the Department of Defense and the University of Hawaii. This mountain offers one of the five best sights in the world from which to observe planets, stars, satellites and the moon."

We walked down to the visitor center below. Inside the small building, the walls were covered with murals, charts and maps. A park ranger was on hand to answer questions. We wandered around outside the building, and I noticed some gray plants nestled among the rocks. Their long, thin petals looked like mini feather dusters.

I knelt down to take a closer look. "These are pretty little flowers," I said.

"They're called silverswords. They grow all over the top of this mountain, but they're an endangered species. They can live up to fifty years, but they only bloom once before they die."

I saw some large, brownish-gray birds searching for food nearby. "What kind of birds are those?"

"Nene geese. They're Hawaii's state bird and are protected as well. The numbers have dwindled, and there are less than a thousand of them left now."

I picked up a baseball-sized, jagged rock lying next to my shoe. It was porous and lighter than I expected it to be. "I've heard that it's illegal to take lava rocks off the island. Is that true?"

Simon reached down and picked up a small one. "It's not a crime, but an old legend deters most folks from carrying them off. It's said that the goddess Pele becomes angry if any rocks are removed from the Islands. At the ranger station we passed coming up here, there are hundreds of lava rocks that have been returned by tourists. Supposedly they started having bad luck after taking them home."

"Superstition can be a powerful thing," I said. "But if it keeps people from carrying off the mountain, so be it."

"That piece you're holding is *a a* lava. It has sharp, pointed edges. The other type is *pahoehoe,* or smooth lava."

I set the rock back down on the ground where I had found it. Though I wasn't a superstitious person, I didn't want to take any chances.

It was after 3:00 when we got back into the pickup to leave. With all the standing, climbing and slow walking we had done, I was tired. Sitting in a comfortable spot next to Simon with the warm sun coming through the glass, I started feeling drowsy. I must have dozed off, because the next thing I knew, Simon was gently shaking me awake.

"Hey, Allie. We're home."

I opened my eyes and found that my head was lying on his shoulder. I raised my head, then started stretching my legs to get the kinks out. My right foot had fallen asleep and wasn't cooperating. I shook it to get the blood circulating again.

"When you sleep, you really sleep," Simon said. "We were driving down the mountain and I was talking up a blue streak. When you didn't respond to my questions, I realized you were out."

A thought occurred to me. "I wasn't snoring, was I?" Kristin had told me that I sound like a bullhorn, but I didn't believe her. However, if I had snored in front of Simon, I would be humiliated!

He smiled and said, "A little. But don't worry, it was a cute snore."

Yeah, right. Snoring tends to run in my family, but I was hoping it had skipped a generation and passed me by. At any rate, I sure felt better after my little nap.

"Are you two going to stay out there all night, or are you coming in the house?" Simon's grandfather hollered out the front door.

"We're coming," Simon said as he opened the door of the pickup. "Allie just needed a minute to get moving again after the long ride."

I climbed out of the truck on his side, and we walked toward the front door.

"Besides getting tired from all the exercise, that thin air on the mountaintop gets to me every time," Trip said, holding the door open for us. "Ella and I always argue about who has to drive home after we've traveled up there. We usually end up drawing straws."

The aroma of apples and cinnamon drifted through the doorway. "I just took an apple pie from the oven, if you two would like a piece," Ella called from the kitchen.

"I don't mind if I do," Simon said. "After that big breakfast this morning, we didn't stop for lunch. How about you, Allie?"

Not needing any coaxing, I said to Ella, "I'd love a piece, but only if you let me help do something."

"If you insist, you can add the ice cream. The utensils are in the drawer by the refrigerator."

I washed my hands, then added scoops of vanilla ice cream to each of the four slices of pie that she had placed on saucers. When they were ready, we carried the desserts and some forks to the table.

Simon was already seated. I set one of the saucers down in front of him, then one down at my spot.

"Thank you very much," he said.

Ella served Trip, then we all started eating.

The tangy apples and flaky crust melted in my mouth. The women I had met in Simon's family so far sure knew how to cook!

We told his grandparents what we had seen and done that day. After visiting with them for almost an hour, it was after 5:00.

"If we're going out tonight, I need to take a shower and start getting ready," I said to Simon.

"And I need to stick a casserole in the oven so that Trip and I will have some dinner after while," Ella said, pushing back her chair.

Simon looked at me and tilted his head toward his grandmother. Somehow I knew what he was thinking. I nodded at him.

"Why don't you and Grandpa go out with Allie and me tonight?" he asked. "It will be my treat."

Trip started shaking his head. "You two don't want a couple of old folks tagging along," he said.

"We'd love to have you come with us," I said.

Ella looked at Trip, and he smiled at her. "Well, if you wouldn't mind, we'd love to go," she said. "The casserole in the fridge will keep until tomorrow, and we can have it after church."

"It's settled, then," Simon said.

We went to The Big Kahuna's and the band there was fabulous! Trip and Ella danced up a storm, and I was having a ball watching them. Simon pulled me out onto the dance floor for a couple of slow dances, then convinced me to try a faster number.

We all chose to eat off the buffet and the selection of food seemed never-ending. The waitress kept bringing us frosty mugs filled with either ginger ale or pink lemonade. Some of the ice cubes in the drinks were molded around maraschino cherries. Simon asked me a question while I was sucking on one of the cubes. When I tried to answer him, it fell out of my mouth onto the table, then rolled onto the floor. We both started laughing. He tried to retrieve it, but before he could get to it, a girl in stiletto heels danced by and squashed it. It was quite a night!

Simon pulled into his grandparents' driveway at 11:15. Though the older couple was still laughing and having a big time in the back seat of Ella's car, Simon and I were worn out. All the activity from the day had taken its toll.

We told his grandparents good night, then Simon walked me to my bedroom door.

"I hope you enjoyed the day," he said, placing his hands on my shoulders. "There are hundreds of things to see on Maui. Since we only have two days here, we'll barely scratch the surface. Before you go home at the end of the month, maybe we can come back again."

"That would be nice," I said. "I had a wonderful day."

As I looked into Simon's eyes, I felt torn. I loved being with him and Traci, teaching at Prince Kuhio and working at the *Hawaiian Star*. The more I saw and learned about the Islands, the more I loved them.

But I also missed my home in Paradise, my family, the dachshunds and so much more that had been a part of my life for so long. Right now, I had the best of both worlds. I wished that I could bring them together, because at that moment, I realized it was going to kill me to have to leave this one behind.

CHAPTER 10

The next morning I awoke before anyone else. I washed my face, then fished my phone card out of my purse. It was already 1:00 p.m. in Oklahoma, and I knew that some of my family members would be gathered at Gramma Winters' house for dinner. I walked into the kitchen and dialed Gramma's phone number.

Until recently, our family members met at her house on the fourth Sunday afternoon of each month, then at Nana Kane's on the second Sunday. However, since everyone was so busy during the summer months, the group at each gathering tended to be smaller. Therefore, my grandmothers each offered to host the dinners twice a month until school started again. The first and fourth Sunday dinners were at Gramma Winters,' and the second and third Sunday meals were at Nana's.

After the third ring, Grandad answered the phone.

"Hi, Grandad, it's Allie."

"What a nice surprise, young lady. It's good to hear from you. I just asked your mama if she had talked to you lately."

"I thought I'd better check in with everyone. What have you been up to?"

"Been helping some of the neighbors clean up debris from the storm that came through. Tired after all that work, Clarence and I sneaked off and went fishing on Friday. How's Hawaii?"

"It's wonderful! Right now, Simon and I are visiting his grandparents on Maui."

"That's great," he said. "Say, why don't you hang on and I'll put you on the speakerphone in the living room. That way you can tell everybody what you've been doing, and they can talk to you."

"Sounds good. I'll wait."

I could hear him tell someone that I was on the line. He asked them to please hang up the phone as soon as he got to the one in the living room. The sound of his footsteps faded away, and I heard a clunk. Someone had picked up the telephone receiver, then dropped it. Scratching noises came across the line, then I heard my niece Brittany speaking.

"Hi, Aunt Allie. Until Grandad gets to the other room, I thought I'd talk to you."

"Hi, sweetie. What have you been doing?"

"Riley and I got to spend the night with Nana and Grandpa A.J. last night. We rode horses yesterday afternoon and played with Sassy's new kittens. It was a lot of fun, even if my eyes did swell up."

Riley was my cousin Michael's daughter. She and Brittany were the same age, and they often played together. Sassy was an old barn cat that Nana had had for almost ten years. Though the nearest male cat lived a mile down the road, they seemed to find each other on a regular basis. All the kids loved playing with the new kittens, but Brittany was allergic to dust, hay and cat hair. Though Nana tried to interest her in other activities when she visited, she insisted on playing in the barn. The consequences for that decision involved red, swollen eyes, sneezing and a dose of allergy medicine.

"I'm sorry about your eyes, sweetheart. What has Ryan been up to?" Ryan was Brittany's twenty-one-month-old sister.

"Well, for one thing, she got hold of a blue ink pen and marked on the couch yesterday morning. Mommy and Daddy were pretty upset about it."

I'll bet. About six months ago, Jamie and his wife, Nicole, bought an expensive, cream-colored leather sofa. It was their Christmas present to each other. Ever since they got married, they had been using one that Nicole used in college. I knew that they were glad to finally be able to afford to replace it with the new one.

"Did your mommy get the marks out?"

"She tried, but nothing worked. She called a cleaning service and they're supposed to come on Tuesday."

My niece Ryan is an explorer. She isn't allowed into several rooms of her house without an escort because she gets into everything. One morning Jamie was getting ready for work, and Nicole was ironing some slacks for him. Ryan wandered into her bedroom across the hall. All at once, there was a crash, then Ryan started screaming.

Jamie told me that they ran in and found her lying on the floor. A big goose egg was forming on the side of her head. She had moved her toy scooter to her dresser, then must have used the drawer handles like rungs on a ladder to climb on top of it. Things had been pushed around, so they figured she had been walking on the surface. At any rate, she slipped and fell off. Aside from the bump on her head, and probably an awful headache, she was okay.

There were some clicks on the line. "I'll talk to you later, Brittany. I love you."

"I love you, too," she replied, then she hung up the phone.

I heard Gramma's muffled voice. "Allie? Can you hear me?"

I assumed I was on the speaker in the living room. "Yes, Gramma, I can hear you. How are you?"

"Tickled that you called. Your mama and daddy are here, as well as about ten others. Say hi to Allie, everybody."

I heard greetings from several voices in the room. A *toot-to-do* sound was among the mix.

"Hi, little girl," Dad said. "How's school going?" Again, I heard the *toot-to-do* noise.

"I'm enjoying it. I have ten students and we've been going through books like crazy."

"Are you busy at the newspaper?" Mom asked. "Be sure and save all the editions you're featured in. I want your articles for your scrapbook." Mom made scrapbooks for my brothers and me, as well as for Brittany and Ryan. The *toot-to-do* was louder this time.

"Yes, I'm working on two stories right now and hopefully there will be a fun human interest project beginning tomorrow. What's that *tooting* sound I keep hearing?"

I heard some giggles, then Jamie said, "That's your youngest niece playing with an empty toilet paper roll. Surely you remember when Mom gave them to us to play with when we were kids."

I laughed. "Yes, and they were a lot of fun. Ryan seems to be enjoying hers."

"She's driving us nuts with it," he said. "But at least it's keeping her out of mischief for a while. Tell us more about what you've been doing."

I hit the highlights about my projects at the *Star,* answered their questions, and then told them about the places Simon and I had visited on Maui. They had all met him when he came to visit me in April.

"Allie, this is your Aunt Edith," I heard her say. She must have been leaning over the telephone, because she was coming in strong.

"Hi, Aunt Edith. How are you?"

"Peachy keen. Glad to get my front yard cleaned up after the pecan tree messed it up. Clarence had to have a new roof put on his house because the hail from the storm did a job on it. I'm trying to talk him and your granddad into letting me help them with it."

Oh, boy. The image of her in the pecan tree cutting off limbs with a chainsaw still made me shudder. Now there was a chance she would climb onto the top of his house and fall off the roof! I hoped that Grandad and Uncle Clarence would keep her busy on the ground.

"Yes, Frankie told me about the pecan tree." If other family members hadn't been listening, I might have done some scolding. "Are you still set to come here on the 16th?"

"Yes, and it can't get here fast enough to please me. The airline contacted me, and they're putting me on another plane, but I don't remember the new flight number right now. Can I call and give it to you tomorrow?"

"It will be easier if I phone you. Can I give you a call before I go to school? That will be around noon in Oklahoma. Will you be home then?"

"Oh, yeah. I always eat lunch at twelve while I watch my story on television." She and Gramma had been watching *As the World Turns* since before I was born.

"Okay, I'll try to call you before the show starts, so you won't miss anything."

"Well, I could miss a whole week's worth of shows and still be able to catch up with the next episode. But I like to watch as much as I can. I'll lay my airline ticket by the phone. Ryan wants to talk to you now."

"Go ahead and talk to Aunt Allie, baby," I heard my mother say to my niece.

"Hi," Ryan said.

"Hi, sweetpea. Have you been playing at Gramma's today?"

There was a scraping noise, then a *wha* sound came through the line. It sounded like she was blowing into the speaker. I guess she was trying to figure out if I was inside the phone.

"I been playing *toot*." The sound of her voice was muffled. I figured her little mouth was probably against the speaker now. Gramma would have to take the phone apart to get out all the drool.

"Toot-to-do's are fun, aren't they Ryan?" I asked.

"She's gone," my dad said. "You know when she's through talking, she just takes off."

I looked at the clock on the wall. "Well, it's getting late, so I need to take off, too. I love you all."

I heard "good-bye" and "love you, too," from various members of the group. The last thing I heard was Jamie hollering at Ryan to get out of the cabinet. I was smiling when I hung up the phone.

I went to shower and start getting ready for church. By the time Simon and his grandparents got up, we only had time for a quick breakfast. Ella put the chicken casserole and some potatoes in the oven to bake while we were gone, then we left for the Lahaina Community Church.

It was a beautiful, clear day. People dressed in all types of attire were walking and jogging on the sidewalk running along Highway 30. On the opposite side of the road, the beaches were crowded and surfers were out in full force. They seemed to be vying for space in the massive ocean. Fun in the sun was the focus of the day.

"Those people ought to be in church," Trip mumbled as he drove past them.

Simon and I were sitting in the back seat. We smiled at each other, but didn't say anything. It sounded just like something Grandad Winters would say.

Simon and I joined his grandparents in their Sunday school class and I enjoyed the lesson. When it was over, we walked into the small sanctuary for the worship service. The congregation sang "Great is Thy Faithfulness," and "Victory in Jesus," then the choir sang a song. Though it was only half as big as the choir at my church, their volume and exuberance equaled ours.

The pastor preached a sermon about the importance of encouraging others. At the end, the congregation sang "Amazing Grace."

"I don't know about all of you, but I'm starving," Trip said as we got into the car to go home. "That toast and jelly I had was gone before we got out of Sunday school."

"I could hear your stomach growling before the pastor stood up to preach," Ella told him. "The two visitors in front of us must have heard it, too, because about that time they turned around and grinned at us."

When we reached the house and walked in the front door, we were met by wonderful aromas coming from the kitchen. I fixed a salad while Ella put the things from the oven on the table. Simon poured iced tea for all of us, and Trip set out the plates, napkins and utensils. In no time, we were seated, and Simon was saying the blessing.

The casserole was a meal in itself. Big chunks of chicken were surrounded by a rich, creamy gravy filled with tiny pieces of jalapeno peppers, chopped Maui onions, hominy, and sliced mushrooms. Each of us loaded our huge baked potato with butter and sour cream. Trip and Simon also added some shredded cheddar cheese to their mounded concoctions. For dessert, we finished off the apple pie left from the day before.

"Thanks for another wonderful meal, Grandmother," Simon said as he carried his dirty dishes to the counter. He walked over and kissed the top of her head. "This weekend has really perked me up."

"You're welcome, sweetheart," she said. "I worry about you working so hard and eating out so much."

"You need to come and visit more often," Trip said to him. "There's nothing like your grandmother's cooking and a change of scenery to help you relax."

Simon took his seat beside me and reached for my hand. "I'm less stressed now than when I left Oahu Friday evening, that's for sure. Comfort food and being surrounded by people you love makes all the difference in the world."

People you love? He wasn't looking at any specific person when he made the statement, but was doing that thing with my fingers that I had become so fond of.

My heart started beating faster. I looked at Ella and she smiled. Trip winked at me.

Simon looked at me. "I thought we'd go down to the waterfront and walk around for a while this afternoon, if you want to. There's all kinds of neat things to see and do around Lahaina."

"That sounds great. Let me help your grandmother clean up the kitchen first. It will just take me a few minutes to change out of my church clothes.

"I'll help with the dishes," Trip said, pushing back his chair. "You two only have a few hours until your flight leaves, so you'd better not dally around here."

"I'll owe you one," I told him. I stood up and looked at Simon. "I'll be right back."

I put on a pair of red shorts and the T-shirt Simon had bought for me the day before. After slipping on my white sandals, I combed my hair and put on fresh lipstick. There were still several pictures left in the camera I had brought with me. I put it back into my purse, then slung the purse strap over my shoulder and hurried to the living room.

Simon was standing there talking with his grandparents when I walked in. He was wearing a pair of khaki shorts and the T-shirt that matched mine.

"I'm ready to go when you are," I told him.

He smiled at me, then said to his grandparents, "We'll be back around 4:00. Our flight leaves at six, so that should give us plenty of time to pack and get to the airport."

We waved good-bye to them, then headed to Trip's pickup. Since we only had a few hours left on the island, I intended to soak up every sight and sound that I could.

We drove past the Pioneer Sugar Mill and turned left on Wainee Street. Simon pulled into a parking lot and stopped the car. We got out and he paid for our space, then hung the ticket on the rearview mirror of the pickup. After locking the vehicle, we walked down to Front Street.

We browsed through a couple of shops, then walked to the Old Lahaina Courthouse. People were sitting on benches under the mammoth Banyan tree in front of it. The canopy was intertwined with twisted, rope-like limbs that stretched downward. Over the years, many of them had attached themselves to the ground and had formed new trunks. I counted sixteen of them.

"The Banyan tree was originally found in East India," Simon said. "Believe it or not, this maze of branches belongs to just one tree. It stands sixty feet tall, and is more than 130 years old. They say it's the largest Banyan tree in the world." The massive umbrella made of leaves shaded the entire block. It was amazing!

The courthouse had formerly served as a customs house during the whaling era. An earthquake caused severe damage to it in the late 1800s. When it was rebuilt, the county started using it as the courthouse. Inside the structure, photos and artifacts were displayed for visitors to view.

After we left, we walked along the docks lining the harbor. At one end, some people were waiting in line to board a ferry bound for Molokai.

"If we had more time, we could take a day trip to either Lanai or Molokai," Simon said as we walked past the group. "The ocean's calm right now and that's the best time to go. When the waves are high, they really rock the boat, and a lot of the passengers spend their time hanging over the rail."

I looked toward the large island looming in the distance. "How long does it take to get to Molokai on the ferry?"

"About an hour. It takes about forty-five minutes to get to Lanai," he said, pointing to the smaller island. "There are lots of things to see on each one."

I took some pictures of The Carthaginian Floating Museum that was tied to the end of the pier. The tall masts stood like beacons in memory of the whalers from days gone by. Though this ship was a replica of the original one lost at sea, I could imagine it coursing through the waters filled with hopeful men searching for whales.

We had been walking for over an hour when I spotted some benches beneath a nearby shade tree. "I could use a short reprieve," I said. "How about you?"

"Lead the way."

The cool breeze blowing off the ocean was refreshing. Several kids were having fun with their boogie boards in the water. A young couple strolled past us, then stopped at a historical marker a short distance away.

When they walked on, Simon said, "Come here; I want to show you something." He led me to the sign that the couple had been reading. It gave information about the Hauola Stone below. "Take a look down there." He pointed to the rocky ridge below.

I looked over the edge of the cliff and took a picture. About twenty feet down, I saw some large boulders lying against each other. In the middle of the group, a place had been carved out of one of the stones. It resembled a chair.

"That is the Hauola Stone," Simon said. "The legend says that if a woman sat in that hollowed out space, she would become more fertile."

I watched the waves wash over the seat, then looked up and frowned at him. "So, you're telling me that if a woman wanted to get pregnant, she would come here, climb down that steep, rocky bank and sit on that stone?"

"That's what they say."

"Hmmm. Well, thankfully the women on both sides of my family don't have any trouble getting pregnant," I said. "But I suppose that if some women had trouble conceiving, they would be willing to try just about anything."

He took my hand, and we started walking across the grassy lawn toward Front Street. "Do you want children some day?" he asked.

I glanced at him. He was looking straight ahead and seemed intent on where we were headed. "Sure, I love kids. How about you?"

"I would like to have three, Richard, Amanda and I have always been close."

"Yes, three is a nice, round number. My two brothers and I usually got along pretty well together."

Had the fertility stone conjured up something in Simon's mind, or was this something he had been pondering for a while? Did I figure into his plan with the three children? I wondered. My heart fluttered in my chest, and I couldn't help but smile at the thought.

He changed the subject and started telling me about the next site we would visit.

The Wo Hing Temple was a beautiful structure that had been built about a hundred years earlier. Inside, we saw displays showing the lifestyle of Chinese workers who had migrated to Hawaii. We looked at the Thomas Edison exhibit, and Simon told me a little about the silent films they showed there. Apparently, the inventor had shot them while he was on the island.

"There's one more place I want to take you to, but I could use a snack first," Simon said. "How about some ice cream while we sit and cool off?"

"Sounds wonderful." I regretted that I hadn't pulled my hair into a ponytail before we left the house. I took a tissue from my purse and dabbed away beads of sweat from my forehead and the back of my neck.

We walked into an air-conditioned ice cream shop. The cool air felt terrific on my hot skin. Simon ordered a double-dip hot fudge sundae with whipped cream and almonds for us to share. I ordered an extra-large root beer with two straws. We found a table for two by the window, then sat down to enjoy our treats.

"So where are we off to after this?" I asked. I glanced at the clock on the wall and hated to see that the afternoon was rushing by.

"A few blocks away is the Hale Pa'ahao Prison. In English it means 'stuck-in-irons house.' It was mostly used for non-violent offenders like drunks, deserters and violators of the Sabbath. Anyone sentenced to more than a year was sent to the prison on Oahu."

I wiped my mouth with my napkin. "It sounds interesting. Let's go." We dropped our trash into the receptacle, then headed out the door.

When we reached the jail, I was surprised at the height of the stone fence. Though the walls were about a foot thick, they were only about eight feet tall. Simon and I walked inside the courtyard and I saw a small wooden structure off to one side. There were individual cells inside it and in each cell, iron shackles hung from the walls.

"These wooden cells wouldn't work today," Simon said as he peered through the doorway. "But from the look of those shackles, I guess the prisoners either cooperated and stayed put, or bore the consequences."

We walked along the edge of the stone wall and Simon told me that convict laborers in the mid-1850s had constructed it. A breadfruit tree that was planted more than a hundred years before still thrived in the courtyard. He said it was called "The Hanging Tree," for obvious reasons.

"Thanks for a great tour," I told him as we walked back to the parking lot.

"I enjoyed it, too. It's been a long time since I walked around down here."

It was after 4:00 when we got back to the Kahala's house. Ella wasn't about to let us fly off hungry, so she had made some roast beef sandwiches and potato salad. We enjoyed our last meal together on the patio, then it was time to go to the airport.

Traffic was congested around the terminal. Trip had to drive around a couple of times before he found a parking space. We all walked toward the security gate together.

When Trip and Ella couldn't go any farther, she turned to me. "We enjoyed having you, Allie. You make my grandson bring you back for a visit again." She hugged me, then turned toward Simon. "Tell your mama and daddy I love them and to come and see us when they can."

"I will," he told her, giving her a hug. "Thanks for the hospitality. I love you."

"I had a wonderful time and enjoyed the delicious food you cooked for us," I told Ella. I stretched my hand toward Trip. He ignored it and put his arms around me.

"Like I told you when you got here, you sure are a pretty thing," he said to me. "You're welcome to come back to see us anytime."

"Thank you. That's very kind of you."

"Grandpa, take care. I love you," Simon said, putting his arms around his grandfather.

"I love you, too, young fella. You be careful chasing after those mean guys. I want to see you in one piece the next time around."

When Simon and I headed for our gate, I had an ache in my chest. I felt like I was leaving my own family behind, and I didn't know if I would ever see them again.

🐾　🐾　🐾

While we were flying back to Oahu, I told Simon how much I liked his grandparents. I hadn't seen any ill effects from the stroke Trip had suffered in March.

"Grandpa is a tough old bird," he said. "Grandmother hovered over him, and he didn't have any choice but to get better."

"They seem very happy. Have they always lived on Maui?"

"They've been in the same house since they got married in 1955. Grandpa worked for C&H Sugar for forty years. Grandmother was an expert seamstress and kept busy sewing for well-to-do ladies on the island. With their jobs, raising four children and their church work, they've led very full lives."

He told me a little about his father's younger sisters, and in no time, we were landing on Oahu.

When we walked through the terminal, we saw the security guard that I had met on Friday. "Hey, don't you ever go home?" Simon hollered at him.

Kelly waved at us. When we reached the security area, he said, "I was supposed to be off today, but Doreen called in sick. She's been fighting a cold all week, and I told her yesterday that she ought to stay home and get well. I guess she decided to take my advice."

I glanced down and saw Abbie lying in her spot near the conveyor belt. Though she continually surveyed the area around us, her eyes often came back to rest on her master.

"You're a good man, Kelly. See you later," Simon said.

"You two take care," he replied. He quickly turned his attention back to the people waiting in line.

On the drive back to Traci's, Simon draped his arm around my shoulders. We were lost in our own thoughts, and neither one of us said much. I felt that our trip to Maui had brought us closer together. But now that we were returning home, Simon would again have to face the cases that had frustrated him for months. I was determined to do what I could to help him solve them.

It was almost 8:00 p.m. when he walked me to the door of the apartment building. "Would you like to come up for a while?" I asked.

He put his arm around my shoulders and turned me toward him. "I hate for this weekend to be over, but I need to go home and make some phone calls. I want to be downtown by 7:00 in the morning, so I'll probably turn in when I'm finished. Would you like to go out tomorrow night?"

"I'd love to."

"I'll call you at the *Star* tomorrow afternoon, and we can discuss what we want to do."

"Well, I may not make it into the office. Mr. Masaki has asked me to try to interview Maynard Desmond. He's starting to build a new exhibit near Diamond Head."

"Congratulations! I'm glad you're getting to do a story that doesn't involve body parts. And I'm also glad you'll be working without Kyle Messenger. I can't stand that guy!"

I smiled at him. "He's not the hardest working individual I've ever been partnered with, but like I've told you before, we're just work associates and nothing more."

"Just be sure it stays that way." He gave me a good night kiss. "If you'll give me a call after you're finished at Diamond Head tomorrow, we'll discuss plans for dinner."

"Will do," I said. I watched him walk back to his Jeep. We waved at each other, then I went inside the building.

❦❦ ❦❦ ❦❦

I let myself into the apartment and saw a note lying on the kitchen counter. Traci was letting me know that she and Tommy had gone to church and would be back around 9:00. She also said that if I was hungry, I was welcome to help myself to the tuna salad in the fridge.

I walked to my bedroom and unpacked my carryon. The dirty clothes were added to the growing mound in the laundry basket inside the closet. Since I hadn't washed any clothes since I had arrived, I made a mental note to do that soon. After putting away the other things in my bag, I went to the kitchen to fix a sandwich. While I was munching on it, Traci and Tommy came in from church.

They wanted to know all about my trip to Maui. I told them about some of the places Simon and I had visited and a little about his grandparents. Even though Traci and Tommy had lived in Hawaii for several years, they had only been to Maui one time. They always spent several weeks each summer visiting relatives in Oklahoma, and that depleted their yearly travel budget. After I finished telling them about my trip, Traci began trying to convince Tommy that they needed to go to Maui for a few days before the baby came. Tommy said he would think about it, then we all decided it was time to go to bed.

Traci walked with me to the door of my bedroom. "It sounds like you had a wonderful weekend. You and Simon are getting pretty thick, aren't you?"

I gave her an innocent look. "I love being with him, and he seems to like being with me, too."

"Has anything beyond *like* been mentioned by either of you?"

"Not the other "L" word, if that's what you mean. His grandmother quizzed me a little, too. She indicated that I must be special to him because he's never brought another girl there for an overnight visit." I was still analyzing the comment that Simon had made at the kitchen table about "being surrounded by people he loved."

"Well, I suspect it won't be long until one of you comes to your senses and takes the plunge," Traci said. "Anyone can see you're meant to be together."

A warm, fuzzy feeling came over me at the thought. But at this time in our lives, I wasn't sure if either of us was ready for a long-term commitment.

I smiled at her and gave her a hug. "Good night," I said. "See you in the morning."

"Sleep tight," she said.

After Traci left, I walked into my room and put on my nightgown. The sounds coming through the open window were different than they had been in Lahaina the night before. The noises from night creatures in the quiet neighborhood there were more like what I heard at home. Though the sounds tonight were not obtrusive, they were louder and busier. Both islands had their own special qualities, and I knew I could get used to being here permanently. Too bad that wasn't going to be an option.

CHAPTER 11

I awoke at 6:30 the next morning with a start. I was gasping for air as I sat up in bed. I had been dreaming that I was trying to climb down the jagged rocks of a cliff. Ocean waves were crashing against me, and I lost my footing. The salt water was washing over me, and I couldn't breathe.

I shook my head and took some slow, deep breaths. *So much for trying to reach the Hauola Stone,* I thought. Evidently the visit to it yesterday had contributed to the crazy dream. I looked toward the window. The bright morning sun shining through it had awakened me several times last week, but today the skies were gray.

Though I figured Tommy had already left for work, I didn't hear any other sounds in the apartment and assumed Traci was still asleep. I threw back the covers, grabbed my robe off the bedpost, then hurried across the hall to the bathroom. I took a quick shower, then dried my hair. I wanted to call Aunt Edith before I left for school, so I only took time for a little mascara and blush. I hurried back to my room to put on the aqua slacks and top that I had decided on the night before. After making the bed, I tiptoed down the hall and peeked in Traci's door. She was snoring softly, so I didn't disturb her.

I walked into the living room with my phone card in hand. I dialed Aunt Edith's phone number. She answered after the second ring.

"Hi, Aunt Edith."

"Hi, Allie. I was just warming up my lunch."

"Something good, I bet."

"I carried home some of Sarah's baked ham, sweet potatoes and angel food cake from yesterday's dinner," she said.

Yummy. My stomach started growling at the thought of Gramma Winters' good cooking. "I just called to get your new flight number."

"Okay, hold on a second. It's right next to the phone in the living room."

While I waited for her to get the number for me, I picked up a scratch pad and pencil that Traci had lying on the end table. Cupping the phone between my chin and shoulder, I sat down on the sofa and prepared to write.

"It's American Airlines flight number 237," Aunt Edith said when she returned. "It's supposed to land in Honolulu at 2:10 p.m. Will you be able to pick me up?"

"I'll be there," I said as I tore the sheet of paper from the pad. I stuck it in my pants pocket. "Anything fun going on this afternoon?"

"Oh, I'm going to watch *As the World Turns,* then I've got a date."

"Really? Who are you going out with?"

"Bubba Phillips from down at the Caterpillar place. We're going skating. A session starts at 2:00, and we don't want to be late. They offer half-priced soft drinks at the concession stand to senior citizens on Mondays. I plan to get my money's worth today."

I glanced at the clock on the wall and saw that it was 7:05. With the time difference, it was just after noon in Paradise. "I've never heard you mention Mr. Phillips. Where did you meet him?"

"Down at the Senior Citizens Center. We've become pretty thick since he came to the luncheon last week. We sat together at church last night, then he took me out for pizza after the service. Bubba really stood out."

The older ladies at church tend to compete for the eligible bachelors in town. "Did something happen at church?"

"Oh, Freda Mitchell was sitting in the choir loft and had her eye on him," she said. "But I can handle Freda. No, it was at the pizza parlor. Bubba has loose dentures and the top plate got stuck in some pepperoni. The dentures popped out when he tried to bite off a piece of his slice."

I had to bite my lip to keep from laughing. I imagine it would have been quite a shock to her and to the people around them to see a set of teeth lying on the table stuck in a slice of pizza.

"Bubba's a pretty nice guy, except for the teeth and hair. When he kissed me good night, his dentures kind of flopped around inside his mouth. But a girl can't be too choosy when she's nearing eighty."

"No, I guess not," I said, smiling. "What's wrong with his hair?"

"He's as bald as a cue ball, except for a gray hairpiece stuck on the top. It has a cute little black streak in the front, just like Jay Leno's. The only problem is, it tends to slide around on the top of his head. I guess he needs to put on more hair glue."

Don't laugh, I thought. "Maybe Gladys could suggest something to help him hold it in place."

"I might have remembered to ask her about it, if there hadn't been so much commotion at the beauty shop this morning."

"Oh? What happened?"

"Well, Gladys had just finished spraying me down with hairspray, when we both smelled smoke. I got up out of the chair, and we both started looking around for the source. Back by the storage shelves where the towels are stacked, we caught Beulah Morgenstern hiding behind the rack smoking a cigarette. Gladys has told Beulah a dozen times that if she caught her smoking in the shop again she would ban her from the place. But I guess since they're cousins, Beulah's not worried and just keeps doing it."

"Was this time the last straw for Gladys?"

"Well, she was doing a lot of yelling at her, but I don't know if they made up or not. We were both pretty busy fighting the fire at the time."

My heart started pounding. *Fire?* A shop full of aerosol cans, containers of chemicals for dying and perming hair and a host of other accelerants weren't a good combination with fire. "You fought a fire?"

"Evidently, Beulah had flicked off some ashes onto one of the towels on the rack, then turned around to finish her cigarette. There must have been a live ember, because some of the towels caught on fire. When Gladys and I got back there, Beulah was batting at the blaze with her hands. But since she was wearing one of those plastic capes that most of us use to protect our clothes, she was really just fanning the flames."

"Aunt Edith, why didn't somebody call the fire department? Fighting fires is what they do! You and everyone else should have fled the building."

"One of the stylists called 911, and I ran back up front and hollered at the two Tammy's to get everybody out the front door. Tammy Williams was in the middle of putting black dye on Mildred Washburn's hair. She and Mildred managed to get out okay. A new customer still had shampoo suds in her hair, but she bee-lined through the door, jumped in her car and never looked back." She started laughing. "Watching all those black capes flapping in the wind was really something to see. It looked like a slew of bats fleeing a barn loft."

"Well, I hope you were one of those fleeing ladies."

The line went quiet and I knew that wasn't a good sign. "Allie, Gladys' Mane Event is a legend in Paradise. I couldn't just run out on her without trying to save it. By the time I reached the back of the shop again, the flames were touching the ceiling and spreading toward the nail polish cabinet. The whole towel rack was engulfed, so I grabbed a broom that was sitting inside the bathroom. Since I'm so short, I climbed up on a chair, then started beating the daylights out of those towels. Gladys was using the spray hoses from two of the shampoo sinks to squirt water on the lower shelves. By the time the firemen arrived, we had the fire out and the ventilation fans turned on."

A shudder ran through me. I knew the two of them could have been burned, or worse. With all the chemicals in there, it was a miracle the place didn't explode in a fireball.

Trying to sound calm, I said, "So the two of you saved the day. Was there a lot of damage?"

"Aside from a charred place on the ceiling that will have to be repaired and the wooden rack with four dozen towels reduced to ashes, you'd hardly know there was a near disaster today."

"Thank the Lord no one was hurt."

"Well, not from the fire. But there was a little incident in the parking lot."

"Oh?"

"Tammy T. was in the middle of rolling up Lena Woodley's hair on perm rods when I hollered for them to get out. Tammy's ring got caught in one of the rods. Lena was so scared, she jumped up and was dragging Tammy along behind her. Tammy kept trying to pull her hand free, but it wasn't budging. She outweighs Lena by a good sixty pounds, so when they were away from the building, Tammy pinned Lena against a car long enough to get the rod out. Lena claimed later that Tammy knocked the breath out of her and was holding her against her will. Gladys told Lena that if she wanted to keep her standing Monday appointment, she'd better get a grip and shut up."

"That sounds like Gladys," I said. "Will her insurance take care of the repairs and replace the merchandise she lost?"

"She told me she's not going to file a claim. Her insurance premiums just went up last month, and she was ticked about it. So she told Beulah that she expects her to buy new towels, a new rack, and to have the ceiling repaired by the end of the week—or else."

"Or else? If Gladys has threatened to ban her cousin from the shop before and not followed through, what makes her think Beulah will do it?"

Aunt Edith started chuckling. "Beulah had a little fling awhile back with Joe Murphy, the barber who cuts Clarence's hair. Joe's wife takes karate lessons at the YWCA in Tulsa and would probably work Beulah over pretty good if she found out about it."

"That sounds like incentive to keep Gladys happy."

"You bet." Aunt Edith was quiet for a moment. "I sure miss having you take me places, Allie. I had to drive myself over to Simpson's Funeral Home last Saturday for Harold Polinski's viewing. Daisy and Clarence were both busy and couldn't take me, but since Harold and I dated a few years back, I just had to go pay my respects. I'm sure if a policeman had stopped me, he would have understood."

I doubt it, I thought. Though most of the policemen in Paradise are acquainted with Aunt Edith, I knew they wouldn't be happy if they caught her driving. Since she had forgotten to renew her driver's license over a year ago, I usually took her to the places she needed to go. Her friend, Daisy Johnson, or Uncle Clarence sometimes helped out, but I was her main chauffeur.

"Will someone be able to take you to the funeral?" I intended to call Frankie and tell him to go by and pick her up if she said no.

"Yes, your grandparents are going, so I'll catch a ride with them."

"That's good. Well, I need to get to school and you need to eat your lunch while it's warm. I'll talk to you later."

"I can't wait to get to Hawaii and try out my new bathing suit. It will knock your socks off! See you soon," she said, then hung up.

Oh, boy! Look out Hawaii, here she comes.

I poured myself a glass of guava juice. I figured the extra vitamin C would make up for the lack of food I didn't have time to eat. I scribbled a note to Traci telling her that I would be back around 5:00, but wouldn't be eating dinner here because I had a date with Simon.

I put my dirty glass in the dishwasher, then grabbed my purse and hurried to the elevator. Some sprinkles fell on me as I walked from the building to the parking garage. By the time I reached the exit of the complex, large drops were splattering on the windshield. Nathan was standing by the curb waiting for me under the shelter of his new umbrella.

Shaking the water from it as he climbed inside the car, he said, "I'm glad it's raining. That way I got to use your present today."

I smiled at him. "How was your weekend? Did you do anything special?"

"Ronald took me to an arcade in Pearlridge Center on Saturday, and we played games for a while. Then we ate tacos at a Mexican place in the food court. It was pretty cool."

"It sounds like you had fun. I had a nice weekend, too."

"What did you do?"

"I went to Maui with a friend of mine."

"I've never been to Maui," Nathan said. "Ronald has been there lots of times while he was working. Maybe he'll take me sometime."

"Maybe so."

We rode along in silence for a few minutes. All at once, Nathan blurted out, "Because you've been so nice to me, Allie, I want to give you a present."

"That's kind of you Nathan, but you don't need to do that."

He was twisting on his pinky ring. "I know, but I want to." He pulled the ring from his finger and extended it toward me. "I'd like you to have this."

We had exited H-1 and were stopped at a red light on Beretania Street. "I appreciate the gesture, but that was a birthday gift from your brother."

"I know, but I want you to have it," he said. "Here. Try it on."

To humor him, I took it and slipped it on my right ring finger. It was way too big.

"I'm afraid I might lose it," I said, handing it back to him. "Since we're going to be seeing each other most mornings, why don't you hang onto it. I can enjoy seeing you wear it."

Nathan seemed to be considering my statement as I drove the last few blocks to the nursing home. I pulled up in front of the building and stopped the car.

"I tell you what," he said, reaching for the hula dancer hanging on the radio knob. "I'll put it on this little girl. That way we can both look at it while we're traveling to work." He placed the ring over the head of the ornament and slid it down to her waist. It was a perfect fit.

"Okay, we can leave it on her while I'm driving the car this month. But it's just a loan, and when I have to return home, I want you to take it back. Deal?" I felt uncomfortable taking the ring from him, but I didn't want to hurt his feelings.

He opened the car door and climbed out. "We'll talk about it later. Have a good day at school." He shut the door and waved as I pulled away.

By the time I reached the school parking lot, the rain had stopped. I grabbed my purse from the back seat. Afraid to leave the ring in an unattended car, I pulled the hula girl from the radio knob and stuck her inside the zipper compartment in my purse.

I walked into the cool building and saw Miss Kahala putting a huge poster on the wall beside the office door. It was announcing the annual King Kamehameha Celebration Floral Parade to be held the next Saturday. Details about it were listed in colorful print. A map of the route was displayed at the bottom of the sign.

"Good morning, Allison," she said, taping the last corner to the wall. "Did you and my nephew enjoy your weekend at my parents' house?"

"They treated us like royalty." I walked up and stood beside her. "Your dad is a charmer, and your mother is a marvelous cook."

"They're great people," the principal replied. "We had a wonderful childhood." She took a step back to survey the poster. "But Simon's dad and I ate too much of Mother's delicious cooking when we were at home. Her side of the family tends to be slim, but Dennis and I took after the robust Kahala side."

Pointing toward the poster, I said, "I'm sure my students would enjoy doing an activity regarding the celebration. Can you tell me where to get more information about it?"

"In addition to this poster, I received a brochure from the Celebration Commission last week. There are some web sites and phone numbers listed on it. I have a meeting at the state education office in about an hour, but I'll put the flyer in your mailbox before I leave."

"Thanks. I appreciate it." I glanced at the clock on the wall. "My students are going to be arriving in about twenty minutes, so I'd better head to the classroom."

"Have a good day," she said, then turned toward the office door.

I walked down the hallway and stopped in front of the library. The only set of books left in the classroom were the ones about the Plains Indians. I walked inside and headed toward the nonfiction section. I stopped when I saw some books on the water cycle. Deciding to use the "teachable moment" with the rainy weather, I picked out an assortment of books relating to water.

On a rack close to the checkout desk, I found a couple of biographies about King Kamehameha and some other books dealing with his monarchy. After signing for all of the books, I carried them to the classroom.

I was looking at some experiments listed in one of the water books when the students started coming in. Seth and Mareko zeroed in on the book in my hand and asked if the class was going to get to read it.

"Yes, you are. After we discuss the *Amelia Bedelia* book you read on Friday, I'm going to let everyone choose a partner, then one of these books on the table. We're going to focus on nonfiction this week."

All the boys cheered.

"Does that mean we get to read about Indians, too?" Seth asked, pointing to the stack of books lying on my desk. He and the rest of the boys in the class had been itching to get their hands on them.

"Yes, we'll read those books, too. Today we'll talk about water. Tomorrow we'll start reading about tribes found in the Midwest, and you can take turns with the bulletin board display."

The students had been eager to work with the Trail of Tears set ever since they saw it the first day of school.

Once the students paired up, they chose their books, then settled in spots throughout the room to start reading to each other. For a few minutes, I walked among the groups and helped with an occasional hard word they encountered. While they continued reading, I browsed through a cabinet where Traci kept manipulatives for math and science. I found three hand mirrors and put them on the counter by the sink.

The rain had started again and was coming down at a steady pace. Droplets cascaded down the windows.

When everyone finished reading, we discussed the water cycle and the different ways we used water every day. They were amazed when I told them that more than half of their body weight was liquid. We discussed ways that our bodies eliminated it, then I handed the mirrors to the three girls.

"I would like each of you to open your mouth and blow onto your mirror," I said to them. "When the foggy spot appears, rub your finger across it."

"It's wet," a timid girl named Jennifer said after performing the task. "I like to do this on the living room window at home, then draw hearts and stuff. It's fun until my mom catches me. Then she hands the Windex to me and makes me clean the whole glass."

I smiled at her. "When I was about your age, my mother would tell me to quit messing up the car windows with my designs."

Each of the boys had a turn with the mirrors. By the time we finished discussing why the vapor from their breath condensed and changed to a liquid, the rain had stopped.

"Hey look, Miss Kane," Seth said, pointing toward the window. "A rainbow!"

All the kids clamored to the window to get a better look. The sun had come out and there was a colorful rainbow in the distance.

"Can anyone tell me how a rainbow forms?" I asked.

Jennifer raised her hand. "God puts it there to remind us that there will never be another big flood."

I had been taught the same lesson in Sunday school many years before. "Yes, Jennifer, God did promise Noah that the earth would never be destroyed by a flood again. Can anyone tell me anything else about it?"

"It has something to do with light shining through the water in the air, doesn't it Miss Kane?" David asked.

"That's right, David."

A clear drinking glass was sitting on my desk full of sharpened pencils. I dumped the pencils onto the desk, then held up the glass.

"Pretend this is a water droplet in the sky. When a ray of light touches the droplet, it spreads out and we see colors. From the ground looking up at a rainbow, we see a half arc. If we were in an airplane, a rainbow would appear more like a circle and the shadow of the plane would be in the center of it."

"Cool," Mareko said. "When I get home today, I'm going to turn on the sprinkler and stand in the middle of it. I want to see if the rainbow is all around me."

"Tell us tomorrow how it goes," I said to him. "Now, let's get the room straightened everyone, because the bell is about to ring."

We picked up the room, then each child chose a new book about water to take home to read that night.

After the students were gone, I walked to the office to use the computer. I needed to respond to the messages that I had received from Doug and Kristin on Friday.

After logging on, I saw that I had two new messages. One was from my cousin Michael. He told me that he was sorry that he had missed talking with me when I called our grandparents' house the day before. But he said he was glad to hear that I was enjoying Hawaii. He also told me that Riley had hit two homeruns in the Champions' T-ball game on Saturday. She had given him orders to be sure to write and tell me about it.

Michael said he had been putting in a lot of hours at Kane Energy and needed a vacation. The quarter was nearing an end and as the controller of the company, that was always a busy time for him. Simon's brother, Richard, had been after Michael to come to Hawaii and go deep-sea fishing with him. Since he didn't mention anything about the trip, I assumed those plans hadn't been finalized.

He signed off without saying anything about DeLana, a teacher whom he had been dating for almost three months. A few weeks earlier he had given me the impression that an engagement might be on the horizon. *Leave it to a man to leave out the juicy stuff,* I thought.

The second message was from Doug. The subject line read: "We miss you, Mama!"

Doug told me that things were pretty quiet around home. Though it was a bit lopsided now, he hadn't had the heart to take out the storm-damaged Bradford pear tree in my front yard. He reminded me that he still wanted to hear more about the "unusual discovery" at the Sacred Resting Place that I had mentioned in my earlier e-mail to him. He assured me that he had been watering my peace lily, been picking up the mail, and had driven my Mustang around the block a few times to keep the battery charged.

I smiled and would have bet money that he had only watered the plant one time just to be able to tell me that he had. My smile turned into a frown as I read on.

Rowdy and Precious were moping around his place like abandoned children. Since Doug had begun his pediatric residency at a hospital in Tulsa in May, I knew he had been putting in a lot of hours at work. He also had a full social calendar, though he said he had cut back on dating since I had left because he felt guilty leaving the pups so much. Though we shared ownership of the dogs and I knew he wasn't complaining, I realized it was going to be difficult for him to take care of them for another three weeks.

While puzzling over the situation, a message from Kristin popped into my inbox. The subject line read "Don't worry!"

For the moment, I closed Doug's letter and opened hers. Though the message was brief, I felt a sense of relief after reading the first para-graph. It said:

Hi Allie,

All week long Joey has been driving me nuts to go see Rowdy and Precious. Now that we're back from Kevin's folks' house, I told him I'd see if Doug would let us keep them for a few days. It won't be easy on any of us when Kevin goes back to Iraq on Wednesday. But I thought Joey might transition a little better if he had some furry playmates.

I hope you're having a great time in Hawaii lying on the beach and eating poi. Please continue enjoying yourself and don't fret about the dogs. Though Joey may wear them out playing with them, he'll make sure they don't get lonely. In the meantime, I'll keep the antihistamine and tissues handy.

We all miss you!

Love, Kristin

"Bless you, Kristin," I said.

She and Doug and I had always been close. I suspect she had called him and found out that he was having a hard time caring for the dachshunds. She was allergic to most animals, and I knew it wouldn't be a picnic for her having them in her house. Though it was a temporary solution, I was thankful that she was coming to the rescue. I wrote back and thanked her for her assistance.

Feeling better about the situation, I wrote to Doug. Toward the end of the message, I gave him some details about how I came to find the thumbs at the cemetery and asked him to please keep it to himself for now. Though I would tell them in due time, I didn't want word getting out about it to my parents and grandparents just yet. They all tend to worry about me a lot as it is.

After logging off, I checked my mailbox. I found the brochure regarding the King Kamehameha Celebration in it. As I walked out of the building toward my car, I read about some of the upcoming events.

On Friday, prior to the Statue Decoration Ceremony, the Royal Hawaiian Band was set to perform at the Honolulu Civic Center. The statue of King Kamehameha would be decorated with long ropes of tropical flowers. Hula performances were also on the schedule.

After hearing the band play in the park last spring, I welcomed a chance to attend another performance. Though I figured another *Hawaiian Star* reporter had already been given the plum assignment, I decided to ask Mr. Masaki if he would consider letting me help cover the event for the paper.

I picked up a burrito and a large Dr. Pepper at a fast-food place on my way to Diamond Head. On H-1, the traffic was heavy and I weaved through the maze of cars while trying to eat the spicy food. It was all I could do to keep the chili sauce from dripping onto my shirt. By the time I exited the expressway, the peppers had set my mouth on fire and the drink was almost gone.

I headed south on 12th Avenue and drove toward the Diamond Head State Monument. Just off Monsarrat Avenue at the base of the crater, I spotted a park on my left. I pulled into the entrance and parked next to a large tour bus. I took the hand-sized tape recorder I had borrowed from the Star from my purse and stuck it into my pocket. Since I wouldn't need anything else from my purse, I stuffed it under the seat, then got out and locked the car doors.

The small lot was crowded with vehicles. Some had rental agency tags on them, but the majority of them were tagged with regular Hawaii plates.

Mr. Masaki had instructed me to look for a sidewalk on the west side of the parking lot. He said it would lead me to the new exhibit area. A short distance from my car, I spotted the walkway.

Strolling through the park, I enjoyed the warm sunshine and the beautiful scenery. Large palm trees dotted the grounds and shaded the picnic tables that were scattered throughout the area. A dozen or so people were eating at various tables and at least twice that many were picnicking on blankets spread on the grass.

I passed a group of Japanese tourists who were huddled around their guide. They stood gazing at a majestic stone statue while listening to his oration. After passing the group, I came to a playground and saw three young women sitting on a bench watching some preschoolers play on the swings.

I topped a small hill and the pavement ran out. A beat-up white van was parked on the grass a short distance away. Taking a chance that the vehicle belonged to Maynard Desmond, I walked toward it.

As I rounded the back of it, I saw a man standing on the grass about twenty feet away. His hands were clasped behind his back, and he was intently studying a huge mound of dirt. He was wearing a tattered straw hat, some lightweight gray coveralls and gardening gloves.

He seemed oblivious to my presence. I didn't want to startle him, so I stopped by the open doors of the van. Stacked neatly inside, I saw a variety of gardening tools and equipment. Sitting beside an assortment of shovels, axes and hoes, there were two rolls of garden skirting. Sacks of fertilizer and peat moss were leaning against the back of each of the captain seats. Pegboard had been mounted on the inside panels and every hand tool imaginable was hanging from it. A long shelf was attached halfway up on one of the pegboards and several pairs of gloves were lying on it. The van was a virtual candy store for gardeners.

"May I help you, miss?"

I jumped when I heard the gruff voice beside me. I had been so caught up perusing the equipment, I hadn't seen the man walk toward me. He was standing less than three feet away, and he had a frown on his tanned face. Wisps of gray hair fell beneath the hat brim onto his ears and the back of his neck. Since he had caught me eyeing the valuable tools in his van, I realized he might be thinking that I was up to no good.

Embarrassed, I stretched my hand toward him. "I'm Allison Kane, a reporter with the *Hawaiian Star*. I'm looking for Maynard Desmond and was told he might be here today. By any chance would you be Mr. Desmond?"

Still frowning, he pulled off the dirty glove covering his right hand. "The one and only," he said, shaking my hand. "I don't mean to be rude,

Miss Kane, but I'm very busy. You must be new here and haven't been told that I don't give interviews to the press."

He put the glove back on, then stepped behind me and reached for a grooved, trenching shovel that was resting on the floor of the van.

Not willing to be put off, I decided to try stroking his ego. I turned around to face him.

"Yes, I've only been working for the *Star* for a week. When I first arrived on Oahu, a friend and I stopped to look at your Portuguese exhibit in the park near the airport. It was remarkable, Mr. Desmond. Surely you would like more people to know about your work."

"Tourists come and go," he said as he reached for a trowel hanging on the pegboard. He slipped the tool into a back pocket of his overalls. "Many of the locals are familiar with my displays. Some of them call me the landscape artist, if you can believe that."

"I think the title fits you. Your displays are works of art. My mother owns a flower shop and nursery back in our hometown. Though she has created some spectacular gardens and raised prize winning flowers, I'm sure she would be impressed by the way you've integrated plants and trees into your designs."

He looked at me for a moment and the frown disappeared. A slight smile began tugging at the edges of his mouth. "She would, huh?" He seemed to be considering my remarks. "Well, Miss Kane, I create what pleases me. But don't get me wrong. Though I don't build my exhibits to try to impress other people, I do appreciate getting opinions from other floral designers."

I was standing in his way, so he walked around me and propped the shovel against one of the van doors. I watched him walk over to the side of the vehicle. He reached for the handle, then gave it a pull, and the door slid open.

I wasn't buying his remark that he only tried to please himself. "Mr. Desmond, I believe you want to share your ideas and inspiration with others, or you wouldn't continue building your displays in such well-traveled, public places."

He dragged one of the bags of peat moss out the door. I watched him hoist it onto his shoulder, then start walking back toward me.

"Is that right?" he said, stopping in front of me.

I hadn't meant for my remark to sound accusing, so I softened my tone. "I'm sure people would love to know the motivation behind your designs. As beautiful as Hawaii is, your exhibits representing the legends of cultures who migrated here make it that much better." His facial expression didn't indicate that I was swaying him in the least. Frustrated, I plunged ahead. "And aside from that, you should let me interview you because I'm helping the detectives who are working on your vandalism cases."

Now where did that come from? I did a mental eye roll and knew I'd have to be sure and let Simon in on this turn of events.

Maynard raised his eyebrows. "Well, I didn't report the vandalism," he said. "Someone from the Parks Department did." He readjusted the heavy bag resting on his shoulder. "But, Miss Kane, you're persistent; I'll give you that. Since you wrote an excellent piece about the Ray Franklin investigation, I'll expect that kind of quality when you write about our interview." He turned around and started heading back toward the mound of dirt. "Now, grab that shovel I set there by you and a pair of gloves from inside the van, and let's go move some dirt while we talk."

An excellent piece? And he didn't tell me to hit the road! With a smile on my face, I grabbed the shovel and a pair of cotton gloves from the shelf, then hurried after him.

"I appreciate your compliment, but I didn't think you liked the press," I said when I caught up with him.

He grinned at me. "Just because I don't talk to reporters doesn't mean I don't read what they write. I subscribe to three different newspapers and read each edition from cover to cover."

We worked side by side and were on a first name basis in no time. So that I wouldn't miss any facts that I might need later for the article, I turned on my tape recorder and set it on a nearby rock while we worked.

Before getting down to the interview, Maynard asked me a few questions about my mother's business. After telling him a little about it, I mentioned that she was also involved with the Garden of Eden project.

He stopped raking and straightened up to look at me. "What is the Garden of Eden project?"

Realizing I had sparked his interest, I wished that I had accepted Nana's invitation to help on the project a few weeks earlier. My knowledge about it was pretty limited, but I decided to give it a whirl anyway.

"In one of the large parks in Paradise, the women's group at my church created four different gardens. Each one has its own theme. One is for flowers, another one is planted with herbs, another one produces different types of food, and the last one is called The Orchard. I think the neatest thing about it is that they have used plants mentioned in the Bible. A tall wooden cross stands in the center and pebble footpaths are intertwined through it. It's pretty neat."

"It sounds like it. I've used lilies in projects, but I'd like to hear more about the other Biblical plants and trees the ladies used."

"Please keep in mind that I don't get to help much, but I do know they planted new olive, apple and fig trees this year. Cedars of Lebanon are planted around the perimeter and I think the hyssop plants are doing well." *At least I hope they are.*

He started raking the plot again. "I'm going to give that Garden of Eden idea some consideration," he said. "That's a concept I'd like to explore further." He set down the rake and opened the bag of peat moss. "Now, since I promised you an interview, I guess we'd better get to it."

Maynard told me some of his ideas for the layout there, then our conversation turned to his other exhibits around the island. When I questioned him about the Portuguese display I had seen, he said that he had built it in honor of a kind man he had known when he was a teenager who had tutored him in gardening. The man was a descendant of the first recorded Portuguese visitor to the Islands, John Elliot de

Castro. In 1814, de Castro had sailed to Hawaii in search of fortune. He became the personal physician of King Kamehameha and a member of the royal court.

The king gave de Castro large tracts of land, but after only two years, his roving spirit led him back to the mainland. Almost a century later, Maynard's mentor inherited a portion of that land. Before he died, he willed it to Maynard and that was where the first exhibit was built.

I had about fifty minutes of conversation on tape when Maynard suggested that we take a break. Deciding I had all I needed for my story, I switched off the recorder and stuck it back into my pocket.

Together we walked to the van, then slipped off our dirty gloves and set them on the rear bumper. I followed him to the right side of the vehicle. He opened the passenger door, and I saw an ice chest sitting in the front floorboard. I waited while he fished out a couple of cans of pop and two Snickers bars from it. After he handed me a drink and some candy, we walked to a nearby park bench and sat down.

Among other things we discussed, he asked me if I had come to Hawaii just to work for the *Star*. I explained that it was my second job, and he seemed impressed when I told him I was a teacher. I told him how much fun the students had had with *The Giving Tree*. He suggested that I bring them to the site on a field trip. He said he would provide an apple tree or two for them to plant.

Soon our conversation turned to the Franklin story. He had been following the various grave-robbing articles in the papers for years. I was shocked when he told me that Ray was his second cousin.

"Ray's dad, Gerald, and I were close when we were kids," Maynard said as he raked the heel of his muddy boot across a patch of grass. "Our mothers were sisters and even though they didn't get along, he and I hung out together once in a while. We both attended the same high school and enjoyed a lot of the same subjects. After graduation, we even talked about joining the Marines. But neither one of us followed through with it. It's probably just as well. Everything between us changed after his mother died, and he inherited what little she had left."

He seemed to be replaying a time that was special to him, yet there was sadness in his voice. I was searching for something comforting to say.

"I have cousins that I'm close to, and no one can ever take away the happy times we shared."

Maynard looked at me. From the expression on his face, I wasn't sure if what I had said had helped, or made him feel worse.

"Gerald started guzzling booze, gambling, and chasing anything in a skirt," he said. "I didn't like his lifestyle and he knew it. Of course, it didn't help that our mothers were enemies." He paused for a moment. "The last time I saw Gerald was at his funeral."

He crumpled his empty soft drink can under the heel of his boot, then picked it up off the ground. He nodded toward the section we had been working on. "If I'm going to finish that area before dark, I'd better get back to work."

I followed him back to the van. Some plastic bags were lying on top of the shelf near the gloves. He grabbed one of the sacks off the stack, then shoved the can inside it.

"It's too bad it turned out that way," I said, handing him my empty can. "If you don't mind telling me, what caused the rift between your mother and aunt?"

"It was stupid, really," he said, shaking his head. "My grandmother, Alhoi Akau, had chosen the men she wanted both her daughters to marry. Gerald's mother abided by her wishes, but my mom was bullheaded enough to defy her. She ran off and married my father. But she paid a price for it; her mother disinherited her. On top of that, my dad thought he was marrying money, so when my grandmother disowned Mom, he took off and left her and me to fend for ourselves. If it hadn't been for my gardening and landscaping skills, we would have been on welfare a lot longer than we were."

The sad expression on his face tore at my heart. "Though I'm sure it must have been hard while you were growing up, your talents have paid off," I said, motioning toward the exhibit plot.

He looked toward the area where we had been working. "Yes, I was blessed to meet some great people during my formative years. My business has grown by leaps and bounds. But things probably wouldn't have turned out so well if Mom had married the man that grandmother chose for her. When I was in high school, Mom told me that he beat his wife and two kids to death, then hung himself."

"Oh how awful!" A sick feeling filled the pit of my stomach. "The police said a ring was taken from Gerald's grave. Do you think that was part of the inheritance?" I didn't say anything about the missing ring finger, though I knew the newspaper articles had mentioned it.

"When Alhoi Akau died, the family wealth was divided among Gerald's mother and my two uncles. When his mother died, I don't think he got much money. She had partied a lot and squandered away most of it. But Gerald did inherit some of Grandmother's jewelry." Though he was looking toward the picnic grounds, he seemed to be remembering another place and time. "If things had turned out differently, the ring that was taken from his grave could have been *my* mother's, then mine."

I heard bitterness in Maynard's voice. Despite his successful career, no doubt his earlier life would have been easier if he had had his part of the family wealth.

I glanced at my watch and saw that it was after 4:00. "I appreciate the opportunity to talk with you today," I said. "I'll try to write an article that will do you justice."

Maynard stepped toward me and stretched out his hand. "I'm sure you will. I have to tell you that I've never enjoyed speaking with a member of the press before now. It's been a pleasure, Allie. And thanks for your help today. I'll have that apple tree here for your kids to plant on Friday."

"They'll love it," I said, shaking his hand. As I turned to leave, I thought of something else. "Since you read so many newspapers, do you recall seeing anything about a grave-robbing incident on Kauai a few years back? An acquaintance of mine mentioned something to me, but my detective friend and I haven't had much luck tracking down anything about it."

"That's probably because it never made the papers. About five years ago, the grave of my great-grandfather, Kawana Kahuku, was dug up. One of my uncle's boys still owns the section of land where the family cemetery is located. He was able to keep the story out of print. Despite the questionable behavior by some of Kawana's ancestors, his name is still revered on Kauai."

"But what about the authorities? Surely there was a police report written up about the incident."

"I'm sure there was. His ring, worth about $200,000, was stolen along with the finger it was on."

Again with the missing fingers. "Thanks for your help, Maynard. We'll see you on Friday."

CHAPTER 12

When I opened the door of the apartment, I could smell oregano and basil coming from the kitchen. Led by my nose and empty stomach, I found Traci putting a large baking dish full of manicotti into the oven.

"Mmmm, that smells terrific," I said to her. "You're trying to punish me because I have another dinner date and won't get to eat any of it, aren't you?"

"Since this is one of your favorite dishes, tonight it's comfort food," she said, smiling. "I hate to have to tell you this, but Simon called a few minutes ago and said he needed to cancel your date. He asked me to have you call him when you got here."

Bummer. Though we had spent the whole weekend together, I had still been looking forward to our date. "Well, now I won't have an excuse to put off doing my laundry any longer. I guess I'll go call him before dinner is ready."

"If you're going to wash some clothes later, I'll go sort some of mine and Tommy's and go with you," Traci said. "I'm not supposed to be carrying anything heavy, so Tommy has to haul everything downstairs then back up again for me. After a couple of loads, he poops out, so I've put off doing towels and sheets for a couple of weeks, and they're starting to pile up. If you don't mind, would you help carry an extra load or two downstairs?"

"Of course I will. After all, you're helping to sooth my disappointment about my cancelled date by fixing manicotti. Besides, it will be more fun if we do laundry together."

Traci walked down the hall toward her bedroom. I flopped down on the couch and called Simon. He picked up the phone after the first ring.

"Hi, it's me," I said.

"I was just thinking about you. Of course that happens a lot these days." I smiled. Since he was often on my mind, it was nice to know that I was invading his thoughts as well. "How did it go today?"

"Maynard put me to work, but I enjoyed every minute of it."

"Got your hands dirty, huh?"

"Metaphorically, yes. It felt good to dig in the dirt. But I was wearing gloves so really my hands stayed pretty clean."

"How did the interview process go?"

"Well, we kind of got off on the wrong foot because he caught me snooping around his van. He has enough equipment in there to stock a small hardware store."

"Uh huh. Though *I* know you wouldn't take anything, he may have wondered about it."

"Yeah, that thought occurred to me a little late," I said.

"Did he give you enough information to write a story?"

"More than enough. Maynard has quite a colorful background, though I won't be including that part in the article. He told me a lot about what inspires him and that is what I'll focus on." I paused for a moment. "He was hesitant about answering my questions until I told him I was kind of helping the detectives working his vandalism cases."

The line was quiet, then Simon cleared his throat. "Well, technically you *have* helped us, though not on those particular cases. I assume that's what you meant when you told him that?"

"I blurted it out without thinking. My mouth gets me into trouble once in a while."

"Yeah, I've noticed that," Simon said. "Will you be able to have the story ready for Wednesday's paper?"

"I hope so. I'll start working on it as soon as I get to the *Star* tomorrow."

"I'm sorry I had to cancel our date. Would you like to go somewhere tomorrow night?"

"Sure. What did you have in mind?"

"How about dinner and a movie? Since I had you to myself over the weekend and we've been neglecting Traci and Tommy, they're welcome to come along, too, if you want to invite them."

"That sounds like fun," I said. "I'll ask them. I assume work is keeping you from me tonight."

"Yes, this afternoon I received the lab report for the glove you found. Eddie is flying over so we can do some work tonight. I'm supposed to pick him up at the airport at 6:30."

"Did they find anything useful on the glove?"

"The soil on it wasn't much help, since most of the Shady Palms Cemetery contains the same type of soil. However, skin cells were lifted from the inside of it, and they show that two different people have worn the glove. There were distinctive DNA markers, and we figure the wearers are closely related. One of them is also a close relative of Ray's."

An odd feeling came over me. I didn't understand enough about DNA to know how close a relative had to be to have similar markers. But from what Simon had told me and from my research, I knew that most of Ray Franklin's relatives were dead. Except for one.

"Allie, are you still there?"

"Yes, I was just thinking."

"For a minute there I thought I'd lost you. I was telling you that Eddie and I are going to try to start tracking down Ray's relatives, but I'm not quite sure where to begin."

Though I wanted Simon to find whoever was responsible for the crimes, I was torn about whether or not to give up the information I had been told today. Trusting that Simon would do the right thing with it, I said, "He was Maynard's second cousin."

For several seconds, the line was silent.

"Did the landscaper tell you that?"

"Yes, and that's not all."

I relayed to Simon everything that Maynard had told me about his relatives. When I reached the part about how he felt that Gerald's ring could have been his had things been different in their pasts, Simon responded. "As soon as I pick up Eddie, we're going to go pay Mr. Desmond a visit."

I was feeling sick at my stomach. In the short time I was with him today, I had grown to like Maynard. I couldn't believe that he was the person involved in the horrific crimes. On top of that, he would know that I was the one who pointed the police his way. I felt like a traitor.

"Simon, you're not going to drag him down to the police station, are you? I can't believe that Maynard would harm anyone, let alone dig up a grave and twist off someone's fingers! Please be nice to him."

I guess he heard the worry in my voice, because his tone grew lighter. "Don't worry, Allie. We'll probably just talk to him for now. Maybe he can tell us about other relatives, because as far as I know, Ray didn't have any left in Hawaii. We'll leave the rubber hoses in the cruiser."

I smiled at his remark and started to relax. Leave it to me to jump to conclusions. If there was one thing I had learned about Simon, he was fair.

"I appreciate that, and I'm sure that Maynard will, too," I said.

"I'll talk to you tomorrow," he replied, then hung up.

Tommy and Traci were eager for a night out and accepted the invitation to join Simon and me the next evening for dinner and a movie. While

Traci fixed some coleslaw, I sliced the garlic bread. Tommy searched through the newspaper to see what movies were playing.

While we ate supper, we each talked about our day. Tommy had been notified that some of his troops were going to be deployed to Iraq. Though he was sad to see them go, he was confident that they were prepared to take on the difficult task. Traci had done some shopping for the baby, and I told them about the interview with Maynard. The huge pan of manicotti was only a memory by the time the meal was finished.

Tommy settled into his recliner to watch a baseball game on television while Traci and I cleaned up the kitchen. When we finished, she stepped to the doorway and called to him. "Allie and I are going downstairs to do laundry."

"Is your basket of linens still in the bedroom?" I asked her. "I'll take them downstairs, then come back and get my dirty clothes."

Tommy put down the footrest and jumped up from his chair. "That's okay, Allie. I'll get our basket and carry it downstairs."

Traci pulled out a big bottle of liquid detergent and a box of dryer sheets from beneath the kitchen sink. She set the items on the counter, then pulled a roll of quarters out of the drawer next to the fridge.

"Since Tommy's going to help, if you can handle your basket, I'll carry this stuff, and we can make it down in one trip," Traci said to me.

Tommy walked back into the living room carrying the basket heaped with linens. He set it on the floor, then picked up my basket full of dirty clothes and put it on top of theirs.

"I'm ready if you two are," he said, lifting the heavy load.

"That's too much for you," I told him, reaching for my basket.

"No, I'll get it. I've been slacking off on my upper body exercises lately, and I'm going to get flabby if I don't start lifting weights again. This will be a good start."

"Okay, if you insist," I said. "Give me a second, and I'll go grab my wallet."

I walked to my bedroom. My purse and car keys were sitting on the dresser where I had left them. I stuck the keys in my pants pocket, then pulled my wallet from the purse.

As I walked back into the living room, I rummaged through the coin compartment. There were only a few pennies in it. I opened the billfold and pulled a ten-dollar bill from inside it.

"I don't have any coins," I said, holding up the bill, "so I'll put this in the drawer to pay for a roll of quarters."

If Tommy's face hadn't been so red from the strain of holding the heavy laundry baskets, I'm sure Traci would have argued about the money. She glanced at him, and I guess compassion won the battle.

"Okay, I'll let you pay this time," she said, opening the apartment door. "Let's go before Tommy gets a hernia."

We rode the elevator to the first floor. When we walked into the laundry room, I could see that every machine was in use. Several people were standing around waiting for dryers to finish so that they could put in their wet things.

"Usually it's not this crowded on Monday nights," Traci said. "I guess everybody was busy over the weekend and decided to clean out their hampers today."

"Is there a laundromat anywhere close by?" I asked her. "Since we made it this far, I hate to carry all these dirty things back upstairs."

"Yes, there's a small place a couple of blocks from here, but I don't have my driver's license or keys with me."

"I do." I pulled my keys from my pocket. "You and Tommy wait here, and I'll bring the car around." They nodded and I headed toward the parking garage.

Though the sun had set, the garage was well lit. The visitor's space that I had been assigned was near the opening, so I had no apprehension about going into the garage alone. I pulled the car to the front door of the apartment building. Within a couple of minutes, the clothes and laundry products were loaded into the trunk of the Malibu. Though the trunk wasn't as large as the one in my Mustang, we managed to squeeze everything in.

Tommy told us to buzz him when we returned, and he would come down and help carry things back to the apartment. We sent him back upstairs to enjoy his ballgame, then Traci and I headed out of the parking lot.

We had only traveled east a few blocks on Moanalua Road when Traci told me to turn left. A short distance up the hill, I saw a small shopping complex on the right side of the road. A health food store, dry cleaners and the laundromat were the only businesses in it. There were a couple of vacant spaces with "For Lease" signs on the doors. I suspected that with the large variety of stores in the Pearlridge Center so close, it wasn't easy for small businesses to survive here.

Darkness had fallen, and I looked for a parking spot next to the building. All the spaces were full. The lights on each side of the doors of the occupied storefronts were dim. Very little illumination extended from them to the parking lot. A few vehicles were parked in the middle and far edge of the lot. After circling once, I found a spot in the shadow of a green Dodge pickup.

"Why don't you go in and locate some washers for us, and I'll start bringing in the clothes," I told Traci.

"They have rolling carts in there," she said. "If you'll wait, I'll bring one out, then help you dump the clothes baskets into it. We can roll the clothes, baskets and laundry products inside and nobody's back will get hurt."

"Sounds like a plan. I'm going to leave the headlights on so you won't trip on something in the parking lot."

Traci nodded, then climbed out of the car and started walking toward the building.

Glad for the bright dome light, I got out and stuck my wallet into the waistband of my slacks. I left the door open so that the light would stay on, then walked to the back of the car. I opened the trunk and was shuffling some clothes around when I heard footsteps approaching.

"Those carts sure are quiet," I said as I lifted out the jug of detergent and turned around. I gasped when I saw Ronald Nowicki standing less than a yard away from me.

He was wearing a baseball cap pushed back on his head. The faint light shining from inside the trunk created shadows on his face and gave it an eerie appearance. His dark hair touched the collar of his shirt, and it looked like he hadn't shaved in a couple of days. His right hand was clasping hangers holding several pairs of jeans draped over his shoulder.

"Well, if it isn't Nathan's teacher friend," he said. He took a step toward me. "Do you need some help with your laundry, Allie?"

I could smell the minty fragrance of toothpaste coming from his mouth. His close proximity made me nervous.

"No, thanks. My friend is inside scouting for available washers and should be here with a cart any time now." Still facing him, I stretched out my arm and lowered the trunk lid so that we weren't hidden from the view of the building.

"You're with a friend, huh?" He glanced toward the building, then back at me. "You seem to have made lots of friends in your short time here. Nathan is quite smitten with you. He told me that he gave you the ring that he got for his birthday."

There was no anger in Ronald's voice, but I wondered if he might be upset that his brother had given away the gift. "Don't worry, it's more like a loan," I said. "Nathan wanted me to have it, and I agreed that I would keep it until the end of the month. Is that a problem?"

He was silent for a moment and seemed to be weighing his response. "I told Nathan to ask you to return it, but he didn't take to my suggestion. Though he rarely backtalks me, he was adamant that he wanted you to keep the ring." He looked down at my hands. "Do you mind telling me where it is?"

I didn't know what his reason was for wanting me to return the ring before I left the island, but I decided right then to be an ally to Nathan. Though a bit slow, he was a grown man, and I knew he was happy that I had the piece of jewelry. "It's safe," I said, looking him square in the eye. "I'll be sure to take good care of it while it's in my possession."

I heard the squeaky wheels of a laundry cart rolling across the parking lot toward us. I turned toward the sound and was thankful to see Traci coming our way. When I looked back at Ronald, he seemed annoyed at the intrusion.

"Well, I'm glad to hear that," he said. He relaxed a little and smiled. "But I would appreciate it if you would consider returning it to Nathan soon. After all, it was my birthday gift to him."

Though I was an outsider looking in at the relationship between the brothers, I felt sure that Ronald insisted on having complete control over Nathan. Whether it involved Nathan's job, shopping, entertainment, and even his friends, Ronald seemed to want to call the shots. Regardless of his reasons for wanting the ring returned, I doubted that it had anything to do with sentiment.

"If you'll excuse me, I need to get started on my laundry," I said to him. Traci had wheeled the cart to the back of the Malibu. "Please tell Nathan I'll see him in the morning."

Not waiting for me to introduce him, Ronald touched the brim of his baseball cap. "Have a nice evening, ladies." He turned and walked to the driver's side of the green pickup, then opened the door.

Traci was staring a hole through him, so I nudged her with my elbow. I knew I would have to answer a barrage of questions from her when he left. In the meantime, I started throwing dirty clothes into the cart.

"Who was that guy?" Traci hissed as she threw towels into the basket. "He didn't seem to want to stick around once I got here."

Some tension left my body as I watched the truck pull out of the parking lot. "That's Nathan's brother," I said, slamming the trunk lid. "He's ticked because Nathan gave me a present and he didn't okay it first."

As we rolled the cart toward the laundromat, Traci said, "Okay, we'll be here for over an hour. I want to hear every detail about this present, and don't leave anything out."

"Yes, ma'am," I said.

When the laundry was finished and we had returned to the apartment building, Traci buzzed Tommy, and he came downstairs to help us. We unloaded the baskets of folded laundry at the front door, then I pulled into the garage and parked my car. They were going inside to hold the elevator for me, so I didn't waste any time.

As I walked toward the tower, I saw a green pickup drive slowly by the entrance of the complex. Moanalua Road is usually crowded with traffic, even at night, so the slow pace was odd. I knew that Nathan lived somewhere close by, and that he may have told his brother where I was staying. An uneasy feeling washed over me.

I hurried inside the building and pulled the door closed behind me. Leaning against it, I could feel my heart racing.

One of the elevator doors was being held open by someone's hand. Traci stuck her head out from inside and said, "Come on, slowpoke. What's taking you so long?"

Riding up in the elevator, I didn't mention the truck. I was sure I was worrying for nothing, and besides, I could handle Ronald Nowicki.

CHAPTER 13

I tossed and turned all night and woke up with a throbbing headache. I didn't waste any time getting ready for school. After taking two ibuprofen tablets with my orange juice, I grabbed my purse, then headed out of the apartment.

It was a gorgeous, sunny day. Though I normally relished the walk from the building to the garage in the fresh air, today I squinted and wished for a pair of dark glasses. The bright light wasn't helping the pain in my head.

When I climbed into my car, I took the hula girl from my purse. I slipped the ring from around her waist and held it up to the window. Rays of sunlight streaming in through the large openings in the garage bounced off the red gemstones. The ring was pretty in a gaudy sort of way. I had seen similar pieces in a glass showcase at Wal-Mart in Paradise when I was shopping for a Mother's Day gift for Mom in May.

Maybe I should insist Nathan take it back, I thought. I certainly didn't want to cause a rift between him and his brother. I put the ring back around the hula girl's waist, then slipped her onto the radio knob.

After I picked up Nathan, he monopolized most of the conversation on the way to work. He was excited about two flats of petunias that were going to be delivered to the nursing home that morning. His boss had informed him the previous day that he was going to get to spruce up the beds surrounding the facility.

I tried to stay focused on what he was telling me, but with the ache in my head it was difficult. I nodded and gave an occasional response, and he didn't seem to notice my lack of enthusiasm. After dropping him off, I was several blocks away before I realized I had forgotten to give the ring back to him.

By the time I reached school, the medicine had taken effect, and I was feeling better. I stuck the figurine inside my purse, then grabbed the King Kamehameha Celebration brochure from the back seat.

After the students arrived, we got down to business reading the different Native American books. They took turns with the bulletin board display. I dug out scissors, some construction paper and jars of paint for them to use. They all worked together to construct a small Indian village, complete with teepees, campfires, and some plastic horses that I found in the rainy day games cabinet.

Before I dismissed the class for the day, Mareko asked if he could report on his rainbow experiment. Glad that he had reminded me, I gave him the floor.

"When I got home from school yesterday, I ate lunch, then dug out an old water hose we had in our shed," he told the class. "Since I couldn't find the sprayer, I just turned on the water full blast, then put my thumbs over the spout."

"I'll bet you got a shower, too," Seth blurted out. Some of the kids started giggling.

"Yeah, I sure did," Mareko said, grinning. "I turned the faucet down a little, then moved my thumbs around. After they were fixed just right, the water sprayed out more evenly."

He reported that when he held the hose level with his eyes, he could see a half-arched rainbow like we had seen the day before. But when he held it waist high, he saw a full circle of light. Since none of my students were used to being a star in the classroom, I could tell he was proud to be able to share this information with us. I intended for all the students to have more self-confidence before summer school was over.

"Everything was going fine, until my dumb sister butted in. I was moving the hose up and down, when she sneaked up and clamped it, causing the water to stop flowing." He paused for a moment and folded his arms across his chest. "But it was worth seeing her scream and run when I jerked it out of her hands, then turned the spray on her! You could hear her screaming a block away!"

Everyone burst out laughing and I had to smile, too. It reminded me of a time when Jamie and I were still at home and he was washing his car in the driveway before a big date. I had slipped up behind him and crimped the hose, just like Mareko had described. But Jamie didn't just spray me to teach me a lesson. He ran after me and dragged me back kicking and screaming. He washed my face with the yucky, soapy rag he had been using on the car.

However, Jamie didn't have the last laugh. Though I was grounded for a week, I got some revenge that night. When he returned home from his date and crawled into bed, his feet hit a gooey pile of shaving cream. I had emptied his entire can between the sheets. He hollered loud enough to wake the dead.

"Thank you for the report on your experiment, Mareko," I said after he sat back down. "Good job!"

When the students were gone, I straightened the room, then walked to the office to e-mail my mother. I had vowed to find out more about the Garden of Eden, and I planned to report my findings to Maynard on Friday. As soon as I sent the message, I logged off, then headed out the door to my car.

I was starving and wanted something more substantial than a burger and fries for lunch, so I stopped by Mr. Omura's deli. Before reaching the counter to place my order, I noticed that he had caldereta on the menu on the wall. I decided to see how his compared to Ella's.

When I reached the counter, Mr. Omura was all smiles. "Miss Allie!

It's good to see you again. I saw your story in the Saturday paper. You're a good writer."

The tables were full and people were glancing our way. Blushing, I said, "Thanks, Mr. Omura. The case I wrote about is a strange one."

"Yes, it is," he said. "I've been following all the grave-robbing stories since they started five years ago on Kauai."

"You know about the one on Kauai?"

"Oh, yeah. My brother lives about two miles from the Kahuku estate. His wife and children planned a big birthday party for his sixtieth birthday, and the grave disturbance was discovered the day before the party."

I couldn't believe this stroke of luck! "So you had some insider information?"

"The Kahuku family tried to keep it quiet, but neighbors talk." He winked at me.

"Would you mind answering some questions for me sometime?"

"If it will help you write a story, I'll do better than that. I'll jot down everything I can remember about it, then you can stop by and pick it up."

"That would be fabulous." A man standing behind me cleared his throat, and I realized I was holding up the line.

"Now, what would you like for lunch today?" Mr. Omura asked me. "Berta just made some fresh crab and noodle salad this morning, if you'd like to try it."

His helper, Berta, who was standing close behind him, smiled at me. Her fiery-red hair was plastered down with a white chef's hat, but the ends refused to be tamed, Strands of hair were sticking out every which way. Her plus-sized waist was only inches away from Mr. Omura's arm.

"Yes, that sounds good," I said. "I love crab salad."

"I obtained the recipe from a friend of mine who is a chef at a resort on Kauai," he said as he put a big scoop on a plate. "He uses buttermilk in the dressing, and it adds just the right zing to the fish."

"I would also like a bowl of caldereta."

"Coming right up."

After paying for my food, I told him I would stop by in a day or two for the information. I was anxious to see what he had to say.

I carried my lunch to a table in the park across from the deli. While watching some kids throw Frisbees for their dogs, I enjoyed the scrumptious meal. When I was finished, I couldn't decide which cook had made the finer caldereta. But I was certain of one thing, it was becoming one of my favorite dishes.

When I arrived at the *Star*, I stopped in to ask Mr. Masaki about my chances of covering the King Kamehameha Celebration on Friday. I was surprised to learn that no other reporters had asked for the assignment. I told him I would love to do it.

"Maybe you can put a unique spin on it, Allie," the editor said. "Covering the annual celebration has become a drag for most of the seasoned reporters here. I welcome your fresh insight. Now, how did the interview with Maynard Desmond go?"

"I think it went very well."

I told him what I had obtained regarding the exhibits and about some of the gardening stories we had shared. I didn't mention anything about what Maynard had said regarding his family, or what I considered personal. But when I reached the part about working side by side with him on this new exhibit and about the invitation to bring my class to the site on Friday, Mr. Masaki was grinning ear to ear.

"I knew it!" he said, thumping his fist on the desk. "If anyone could get an interview from him, you could! This is wonderful, Allie!"

"I'm tickled myself. Maynard's a great guy."

"Do you think you'll have a draft ready for me to look at this afternoon?"

"I plan to." I rose from my chair. "I'll check in with you in a few hours."

When I walked out of Mr. Masaki's office, he was humming. He made me feel like I had made his day.

When I climbed the stairs and walked past Kyle's office, his door was closed. I didn't hear any noise coming from inside and assumed he was out somewhere covering a story. *It's a good thing we aren't partnered on this piece,* I thought. If I had to depend on Kyle's help, there's no way it would be ready for tomorrow's paper.

I walked into my office and flipped on the computer. While waiting for it to boot, I pulled my tape recorder from my purse and rewound the tape. I fast-forwarded past the conversation about my mother's business and the Garden of Eden project. When I got to the part where Maynard was telling me about his exhibits, it was like magic. He was a master storyteller drawing his audience ever deeper into his tale.

Listening to his smooth voice, I started typing. Often I paused and rewound the tape to be sure I was getting all the facts down right. It was very important to me that Maynard like this piece. One miscue and he might not trust me to ever write about him again.

When I looked up from the screen at the clock on the wall it was almost 3:3o. My fingers were aching and my shoulders were tense from sitting in the chair for over two hours without a break. With both hands, I rubbed the back of my neck to help relieve some of the stress that had crept up both sides of it. After rolling my shoulders forward several times, I felt more relaxed.

"It's time to take a break, Allie," I said out loud to myself.

I stood up and reached toward the ceiling, then bent down to touch my toes. After a few repetitions, I straightened back up and walked toward the window.

The view of the ocean that had mesmerized me the first day at work was just as impressive as it had been then. The massive flower garden in the center of the park across the way was bursting with orchids and other tropical plants.

Knowing I wouldn't get another break for a while, I stretched some more, then turned my back to the window and did a few jumping jacks. Winded after twenty-five of them, I turned back around, huffing and puffing, and saw that a small audience had gathered in the parking lot below.

Sammy Cho and his uncle were standing outside the door of the laundromat watching me. The uncle started clapping, and Sammy stuck his hand in the air and gave me a "thumbs-up."

Though I felt like a nut, I bowed, then waved at them. They started laughing.

Shaking his head, the uncle went back into the laundromat, and Sammy waved as he headed toward his car.

Nothing like putting on a show for the neighbors. Oh, well. I felt like a new woman after the exercise, and I was ready to get back to work.

The story flowed from me like none other that I can ever remember writing. It was as if Maynard was sitting across from me telling me word-for-word what to say. After rereading it and making a few corrections, the piece was done.

As the sheets came off my printer, I looked at the clock. I couldn't believe that I had written the story in less than three hours.

I took a copy to Mr. Masaki and while he read through it, I proofread my copy again. Finishing at about the same time, I could tell by the look on his face that he was pleased.

"Very good," he said, leaning back in his chair. "I want to run your piece on the front page of tomorrow's paper. Since we don't have a picture of this new project, I'll dig into the archives and pull out something recent from one of Mr. Desmond's other exhibits. With his popularity and the warm way you've portrayed him, I expect to sell an additional four to five thousand copies of this edition."

I was humbled by the editor's praise, but also proud. I knew it was a great story. Not because I had written it, but because of the subject.

"Thank you, Mr. Masaki. It was a pleasure to do this article."

"I just saw one minor mistake that you need to fix," he said, handing his sheet to me. "After you do that, please e-mail it to the copy editor, and he'll take it from there."

All weariness had left me by the time I returned to my office. I made the correction, then e-mailed the story to the copy desk. After filing away my notes, I turned off my computer, then grabbed my purse and headed back downstairs. While walking to my car, my steps were light, and I had a smile on my face. This was turning out to be a great day!

When I walked into the apartment, I detected the faint smell of lemon Pledge. A Windex bottle and a roll of paper towels were sitting on the kitchen counter next to a large bag from Mr. Omura's deli. The carpet had been vacuumed and nothing was out of place in the living room. Traci was in the dining area setting the table for supper. A pale blue linen tablecloth that I knew she reserved for special occasions had been placed on the table.

"You're just in time," she said. She was folding a matching linen napkin.

"It looks like I'm a little late." I slipped off my shoes, then stooped down to pick them up. "The table looks great, and you've picked up food for dinner. You've been dusting, cleaning windows and doing heaven knows what else today. I hate to walk on the carpet because it might flatten down the pile."

"Ha ha," Traci said, waving one of the linen napkins at me. "Since I don't get in the domestic mood too often, when it hit me today, I took advantage of it. I cleaned all the baseboards, vacuumed up all the dust bunnies from beneath the furniture, swept away the cobwebs lurking in the corners, and polished every piece of wood in this apartment."

"And what do you think caused this mysterious mood to overtake you?" I asked, walking toward her.

"Well, I could blame it on the mood swings resulting from the pregnancy, but really I think it was just plain guilt. Spring cleaning was long overdue. Since Tommy and I are going to travel to Oklahoma next week, I wanted to leave a clean place for you and Aunt Edith."

I placed my hand on her shoulder. "I have felt at home from the moment I landed on this island. A few specks of dust don't matter to me in the least, but rest assured, Aunt Edith and I will keep things tidy while you're gone."

It surprised me to see tears well up in Traci's eyes. She brushed them away. "Darn these crazy hormones! I've been crying at the drop of a hat all day! Dr. Phil had four guests on his show today that have been on a special weight-loss program. I started bawling when they were telling their stories!" She dabbed her eyes with one of the napkins she was holding.

I was trying to understand my friend's emotional state. "What was wrong? Hadn't they lost the weight they were striving to lose?"

"Oh, yeah, they had surpassed their goals. They looked great! I started boo-hooing because I was so happy for them!"

I decided right then that if I ever got married and became pregnant, I would remember this moment. If a person as strong and levelheaded as Traci could be reduced to a blubbering puddle because of body changes, I knew I was probably doomed.

"Oh, good grief," Traci said, wiping her eyes with the back of her hand. "Tommy and Simon will be here any minute, and I probably have mascara running down my cheeks."

"I tell you what," I said. "You go and freshen up. I'll take care of putting dinner on the table." I could hear voices outside the apartment door and knew that one or both of the guys had arrived.

"Thanks, Allie," Traci said, hugging me. "I'll be right back."

She managed to make it out of the room before Tommy and Simon walked in. Shaking my head and smiling, I walked toward the door to meet them.

"Well, isn't this a nice welcome," Simon said when he saw me. He pulled me to him and gave me a big kiss.

"The little woman was waiting at the door for you after a hard day's work," Tommy said as he sat down in his recliner. He looked around the room. "That's the way it should be. They should meet you at the door with your slippers and a cool drink in hand. Speaking of which, where is my blushing bride?"

"She'll be back in here shortly," I said. "And in regard to doing a hard day's work, Traci has been working herself to the bone today, so you might want to compliment her efforts."

I knew that with the unstable mood she was in, it was probably a good thing that she hadn't heard his "little woman" speech.

Simon helped me set the food on the table and fix the drinks. When Traci joined us, she was smiling and seemed to be feeling better.

"So did you and Eddie get a lot of work done last night?" I asked Simon as I passed him the bowl of lomi lomi salmon.

"Yes and no." He scooped diced fish, tomatoes and onions onto his plate. "My first priority after picking up Z at the airport was to drive to Maynard Desmond's house to talk with him. But we were delayed by an incident inside the terminal."

Tommy took the bowl from him. "What kind of incident?" he asked. He helped himself to a large spoonful of the salmon mixture.

"While we were walking toward the front doors, we heard two gun-shots fired."

"Gunshots?" I nearly dropped the platter of egg rolls I was holding. Traci and Tommy, each holding a bowl of food in mid-air, looked as shocked as I was.

Simon reached over and took the platter from my hand. "We deter-mined that the shots came from the security check area. When we arrived, the suspect was being held to the floor by a couple of hefty Marines. His gun had been wrestled away from him, and one of the security people, Doreen, had it in her possession."

"Was anyone hurt?" Tommy asked.

Simon looked at me and I could tell by the look on his face that the news wasn't good. "One of the other security guards on duty, Kelly Hugo, was hit in the arm. It was a nasty wound."

"Oh, Simon, how awful!" I said. "I hope he's going to be alright." I couldn't believe what I was hearing.

"I stopped by the hospital to visit him this morning. The bullet fractured the bone, and tore a hole the size of a quarter through the back of his upper arm. His doctor told him he should recover, but he's going to be carrying around a big scar the rest of his life." He glanced down at the platter he was holding in his hand, then looked back at me. "Kelly was hit by the second bullet—Abbie caught the first one."

"Oh, no!" I said. "Please tell me she's going to be alright, too."

"Last night the veterinarian didn't seem very hopeful. I stopped by the animal hospital after visiting Kelly today, and the doctor said that Abbie had done well during surgery. However, he said the bullet nicked one of her heart valves and there was a lot of internal bleeding. It's still touch and go."

Tears were stinging my eyes, and my heart ached for both Abbie and Kelly.

Simon looked at Traci and Tommy. "Abbie is the police dog that has been living and working with Kelly for more than four years. You never saw him anywhere without that dog. I'm sure she probably saved his life."

"And possibly many others," Tommy said. "No telling what the bad guy intended to do with that gun."

"Doreen told me that everything was progressing like any other day, when all of a sudden, Abbie started growling," Simon said. "She barked once, then leapt at the suspect. Doreen said that it all happened so fast, none of the guards knew anything was wrong until they heard the shots."

"How do you think Abbie knew the guy had a gun?" Traci asked, wiping a tear from her cheek. I knew this conversation wasn't helping Traci's delicate state.

"I guess she smelled something, or detected a movement that the guards didn't notice," Simon said. "Dogs are amazing animals. They have an extraordinary sense for danger."

"They ought to lock that guy up and throw away the key, if you ask me," Tommy said, echoing my thoughts.

"In most states, Hawaii included, a crime committed against a police dog is the same as against an officer," Simon said. "Recently in Virginia, a man was committing a burglary when an officer and his dog happened to drive by. The guy shot them both and received an additional five years on his prison term for shooting the dog. The suspect in this crime will probably be charged with attempted manslaughter for shooting Abbie and Kelly as well as firearm charges. He was carrying a fake I.D. After we fingerprinted him, we determined he had some associates connected with al Qaida. He's been on the CIA and FBI watch lists for a while, but the authorities had lost track of him. Apparently, he's been hiding here on Oahu for some time."

"I wonder if he had planned to hijack the plane?" Traci said. "It gives me goose bumps just thinking about it."

Okay, it's time to call a halt to the grim thoughts and conversation, I thought. I looked at everyone around the table and noticed that they were all still holding containers of food in their hands. Traci had had enough tears for one day. It was time to turn this evening around.

"It's tragic what happened last night, and we all need to remember Kelly and Abbie in our prayers," I said. "But I vote for more pleasant dinner conversation now." I took the bowl of moo goo gai pan from Traci.

"She's right, you guys," Simon said. "I apologize if I put a wet blanket on the party. Let's dig into this wonderful feast and start enjoying ourselves. I'm starved!"

We pushed away the gloom and in no time, we were joking and laughing with each other. Traci asked me about the article I had turned in for Wednesday's paper. Everyone put down their forks and clapped when I told them my story would be on the front page. Traci kidded me that I would probably be hard to live with now, given my new celebrity status. I assured them all that I'd try to remain humble when the *New*

York Times offered me a six-figure columnist job. They might even get an occasional Christmas card after I moved to the Big Apple.

"Well, I'm stuffed!" Traci said, pushing back her plate. "I hope this baby appreciates getting the finest food on Oahu." She gently stroked the baby bump with her hand. "And that reminds me, Allie. Mr. Omura asked me to tell you that he'd have the information you wanted by tomorrow afternoon. Sorry I didn't tell you before now."

"Oh, that's okay. I didn't expect him to have it so quickly. I'll go by on my way to the *Star* and pick it up." I turned and looked at Simon. "When I stopped by the deli for lunch today, Mr. Omura told me he saw my story about Ray Franklin in Saturday's paper. He said that his brother lives a couple of miles from the Kahuku estate and that he was on Kauai for a birthday party the day after the grave disturbance was discovered. He's going to tell me all he knows about it. Maybe it will be another piece to this crazy puzzle we're working on."

"I don't know what I'd do without you, Miss Kane," Simon said, leaning toward me. He put his arm around my shoulders. "I told you the first night we had dinner together that the crime rate would drop faster if you moved here and helped me. You need to forget about the *New York Times* and consider that idea."

He kissed me and even though I knew we were putting on a show for Traci and Tommy, I wasn't embarrassed one bit.

Tommy coughed. "Okay, you two. Some of us are trying to eat here." Though the rest of us had finished, Tommy was still munching on the last egg roll.

Simon and I separated, but from the look in his eyes, I figured this conversation would resume later when we were alone.

Traci pushed back her chair and stood up. "Come on, Tommy. The *little woman* needs your help in the kitchen."

I couldn't help smiling when I saw a worried expression come onto Tommy's face.

"So you heard that comment, huh, muffin? Now you know I only meant it in the most gracious way." He started loading his arms with dirty plates and serving bowls.

"Uh huh," Traci said. She winked at Simon and me as she headed toward the kitchen carrying the empty glasses.

With the four of us working together, the kitchen and dining area was soon clean. We gathered back in the living room and watched an old Cary Grant movie on TV. Though it was a chick flick, the guys didn't act like they minded too much. During commercials, they talked baseball and golf while Traci and I chatted about girl stuff.

When the movie was over, Simon stood up to leave. He thanked Tommy and Traci for their hospitality, then I walked him to the elevator.

Holding my hand as the car descended to the first floor, Simon said, "You'll be happy to know that Eddie and I were polite to Maynard Desmond when we talked with him this afternoon."

I continued staring at the elevator door. I still felt like a traitor for giving up Maynard's information, and though I knew Simon was going to question him, I hadn't asked him about it.

"He didn't object to going to the lab to give a DNA sample," he continued. "He also gave us the names of a couple of relatives here that we didn't know anything about."

"But you're still considering him to be a suspect," I said, turning to look at him.

He lifted my hand that he had been holding on the ride down and placed it in the crook of his arm. While gently bending my fingers back and forth, he said, "Too many things connect him to the crimes for us to rule him out. Not only is he a relative of the victims, but in his profession, he knows all about the soil here. We know that whoever dug up those graves came prepared for a hard task. He also has motive because he was cheated out of his inheritance." He stopped bending my fingers and pulled me closer to him. "And while we were there today, we discovered another possible link."

My heart was pounding. *Please, no more links!*

Simon turned my chin so that I was forced to look at him. "You told me the other day when you helped with the exhibit that he gave you a pair of gloves to wear. Do you recall if they were like the one you found at Shady Palms?"

Without hesitation, I shook my head. "Not one bit! There was nothing that I saw or anything that happened that day to make me think Maynard had anything to do with the crimes." I pulled my hand from his and crossed my arms. I had the feeling he was about to object to my behavior when the elevator stopped on the fifth floor and the doors opened.

Two teenagers, one with a purple Mohawk and a lip ring and the other one with tattoos covering both arms, were waiting to get on. I stepped back to give them more room. Simon nodded at the two boys, then moved closer to me.

In the silence of the elevator, a nagging voice inside my head was whispering, *Whose side are you on?* Simon was just doing his job. I was resisting the possibility that Maynard was involved. What was the matter with me?

The elevator stopped at the first floor and the doors opened. The boys walked out, and I followed them. A few steps into the foyer, Simon again reached for my hand and led me to a bench near the tenants' mailboxes.

"Okay, have a seat," he said, pulling me down next to him. "We need to get something straight right now."

He was still holding my hand. I considered pulling it away again, but when I looked into his eyes, I thought I saw a "Don't do it again," look there. So I decided not to press my luck.

"I'm not the enemy," he said. "I know you like the landscaper as most of the people who live on this island do. Hey, I like him, too! But the best way to rule him out is to check him out. That's what Z and I are doing."

I felt like a heel. *Maybe a girl doesn't have to be pregnant to have hormonal problems,* I thought. Better to blame it on some physical imbalance than to admit I'm acting like a two-year-old child. Or else, maybe I needed to find an altar and get some spiritual guidance really quick. I decided I'd better pray twice as long before I fell asleep tonight.

"I'm sorry for the way I've been acting.," I said. I gave him a charming smile, then leaned forward and kissed him. He grinned and I took that as a sign of forgiveness. "They were run-of-the-mill cotton gardening gloves. Why do you ask?"

"Today the doors of Desmond's van were open, and I saw the array of tools you mentioned that he owned. I spotted two stacks of gloves on a shelf. I asked him if I could take a look at them, and he said I could. One stack was the cotton variety like you're describing, but the other stack consisted of the heavier, canvas-type. The brand name on the cuff of those gloves was Heman."

And there, folks, you have it! As much as I wanted Maynard to be blameless, it didn't sound good.

Simon and I talked for a few more minutes, then he kissed me good night. Before he left, he said he would call me the next day at the newspaper.

As I rode the elevator back upstairs, I thought about what he and Eddie had discovered. Despite that, I was determined to hold onto the premise that a person is innocent until proven guilty. It was time for me to dig deeper for the truth, because time was running out.

CHAPTER 14

At school the next day, I read part of one of the King Kame-hameha biographies that I had checked out of the library to the class. Though I didn't dwell very long on the portions dealing with the king's bloody battles, the boys were impressed with the warrior. Annie wanted to know why Kamehameha didn't have a first name. After the restroom break, the children paired up, then chose one of the other selections to read.

As I walked among the students, I heard confidence in their voices as they read to their partners. When I walked by Mareko, he was help-ing Seth sound out the word "conquer." Seth was enamored with his buddy for knowing that "qu" sounded like "k." I stopped for a moment and listened to Mareko explain to him what conquer meant. I was impressed with the fine job he did.

I smiled at them, though they didn't notice. I remembered how Mareko had announced on the first day of school how much he hated reading. "I stink at reading" were his exact words.

I walked toward David and Annie, who were huddled together by the front window reading together. Annie was explaining to David what a "kahuna" was. Though I was certain both the children had heard the word, I suspected that Annie had figured out that it meant "priest" from using context clues in the passage she was reading.

"I'd rather clean the bathroom than have to try to read a book," she had told the class the first day. Listening to her now, I doubted that the statement was still true. When everyone was finished, we discussed some of the highlights from the books. I put facts they had learned about the monarch on the board.

"Did anyone learn what Kamehameha means?" I asked.

Danielle was the first one to raise her hand. "The lonely one," she said. "But how could he be lonely with all his soldiers around him, Miss Kane?"

"That's a good question. Does anyone have an idea about that?"

Mareko raised his hand. "Maybe because he didn't have any brothers or sisters. But I'd be glad to give him my yucky old sister anyday."

Some of the kids snickered. I smiled because I remembered I had felt the same way about my younger brother, Jeff, when I was Mareko's age.

We discussed how the king overthrew the rulers of each island, one by one, beginning with the Big Island of Hawaii where he was born. Seth was proud to tell the class that Kamehameha had conquered Maui and Molokai next. I could tell he was tickled to get to use the new word.

"When did he come to Oahu?" Annie asked. "That part wasn't in our book."

"It was in mine and Cindy's," Danielle spoke up. "In 1795, his army invaded the shores of Waikiki beach."

"Good job, Danielle," I said. Her book hadn't gone into a lot of detail about that invasion. I had held back one of the books that talked about the hundreds of Oahu warriors who were killed during that battle. The king's army had driven them over the Pali cliffs. Since we were studying about the king because of the upcoming celebration, I didn't want them to focus on war. Some day they were bound to find out the gory details, but I didn't want it to be today. I had no doubt that when I saw the cliffs that night when Tommy, Traci and I traveled on the Pali Highway to Kaneohe for church, images of falling soldiers would appear to me.

"One last question, then we're going to make some posters," I told them.

David raised his hand. "Why didn't the king just let all the other kings keep ruling their own islands? Why did he think he had to take over everything?"

The age old question of man conquering man, I thought. "Well, David, I can't tell you what was on the king's mind, but throughout time, some men have been so greedy they would kill to get land and wealth from others. They usually weren't happy getting just a portion of the land; they wanted more and more, regardless of who they hurt to get it."

"That stinks, Miss Kane," he replied.

"Yes, I agree." I looked around the room, pausing a moment to focus on each youthful face. "Boys and girls, I hope that as you grow up, you'll try your best to get along with people. It's not always easy, and sometimes you have to give in to keep the peace, but I hope you'll try your best to be kind to others."

"Not to my dumb old sister, Miss Kane," Mareko blurted out without raising his hand.

"At least, please give it a try, Mareko."

He rolled his eyes. "Okay, but it won't be easy."

I smiled at him, then walked to the activity table in the back of the room. That morning I had found some large sheets of white posterboard in one of Traci's cupboards. I began handing out the sheets to the students while the three girls passed out boxes of markers and crayons.

"Before you start drawing, I'd like you to take a couple of minutes to think about something that impressed you about King Kamehameha," I said after all the supplies were distributed. "If you choose to go the warrior route, no gory pictures." I heard a couple of the boys sigh. "You have thirty minutes until the bell rings. Fill your space, add lots of color and please remember to put your name on the back of your posterboard."

The words were barely out of my mouth before Seth and Mareko started drawing. A few of the kids contemplated a minute or two before beginning. I walked to my desk and sat down to do lesson plans while the students worked.

🐾 🐾 🐾

After school, I stopped by Mr. Omura's deli. When I walked in the door, I noticed that a new checkout stand had been erected. A young, Oriental girl was at the cash register taking money from customers.

Mr. Omura and Berta were up to their elbows serving noontime patrons at the counter. He looked up and smiled at me. "Allison, I'm glad you came by. Right there by the new register is a manila envelope. My notes and some old newspaper clippings I found are in it."

"Thanks, Mr. Omura." I walked to the register, and the girl handed me the envelope.

"What can I get you for lunch?" he asked me.

The number of people crowding into the deli was growing. I didn't want to risk making someone angry if Mr. Omura tried to serve me first. "I'll just grab one of your pre-packaged sandwiches here in the glass case," I said. "I need to get to the paper soon."

I stuck the manila envelope under my arm, then headed toward the refrigerated case. When I opened the door, I saw several different types of sandwiches displayed on the shelf. I selected one that had turkey and cheese on it. Paper-thin slices of meat were piled onto the large, homemade bun. A packet of mayonnaise and a sweet pickle had been wrapped separately in cellophane and placed inside the bag with the sandwich.

"Everything in the case was made fresh this morning," Mr Omura said.

"It looks great," I told him as I shut the glass door.

He turned his attention from me to the man standing in front of him at the counter. I grabbed a bottle of root beer, paid for my lunch, then walked across the street to the park.

It was a windy day, so it was all I could do to keep my napkin, sandwich and the envelope on the table. I was anxious to see the contents in the package, but knew better than to open it here. Though my body would benefit from the exercise, I wasn't in the mood to run after any papers that might fly away.

After the food and last swig of pop was gone, I threw all my trash into a nearby can, then headed to my car.

When I turned into the alley running beside the *Star* building, I saw Kyle's silver Chrysler coming toward me. I hadn't seen him all week and expected him to be in the office today. Since I had no other assignment until the celebration on Friday, I had planned to spend today and tomorrow doing some research regarding the grave-robbing cases. Kyle and I were supposed to be working on it together, but lately, I had been flying solo.

As he pulled up beside me, he rolled down his window and stopped. Loud rap music was blaring from his stereo, and I could feel the vibration from the heavy bass on the floorboard under my feet. I rolled down my window and heard a man singing in a monotone voice, "I was ridin' down the road, with such a heavy load, but I forgot the code, hey, baby."

"That's quite a song," I said to Kyle.

"What?" he yelled at me.

"That's some song," I hollered back at him.

"Wait a minute," he yelled back. "Let me turn down the music."

Music? That's a matter of opinion. He adjusted the volume and my feet stopped vibrating. "Where are you going?" I asked. "I thought we might do some research this afternoon."

"Sorry, no can do. On Sunday, while I was playing golf, I pulled a muscle in my back. That's why I haven't been at work all week."

"I'm sorry to hear that. Have you seen a doctor?"

"I went Monday afternoon, and he gave me some muscle relaxants to take. Afraid that the pills alone might not ease all the pain, I stopped at a gas station on the way home and picked up a six-pack of beer. I was really hurting at the time and considered popping open a can and drinking it on the way home. But I came to my senses before I did anything stupid."

In Oklahoma, if you are caught drinking while driving, it's an automatic trip to jail. I assumed the laws were similar in Hawaii. "Thank goodness for that," I said. "I'm glad you reconsidered. You could have had a wreck, or been stopped by the police."

"Please don't say anything to Mr. Masaki about it. I'm still on probation until the end of the month, so he might not want to make the job permanent if he thought I had pondered doing something like that."

Though I had seen some of Kyle's character flaws, this time he hadn't actually done anything wrong. If we were judged just for thinking something wrong, we'd all be up a creek. I knew that Mr. Masaki would make his own decision about Kyle, and I didn't intend to interfere.

"Don't worry about me," I told him. "How long do you think you'll be off work?"

"The doctor told me to take it easy for a couple of days, so I won't be back until Monday. I just came in to grab some files in case I wanted to do a little work at home."

A couple of days? This was already day number three. And I had never asked, but I assumed no files were supposed to be taken from the office. Maybe under the circumstances, Mr. Masaki had given him permission to do it.

"Well, take it easy and get some rest," I said. "See you later."

"See you." He turned up the volume on his stereo again, and the bass was thumping when he pulled away.

As I drove into the parking lot behind the building, I saw Sammy walk out the back door of the laundromat. I picked up my purse and the manila envelope, then climbed out of the car. He was walking toward me.

"I just finished reading your story on the front page of today's *Hawaiian Star*," he said. "Congratulations. It was very interesting."

"Thanks. I had a lot of fun doing it."

"Even though I've seen all of the landscape artist's exhibits many times, your article makes me want to run out and look at them again. For a while, the police will probably have to set up crowd control at all the locations." He had a big grin on his face.

I smiled at him. "Well, I doubt if it will come to that, but the piece should help promote his newest endeavor."

"I'd better let you get to work. I need to hit the road, too. Besides the hours at the gas station, I'm working every night at a beach show in Waikiki. It's still not enough hours, but it's helping until I find a full time job."

"It was good talking with you again," I said. "See you later."

He waved, then turned around and left.

Anxious to see what Mr. Omura had enclosed in the envelope, I hurried to my office. I turned on my computer, then opened the package. Inside I found three sheets of paper with notes scribbled on them, along with a five-year-old Kauai newspaper. A yellow sticky-note with "Birthday Party" written on it had been placed on the edge of one of the pages of the newspaper. I opened it to that section and saw the article about Mr. Omura's brother's party. It must have been a slow news day, because quite a spread had been dedicated to the affair. There was a festive picture showing a smiling birthday boy holding a piece of cake. His right arm was draped over the shoulders of his brother. The caption under the picture read: Tam Omura and his brother, Luu. A long list of party attendees followed in the article below it.

After reading the story, I searched through the paper trying to find something regarding the Kahuku grave disturbance. There wasn't a word about it anywhere.

Not too surprised, but a little disappointed, I set the newspaper aside and focused on the handwritten sheets. Expecting them to contain more information about the birthday party, I was confused when I reached the end of the first page.

Mr. Omura was telling me things about his grandmother that had taken place in the mid-1950s. He wrote that as a teenager, he often visited her when she lived in the Nahoa Nursing Home. I knew from dropping Nathan there that the facility was old. For several years, Bea Omura had shared a room with a woman named Fae Song and they became close friends. He said that he never saw anyone visit his grandmother's roommate, so whenever he took a card or gift to Bea, he always took one for Miss Fae, too.

"That's sweet," I said out loud.

One day Miss Fae fell and broke a hip and had to go to the hospital. While she was away, Mr. Omura visited his grandmother. He had asked about Miss Fae's condition, then inquired about her family. Bea told him that Fae had never married, but did have one son and three grandchildren. She also told him that Fae had worked as a domestic servant most of her life.

I'll bet she had a rough time, I thought, rubbing the back of my neck with one hand. In the early 1900s, a child born out of wedlock was taboo. The children often bore the brunt of cruel criticism and were considered "marked," which seemed ridiculous to me. It wasn't the child's fault if his or her parents weren't married.

Concentrating hard on what I was reading, I jumped when the phone rang.

"Hello?"

"Are you hard at it?" Simon asked.

"I'm in the middle of going through the information I picked up from Mr. Omura. So far it's been very interesting, but I'm puzzled because I'm not sure what he's trying to tell me."

"Hang in there," Simon said. "I'm sure it will come to you."

"After our little misunderstanding last night before you left, I didn't get a chance to ask you if you'd like to come to church with Tommy, Traci and me tonight. Do you have anything else going on?"

"I appreciate the invitation, but I'm taking Eddie to the airport to catch a 5:30 flight back to Maui. We interviewed one of the relatives that Maynard told us about."

"Is he a suspect?" I silently berated myself for wishing he was, but I wanted Maynard to be off the hook.

"I don't think so. The guy was in a car wreck over a year ago, and he's in a wheelchair. There's no way he could have done the last two jobs alone. Neither Eddie nor I feel like he's connected to the first two either, or that he had someone do it for him. It doesn't make any sense."

"If that's the case, why do you think Maynard mentioned him to you?"

"Well, he told us that he had read about the car wreck in the newspaper, but hadn't seen the guy. I doubt if he knew that his relative was in a wheelchair."

"What about the other person?"

"We haven't been able to locate the other one yet, but Eddie has another case he needs to get back to. After I drop him off at the airport, there's another case I need to go help with."

"A detective's work is never done," I said.

"You can say that again. Two homeless men have been mugged near a park in Waikiki in the last three days. They were both beat with a baseball bat. The latest one is barely clinging to life. A half dozen officers are scheduled to patrol the area tonight."

"Why would anyone want to prey on defenseless homeless men? I can't imagine that they would have any valuables to take."

"Neither one of them did. From the way it looks, whoever beat them up did it out of pure meanness. Marshall, Dave and I are going to canvas the bars and nightspots tonight near the area to see if any regular patrons noticed anything out of the ordinary."

"Well, since you're joining the investigation team, I'm sure the culprit will soon be found."

"Thanks for the vote of confidence," he said. "To make up for turning down your invitation tonight, how about going to the Kuhio Beach Torch Lighting and Hula Show with me tomorrow night?"

"I'm sure I'd like to. It sounds interesting."

"Every night at Kuhio Beach in Waikiki, a torch lighting and conch shell ceremony is performed. There's plenty of Hawaiian music, hula dancing and other entertainment and it's all free. People sit on the grass, or bring lawn chairs. I've been many times and I think you'll enjoy it."

"It sounds like fun," I said. "I've always admired the graceful way those hula girls move. I've never been much of a dancer, but I wouldn't mind learning how to hula."

"You'd probably be good at it. A lot of people say that the hands tell the story, but the chant is just as important. During the show, the performers pull a few folks from the crowd onto the stage. I'll see if I can get one of the girls to give you a few impromptu pointers."

I had to open my big mouth. "Oh, that's okay. I'll just watch the professionals, then practice a little on my own."

"Well, we'll see when we get there. I'll pick you up about 5:45."

"I'll be ready. Don't work too hard tonight and stay safe."

After I hung up, I returned to my reading. On the top of the second page, I snapped to attention.

When Fae Song was in her twenties, she was a servant for a rich family on Kauai. She told her friend, Bea, that the master of the house often "took advantage her." She feared losing her job, so she didn't tell anyone what was happening. But one day the master's wife figured it out. Fae was in her sixth month of pregnancy and couldn't keep it hidden any longer. She was forced to leave the estate with only the clothes on her back.

Mr. Omura concluded the story by writing that Fae recovered from the hip fracture, and returned to the nursing home. However, a week later, his grandmother suffered a massive heart attack and died in her bed. The nurses at the home found Fae lying across her friend's chest sobbing. She was so heartbroken she refused to eat. When Mr. Omura took her home after his grandmother's funeral, she had pleaded with him to be buried beside her friend when her time came. Bea was laid to rest next to her late husband in the Waiakai Cemetery. Ten days later, Fae was buried on the other side of her.

I had tears in my eyes when I laid the pages down on my desk. My heart ached for this single mother who had probably struggled most of her life. Though she never married, I wondered if she had ever experienced true love. Where had her son and grandchildren been during her last days? Memorial Day had just passed. Did anyone decorate her grave, or was she one of the forgotten ones buried in the Waiakai Cemetery?

The Waiakai Cemetery. Where had I seen that? I pulled out the file that contained all my notes regarding the grave-robbing cases. As I thumbed through the information, there it was. Alhoi Kahuku Akau, Maynard's grandmother, had also been buried there.

I stared at the materials strung out on my desk. I sorted through the information and jotted down more notes. There had to be some connection in this maze of documents that I wasn't seeing. Mr. Omura must think so, too. Why else would he have told me the story about Fae Song?

I searched the Internet and found a genealogy site. I entered Fae Song's name, but no records were found. Since she had worked all her life as a domestic servant, I knew she might not have ever had a social security number. She probably worked cheaply and her employers saved money by not reporting the wages.

By 5:00, I hadn't made any more progress. Frustrated, I put the folder back in my desk and shut down the computer. Maybe sleeping on it would help. But before then, I intended to ask for some divine intervention, and what better place to do that, than tonight at church.

The next day, I sent home permission slips with the students regarding the field trip we were taking to Diamond Head on Friday. Though I try to do that several days ahead to ensure they are all returned, it had slipped my mind. After stressing the importance of getting them back, or risk being left behind to sit in the office, all the students promised to get the slips to me the next morning.

Before leaving at noon, I checked my e-mail. Doug had written to me and was asking me to consider letting Rowdy and Precious join me when Aunt Edith came the following week. He was still feeling guilty that he had to leave them alone so much. Despite taking antihistamines, Kristin's allergies were killing her when the pups were there, so that wasn't an option anymore.

Doug had paid for obedience lessons for the dogs, and their behavior had improved over time. Rowdy had been notorious for chewing furniture and my clothing when we first got him. Now he was content with his chew toys. With Aunt Edith staying at Traci's apartment with me, I knew she probably wouldn't mind keeping an eye on them while I was away. I hated to ask Traci, but it looked like the only solution. I sent a reply to Doug telling him I was sorry for his dilemma and that I would let him know soon if he could send them over with Aunt Edith.

Mom had e-mailed a list of the plants and trees used in the Garden of Eden to me. She wrote that a patch of qaneh, or giant cane, was planted in one corner of it. Frankincense and myrrh were also among the mix. A few items that I had never heard of were also listed. I printed off the sheet, then stuck it into my purse to give to Maynard the next day.

Mom continued writing:

> Allie, your Nana was a hero yesterday at the Circle K. Your dad spoke with your grandpa on the phone last night, and he told him the whole story. It seems that A.J. was out at the paddock checking on Goliath. (The old bull's improving from his back injuries, by the way.) Your grandpa sent Brittany and Riley, who had come out after school, to the house to fetch your grandmother. He needed her help to pull Goliath away from the gate. I guess the straps on the bull's halter were tangled in the chain holding the gate closed. Anyway, Susanna came out and climbed into the paddock and started trying to pull it free.
>
> All at once, Nana yelled at Riley to run. Susanna started whooping and stomping the ground with all she was worth. A.J., Brittany

and Riley just stared at her like she had lost her mind. When she finally stopped jumping, they saw that she had pounded the head of a copperhead snake into the ground with her boot heel. A.J. grabbed a hoe sitting next to the barn and jumped in there and chopped off its head. According to the girls, the body of the snake wriggled around for quite awhile.

A.J. told your daddy that Susanna probably saved Riley from getting bitten. Anyway, she's a hero now. (As if she wasn't the family's hero before.)

Take care, and call your daddy and me when you can.

Love, Mom

Good for Nana! I knew that despite Grandpa's efforts to rid the ranch of snakes, some years copperheads and water moccasins were thick at the Circle K. When I was younger, my cousins and I often rode horses out there during summer vacation. Many of those times, we saw snakes in the pastures while we were riding.

I wrote back to Mom and thanked her for compiling the list of plants for me. I also asked her to tell Nana that she would always be a hero to me. After logging off, I headed toward the car.

As I drove toward the *Hawaiian Star,* I thought about the upcoming King Kamehameha Celebration. Today I was planning to search the newspaper's archives and read some of the stories written about the past events. Part of my article would reiterate activities that were annual traditions. I wanted to create an outline ahead of time to help me determine what to watch for. After writing about those things, I hoped to be able to find something fresh and new about the event to bring to readers.

I pulled into the parking lot, then walked into the building. Since I hadn't taken time for lunch, I stopped at the vending machine near the copy desk and bought a package of Fritos. The soda pop machine next to it had a variety of soft drinks and juices in it. I chose a can of cranberry juice, then carried my goodies upstairs to my office.

While munching on the chips, I read the stories covering the past six celebrations. A different reporter had written each article, and all of them were upbeat and informative. I knew I would have my work cut out for me to be able to top any of them.

I prepared an outline and put it into a folder along with other materials I would need the next day. The story would have to be completed in time to run in Saturday's paper. In order to do that, I would have to come back and work late on Friday night.

Though I was trying to center my brainpower on the task at hand, the information from the previous day about Fae Song kept nagging at me. Confident that I was prepared for Friday's assignment, I pulled out the folder containing Mr. Omura's notes. While reading through it, an idea hit me. I picked up the phone and called Simon's cell. It bounced directly to voicemail. Rather than leave a message, I called Honolulu P.D. and asked to speak to Marshall. After three rings, he picked up.

"Hi, Marshall. It's Allie."

"Hi, Allie. If you're looking for Simon, he's in a meeting with some top brass."

"I tried his cell phone, but since he didn't answer, I assumed he was busy. But that's okay because you can probably help me."

"Sure. What do you need?"

"I'd like the directions to the Waiakai Cemetery."

He paused for a moment. "Waiakai Cemetery? It's in the center part of the island just outside of Mililani Town. Where will you be traveling from?"

"I'm at the *Hawaiian Star* right now."

"Take H-1 north past Pearl City. When you see the junction for H-2, get on it. Mililani is about seven miles north of that point. Exit off H-2, then follow the signs into town. Waiakai Cemetery is two miles east of Main Street on Auhana Road."

I had been taking notes on a scratch pad while he talked. "Thanks. I appreciate your help."

"Do you know someone who's buried there?" I could almost hear the wheels turning in his detective brain.

"No, but I've been working on something, and I'm hoping I might get some direction there."

"Uh huh." He was quiet for a moment. "Well, I've been able to get inspiration from lots of places, but never from a cemetery."

I realized that Marshall must be thinking that I was going there to pray or to meditate. I didn't know myself what I was looking for. If I came up empty-handed, praying might not be a bad idea.

"Thanks again for your help. I'll talk to you later," I said.

"You're welcome. I hope you find what you're needing."

That makes two of us, I thought.

After I hung up, I shut off my computer, then grabbed my stuff. On the way out to my car, I tossed my empty juice can into the recycling bin. As I pulled out of the parking lot, I saw Sammy walking out the back door of the laundromat carrying a colorful costume over his arm. I assumed it was what he wore at his new job. I waved as I drove past him.

Following Marshall's directions, within a half-hour I was in Mililani Town. I passed Auhana Road and had to circle the block. Two miles east of Main Street, I entered the pristine Waiakai Cemetery. There was only about a hundred graves in it.

Old headstones marked most of the graves. As was the tradition at the Valley of the Temples Cemetery near the Byodo-In Temple, some of the graves were adorned with flowers, ornaments and toys. Bits of paper and pieces of floral arrangements littered the grounds. I saw a groundskeeper in the distance picking up the blowing trash.

I parked my car on the side of the narrow, dirt-packed road. As I walked toward the caretaker, I noticed some of the dates on the elaborate headstones. A few of the grave's occupants had been there for nearly a century. Others had been there for several decades. The newest grave I saw dated back to the early 1960s.

The caretaker had been watching me as I progressed toward him. When I reached him, I smiled and said, "Aloha. It looks like you're working hard."

He propped the large trash bag that he had been dragging along behind him against his leg. Wiping beads of sweat off his forehead with the back of his hand, he said, "Aloha. Yes, there's always more work to do around here after Memorial Day. Folks don't always anchor their arrangements properly, and pieces come loose and blow away. The wind has also been picking up debris from the neighborhood across the road. It's been a full time job lately keeping the place looking nice."

I noticed that the section behind him was neat and free of trash. Sweeping my hand toward the back fence, I said, "It looks like you're making headway."

He glanced that way, then back at me. "Yes, ma'am, but it will probably need to be redone tomorrow. I don't mind, though; that's job security."

I nodded and smiled. "Do you happen to know where I can find the grave of Bea Omura?"

"Oh, sure. The Omura plots are there on the east side where I've already cleaned. Come on. I'll take you there."

Together we walked to the back of the cemetery. Nine plots on the last row were dedicated to the Omura family. The grass around each headstone had been trimmed. An eight-foot-tall monument with the family name and crest on it stood in the center.

"There she is," he said, pointing toward the grave closest to the pillar. "Miss Bea has been here since I was a teenager. Her husband, who is lying next to her there, was the first one buried in this row."

"Beloved Wife, Mother, and Grandmother" was carved into the headstone, along with the date that she had been born and the date she died. A large wreath of yellow roses intertwined with white orchids had been placed against the marker.

I walked to the plot next to hers. A smaller wreath of yellow roses was lying against the headstone. The marker was less elaborate than Bea's, but was made from the same type of material. "A Dear Mother and Friend," had been engraved below Fae Song's name. Her birth and death dates were listed last. A red plastic hibiscus blossom had been placed in the dirt beside the wreath.

"When I mow, I lay the large arrangements on top of the markers, then put them back on the graves when I'm finished trimming," the worker said. He motioned toward Fae's grave. "But I discard those little ones, because they get loose and blow away before I can get back to secure them. However, with this grave, someone always comes in here after I'm gone and replaces the flower."

"Hmmm. Have you ever seen who does it?"

"Never have, though I'm here early and sometimes stay until almost dark," the man said, shaking his head. "But it never fails. The day after I mow, I know there's going to be a new flower on there."

Though I suspected that the rose wreath had come from Mr. Omura, I doubted that he had anything to do with the reappearing red hibiscus. The groundskeeper was enjoying telling me about each new addition to the section. He pointed out where Mr. Omura's parents were buried and said he had often shopped at their grocery store. Bea's two daughters and their husbands were buried in the remaining four plots.

He glanced at his watch. "Well, if you'll excuse me, I'd better get back to work or I'm not going to finish tonight. Take your time; you can stay as long as you like."

"Thanks. I appreciate your help."

After he walked away, I stood looking at Fae's grave. I wished I could have just one minute of conversation with her. I felt there was a tie between her past and the grave-decimation crimes that had occurred over the past five years. Though I willed her to communicate with me, of course, it didn't happen.

It was after 4:30, and I needed to go home to get ready for my date.

As I turned to walk back toward my car, a voice as clear as could be said, "Take the flower."

I looked around, but didn't see anyone in the cemetery except for the caretaker picking up trash near the entrance. *Get a grip, Allie.* I took a couple of steps, then again heard the voice say, "Take it."

Okay, this was getting too weird! I glanced back at Fae's grave. Was she trying to tell me something? I looked at the lone, red flower sitting there. The caretaker had said he would be throwing it away when mowing time came. I hesitated for a moment, then reached inside the pocket of my slacks and pulled out a tissue. I knelt down and wrapped the tissue around the flower, then pulled it from the dirt. Holding it up, I could see nothing unusual about it. But still I felt compelled to take it with me. I stood up and stuck it inside the pocket of my slacks.

"Stealing flowers from graves now, Allie?" said a different voice inside my head.

"Hey, I'm just doing what I was told," I said out loud to the accusing voice. With my head held high, I turned around and headed toward my car.

Along the way, I came upon a large, granite monument with a Hawaiian family crest attached to the front of it. The diameter of the emblem was about three feet in length. An ancient warrior wearing a feather headdress and holding a spear at his side stood in the center of it. Intricate scrolls on the crest were inlaid with polished brass. Though the metal had tarnished a bit over the years, the object as a whole was still impressive. I did a double take when I saw the name below it. The monument was marking Alhoi Akau's grave. Though it had been two years since the grave had been disturbed and the jewelry stolen, a few patches of bare earth still remained. Unlike the graves all around it, there were no flowers on it.

With a bulging trash bag thrown over his shoulder, I saw the groundskeeper walking toward me. "That plot must be cursed," he said as he drew near to me. "Somebody keeps destroying or stealing anything placed on it. On the day after Memorial Day, I found the wreath on her grave shredded to pieces."

"I assume no one reported seeing anyone do it?"

He shook his head. "Another phantom, I guess."

Guilt was weighing on me. I pulled the plastic hibiscus from my pocket. "Since you said you would be throwing this away in a few days, do you mind if I take it? I'm trying to write a story on the grave disturbances and somehow I feel like this flower may be connected."

"Sure, you're welcome to it. It wouldn't surprise me to see a replacement on the plot when I get here in the morning, though." He scratched his head. "So you're a reporter, huh? I took you to be a schoolteacher."

"Actually, I am a schoolteacher slash reporter."

He motioned toward Alhoi Akau's grave. "My intuition tells me that whoever is destroying or stealing the flowers from this grave hates its occupant. Pure rage ripped that wreath apart the other day."

His revelation was disturbing. I couldn't help wondering if the "phantom" was also the jewel thief.

"Well, I need to go," I said. "You've been very helpful, and I enjoyed visiting with you today."

"My pleasure. Come back anytime."

As I drove toward Traci's, I thought about the flower I had felt the need to take. Now that I had it, I didn't know what to do with it. I hoped that the same voice that had told me to take it would give me further instructions later.

CHAPTER 15

When I reached the apartment building, I only had thirty minutes until Simon was due to arrive. Traci had left a note telling me that she had driven to the pastor's house in Kaneohe to check on his wife. At church the night before, the pastor told the congregation that she was battling bronchitis, and he had requested prayer on her behalf.

I hurried to my bedroom and stripped off my clothes. When I removed my slacks, I took the flower from the pocket before tossing the pants into the basket inside my closet. I laid it on the dresser, then hurried to the bathroom. I fixed my makeup, brushed my hair and was ready to go in ten minutes flat. Before leaving the room, I picked up the blossom from the dresser and stuck it inside my purse.

I was standing outside the front door of the tower enjoying the evening breeze when I saw Simon pull into the complex. Not wanting him to waste time getting out to open the car door for me, I hurried to the passenger side when he stopped in front of the building.

"Hello, beautiful," he said when I opened the door.

"Hi, handsome." I leaned over the middle console and kissed him.

He looked at me and smiled. "I'm not complaining, but what was that for?"

"Does a girl need a reason to show some affection?" I said as I buckled my seatbelt.

"Not at all. Feel free to kiss me anytime you want to."

He did a U-turn and headed out of the complex. After turning left onto Moanalua Road, he headed east toward H-1.

I asked him if anything new had turned up in the Waikiki mugging cases. He said they got a lead from a police informant who was a regular at the Watering Hole Lounge near the park where the beatings had occurred. The man had overheard a couple of college kids laughing about bashing a guy. He gave Simon a general description of the two boys.

"Marshall and Dave went to the Student Union on the University campus today," Simon said. "They talked to several students and picked up a couple of names. The school counselor gave them the addresses of the two boys. When I left, Marshall and Dave were leaving the station to go pay them a visit."

"I hope you catch whoever is doing this before they strike again."

"Me, too."

We discussed my day at school, then I told him about my visit to the cemetery.

"I was planning to ask you about that," Simon said. "Marshall told me you called and asked for directions. Why did you go there?"

"Partly because of what was written on the sheets that Mr. Omura gave me. I did find something, though I'm not sure if it will be helpful." I pulled the tissue-wrapped flower from my purse and held it out to him. "Mr. Omura told me an interesting story about a woman who is buried there, I found her grave and took this from it."

Though he was trying to manipulate through heavy traffic, he looked at me and frowned.

"Don't worry, I received permission to take it," I said.

"The lady in the grave told you it was alright?"

I thought about that for a moment. "Well, actually, I think she did. A voice as clear as yours told me to take this flower. No one was around but the caretaker, and he was on the other side of the cemetery. But I didn't steal it. He said it was fine to take it because he would be throwing it away when he mowed anyhow."

I wasn't sure if I was trying to convince Simon, or myself that what I had done was okay. Hopefully, the end would justify the means.

"Well, if the groundskeeper needed it out of his way, then you're safe," he said. "Why do you think you were told to take the flower?"

I told him what I knew about Fae Song and how I felt that something in her past might be connected to the grave-robbing cases. Simon didn't interrupt while I bounced the details of my theory off him. By the time we pulled off H-1 onto a street called Uluniu Avenue, he seemed convinced that my theory was worth exploring. As he pulled into a parking space, he asked me to give him the flower so that he could take it to the lab for analysis. I was happy to place it in his care.

"Now that we have that settled, let's go listen to some music," he said. He reached for a folded towel that was lying in the back seat. "We'll use this to sit on when we get to the beach." He climbed out of the Jeep, then walked around to open the car door for me.

I stepped onto the sidewalk. "Uluniu," I said, reading the nearby sign. "That's an unusual name for a street."

Simon glanced at the sign. "It is unless you know the story behind it," he said, reaching for my hand. "The statue of Duke Kahanamoku was erected in the park where we're headed. He was an Olympic champion in the early 1900s. One time he was accused of being reckless when he rode thirty-foot waves on the North Shore. A guy told him, 'Duke, you loony, you. You're crazy to get out on those waves.'"

I looked at Simon and he had a solemn expression on his face.

"So they named the street Uluniu," he continued. "When I was in grade school, some of the kids called each other 'Loonies,' in honor of Duke."

"They did, huh?" I said, smiling. "Well, I'd have to be loony to believe that story." I nudged him in the ribs. "That's a tall tale if I ever heard one."

He looked at me and grinned. "But I had you going for a while, didn't I?"

When we reached the park, there were lots of people sitting on the ground, in lawn chairs and leaning against trees. We had a few minutes before the ceremony was set to begin, so we walked to the statue. Simon said that Duke Kahanamoku had won a total of six Olympic medals and was known as the Father of International Surfing.

We found a vacant spot on the beach and sat down. The crowd grew quiet when the sound of the *pu,* or Hawaiian conch shell, was blown. A handsome, bare-chested young man dressed in a ti-leaf skirt with a lei around his neck was sounding the call. He blew the conch shell two more times, then the torches were lit. Soon a troupe of dancers converged on the scene. The colors in the costumes and the energy of the dancers stirred up the excitement already running through the crowd. The backdrop of the fiery sunset made it even more magnificent.

The mood changed when a dozen hula dancers made their way onto the beach. They drew people from the audience onto the stage. Some were going willingly while others were being prodded by their companions to take the plunge.

"Don't look now, but I think you're about to be kidnapped," Simon said to me. I looked up and saw Sammy Cho walking toward us.

"Hello, Detective; Allie," he said when he reached us. He stretched his hand toward me. "It would be my pleasure to show you some hula steps."

I looked at Simon. "Go ahead," he said. "You'll have fun,"

Shrugging, I extended my hand toward Sammy. "So this is your new part-time job?"

He pulled me up from where I was sitting. "Yes, and I love it! Every night I get to meet a new batch of pretty girls and get paid to do it. You can't beat a job like that!"

"Amen, brother," I heard Simon say behind me. I turned around and gave him a dirty look. "What?" he said with an innocent expression on his face. "I meant for Sammy, not for me."

"No, of course not," I said, grinning at him. "I turned back around and looked at Sammy. "I'm ready to learn the hula. Let's go!"

He led me to the stage, and I joined a group of other people already gyrating their hips and wiggling their arms in all kinds of crazy motions. Sammy draped a grass skirt around my waist and fastened it in the back. Though I felt silly, I followed his lead and was soon swaying with the rest of them. A man close by was getting a little carried away and bumped into me. I scooted closer to the edge of the stage to give him more room.

Some of the strands of grass on my skirt got caught in the strap of one of my sandals. One minute I was dancing and laughing with Sammy on stage, and the next minute I was falling off it into the arms of another male dancer. He looked as surprised as I was.

Smiling at me, he set my feet down in the sand, then pulled the leaf headdress he was wearing off his head. He placed it onto mine, then gently kissed both of my cheeks. Though I knew the act of kissing someone after presenting him or her with a gift was a Hawaiian tradition, I felt my face heating up.

Sammy came to my rescue. "I think I'd better take you back to your date, before he starts arresting some of our performers," he said, nodding toward the dancer who had caught me. I handed the headdress back to the dancer, then followed Sammy back to where Simon was sitting.

When I was seated beside him again on the towel, Simon said, "Well, that will teach me not to push you into something like that again." He wrapped his arm around my shoulders and pulled me to him. "I pushed you right into the arms of another man."

When the ceremony was over, we headed back to the Jeep. Simon drove to a Japanese restaurant a few blocks away. Only three spaces in the large parking lot were vacant.

"This place has won several awards over the past ten years," he said as he pulled into one of them. "I hope you like it."

"I'm sure I will. Out of all the places we've been, I haven't been disappointed yet."

When we got inside, other people were waiting to be seated. Within ten minutes, the hostess led us to a table for two on the back porch overlooking the ocean. The swish of the waves lapping the shoreline was relaxing. Dusk had settled in and the lights of the various businesses along the waterfront looked like stars twinkling in the water.

Instead of ordering from the menu, we chose to go through the buffet line. With more than forty items to choose from, we both ate more than our money's worth. After enjoying the wonderful dinner, we took a drive up Highway 93 along the West Coast of the island to Waianae. Simon pulled into a small park there, and we walked along the beach for a while. It was a wonderful evening.

When we got back to the apartment, Simon said, "So tomorrow is the big field trip to Diamond Head."

"Yes, and the kids have been looking forward to it all week." I didn't elaborate, but I had been, too. "You don't have any qualms about us being around Maynard Desmond, do you?"

"Though he's still at the top of our suspect list, my gut tells me that he's not dangerous." He stroked my cheek with his forefinger, then wrapped his arms around me and softly kissed me. "It's time for you to go inside now," he said, stepping back. "You're the one who's dangerous when we're alone."

I guess it gave me a sense of power knowing how I affected him. But despite what he thought, I knew that he was really the one holding the power over me and had long ago conquered my heart.

🐾 🐾 🐾

On Friday, I couldn't have ordered a more perfect day. When I walked to the parking garage, the birds were singing and the sky was a brilliant blue. Nathan was in a joking mood, and we chatted all the way to the nursing home.

When the students and I boarded the van in front of the school, we all had smiles on our faces. It took about twenty minutes to reach the park near Diamond Head. The van driver let us out by the sidewalk leading to the exhibit location, and Maynard was there to greet us. He was wearing the same tattered straw hat that he had worn the day I met him. I noticed he was also wearing Heman gardening gloves.

"Boys and girls, I'd like you to meet Mr. Desmond," I said to them.

"Aloha, children," he said. "Welcome to my newest venture on Oahu."

"Aloha," everyone replied.

"You're the landscape artist," Annie blurted out.

He smiled at her. "That's what some people say."

I stepped toward him. "Thank you for having us today. Before I forget it, my mother sent me a list of plants used in the Garden of Eden at home." I pulled the folded sheet of paper from my purse and handed it to him.

He took it from me. "Thank you. I've already purchased what I could on the island. This will be helpful when I start ordering things from the mainland." He turned toward the students. "If you'll all follow me up the hill, I have a surprise for you."

He led us to the exhibit area, and I was amazed at the amount of progress that he had made since I had been there. The huge mound of dirt had been reduced to a small hill. Just like the one at home, he had built four separate gardens. Signs had been placed in each section designating the type of plants he wanted to use.

Maynard stopped in front of the largest plot. Three young apple trees in large pots filled with dirt were sitting beside a sign that read The Orchard. He motioned toward the plot. "Children, this is where I need your help today. I plan to include at least three different types of fruit trees in here: apple, fig and olive."

Before he could continue, Seth raised his hand. "I didn't know olives were fruits." Most of the other students murmured that it was news to them as well.

He smiled at them. "I know you probably think of fruits as being sweet, like bananas, papayas and apples. But olives are also considered to be fruits. That's why the trees will fit nicely here. Miss Kane told me that you read *The Giving Tree* in class. I've read that book, too, and it's a good one. As you can see, I have three apple trees here. I'd like to split you into small groups and would appreciate it if you would help me plant them."

Earlier I had told the students that they would get to help plant one tree. They clapped and cheered after Maynard's announcement.

His van was parked a few yards from the plot. He walked to the back of it and reached inside. He asked me to pass out pairs of gloves to each child while he passed out the tools. Rather than the adult-sized gloves he and I had used, he handed me ten pairs of cotton, kid-sized gardening gloves to give to them.

"You get to take the gloves home with you," he told the students as he passed out shovels and rakes. His statement was followed by another round of whoops and hollers from the kids.

We split the students into three groups. I followed Maynard's instructions and helped supervise one group's digging while he assisted the other two groups. The seven boys insisted on lifting and placing the trees in the holes. They adhered to Maynard's helpful directions and I was proud of them. The girls fertilized and watered the three trees. All the children helped in the anchoring process. Soon we were standing back admiring the first additions to The Orchard.

"Looks pretty good, doesn't it, Miss Kane?" Mareko said, his arms folded across his chest.

"It looks fantastic, Mareko," I said. "Everyone worked hard and it shows."

"We're not quite finished," Maynard said.

He walked back to his van and opened the passenger door. He lifted out a small sign that was attached to a two-foot-tall wooden post. As he walked by the back of the van, he picked up a wooden mallet. He carried it and the sign to the cluster of apple trees. The message on the sign said, "Planted by students from Prince Kuhio Elementary."

"Hey, that's us!" Danielle said.

"I thought it was fitting to give credit to whom credit is due," Maynard said. He drove the stake into the ground next to the group of trees.

"I think we owe Mr. Desmond a great big thank you, don't you?" I asked the students.

Amid the "thank yous" and "I sure had fun," statements, everyone either shook his hand, or gave him a hug. I could tell he was overwhelmed with the adoration from the youngsters. He brushed a tear from his eye when I announced it was time for us to leave.

Maynard and I walked together behind the group toward the van. "You made a big impression on these kids today," I told him. "The gift of the gloves and the chance to add their own touch to the project will be something they'll remember for a long time."

"They couldn't have had more fun than I did. Thank you for bringing them."

"Thank you for your time. We all enjoyed it."

As I opened the passenger door to get in, he said, "Don't be a stranger. I can always use an extra pair of hands."

I smiled and waved, then the driver pulled away. Riding back to school, the kids were quieter than they had been during the ride to the park. After all their hard work today, I figured they would probably sleep well tonight.

As I stared out the window, I thought about the way Maynard had acted with the kids. *Simon, please hurry and solve those cases,* I thought. I wanted Maynard to be cleared as soon as possible. "I just can't believe he could hurt anyone."

"Did you say something, Miss Kane?" the van driver asked. He was looking at me through the rearview mirror, and I realized I must have spoken out loud.

"Don't mind me," I said. "I was just talking to myself."

He grinned and nodded. "I do that all the time."

🐾 🐾 🐾

That afternoon, I worked at the newspaper for a couple of hours, then headed to the Honolulu Civic Center. The Royal Hawaiian Band was warming up when I arrived. The crowd was growing, so I ambled through it and picked out some people to interview. I wanted to get some feedback from both tourists and locals about the celebration festivities for my article. By the time the band had performed and the statue decoration ceremonies were concluded, I had eight pages filled in my notebook.

Mr. Masaki had let me bring one of the *Star's* cameras to use. The colorful displays and costumes, both inside and outside of the building, were a photographer's delight. I took almost fifty shots before I returned to the office.

The darkroom technician told me she would develop the film and bring the pictures to me. I thanked her, then walked upstairs to my office to start transcribing my notes.

It was nearly 6:00 when the technician brought the pictures to me. I had been so intent on my work, I almost didn't hear her knock on my door. I invited her inside, then I spread the pictures out on my credenza. She seemed pleased when I asked her opinion about the best pictures to use. We settled on six possible choices, then she left. Though I had kept her late, she told me she appreciated the opportunity to help me.

Around 7:00, I walked down to the vending machines and bought a root beer and a package of peanut butter crackers. My stomach had been growling for more than an hour and I couldn't put it off any longer. I figured I had at least another hour's worth of work to do, so I decided to appease it and have a snack.

Wanting to stretch my legs, I moseyed toward the front offices. I could hear the presses humming and knew that in a matter of hours they would be churning out Saturday's newspaper. Mr. Masaki had told me that the assistant editor would be there to okay the final draft of my story. When I walked by the man's office, I saw him talking on the telephone.

Finished with my snack, I dropped my empty pop can into the recycling bin, then walked back upstairs to finish the article. While taking the break, I had decided which picture I wanted to use. I picked up the one showing a group of students ranging in age from six to eighteen standing in a circle around the freshly decorated King Kamehameha statue. Each person had a smile on his or her face and looked happy to be there. Though wearing regal robes and made of stone, the king seemed to be just another friend in the group. It was a down-to-earth shot that I thought my boss would be happy with.

I completed the article and proofread it for mistakes. I printed off a copy and carried it downstairs to the assistant editor's office. He glanced at the wall clock when I knocked on his door.

"You made it ahead of time," he said.

"Well, you haven't checked it for errors yet. After you do, I may be lucky to make the deadline."

"From what I've seen and heard about you from our boss, I doubt if I'm going to find many errors." He motioned toward a chair in front of his desk. "Please have a seat and I'll take a look."

I watched him read through the copy and was pleased when he didn't make a single red mark on it. He scanned it one more time, then handed it back to me. "Looks great to me. It's upbeat and I like the picture you've chosen. Those kids look like they're having a terrific time, and that's what the annual celebration is supposed to be all about."

"I had a good time doing the piece," I said. "If you don't have any changes, I'll go upstairs and e-mail it to the copy desk, then head home."

"Send it on its way, and have a nice evening."

I walked back upstairs, e-mailed the story to the copy editor, then shut down my computer. After putting the remaining pictures lying on the credenza in the folder with the article, I grabbed my purse and headed home.

Traffic was heavy on H-1 and wasn't any better when I exited onto Moanalua Road. I pulled into the entrance of Traci's complex and drove past the row of eight single-story garden condominiums. I had often admired the small, manicured yards in front of the units. Grass and shrubbery extended around each end of the building and added a nice touch. Behind the condos, covered parking was provided for the tenants.

I parked in my space in the garage, then walked across the parking lot toward the tower. I noticed that someone had backed a pickup against the end unit of the condominiums instead of pulling around to the back. Though it was dark, I could see the silhouette of someone sitting inside the truck. The tailgate was almost touching the wall, and I knew that flowers and shrubs must have been crushed when the truck backed into that position.

Buddy, there's a reason they have designated parking here, I thought, shaking my head. As if he heard me, the engine roared to life and the headlights came on. The driver flipped on the brights, and even though the truck was thirty yards away, the glare was blinding.

The truck started crawling toward me. Figuring the driver would U-turn, then head out of the complex, I just shielded my eyes with my hand and continued walking toward the tower. I was shocked when the vehicle accelerated and starting racing toward me. It screeched to a halt in front of me, blocking my way to the front door. The driver rolled down his window.

Frightened from the erratic way the truck had come barreling toward me, my heart was beating double time. It didn't help when I saw who was driving it, Ronald Nowicki was sitting behind the wheel.

"Good evening, Allie," he said. "I didn't scare you, did I? From the smirk on his face, I figured that was what he had hoped to do.

I didn't say a word; I just stared at him. He stared back at me and several seconds passed without either one of us looking away. I was reminded of the game I had played as a kid with my cousins. We'd stare at each other to see who could keep from blinking the longest. No matter who I was up against, I always won.

I saw Ronald's eyes start to water. He licked his lips, then pulled his gaze from me and started rubbing his eyes.

"What do you want, Ronald?"

"I was driving by and didn't see your car in the parking garage. I thought I'd try to catch you when you got home and ask you about Nathan's ring."

He was driving through the garage checking up on me? I didn't like the sound of that. I made a mental note to be sure that the complex security office knew about it.

"I thought we had that settled," I said. "Didn't I tell you that I would return it before I go home at the end of the month?"

"I've been away for a couple of days, and I thought that after our talk the other night, you might have changed your mind."

Even though I had considered it, his hounding was getting old. I was holding my purse against the side of my leg. The hula girl was tucked inside it. I might save myself some grief to just return the ring to him and be done with it. But on the other hand, I knew that Nathan would be upset if I did, and I wasn't going to do that to him.

I didn't say anything, and I guess Ronald got the message. "Well, okay." He paused as if to give me a second chance to come up with it. "I'll see you later. Have a nice weekend, you hear?"

"I plan to," I said.

He shifted into reverse, then backed up and turned around. I didn't move from my spot until the truck had reached the exit.

I was emotionally drained when I reached the apartment. Traci and Tommy were watching a movie on television and didn't seem to notice. I plopped down on the sofa and tried watching it, too, but my mind kept drifting back to my encounter with Ronald. In the middle of a McDonald's commercial, I fell asleep. Around midnight I woke up and the room was dark. I was covered with an afghan that Traci's grandmother had crocheted years before.

I dragged myself to the bathroom to wash my face and brush my teeth. Like a zombie, I trudged to my bedroom and pulled off my clothes. I was asleep by the time my head hit the pillow.

CHAPTER 16

I woke up bright and early on Saturday morning. Traci, Tommy, Simon and I were going together to the King Kamehameha Celebration Floral Parade that started at 9:30 a.m. in Honolulu. I could hear Traci in the kitchen, and the shower running across the hall. I figured if I didn't want to keep everyone waiting, I'd better get a move on.

I was showered, dressed and had my hair done when Simon arrived at 8:00. I pitched in to help fix some toast while Traci set a variety of jams on the table. Simon poured everyone some orange juice, and in no time, we were all seated at the table eating breakfast. When we were finished, we stacked the dishes in the sink, then headed downstairs to Simon's Jeep.

On the way to the parade, I asked Simon about Kelly and Abbie.

"Marshall told me that when he was at the airport yesterday, he saw Kelly working. He said he was wearing a sling, but it didn't seem to be hindering him. When he talked to him, he said Kelly was as chipper as he always is. I imagine part of his good mood had to do with the fact that he was supposed to go pick up Abbie at the vet's office yesterday evening. He told Marshall she's recovering nicely from the chest wound and will be able to come back to work with him by the end of next week."

"Thank the Lord for that," Traci said.

"Isn't that the truth," Tommy said.

When we arrived at the Ala Moana Center, Simon pulled into the parking lot on the lower level. We circled around and found that most of the spaces were already filled. However, he managed to find a vacant one on the southeast corner of the lot.

"The parade will begin at King and Richards Streets, then travel down Ala Moana Boulevard," he said. "It will end at the Queen Kapiolani Park. I figured we could watch the biggest part of it from a spot down the street, then walk to the park for the awards ceremony."

"Let's go," Tommy said, taking hold of Traci's hand. Simon reached for mine, and we were off.

There were bands from many different states marching in the parade. Colorful floats covered in flowers, seeds and other natural things lined the street. A group of cowboys riding beautiful thoroughbred horses rode past us. Though I was used to seeing riders in parades in Oklahoma, I was surprised to see them here. I mentioned it to Simon.

"Cattle were brought to Hawaii in the 1700s," he said. "King Kamehameha issued a royal ban preventing the locals from capturing them. They were free to roam and reproduce until about 1830. Around that time, the Spanish and Portuguese vaqueros, or cowboys, were brought to the Islands to teach the natives how to round up the wild cattle. The king referred to them as *paniolos*, which means 'cowboy' in Spanish."

"I imagine the *paniolos* were a godsend trying to corral cattle on Maui," I said, thinking about the enormous ranch that we had seen as we drove to the top of Haleakala.

"No doubt about it," he said.

After watching the parade and the awards ceremony, we walked back toward the Ala Moana Center. Along the way, we talked about what we had enjoyed most about the two events.

"The floats were beautiful," Traci said. "I think they get better every year."

"They were nice," Tommy said, "but I don't think you can beat the two that Oklahoma had in the New Year's Day Tournament of Roses Parade this year. Even though we only got to watch it on TV, they were spectacular!"

"Yes, they were both gorgeous," I said. "The enormous Indian head-dress and the revolving birthday cake were my favorite things on them. But don't tell Dad—considering the family business, he would expect me to like the oil well that was on the Unique History float the best. Did you know that the retired state senator who lives near Paradise rode on it?"

"No kidding," Tommy said. "The television announcers mentioned a few Oklahoma celebrities, and I saw the governor and his family riding on one, but I didn't see the senator. How cool!"

"All the townsfolk were sure proud that he represented our little section of the state," I said. "He and Grandpa A.J. have been friends for years, even if they don't always see eye to eye on politics."

"This year is a special year for Oklahoma, isn't it?" Simon asked. We had reached the Ala Moana Center and were starting to look for a place to eat lunch.

"One hundred years ago Oklahoma became a state," Traci said. "Mom and Dad have been keeping us informed about different celebrations that are supposed to take place in northeastern Oklahoma this year. Since Tommy's folks live in Lawton, they let us know about things going on in that part of the state." She gave a little sigh. "Even though Tommy and I are happy living here in Hawaii, we'll always be Okies at heart."

"The Punahou High School marching band and color guard from Honolulu was in that parade, too," Simon said. "They had more than 240 members involved."

I looked at him and frowned. "I wouldn't have taken you for a man who watched parades on television. New Year's Day football games yes; parades no."

He grinned at me. "You have me pegged pretty well. I don't usually watch them, but Marshall has a nephew who plays saxophone in the band, and he strong-armed some of us who were working that day into watching it with him."

We decided on a sandwich place in the Center's food court for lunch. "Have you had any luck finding Ray Franklin's other relative yet?" I asked Simon after I swallowed a big bite of my fish fillet sandwich.

"That guy is like the wind," he replied. He wiped his mouth with his napkin. "We weren't having any luck catching up with him, so on Wednesday afternoon, Eddie checked all the major airlines to see if he might have left the Islands. None of them had a record of him booking a flight. So then he called both Aloha and Hawaiian Airlines, thinking the guy might have flown to another island. His name didn't appear on any of their manifests."

"Maybe he used a different name."

"Possibly, or he may still be tooling around Oahu laying low. We went to his house, which is in Aiea by the way, and talked with his brother. But he didn't know where he was, or when he would be back. Eddie and I staked out the house off and on, but the guy never showed." He wadded his ham sandwich wrapper into a ball and tossed it into a nearby trash can.

"He might be hanging with friends," Tommy said. He glanced down at Traci's half-eaten chilidog. "Are you finished with that coney, babe?"

She pushed it toward him. "It's all yours; the salad I ate first filled me up." With a smile on his face, Tommy popped the chilidog into his mouth.

"The guy could be staying with a girlfriend," Simon continued. "His brother told us that he dates a lot, but didn't know any of the girl's names. We don't have the manpower to have an officer watching the house around the clock, but a cruiser is driving by several times a day to try to catch him if he comes home."

After lunch, the four of us decided we wanted to go to the beach. We picked up three six-packs of pop and a cheap, Styrofoam ice chest before we left the mall. Simon said he had a bag of ice in his freezer just waiting for a party. He drove us back to the apartment to change into our swim gear, then we went to his house for him to change clothes. I had never been to his place, so I snooped around in the kitchen while he was in the bedroom.

"For a bachelor, he sure keeps a tidy house," Traci said, surveying the living room. "Before we got married, Tommy's apartment was a pig sty. While we were dating, his mother was always after me to clean it when I was over there. But, hey, I was still living at home at the time, and my mom rode me to keep my own room clean and neat. It didn't matter to me how Tommy chose to live."

Simon walked into the room and caught me looking inside his refrigerator. "I hope you're not hungry, because it's pretty bare in there," he said to me. I slammed the door and caught the sleeve of the cover-up I was wearing in it. Tugging it free, I turned around to face him.

"I was looking for the bag of ice," I said.

He walked over and opened the freezer door. "I keep it up here where it will stay frozen," he said, grinning at me.

"Okay, so I was snooping around to see how you live when you're not with me."

"Not very well," he said, reaching for my hand.

"Hey, you two are wasting valuable sunlight here," Tommy said, heading toward the door. "Grab that bag of ice and let's go hit the beach."

We followed him out the door to the Jeep. Simon passed the ice to Tommy, and he pounded the bag on the pavement. When the pieces were loose, he tore open the bag and emptied it into the ice chest. Simon pulled the cans of pop from the plastic webbing that held them together, then pushed them into the bed of ice. After everyone was settled in the car, Simon drove us to the same beach that he and I had gone to when I had visited the island back in March.

We walked along the water's edge and listened to Simon tell about his family's excursions there while he was growing up. Though I had heard some of the stories, I enjoyed hearing them again. When he mentioned that his sister, Amanda, had had her marriage ceremony on this beach, Traci asked him all kinds of questions about it.

All afternoon we swam, walked the beach, drank pop, and laughed. Traci had to put on her straw hat and sunscreen to keep from burning, but she made it fine. We all had a terrific time. When we had had enough, we headed back to Aiea. While Traci, Tommy and I showered and changed clothes, Simon went home to do the same. He was going to rejoin us around 6:00. We had decided to spend the evening at Traci's instead of going out.

While I was showering, I noticed that my throat was a bit scratchy. Blaming it on the talking and laughing I had done that day, I ignored it. I blow-dried my hair and put on makeup. My eyes kept watering, and I had trouble putting on mascara. I assumed the excess tears were due to the earlier exposure to the salty air. Though Simon had seen me in all my rough glory at the beach, I wanted to look pretty tonight. I dressed in a royal blue weskit top that had classy gold buttons on each shoulder. The skirt had a nautical pattern embroidered on it in the same rich, blue color. In the past, people had told me that when I wore blue, it enhanced my eyes. My mission in choosing this particular outfit was to try to sweep Simon off his feet.

He arrived downstairs at 6:00 on the dot. When I let him into the apartment, he was carrying the ice chest. On the top of the lid was a sack from a submarine sandwich shop located in Pearlridge Center.

"I thought we might as well drink the rest of this cold pop tonight," he said. He set the ice chest down on the kitchen counter, then lifted off the bag of food. "I didn't want you and Traci to have to cook and clean up, so I stopped and picked up some sandwiches."

"Bless your heart, Simon," Traci said as she walked into the living room. "I didn't feel like eating out, but I knew there weren't many cold cuts in the fridge. You saved the day again as usual." She reached up and patted his cheek.

"Glad to be of service, madam," he said.

Traci pulled some paper plates and napkins from the pantry. "You know, since you're often bringing food for us, after Allie goes home you're going to have to keep it up." She stopped in the middle of what she was doing. "Good going, Traci," she murmured to herself. "Open mouth; insert foot."

Simon didn't comment. He walked over and put his arms around me. "Traci, I don't want to think about Allie going home."

A lump formed in my throat and I couldn't swallow. I leaned against him.

Traci set the plates and napkins on the counter. "That was a stupid thing to bring up," she said. "I don't want Allie to go home, either. I want her around to see my baby every day." She walked over and put her arms around my waist.

When Tommy walked in, he stopped short at the doorway. "What did I miss? You all look like you just lost your last friend."

Traci dabbed her eyes and picked up the things she had set on the counter. "No, I just opened my big mouth and brought up a very unpleasant subject."

"Don't worry about it Traci," I said. I lifted my hands in the air and started sashaying around the kitchen. "Now, it's time to get this party started!" I bumped my hip against hers, then strutted over to Simon and bumped his. Everyone started laughing.

We had a great evening together. When I walked Simon to the elevator, I was tired, but happy.

"I had loads of fun today," he said to me.

"Me, too. Let's do it again sometime."

"How about tomorrow?" he said, draping his arms over my shoulders.

"Tomorrow is good for me."

"I'll meet you at church, then we can all go somewhere." He glanced down at my clothes. "I don't think I told you how beautiful you look tonight."

Yes! The outfit had worked! "While we were on the lanai and you were fiddling with my hair you said I looked scrumptious. I took that as a compliment."

He smiled at me. "I intended it to be." He lowered his head and kissed me. I heard someone close by clear her throat. Simon stepped back, and we both looked over and saw Traci's next door neighbor standing there with a frown on her face.

Simon looked back at me. "I guess I'd better go." He gave me one more quick peck on the lips.

The elevator doors opened and Simon motioned for the woman to enter the car before him. She didn't say anything, but the disapproving look on her face hadn't changed when she turned around to face me. I waved at Simon as the doors started closing, then I turned and walked back to the apartment.

"Your neighbor thinks I'm a hussy," I told Traci when I walked into the living room. "She didn't appreciate seeing Simon kissing me in the hallway."

"It's probably because she was jealous that it wasn't her he was kissing," Traci said. "The old busy body. Evelyn Hunter complains more and tries to stir up more trouble in this building than anyone else. I try to avoid her whenever I can."

"I rode up in the elevator with her the other evening," I said. "I smiled and said hello to her, but she didn't respond. Even so, if I see her again, I'll tell her I'm sorry if we offended her tonight."

"Allie, I have to hand it to you. You practice the good lessons that you've been taught. You never want to offend or impose on anyone. I'm still practicing."

After she said that, I remembered that I hadn't asked her if the dachshunds could come to stay with me. "Speaking of imposing, Doug is having a hard time with the puppies. I hate to ask you this, but would you mind if they came over with Aunt Edith and spent the remaining two weeks here? They're potty trained now and since they've had the obedience lessons, they don't chew on anything they're not supposed to."

Traci started smiling. "Of course I don't mind. We had a dog until she died about a year ago. Precious and Rowdy are welcome to come and stay with you."

One more obstacle had been overcome. "Thanks, Traci. I appreciate it. Some of the family will be having dinner at the Circle K tomorrow after church. If Doug is there when I call, I'll let him know the good news. I know he'll be relieved."

"Well, Tommy has already hit the hay, so I'm going to join him," she said. "Are you feeling okay? Your cheeks are pretty red."

I had had a headache for the last hour. "It's probably from all the sun today, but I'm not feeling the greatest. I'm ready for bed, too."

"Well, sleep tight and I'll see you in the morning," Traci said, turning toward the hallway.

"You too."

🐾   🐾   🐾

On Sunday morning, I woke up with a sore throat and my nose was running. I took a hot shower and it helped ease my aching muscles. *You haven't got time to be sick, Allie,* I thought as I toweled off. Before doing my hair, I took some ibuprofen that I found in the medicine cabinet. By the time I was dressed, it was starting to take effect.

Traci was in the kitchen banging pots and pans when I walked in. "Good morning. Are you feeling better?" she asked.

"A little, I think. I slept well, and I just took a pain reliever that I found in the bathroom."

"That's good. There are some cold tablets in there, too, if you want some later."

"I'll keep it in mind. I'm hoping I'll continue to mend after eating some breakfast."

"I'm going to fry some sausage, if you want to stick some buttermilk biscuits from the freezer into the oven."

"That sounds good," I said. "By any chance are you going to make gravy?" I gave her a charming smile.

She grinned at me. "You bet. Tommy asked me the same thing awhile ago. What are biscuits without gravy? Grandma taught me that."

When we were growing up, Traci and I had spent many nights with her Grandma Ruthie. The crash of pots and pans and the smell of frying bacon would always awaken us the following morning.

"You can take the girl out of Oklahoma, but you can't take Oklahoma out of the girl," I said as I walked over to the refrigerator.

"Preach it, sister," she said, laughing.

I put eight frozen biscuits onto a cookie sheet. Cocking my head to one side, I reconsidered the amount and added a couple more. Traci had already turned on the oven, so it was at the right temperature when I set the tray inside it.

A pitcher of fresh guava juice was sitting on the counter, so I poured each of us a big glassful. I knew the extra vitamin C would be good for me, and it might keep Traci and Tommy from catching my cold. I set the glasses on the table, then walked back to the kitchen for the plates, silverware and napkins.

Tommy had been sitting on the lanai reading the *Hawaiian Star*. He walked back inside while I was setting the table. "You did a fine job on your King Kamehameha story, Miss Reporter," he said to me. "I like the picture, too."

"Thanks. I may take up photography in my spare time."

"What spare time?" Traci asked. She carried a bowl of gravy and plateful of sausage patties into the room and set them on the table.

"My schedule has been a bit tight, hasn't it?"

"That's an understatement," Traci said.

I looked at the food on the table. "I'm sure after this yummy meal, I'll be fit as a fiddle."

"Well, let's get some food into you, then," she said. "You two sit down, and I'll bring in the hot biscuits."

When she set the cookie sheet down on the table, I noticed that two more biscuits had been added to the tray sometime after I left the kitchen. I mentioned it to her, and she said she didn't see any reason to leave only two in the package taking up freezer space. After Tommy said grace, we all dug in. None of the food was left by the time we were done.

We all rushed to finish getting ready for church. While I was trying to brush my teeth, I kept sneezing. By the time I was done, specks of toothpaste were all over the mirror. After I cleaned them off, I took a couple of the cold pills that Traci had offered earlier, just to be safe.

By 9:15, we were on the road headed toward Kaneohe. No one said much during the thirty-minute ride over. I had stopped sneezing and sniffling by the time we arrived at church.

Simon was standing in the parking lot waiting for us. After we exchanged greetings, he and Tommy headed for the young adult's class. I followed Traci to her Sunday school class, and I couldn't help wondering how Kristin had made out with my group back in Paradise that morning. It was mid-afternoon there now, and I knew she was probably jamming with my cousins at Nana's house.

Sunday afternoon jam sessions are the norm when we have dinner at Nana and Grandpa's house. On one end of the second story, there is a huge music room containing Nana's baby grand piano, a full set of drums and a Hammond organ. A variety of wind, string and brass instruments are also there. Since Nana and Gramma grew up playing instruments, they were determined that their children and grandchildren would have the same opportunity. At one time or another, we all took piano lessons from them.

A few of my cousins chose to switch from the keyboard to trumpets, clarinets, flutes, or violins. Kristin and I, along with a few others, stuck with the piano and organ. Some of the boys took drum and guitar lessons. We all participated in school and church choirs and won our fair share of awards at contests.

After Sunday school was over, Traci and I joined Tommy and Simon in the small sanctuary. The pastor preached a sermon about vengeance belonging to the Lord. He reminded us that even though the flesh desires to "get back" at people who do us wrong, we need to give the hurtful situations to God and let Him handle them. Looking down at Simon's hand wrapped around mine, my mind drifted to the cases that had been plaguing him. No doubt the perpetrator of those crimes was seeking revenge.

I must have dozed off, because I was jolted back to the present when I felt Simon tugging on my arm. He was standing up, along with everyone else in the church. The final song, "Lord, I'm Coming Home," was being sung. Embarrassed, I stood up beside him.

"You were a million miles away," Simon whispered to me.

"Sorry about that," I whispered back. "I guess the cold tablets I took made me drowsy." We focused our attention back on the service, and soon it was time to leave.

When we stopped for lunch, I was still feeling a bit tipsy from the medication, and didn't have much appetite. The others raved about how delicious everything tasted, but my stuffy nose made the food taste odd.

We discussed going to a movie, but decided on taking a drive around the North Shore instead. As we walked to the car, Simon suggested that we take his Jeep. He said he would bring Tommy and Traci back to pick up their car later.

As we drove up the coast, Tommy and Simon discussed golfing strategies. We crossed a bridge that spanned a stream near Waiahole. There was a quiet cove beyond the bridge with hardly any people there. Traci said she wished we had brought our swimsuits. The top was off the Jeep and the cool salt air felt good blowing in my face. Both the ibuprofen and the cold medication had worn off, and my body was aching again. Still several miles from the North Shore, I started sneezing. I had used up all the tissues I had in my purse. Simon came to my rescue when he pulled a small package of them from the glove compartment.

He looked at me and frowned. "I wish we hadn't come this far. I can tell you're miserable. You need to be at home getting some rest." He pulled off the side of the road and turned around.

I tried to protest, but the need to sneeze again overtook me, and I couldn't get any words out.

From the back seat, Traci leaned forward and put her hand on my forehead. "Allie, you're burning up! Why didn't you tell us you were so sick? We could have driven here another time when you could enjoy it, too."

I wiped my raw nose with a wet tissue. "But there might not be another time. You and Tommy are flying to Oklahoma on Thursday, and we all have to work every day until then. I thought I'd be okay once we were on the road. And besides, I didn't want to keep you guys from enjoying your Sunday afternoon."

Simon reached across the console. He took hold of my hand still holding the soggy tissue. "That's one of the things I love about you; you're always thinking of others. But now, I want you to lean back and relax until I get you home."

I wanted to protest, but I just didn't have the strength to do it. I laid my head against the headrest and was asleep before we reached the bridge.

"Allie, you're home," I heard someone say.

I opened my eyes and saw Simon's face above me. I stretched, then straightened up in the car seat. "That was quick. You must have flown to get us here so fast."

He smiled at me. "You've been asleep for an hour. You didn't budge when I dropped Tommy and Traci back at their car, or when the two fire trucks passed us on H-3 with their sirens blaring."

He climbed out of the car, then walked around to open my door for me.

"I'm sorry I ruined your day," I said as I stepped out.

"You didn't ruin my day, silly girl. Just being with you is nice. I don't have to be entertained, too."

As we walked toward the building, Tommy and Traci drove by us. Tommy tooted his horn and waved. Simon and I reached the front door and stood waiting for them. I was feeling lightheaded, so I leaned against the door for support.

"Would you like to come up for a while?" I asked him.

"No. You need to go to bed."

Traci and Tommy had reached the building. "I'll fill her up with juice and cold medicine, then make sure she takes it easy," Traci said.

"Do you have any plans for the rest of the afternoon?" Tommy asked Simon as he unlocked the door.

He shrugged and said, "Not really. What did you have in mind?"

"How about a game of golf? I'd like to try out some of the pointers you told me about earlier." He looked at Traci. "You don't mind, do you, hon?"

"Of course not. You guys go ahead and chase that little white ball around the pasture this afternoon if you want to. Allie and I will be fine."

Tommy opened the door, then turned to Simon. "I'll run upstairs and get my clubs and shoes. Do you want to go pick up your stuff and meet me at the course across the highway?"

"I'll see you there," Simon said. He turned to me and kissed my forehead. "I'll check on you later."

"Okay. Good luck with your game."

"Hey, no fair," Tommy said as he followed Traci and me into the foyer. "That guy is hard enough to beat without you wishing more good luck on him."

When we got upstairs, I headed to my bedroom. By the time I had my church dress off and had put on some shorts and a T-shirt, Traci was poking pills and juice down me.

"I'll check on you pretty soon," she told me as she shut the shades on the window. "Holler if you need anything."

"Thanks, I will. After a little nap I'll probably be fine." I was nestled under the covers and asleep by the time she left the room.

🐾 🐾 🐾

It was dark in my bedroom when I awoke. I looked at the clock and it read 7:30. I looked toward the window and tried to figure out if it was morning or evening. With the shades drawn, I couldn't tell.

I sat up in bed and pushed back the covers. I walked to the window and pulled open the shades. When I saw the cars on H-1 with their lights on, I remembered that it was Sunday and why I was in bed at this time of the day.

I walked into the bathroom and splashed some cold water on my face. My hair looked like a rat's nest, so I brushed out all the tangles. Looking and feeling better, I walked into the living room and saw Tommy sitting in his recliner watching television. Traci was in the kitchen.

Tommy looked away from the screen toward me. "Hey. Are you feeling better?"

"I think so. I'll know after I've been up awhile."

"Hey, sleepyhead," Traci said, walking into the room. "I kept some supper warm in the oven for you, when you feel like eating."

I sat down on the sofa. "I'm hungry now. Can I help you fix it?"

"No, you just sit where you are and I'll bring your plate to you. You do still like meatloaf, don't you?"

"You bet. It smells wonderful."

"It was," Tommy said as Traci turned around and walked back into the kitchen. "I ate three helpings. I was as full as a tick when we finished eating, but now I'm considering having a meatloaf sandwich so you won't have to eat alone."

"No you aren't, Tommy Morris," Traci said. She had put my plate of food, drink and utensils on a TV tray and was walking toward me with it. "I need the rest of that meatloaf for your lunch sandwiches tomorrow.

You can have another piece of chocolate cake if you feel like you need to eat with Allie."

"You talked me into it," Tommy said. "Would you please put a scoop of ice cream on the side, too?"

Traci set the tray down in front of me. She turned to look at Tommy and put her hands on her hips. "The last time I checked, your legs weren't broken."

Tommy had a sheepish look on his face. He smiled at her. "Yes, but pumpkin, you do it so much better than I can. Please?" He stretched out his arm and wiggled his finger in a "come here" motion.

She walked over to him. He took hold of her hand and pulled her toward him. She leaned down, and he kissed her. Raising back up, she said, "Okay, big boy. I'll get it for you."

As she turned to walk back to the kitchen, Tommy said, "On second thought, you might make it two scoops of ice cream. I wouldn't want my stomach growling later in bed; it might wake you up."

"I'll think about it," Traci said. She winked at me when she walked past.

While Tommy and I were eating, Traci told me that my mother had called to check on me. I had intended to call the Circle K before we left for church that morning. In the rush to get ready, I had forgotten to do it.

"Your mom said that Riley told her to be sure and let you know that she hit a grand slam in her T-ball game on Saturday morning. She said she was there watching the game and when it happened, the crowd went wild. The Champions were behind seven to four, but when Riley hit her home run, they ended up winning."

"She'll be on Cloud Nine all week long," I said. "I hope her daddy took her somewhere to celebrate."

"Your mom said that Michael treated the whole team to lunch at Poncho's Pizza Palace afterwards. Later, Kristin took her, Brittany and Joey roller skating. It sounded like they had a fun day."

"Yes, it does. It's too bad I couldn't be in two places at once. I want to be here, but I also hate missing the kids' games."

Simon called later to see how I was feeling. He told me that after his golf game with Tommy, he had driven to the house of Maynard's elusive relative and staked out the place for several hours. While he was there, he had called Eddie and asked if he could come back to Oahu on Monday. Eddie told him he had already made his reservation and would be there by 8:oo a.m.

I watched television with Traci and Tommy, then turned in when the news came on.

CHAPTER 17

I woke up before my alarm sounded the next morning. When I got out of bed, I felt better than I had the day before. The sniffles were gone and my head wasn't hurting. I walked to the bathroom and took a hot shower. After I was dressed, I stuck some cold and ibuprofen tablets into my purse. I wanted to be prepared in case I needed them while I was away.

Tommy had already left for work and Traci was still asleep. I decided I was in the mood for a glass of chocolate milk, but after searching the cabinets, I discovered that there wasn't any chocolate syrup or Nesquik anywhere. I settled on a plain glass of milk and a piece of leftover chocolate cake. By 7:15, I was heading to the elevator.

When I stepped outside the building, there was a heavy drizzle coming down. I hadn't brought my umbrella, so I hurried to the parking garage. After taking the hula girl from my purse and putting her back on the radio knob, I pulled out of my parking place and headed toward the exit.

Nathan was waiting in his usual spot when I arrived. "Good morning," he said as he climbed inside the car. "It's like soup out there this morning." Water was beading up on his hair, and his shirt was damp.

"Not like the pretty, sunny day we had yesterday," I said. "How was your weekend?"

"It was okay, but I've had better." He reached for the hula dancer. "I'm glad to see that our little lady is still riding with us. No matter what, I want you to keep this ring until you have to go back home."

I glanced over at him. "Nathan, I don't want to cause any friction between you and your brother. Even though we agreed that it's just a loan, I think his feelings are hurt that you aren't wearing his gift. We've both enjoyed looking at the ring every day. Why don't you go ahead and start wearing it again?"

"No way, Allie!" Having only seen a gentle side of Nathan, his angry response surprised me. "I may not be the quickest guy in the world, but I can still make my own decisions!" He placed the dancer back on the knob. "Ronald comes and goes as he pleases and does anything he feels like doing without asking me. He may have given me that ring, but he's stingy with other things. He won't even let me see the rainbow that he carries around in his pocket."

I gave him an odd look. "A rainbow?"

"Yeah, about a week ago I woke up in the middle of the night and saw the kitchen light on. I walked in there and saw a rainbow dancing on the ceiling." He looked out the side window of the car. "Ronald was sitting at the table with his back to me. When he heard me, he stuck something into his pocket and the rainbow disappeared. I asked him about it, but he just yelled at me to get back to bed." Nathan had a sullen expression on his face as he stared out the window.

What could have caused the rainbow on the ceiling? While we rode along in silence, I puzzled over it.

Before long, Nathan was back to his jovial self. He talked about the gardening work he had been doing at the nursing home. When I stopped in front of it to let him out, I could see a big difference. I praised him for his efforts, and he was beaming when he climbed out of the car.

When I reached the school, I put the hula dancer back into my purse, then walked inside. The first hour of the day was productive, but then the students became more rowdy than usual. I hadn't checked out more books from the school library for them, so I let them choose something from Traci's bookshelf to read.

When they were done with their books, I decided to give them some free time. The three girls wanted to listen to stories at the listening center. I let them choose from several different sets of books with tapes that I found in one of the cabinets. Four of the boys chose to work together to create a mural about the King Kamehameha events they had seen on Saturday. The other three boys wanted to act out a play they had found in a book on Traci's shelf. I moved the activity table against the wall to give them some extra space and asked them not to get too loud while they practiced.

With the children busy doing their own activities, I sat down to do the weekly lesson plans. By the time the noon bell rang, my head had begun to hurt again and my nose was running. After the students left, I pulled the cold pills from my purse, then walked down the hall to the water fountain. I took the medicine and hoped it would carry me through the rest of the afternoon. Before going back to the classroom, I walked into the library and checked out the sets of books we would need for the rest of the week.

The room was straight, so I grabbed my purse and walked to the office. I logged onto the computer and e-mailed Doug that it would be okay for him to send the puppies to me. I asked him to please check with Aunt Edith to be sure she didn't mind babysitting them once they all arrived. I told him I would shop for dog food, but to please send their toys and dishes with them. After sending the message, I logged off, then signed out and left.

When I stepped inside the *Hawaiian Star* offices, I saw Mr. Masaki standing near his office door. I walked over to him.

"Allison, your piece in Saturday's paper was terrific," he said. "Who took the picture for you?"

"I'm afraid I'm the one to blame for that," I said, smiling.

"You did a good job. The kids in the picture looked like they were enjoying themselves."

"They were great subjects. I was wondering if you have a new assignment for me?"

He stepped inside his office and motioned for me to follow. He picked up a stack of papers and thumbed through them. "So far, today has been a slow day," he said. "How is your research coming on the missing jewelry cases?"

"I got a lead last week that I'd like to check out." I paused and reached into my pocket for a tissue. I sneezed twice into it. "Excuse me. I've been battling a cold for a couple of days now. I'd like to do some research on a woman whose grave I visited the other day. The detective I've been working with on the cases is having a flower from the grave analyzed. I still don't have any results back on that yet." I dabbed at my nose with the damp tissue.

"That sounds like a good task for you then. But if you start feeling bad and want to go home, feel free. You can continue the research tomorrow."

"I appreciate your offer, but I'll try to stick it out. If I do need to leave early, I'll let you know."

I walked to my office and turned on my computer. I flipped through the materials in the case file while I waited for it to boot. As the images filled the screen, the phone rang. It was Simon. "Are you feeling better today?"

"I think I am, then the symptoms come back. Did Eddie get to Oahu alright?"

"Safe and sound. We've been reviewing the information again in the files, and we have a meeting with the captain at 3:00."

"Reviewing the file is what I'm doing, too," I said. "Have you received the report on the flower from the lab yet?"

"When I called them this morning, they promised that we'd have it sometime this afternoon."

"Will you call me when you get the results?"

"I'll try," Simon said. "It sounds like you're still stuffed up. Why don't you call it a day and go home and get some rest?"

"I want to do some work first. I'll talk to you later, okay?"

"Sure. Drink some hot chocolate when you get home. That helps me feel better when I'm sick."

After I hung up, I logged onto the Internet. Since last week's search hadn't pulled up anything on Fae Song, I decided to try a new approach. I typed in "Song Family in Hawaii." Maybe if the search engine had more to work with, I'd get some results. I was pleased when some records popped up.

A Polynesian-based genealogy site was listed. I clicked on it. Records for a person named Sak Song came up. He had had two daughters and one son. The girls were named Luna and Finna, and his son's name was Hiram. I sat and stared at the four names on the screen. Sak, Luna, Finna and Hiram. Something about those names was nagging at me. I rubbed my temples with my forefingers. *What was it?* I had heard one of those names before, but I couldn't remember when, or from whom.

There were other generations of children listed below their names. I printed out the page, then jotted down the web site information on the bottom of the sheet. I decided to try a search from the Kahuku side. Maybe I'd have better luck.

When I typed in Kawana Kahuku, I was delighted when a host of information popped up on the screen. Whoever had done the research—family members, friends, historians, or a conglomeration of them all—had provided a wealth of details. There was information about the land holdings, the mansion on the estate, the servants and their quarters, and more. Even the livestock on the estate was all listed. I was amazed at the amount of land the man had owned. It was nearly an eighth of the island of Kauai.

Tired of reading land descriptions and cattle pedigrees, I skipped to the list of relatives. Under his daughter Alhoi Akau's name, four children were listed. I spotted both Gerald Franklin's and Maynard's mother's names. There was a variety of other offspring listed as well as marriage, birth and death dates of most family members. I figured one of them was the man in the wheelchair that Simon had interviewed. All of these people had similar DNA, and I was sure that one of those still alive had to be the person who had desecrated the graves.

I started scanning the list of servant's names, but had to stop long enough to get a dry tissue. My nose was raw from rubbing it, and my eyes were watering. I was about to give in to the temptation to quit for the day and go home, when a name on the servant's list jumped out at me. Fae Song. She had served as a maid in the mansion from 1889 until 1892.

I pulled out the sheet showing the Song Family descendants. Sak Song had been born in 1892.

I printed off the Kahuku family information, then did a search for the State of Hawaii Legal Records agency. I figured that even if Sak had been illegitimate, there would be a birth certificate on file. With some luck, it might show a father's name.

After typing in Sak Song's name on the site, a "Processing information...please wait" message appeared on the screen. I drummed my fingers on the desk as the message continued to taunt me. Finally, a picture of the birth certificate popped up. The line where the father's name should be was blank.

"Shoot!" I said aloud. Though I wasn't totally surprised, I was hoping for confirmation. Just as I was about to close the file, I looked at Sak's middle name. It was Kawana. *Yes!* Even though Fae didn't list the father, she still made sure her son had his name!

I looked back at the sheet listing Sak's descendants. I focused on later generations of names. His son, Hiram, hadn't had any children, but both of Sak's daughters did. Luna had three children and Finna had one; a daughter named Lorraine.

Lorriane and Hiram. Nathan and Ronald Nowicki's mother and great-uncle!

I grabbed the phone and punched in Simon's number. It rang once, then transferred to his voicemail. He said he was in a meeting and asked the caller to please leave a message. My message would have been too long, so I didn't leave one. I shut down the computer, then grabbed my purse and the file I had been using. I stopped in Mr. Masaki's office to tell him that I had a lead on the story and that I was taking the file with me. I also told him that I wouldn't be back the rest of the day.

Rain was coming down hard when I stepped outside the building. I raised my purse above my head and held the file close to my body. I dashed across the parking lot. By the time I reached the car, both my purse and hair was dripping, but the file was dry. I tossed everything into the passenger seat, then headed toward the Nahoa Nursing Home.

Nathan got off at work at 2:00 and it was already after 3:00. My plan was to go to the personnel office and see if I could convince the director to give me his home address. If not, maybe she would at least call his house and let me talk to him.

When I was about a block away from the building, I spotted Nathan's yellow umbrella. He was crouched beneath it leaning against the side of the plexiglass shelter at the bus stop.

"Thank you, Lord," I said as I pulled up next to the curb. Nathan was looking down at the sidewalk, so I honked my horn. He looked up, and when he saw me, he smiled.

I rolled down the window and motioned to him. He walked over to the car. "How about a ride home?" I said.

"Gee, thanks!" He shook the water off his umbrella, then climbed inside the car. "At the nursing home, there was a leak in the roof in the dining room. I've been mopping up water all day. It's nice to get in out of the wet."

"So you worked some overtime, huh?"

"Yeah, the night custodian called in sick. I finally convinced my boss to ask a couple of the nurse's aides to keep an eye on the area tonight. When I left, they were griping that they didn't want to have to keep emptying the bucket catching the water, but I couldn't stay there and do it all night!"

While trying to manipulate the car through the heavy traffic, I glanced over at Nathan. "Speaking of the nursing home, when you're working on the grounds, do you use gardening gloves?"

He gave me a funny look. "Sure I do. I like those heavy Heman gloves. They hold up better than the thin, cotton ones."

Strike one. "Does Ronald use gloves on his job?"

"Yeah, but he can't keep up with anything and is always bumming a pair from me," Nathan said. "Sometimes after I've done yard work at the nursing home, I stick the gloves in my back pants pocket. I don't always remember to put them in my locker before I leave. I learned my lesson awhile back about loaning anymore gloves to Ronald, though. He lost one of them, and I never got it back."

I thought about that for a minute. *Could it have ended up at the Shady Palms Cemetery? If both men had worn the same pair of gloves, that would account for the similar type of skin cells inside the one I found. Strike two!*

"Nathan, one time you mentioned your great-uncle Hiram to me. Did you know him very well?"

"No. He moved to Minnesota when Mom was still a teenager. She talked about him once in a while, but I never met him." He was silent for a moment. "But Ronald has talked to him on the phone a few times."

Strike three! I exited onto Moanalua Road. "I know you don't live too far from the bus stop. Tell me where to turn before we reach your street."

"It's about a mile from here," Nathan said. "It's the third road on the right after you pass Pearlridge Center."

I saw the shopping center coming up on our left, so I mentally started counting the streets.

"This is it," Nathan said when we reached his road. I turned right, then we started up a steep grade. "It's that brown house with the pansies along the driveway."

When I turned into the driveway, Nathan's hard work in the yard was evident. The lush purple and yellow pansies looked well cared for. Lining the front of the house, I saw hot-pink petunias and impatiens. Small flowerbeds encircled the two trees in the yard.

Nathan started fishing in his left front pants pocket. "I can't seem to find my house key," he said. He shifted his body and started searching in the other pocket. "I guess I left it lying on my dresser."

"Will Ronald be home from work anytime soon?" I was dying to confront him with my newfound evidence. But then again, unsure of how he would react when he heard my allegations, I figured I should probably let Simon know my theory first and let him handle it. *Probably?*

Nathan frowned. "I don't know when Ronald will be home. He's been gone for a couple of days now. He called last night and said he'd be home tonight, but he didn't tell me what time."

Excruciating pain had developed behind my eyes. I was out of tissues and my nose was threatening to drip. "Why don't you come home with me? I don't want you sitting outside in the rain waiting on him." It was still coming down steadily.

He thought about it for a few seconds. "No, I'd better not. Ronald will be upset if he comes home and I'm not here."

A thought struck me. I reached into the back seat and picked up my purse. I started rummaging inside it until I found a large paper clip. I held it up in the air. "Do you want me to try to open the door for you?"

He smiled. "Do you know how to pick a lock?"

"My cousin is a detective back home. When he first joined the force, he learned all types of handy tricks. I bugged him until he taught me how to do it. I haven't tried it in years, but I think I still know how. Come on; let's go see."

Nathan was still smiling when we walked up onto the front porch. I opened the screen door and was glad to see that the lock was similar to the ones I had practiced on years earlier. I uncurled the paper clip so that it resembled a fishhook. I stuck the long wire into the lock, then placed my ear against the door close to it. I listened for the click that occurred just before the mechanism released. I tried jiggling the clip, but it wasn't working. Stepping back, I pulled out the clip, then stuck it in again. I placed my ear a little closer to the catch, and this time when I turned the wire, I heard the tumblers release.

"There you go," I said. I pulled out the paperclip and slipped it into my pants pocket.

"Man, you're something, Allie. Thanks for your help."

While I had been working on the lock, a steady stream of water had been dripping down through a hole in their porch roof onto us. Both of our shirts were soaked. I looked at Nathan. "You'd better get inside now and dry off and change your clothes."

"Wait a minute. Why don't you come inside and I'll give you a towel." Without waiting for my answer, he opened the door and walked inside.

I really wanted to go in and take a look around. If my hunch was right, Ronald was the culprit in the crimes. Then again, if he came home and caught me snooping around or drilling Nathan for more information, I'm sure it wouldn't be pretty. *Try to call Simon again,* a little voice was telling me.

Ignoring the voice, I walked into the small living room. I could hear Nathan rummaging around down the hall.

He walked into the room. "Here you go," he said, tossing me a worn, bath towel.

"Thanks." I pulled out the band holding up my ponytail, and started running the towel over my head. After I fixed my hair back into place with the band, I ran the towel across my damp shoulders.

"You know, I could really go for some hot chocolate," he said. "Ronald won't let me use the stove when he's not at home. If I find a pan for you, would you make us some?"

I knew that Traci was out of chocolate syrup, and I really wasn't in the mood to go to the grocery store. I decided to take him up on his invitation. Maybe I could ask him a few more questions in the process. "Sure, I'll fix us some. Point me toward the kitchen."

He led me to the back of the house. He reached into the cabinet next to the refrigerator and pulled out a bottle of chocolate syrup. After setting it on the counter, he reached into a large drawer by the stove and pulled out a small saucepan. "If you don't mind, I'm going to go change out of these wet clothes," he said. "I'm about to freeze to death."

"It will take a few minutes to fix this," I said. "Feel free to take a hot shower, if you want to."

He sneezed a couple of times. "I think I will. Just make yourself at home."

I opened some of the cabinet doors and looked inside. *Allie, what do you think you're doing? Stop snooping!* Though that little voice was starting to annoy me, I knew it was right. I located some coffee mugs in a cabinet next to the sink. After setting them on the counter, I walked to the refrigerator and pulled out the gallon of milk that was sitting on the top shelf. There was a jar of mustard, a bottle of ketchup and some other condiments on the second shelf. A jar of pickles, a loaf of bread and a six-pack of beer was on the bottom shelf.

I walked to the stove and poured a generous amount of milk into the pan. When I returned the jug to the refrigerator, I noticed two dark-brown glass jars sitting behind the beer. I knelt down to take a closer look. They caught my eye because I had seen similar jars in the china hutch at Gramma Winters' house. Each one was round and the tops of the tight-fitting glass lids had pretty scrolled edges on them. Gramma had once told me that back in the 1950s, many drug companies used similar glass bottles when dispensing medications. The ones in her hutch had contained vitamins.

Curiosity was getting the best of me. *Mind your own business,* the little voice was whispering to me. Ignoring the warning, I moved the six-pack aside, then reached behind it and pulled out one of the jars. I lifted it in the air so that the kitchen light shined through it. I could see the outline of the objects inside it, and they looked like little pickles standing side by side.

"Hmmm." I lifted the lid off the jar. The first thing I noticed was the nauseating smell. I recognized it from the time I had accompanied Frankie to the morgue. It was formaldehyde. I stared at the contents in the jar. Standing at attention like miniature soldiers, eight fingers were lined up inside it.

"You're holding a jar of sweet revenge," I heard a voice behind me say. I jumped. The jar slipped from my hand. *Crash!* It shattered into a jillion pieces when it hit the tile. Splinters of glass shot everywhere. The fingers laid haphazardly among the spilled liquid and shards of glass on the floor.

Both of my legs were burning. I looked down and saw chips of glass embedded in my skin. Dozens of puncture holes were oozing red. Blood from the larger wounds started dripping down each leg.

Ronald sauntered toward me. "You scattered my hard work all over the floor, Miss Kane." He stooped down and picked up one of the fingers. He stood back up and held it in front of my face. "Is that any way to treat the dead?" His voice sounded flat, and he had an empty look in his eyes.

I was speechless. I watched him kneel down and start picking up the scattered fingers. Cupping them in his hand, he seemed oblivious to the slivers of glass stuck in them that were nicking his own fingers. By the time he had picked up all of them, drops of his blood were falling to the floor. The crimson liquid dispersed when it mixed with the embalming fluid.

He walked to the counter where I had placed the mugs. One by one, he set the fingers down on it. "Oh, how I loved twisting these off Ray," he said, smiling. "Though I was the hard-working son, Gerald never claimed me. It was a pleasure taking them from that slacker half-brother of mine."

My legs were shaking, and I knew it was as much from fear as it was from the wounds. I forced myself to ignore the pain. The shower was still running, so I knew that Nathan wouldn't hear me if I screamed. It was time to figure a way out of here on my own.

"So you're the one who put the thumbs on the statue at the Sacred Resting Place Cemetery." I said.

"Yeah," he replied, looking down at the fingers lined up on the counter. "I'm sure you noticed how nice and neat these fit inside the jar, just like those little wieners in the can. But there wasn't room in the jar for the thumbs." He looked over at me. "Then I started thinking that if I put them in a public place somewhere, there was a good chance that someone might find them and report it. That would give the police something else to stew over. But even if the thumbs hadn't been found, they would have made a tasty meal for the birds."

After hearing his explanation, I knew I'd never eat Vienna sausages again. His contempt for the police must have helped fuel his sick passion.

"What about the ring you tried to sell in Los Angeles? Surely you knew it would be reported as stolen property."

"I was betting that the pawnshop dealer had a streak of greed in him. I figured he would want to get his hands on that choice piece so badly, he wouldn't call the police even if he found it on the stolen property list. It cost me a few extra bucks for the middleman, but that ring traveled through several hands before it reached that little Jamaican girl who took it into the shop. Even if the police had got hold of it, my prints weren't on it. They wouldn't have been any closer to me than they are right now, which might as well be a million miles away."

Though I'm against physical violence, right then I would have enjoyed slapping Ronald's smug face. The frustration and man-hours that he had cost Simon, Eddie and a host of other people didn't matter to him. He was just playing a game. His gloating was turning my fear into anger.

"But since I've been so careful with that ring, I blew a fuse when I found out that Nathan had given it to you."

It suddenly dawned on me. *The ring on the hula dancer!*

"Now that you're in on my little secret, let me show you something else I've kept from the cops." He reached into his back pocket and pulled out a small plastic bag. It looked like there was a white napkin inside it. When he pulled out the contents, I saw that it was tissue paper wrapped around something. He set the package down on the counter and started unwrapping it. The most beautiful necklace I had ever seen in my life fell onto the counter. Colors were bouncing off the wall behind it. It had to be "the rainbow" that Nathan had seen.

"Alhoi Akau's necklace," I said.

He looked at me and grinned. "Very good, Allie. I see you've been doing your homework. But you're wrong about the ownership. As far as I'm concerned, it should have gone to Grandma Fae."

"You think in committing all these crimes you're her vindicator?"

"Not only hers," he said, nodding his head. "I'm the avenger for all the family members who came after her. It was a pleasure taking the ring with the family crest from Kawana Kahuku. I didn't intend to take the bony finger it was on, but it popped off when I removed the ring. But that was okay—it made a nice little souvenir. It's with the others in the other brown jar in the refrigerator."

Oh, boy! I needed to sit down. But there was no time to give into a weak stomach. The evil I saw in Ronald's eyes reminded me of my predicament. I started running toward the front door.

"Oh no you don't," he yelled. He twirled around and grabbed the back of my shirt as I ran past him. With his other hand, he grabbed my ponytail. My head jerked back and tears sprang into my eyes.

He turned me around and pushed me hard against the edge of the counter. The blank stare in his eyes had been replaced by rage. My blood ran cold. I had only come this close to evil one other time. Last spring, my deranged neighbor cornered me in my own kitchen. I had been delivered from that situation. I knew it would take a miracle if I made it out this time.

Ronald grabbed my neck with both hands. "Now you know I can't let you out of here," he said. His fingernails were digging into the skin on the back of my neck. I tried to fight back, but he had my arms pinned against his legs. I tried to lift first one knee, then the other one. They were both wedged between him and the cabinet.

I couldn't breathe. My lungs were burning. It felt like my windpipe was being crushed. I thought about Simon and felt tears falling on my cheeks. *I'm not going to get to see Traci's new baby,* I thought. *Aunt Edith will arrive, and I won't be there to meet her.*

I closed my eyes and silently prayed. Our Father, Who art in heaven, hallowed be Thy name. Thy kingdom come, Thy will...

🐾 🐾 🐾

"Allie?" I heard a soft, comforting voice calling my name.

"Yes, Lord," I whispered. There should be a light. "Lord?" I was lost in a dark tunnel. My legs and arms wouldn't move. Darkness was smothering me. I started crying. "God, where are You?" I screamed.

In the black pit, I felt someone's arms cradle me. They were holding me, and I was being rocked back and forth. The touch was reassuring. My fear began melting away. *Coming home, coming home, never more to roam.*

The gentle voice spoke to me again. "Allie, I'm here; don't be afraid. Everything is going to be alright." I felt secure now. The voice was soothing.

Open wide, Thine arms of love. Lord, I'm coming home. I let myself fall deeper into the abyss. I knew that when I opened my eyes, I would be in heaven.

CHAPTER 18

"There's no way of knowing how long she may have been without oxygen," I heard a voice say. "According to the bruises on her neck, a lot of pressure was placed on her trachea. It's a miracle that it wasn't crushed. From the tests we ran, there doesn't seem to be any brain damage. But until she wakes up, we won't know for sure."

I could hear someone crying. I tried to open my eyes, but it was just too hard. It was like my eyelids were glued shut. A soft hand was holding mine and I wanted to squeeze it, but it just took too much strength.

"Allie? Allie, sweetheart? Please open your eyes."

The deep voice was coaxing, pleading. The soft hand was gone and had been replaced by a larger, stronger one. Somehow I knew that the gentle male voice was connected to this hand. I squeezed it, then tried to open my eyes.

"Come on, Allie, you can do this," another voice said. "Come on. Open your eyes!"

"Traci?" I whispered.

"She's talking!" I heard her yell. "Someone go get the doctor! Hurry! Someone go get the doctor!"

My eyelids fluttered, and I could see blurry images in front of me. I forced them open. Traci was standing there crying.

"Traci?" Man it hurt to talk. "Why are you crying?"

"Oh, Allie!" She was leaning over me and squeezing the daylights out of my arm. "I was so worried about you!"

Her teardrops were dripping on me. "You're getting me all wet," I whispered.

She started laughing, but didn't move. "Just deal with it, Miss Detective! I may drown you in our swimming pool after you get better!"

The hand holding mine started bending my fingers back and forth. "You've had me pretty worried, too, Allie."

I turned my head. Simon's legs were anchored against the side of the bed. There were tears in his eyes. I could see a shadow of whiskers on his face. I looked around the room and realized I was in the hospital. "Will someone please tell me why I'm here?" I croaked. My throat was sore and I had a yucky taste in my mouth. It felt like someone had gagged me with cotton.

Before anyone answered me, a doctor rushed into the room. He started poking and prodding me and asking me a myriad of questions. With each poke, my answers became more curt. He asked my visitors to leave, but I told him I wanted them to stay. Simon overruled me and told the doctor that the room would clear out shortly.

"Yes, you're going to be just fine," Traci said after the physician left. "You never could stand doctors jabbing you and you didn't mind letting them know it."

"I'm thankful you're awake and talking now," Simon said. "You were unconscious for almost four hours."

I reached up and rubbed my neck. "Ow! What's the matter with my neck?"

"You had a run-in with a madman," Simon said. "Thanks to Nathan Nowicki, you were rescued from him before he did any permanent damage."

I remembered being at Nathan's house fixing hot chocolate, then

Ronald coming in. It was pretty fuzzy after that. I yawned real big. "Excuse me. I don't know why I'm so sleepy."

"We're going to leave now, so you can get some food, then a good night's sleep," Simon said. He leaned over and kissed my forehead, then stroked the side of my face with his fingers. "I'll be back in the morning and we'll talk then. You saved the day again, Allie."

I didn't know what he meant by that, but I was so hungry and tired, I didn't question him about it.

After they left, a nurse brought me a light dinner. I protested when I uncovered the dishes and saw only a cup of soup, some Jello, and a carton of milk. However, after the first mouthful, I was glad for the soft meal. It was very hard to swallow.

When the nurse came to take my tray away, I asked her to help me get out of bed so I could go to the bathroom. My legs were shaky, but with her help, I managed to make it in there. While I washed my hands, I looked into the mirror and saw raw, red marks on my neck. I traced the marks with my finger, and suddenly remembered how they got there—Ronald Nowicki's hands had been wrapped around my neck. Simon said that Nathan had rescued me. As I stood there tracing the wounds, I wondered what had happened to Ronald. I'd have to be sure and ask Simon about that in the morning.

Back in bed, I laid in the darkness and listened to the strange sounds around me. I started piecing together what had happened at Nathan's house. I remembered seeing the severed fingers and the jewels, but was still foggy about the rest.

🐾 🐾 🐾

The next morning, I was ready to get out of the bed. After a soft breakfast, I showered and washed my hair. As I was finishing in the bathroom, Traci came to visit.

"Good morning," she hollered through the bathroom door. "I

brought your robe and a set of your pajamas. I also brought some other things I thought you might need."

"Thanks. You're just in time." I opened the door and stuck out my arm. "Would you please hand the pajamas to me? I'll get dressed, then be right out."

She handed the clothing to me, along with my hairbrush. I dressed and brushed my hair. When I emerged, I felt like a new woman.

"You look pretty good, all things considered," Traci said. "Has the doctor been in today?"

I climbed back into bed and covered up my legs with the sheet. "Yes, and he said I have to stay here one more night. I'm ready to leave now."

"According to Simon, you experienced quite an ordeal. It won't hurt for you to rest here another day."

Just then, Simon stuck his head in the door. "Is everyone decent?"

"Come on in," I said.

He walked in carrying my purse.

"That's a new look for you," Traci said, grinning at him. "But I like a man who isn't afraid to express himself with some added accessories."

"You're hilarious, Mrs. Morris," Simon said, shaking his head. When he reached the side of my bed, he set the purse down next to me, then leaned over and kissed me. "Marshall found your purse and your keys inside your car at the Nowicki house. He gave them to me to return to you."

"He's so sweet," I said. "When you see him, please tell him I appreciate it."

"I will. He was pretty concerned when he heard about what happened to you yesterday."

"Where is the car now?" I asked. I hoped that since it was a loaner from the school it was in a secure place.

"Dave drove it to our offices downtown. After you're released from here and feel like driving again, I'll take you down to get it," Simon said.

"How are you feeling today? You look much better than you did when I left you last night."

"Gee, thanks." I grinned up at him.

"You know what I mean."

"I feel better. But I have a load of questions to ask you, so grab a chair."

Traci was already sitting in a chair next to the bed. He dragged the other one over next to me.

"First of all, I remember enough of what happened to know why I needed to come to the hospital. But Nathan doesn't drive, so how did I get here?"

"Nathan told Eddie and me this morning that he walked into the kitchen and saw Ronald strangling you," Simon said. "He hit Ronald over the head with a kitchen chair, then called 911. Eddie and I were already headed toward their house when the call came in. The dispatcher recognized the address and called my cell to alert us of the situation."

I frowned. "Why were you and Eddie going to Nathan's house?"

"Remember when I told you that we had been staking out Maynard Desmond's other relative?" I nodded my head. "Well, Ronald Nowicki was the guy we were watching. A patrolman had driven by and seen Ronald's green pickup in the driveway. He called us, and we were on our way to pick him up." He leaned over the edge of the bed and took hold of my hand. "I wish we had arrived a lot sooner."

That makes two of us, I thought, squeezing his hand. "So you and Eddie brought me to the hospital."

"Nathan carried you from the house and was walking across his yard when we arrived. I grabbed you from him, then held you in the back seat of the cruiser while Eddie drove us here." He shook his head and grinned. "I use the word drove very loosely. Z was jumping sidewalks and nearly ran two cars off the street as he drove up Moanalua Road. Once he hit H-1, he drove 90 miles an hour all the way to the hospital."

I smiled at him. "I'll have to be sure and thank him the next time I see him."

"He hated to go back to Maui without talking to you, but he needed to get back to close the case on Gerald Franklin.

"Tell her about the song," Traci said.

"What song?" I asked.

Simon grinned at me. "In the car, you were in and out of consciousness. When I rocked you in my arms, you started singing."

"Singing? With the condition that my neck was in, I'm surprised I could even talk."

"Well, all the words weren't legible, but the melody was familiar. Remember the invitation song at the end of the service on Sunday morning?"

I smiled. "Lord, I'm Coming Home." I paused for a moment. "I remember calling out to God. I was in a dark tunnel and couldn't find my way to Him. I heard a choir singing. I guess I was remembering the song from Sunday, and it fit the situation I was in." I squeezed his hand again. "At the time, I thought I was on my way to heaven. Though I want to go there someday, I'm glad that my trip has been postponed."

"I'm thrilled it was, too," Traci said. She patted her stomach. "I'm still trying to figure out a way to keep you here past the end of June."

A nurse came into the room to check my vital signs. When she finished, she told me I needed to get up several times during the day and walk. She also said that the doctor wanted me to sit in a chair, instead of lying in bed, for at least part of the day.

"We'll walk with her right now," Simon told the nurse. "Right, Traci?"

"No time like the present," she said. She handed my robe to me. "Let's go, young lady."

We started down the hallway. Simon was on one side of me and Traci was on the other. My legs were a little stiff at first, but soon I was enjoying the exercise.

I looked at Simon. "What happened to Ronald?"

"It didn't take him long to come to after the hit on the head. The paramedics arrived and checked him out, then Dave and Marshall took him into custody."

"I guess you found Ray Franklin's fingers," I said. "Did you find the other missing ones in the fridge?"

"Marshall did. After Nathan handed you off to me, he went back inside and showed Marshall where the other jar was. Nathan told him that Ronald had warned him about looking inside the jars. After he saw the broken pieces of glass on the floor and the fingers lined up on the counter, he put two and two together."

"Poor, Nathan," I said. "He is such a wonderful person. I'm worried about what's going to happen to him."

While we walked the halls of the hospital, Simon told me that Ronald confessed to all four of the crimes. He said that he was "the keeper" of Fae Song's grave and made sure a red hibiscus was always on it. He told them that he "was due" the riches, since his great-great-grandmother had been hurt by the wealthy landowner and her descendants had been cheated out of their inheritance.

Simon said that the lab confirmed that the prints on the flower, as well as the ones inside the glove found at the Shady Palms Cemetery, belonged to Ronald. When Eddie asked him about the glove, Ronald said he had stuck both of them in his back pants pocket. He said that since he was working with minimal light digging up the grave, he didn't even notice when one dropped out beside the hedge when he left.

"Did you ask him about the water pattern we noticed on the grass?" I asked.

"Yeah, once Ronald opened up, he let it all go. According to him, it was kind of like how you described your custard sloshing out of the piecrust. He said he carried five-gallon bucketsful of water back and forth to Ray's gravesite from a small tanker truck he had leased. During some of the trips, water had sloshed out forming the checkerboard pattern."

Simon said that the police had searched the Nowicki's house and found all the missing jewelry in a box hidden in Ronald's closet. The fingers they recovered were all taken to the medical examiner's office.

"That guy is nuts," Traci said as we headed back toward my room. "Thank goodness he's locked up now." Simon and I both nodded in agreement.

After we reached my room, I sat down in one of the chairs. Traci said she needed to go to the grocery store so that there would be some food in the house when I arrived home the next day. She also had some errands to run before she and Tommy left for Oklahoma in two days.

"Thanks for coming and for bringing my things," I told her.

She hugged me. "Tommy and I will come back this evening and visit. Until then, take it easy and rest."

After she was gone, Simon told me that Ronald was an independent contractor and often worked for the State of Hawaii opening and closing graves.

"Really?" I said. "So no one would question it if he was in a cemetery at odd hours."

"Exactly," Simon said. "But we still haven't figured out how he knew which graves to target. There are lots of descendents from Kawana Kahuku buried throughout the Islands. We're not sure how he knew which ones were buried with anything worth stealing. It could just be the luck of the draw, but we think he had some insider information."

An idea occurred to me. "When I was in Pearlridge Center one evening, I saw him flirting with a group of girls. Though he didn't appeal to me, they were falling all over themselves for his attention. Maybe he has a girlfriend or two in the offices that keep the burial records. Don't they document if jewelry or other things are buried with a person?"

"Yes, they do," Simon said. "That would explain his easy access to the records." He leaned down and kissed me. "Now, I need to get to work, and you need to get some rest. Aunt Nalani said she would be by to visit you this afternoon. I called Mr. Masaki this morning and told him about your accident, and he said he would also come by. I'll be back late this evening."

I thought of something that I needed to share with him. "Before you go, would you please hand my purse to me? I need to give you something."

He looked at me oddly, but did as I asked.

I reached inside the purse and pulled out the hula doll. "This is the ring that the pawnshop dealer in L.A. saw," I said, pulling it off the dancer. Before handing it to him, I looked inside the band. It had the same family crest that I had seen on the monument marking Alhoi Akau's grave.

He took it from me. "Please don't tell me where you got this," he said. "That way you're not an accessory to anything."

"Okay, you've got a deal. I'll see you this evening."

❦ ❦ ❦

At noon, I was getting hungry and hadn't seen any sign of a lunch tray. I buzzed the nurse's station and asked about it. The person answering my call said that food was on the way down.

"Knock, knock," I heard someone say. Mr. Omura stuck his head inside the door.

"What a nice surprise!" I said when he stepped into the room.

"I heard you were in the hospital, and I know that hospital food isn't the best." He held up a white paper sack. "I brought you a tuna melt sandwich and a bottle of milk. I called to find out if you were on any kind of special diet. I was told that as long as the food wasn't too crunchy or hard, it would be fine."

"Thank you so much, Mr. Omura. That's very thoughtful of you."

He insisted that I go ahead and eat. I told him some of the events that had happened from the day before. He was shocked, but relieved that I would completely recover.

Right after he left, Miss Kahala came by to visit. She had taught my class that morning and brought me a colorful card that the students had made. Inside it, they had written their own special messages, and my heart was touched with their concern. The principal assured me that she would take care of the class until I was able to return. I told her that the doctor said I should be able to go back to work on Thursday.

Nathan called me from the nursing home. He told me that he felt like he was to blame for what had happened to me. I assured him that no one was to blame, then I thanked him for coming to my rescue.

I asked him if he had somewhere else he could stay for a while. He told me that his supervisor had insisted that he stay at her house when he wasn't working. She had gone to his house to clean up the mess in the kitchen, but she didn't want him staying there alone. He had always lived with a relative, and I didn't know if he was capable of caring for himself.

I called his supervisor that afternoon. We discussed possible living arrangements for Nathan. She told me that she had contacted Nathan's great-uncle Hiram Song in Minnesota.

"That's wonderful news," I said.

"Yes, it was almost like fate," she said. "Mr. Song said that for some time he has been thinking about moving back to Hawaii. In fact, he put his house up for sale a few months ago, and just last week a young couple made an offer on it. He accepted their offer and made reservations to come to Oahu later this month to start looking for a place to rent."

She told me not to worry about Nathan in the meantime. Over the years, there had been other times he had stayed with her when Ronald was away. He felt at home with her, and she enjoyed having him.

I was tired of watching television, and I had worn a rut in the hallway walking back and forth. I walked to the nurse's stations and asked for a pad of paper. When I returned to my room, I pulled a red pen from my purse. I sat down cross-legged on the bed and started writing. Though I didn't have the file from my office at the *Star* to refer to, I had enough facts fresh on my mind to begin the story.

My hand could barely keep up with my thoughts, and I filled ten pages of the legal pad. I reread the information and filled in some gaps, then reread it again. I scratched out some phrases and put in better terminology. After rereading it for the fourth time, I decided it was finished. Just then there was knock on the door and Mr. Masaki walked in.

"Allie, I have to say that you go the extra mile for a story," he said, smiling. "Detective Kahala called and told me what happened to you."

"Mr. Masaki, I'm glad you came by." I tore the pages from the legal pad and handed them to him. "That is ninety-nine percent of what you'll need for a story regarding the grave-robbing cases for tomorrow's paper. If you don't mind typing it and adding your own comments to it, I think it will be ready to run."

He sat down in one of the chairs still sitting beside my bed. "Do you mind if I go ahead and take a look at it?"

"I'd like you to."

He took his reading glasses from his pocket, then started reading. I laid back down on the bed. The adrenaline was pumping, and I was excited that the case was finally closed.

After he finished reading the piece, he folded the pages in half. "I'm sorry for what you went through, but this piece is excellent. The passion in it makes the words jump right off the page. It's a spectacular story, but the outcome it represents is also a blessing to the Islands. You helped take a criminal off the streets. You went way beyond the call of duty."

"Thank you for your kind words. I appreciate the confidence you've placed in me."

I asked him if Kyle had returned to work. He said that he fired him because of several indiscretions.

"Apparently, he had been meeting with a reporter from another newspaper looking for a better job," Mr. Masaki said. "He was also taking advantage of the *Hawaiian Star* with his extravagant lunches." He shook his head. "Kyle was rarely around when I needed him. That boy had more doctor and dentist appointments in one month than I've had in five years! I'm usually a good judge of character, but he sure had me fooled."

I felt bad for Mr. Masaki. He was a kind, honest person, and he didn't deserve to be tricked.

After he left, I received a huge bouquet of flowers from Eddie Zantini. The card said that he'd be glad to work with me again anytime. Mom and Dad called me, and we talked for nearly thirty minutes. Traci had notified them that I was in the hospital, and had given them a brief summary of why. A beautiful flowering plant arrived from Maynard while I was talking to them.

That evening, Simon, Traci and Tommy came to visit me. Simon feigned jealousy over the bouquet from his friend. He told me that he had been so busy that he forgot to order flowers for me. I told him being with him was better than flowers any day.

Lying in bed that night, I thought about all the people who had shown their love and concern for me during the day. I fell asleep with a smile on my face.

🐾 🐾 🐾

The next morning, Traci was at the hospital early to take me home. The nurses provided a cart so that we could roll the flowers to her car. An orderly wheeled me to the lobby in a wheelchair.

When we reached the apartment building, we each carried in a batch of flowers. I also carried in the small sack containing my dirty clothes. It felt good to be back home.

Since Mr. Masaki had insisted that I not come into work yet, I attempted to help Traci clean the apartment. She allowed me to dust, but when she caught me trying to vacuum my bedroom, she shooed me to the couch and insisted I take it easy. By late afternoon, she needed to pack for their trip. After a little persuasion, I was able to convince her that I could sit and watch a couple of loads of laundry while they washed downstairs in the laundry room.

Simon came over that night, and we all had dinner together. Since

Tommy and Traci had to catch an early flight the next morning, he was gone by 10:00.

On Thursday, the kids were excited to see me back at school. I tried to play down my absence, and soon we were back on track with the lessons.

Before I left school that day, I called to check on Nathan. He was excited because his great-uncle had arrived on Oahu that morning. He also told me that Maynard had come by to visit him.

"I didn't know I was related to the landscape artist, Allie," he said. "Isn't that great?"

"It sure is, Nathan, and Maynard is a great guy."

"He met Uncle Hiram, too, and we're all going out to dinner tonight. I can't wait!"

I hoped that the three men would become close friends. There were so few members of their family left, it seemed only right that they should be a part of each other's lives. I told Nathan to call me the next day to let me know how the dinner went.

I left school, grabbed some lunch, and then headed to the airport to pick up Aunt Edith. On the way there, I thought about Nathan, his brother, and the case that had just been solved. "The Sins of the Fathers." Kawana Kahuku had transgressed against Fae Song and Sak had been born. Sak was cheated out of his birthright, and he and his descendants were cheated out of their inheritance. Gerald Franklin never acknowledged Ronald as his son. Bitterness and hatred filled Ronald and eventually he took revenge. Maynard Desmond's father abandoned his family. Maynard was robbed of a relationship with his dad. At least, in the end, Maynard had overcome adversity and prospered.

I found a parking spot at the airport, then walked inside to the security area. I saw Kelly working, and his faithful companion, Abbie, was lying next to his feet.

"Aloha, Kelly," I said to him. He was standing by the X-ray machine. "I'm glad to see that Abbie is feeling better and back at her post." She was lying next to a folding chair sitting beside the machine.

"That makes two of us, Allie." He reached down and stroked his dog's head. "What are you doing out here?"

"My great-aunt is coming to spend a couple of weeks here with me. I'm headed to the baggage claim area to wait for her."

He stepped closer to me. "Why don't you go meet her at the gate?" he whispered.

"Are you sure it's okay?"

"Hey, I know you aren't a terrorist. Go ahead, it's fine."

"Thanks, Kelly, I appreciate it. Take care." I looked down at Abbie, and pointed a finger at her. "You be careful, too." She wagged her tail at me.

I glanced at the clock on the wall and saw that it was already 2:00. I checked the monitor to see which gate Aunt Edith's plane would be coming to, then I hurried that way. Just as I reached it, I saw her.

"Aloha, Allie. Alooooha!" She was wearing the grass skirt that I had given to her last spring, and she had an orchid lei around her neck. I was surprised to see my cousin Michael trailing behind her. Aunt Edith was being escorted by one of the pilots from the plane. The two of them were talking and laughing as they made their way toward me. From the look on the man's face, I suspected that Aunt Edith had made his flight an adventure.

Ready or not, Hawaii, here she comes!

A NOTE FROM THE AUTHOR

Thank you for joining Allie, Simon, Aunt Edith and the gang for another adventure. I hope you were held in suspense, laughed, and thoroughly enjoyed yourself. Please watch for the third book in the series, *Justice in Paradise*.

If you'd like to find out more about me and the Paradise series, please go to my web site at www.terryerobins.com. There you can give me your feedback, sign up for the informative quarterly newsletter, find out the places where I'll be appearing, print off the Kane and Winters family trees, and much more. Or, if you prefer, you may write to me at:

P.O. Box 335
Chelsea, OK 74016.

Although Allie was fortunate to have her puppies, Rowdy and Precious, join her in Hawaii, the State of Hawaii Department of Agriculture has a strict quarantine policy regarding animals brought to the Islands. If you decide to take a trip to Hawaii and want to bring along your pet, please check with the agency at least four months in advance of your departure for the guidelines.

BIBLIOGRAPHY

Silverstein, Shel. The Giving Tree. New York: Harper and Row Publishers, Inc., 1964.

Silverstein, Shel. Where the Sidewalk Ends Poems and Drawings. New York: Harper and Row Publishers, Inc., 1974.

Munsch, Robert. Love You Forever. Willowdale, Ontario: Firefly Books, Ltd., 1986.

Parrish, Peggy. Amelia Bedelia. New York: Harper & Row Publishers, Inc., 1963.

Television Shows:
As the World Turns. CBS, Los Angeles, 2007.
Dr. Phil. CBS, Los Angeles, 2007.

Songs:
Arlen, Harold & Harburg, E.Y. "Somewhere Over the Rainbow." EMI April Music, Inc. Copyright unknown.

Hine, Stuart W.K. "How Great Thou Art." Manna Music, Inc. Copyright 1953, renewed 1981.

Lane, Burton & Lerner, Alan J. "On a Clear Day." Chappell & Co., Inc. Copyright unknown.

Kirkpatrick, William J. "Lord, I'm Coming Home." Copyright unknown.

Chisholm, Thomas O. & Runyan, William M. "Great is Thy Faithfulness." Copyright 1923, renewed 1951.

Bartlett, Eugene M. "Victory in Jesus." Albert E. Brumley & Sons. Copyright 1939, renewed 1967.

Newton, John. "Amazing Grace." American melody from Carrell & Clayton's "Virginia Harmony" 1831.